W9-CBG-102

DRIVING THE DEEP

DAW BOOKS PROUDLY PRESENTS
SUZANNE PALMER'S FINDER CHRONICLES

Finder

Driving the Deep

DRIVING THE DEEP

Book Two of the Finder Chronicles

Suzanne Palmer

PAPL DISCARDED

DAW BOOKS, INC.

DONALD A. WOLLHEIM, FOUNDER

1745 Broadway, New York, NY 10019
ELIZABETH R. WOLLHEIM
SHEILA E. GILBERT
PUBLISHERS
www.dawbooks.com

Copyright © 2020 by Suzanne Palmer.

All Rights Reserved.

Jacket art by Kekai Kotaki.

Jacket design by Adam Auerbach.

Interior design by Alissa Rose Theodor.

Edited by Katie Hoffman.

DAW Book Collectors No. 1852.

Published by DAW Books, Inc.
1745 Broadway, New York, NY 10019.

All characters and events in this book are fictitious.
Any resemblance to persons living or dead is strictly coincidental.

The scanning, uploading, and distribution of this book via the Internet or any other means without the permission of the publisher is illegal, and punishable by law. Please purchase only authorized electronic editions, and do not participate in or encourage the electronic piracy of copyrighted materials. Your support of the author's rights is appreciated.

First Printing, May 2020
1   2   3   4   5   6   7   8   9

DAW TRADEMARK REGISTERED
U.S. PAT. AND TM. OFF. AND FOREIGN COUNTRIES
—MARCA REGISTRADA
HECHO EN U.S.A.

PRINTED IN THE U.S.A.

To JT and Robin, for so much.

Chapter 1

In the center of the spindle tube between two sections of the Shipyard, tumbling with the casual grace of zero gravity, there was a giant, magenta, inflatable hamster. Fergus Ferguson reached out to a wallbar to slow himself before he collided with it; the last unattended animal he'd run across had been a four-meter-long robotic snake that had chased him through three sections of hab before he managed to lock himself in a closet. The footage—perspective of the snake, naturally—was looping on all Shipyard vid monitors for a week.

"Maison?" he called.

There was no answer, no sound of snickering from beyond the next set of blast doors.

Wary, he moved closer, inspecting it from arm's length. There was no faint, resonating buzz in his gut to indicate something electrified, no detail that stood out to suggest it was anything other than the obvious. Fergus backed away, skirted along the smooth gray-blue wall until he was well past it, then shoved off through the doorway with only a few paranoid glances behind him.

The hamster didn't explode, didn't call out to him, and best of all, didn't follow.

In the two months or so that he'd been back there, Fergus had explored far more of the Shipyard than he ever had before, but still figured he'd seen less than twenty percent of it. Most of the remaining spaces weren't easily accessible and, even if they had been, too dangerous for casual, solo adventuring. The army of bots doing the heavy work of building spaceships vastly outnumbered the tiny handful of people doing the thinking and inventing and goofing off, and it was best not to get in their way.

From the spindle that ran the length of the orbital station, he dropped into a connecting corridor that led to one of the habitable rings, and as he floated down, he admired, for the thousandth time, the edge-on view through the thick portals of Pluto's surface below.

The planet—hundreds of years later, there was still active resistance to its demotion to microplanet—was a beautiful tapestry of browns and blacks and tans spun together like a rich, poorly stirred hot chocolate, even down to the tiny hint of foam at its polar cap. There were only a few lights visible from there, nav beacons and communications boosters and automated science stations, none of them designed for occupation. Pluto and its partner rock, Charon, were positioned in precisely the sweet spot, in terms of privacy, of being far enough out that, if you were going to go this far, odds were good you'd just keep going until you found brighter skies again around some other star, and never even notice it as you passed it by.

Between spindle and ring, the artificial gravity kicked in, and he walked rather than floated into the main lounge. Noura and Kelsie were both there, hunched over a holo display with data scrolling rapidly past underneath an undulating set of blue lines drawn in air.

"Hey, Ferg," Kelsie said, glancing up from the console. The roundness of her face was accentuated by her close-cropped blond hair and nearly consumed by the omnipresent wide grin that was the essence of Kelsie to the core. Noura was her opposite, with long, tight springs of black hair that, when not painstakingly tied down in tiny braids, spread out in a glorious halo around her olive-tone face, as it was now. Her expression was somber, her brow furrowed in puzzlement.

"You two know anything about the giant hamster floating in corridor nine?" Fergus asked.

"Did you touch it?" Kelsie asked.

"No."

"Then no, I know nothing about it. You'd have to ask Maison."

Noura waved her hand through the screen, and both pattern and dataset changed. "You have a message," she said without looking up.

"Me?"

"Yes, you."

"Who from?"

"Do you really think we'd violate your privacy by watching your personal messages?" Kelsie asked.

"Yes," Fergus said.

"Then it's from your friend Mari," Noura said. "We like her."

Fergus headed over to Ignatio's console, brushed green fur off the chair, and sat. His leg ached dully from the transition into grav, but he was grateful he still had a leg at all. For a while, it wasn't clear he would.

"Tomboy?" he asked.

The steady green iris above the console stared at him. "Good morning, Fergus," the smooth, ungendered, artificial voice of the station intelligence said. "Have the others already informed you that you have a message?"

"Yes, thanks," he said. "Could you play it for me?"

"I would be happy to," Tomboy said.

Mari's face appeared on the screen. She looked different. Not older, he thought, but less unsettled. Not the same surly nineteen-year-old he'd been dragged through a war with. "Hey, Fergus," she said. "Calling with the news, as you asked. We've finally permanently reconnected the Wheel Collective and Blackcans to Cernee's halo, and we're using what salvage we can pull from the destroyed habs to repair the others. No sudden decompressions anywhere in more than a week, so I think we're making progress."

Cernee was a deep-space settlement made of strung-together junk that barely held its air under the best of circumstances; the war there had pushed survival to the very brink.

"The good news is that the Governor thinks we can repair the sunshield that got bombed," Mari continued. "The bad news, of course, is we can't afford to, not for a while. But for now, the shell seems stable, so eventually we'll get there. Oh, and the Shielders gave me something for you." She turned away from the camera, rummaging through something out of sight.

"This is the best part," Kelsie said from over the display.

"Shhhhh," Noura said. "I'm concentrating."

Mari sat up again, and held a large square of velopaper in front of her. On it was a drawing of a figure in a suit, small lightning bolts coming out of his fingers, near one edge of the paper. On the opposite side was a shape clearly meant to be a sunshield, although Fergus conceded it was possibly also a giant space banana. Between them were a large quantity of stars.

"They tell me to tell you that they've drawn you staying far away from Cernee, and of course as you know, once something has been added to their Narrative, it must be so," Mari said. "I think they're still mad at you."

Fergus thought that likely and couldn't say one way or the other if he deserved it.

"Aaaanyway, the Shielder who gave me this? I showed him how if I folded it just right, I could hide all the stars and put you right next to the sunshield," she said, demonstrating. "He actually screamed and ran away."

She set down the paper out of sight. "We could use someone with your problem-solving skills, if you ever do come back. Mr. Harcourt and the Governor and Ms. Ili seem to be working together for now, but the cracks are showing. The miners and other people who worked under Vinsic but weren't part of the coup attempt have banded together and seem to have nominated Tobb— Bale's brother?—as spokesperson. He's doing okay with it, though Bale has had to keep him and Harcourt from hitting each other a couple of times. Everyone is still on edge, whether they'll admit it or not. You probably won't believe me, but sometimes it's really nice to be back home in the peace and quiet of the family farm."

"What do they grow that far from their star?" Noura asked.

"Genmod lichen," Fergus answered. "Now hush."

"Uh, that's really about it," Mari continued. "The usual people say hello. If you're not still at the Shipyard, I guess they'll forward this on or save it for when you get back. If you're still there, call back and let me know why the hell you're procrastinating and getting on everyone's nerves instead of doing what you need to do. You know what I'm talking about."

The message ended. Fergus stared at the screen until Tomboy spoke up. "Would you like me to play it again?"

"No, thank you," Fergus said, and got out of his chair. Both Noura and Kelsie were watching him, leaning back in their seats and looking unsatisfied.

He went over to the kitchen alcove, made three bulbs of coffee, and set down two of them in front of the women before taking an empty seat. "What are you two looking at?" he asked.

"Either we've stumbled across a whole new phenomenon in physics, or we've got bad data from a sensor calibration problem on *Falconer*," Kelsie said. "So, yeah, trying to figure out how the sensor went *whumpf*. Here, look. Running this in super slo-mo."

She waved her hand through the console again, and a curved

field appeared above it, a smooth grid of lines widening out. Just before the field popped, there was the briefest flash of something. Kelsie backed it up, and Fergus could now make out a tiny break in the lines of the grid. "Looks like a pothole," he said.

"Lasts about a thousandth of a second. A few dropped data packets, is all. Can't reproduce it."

"Except you can, but only running the exact same sequence along the exact same trajectory," Noura said, "which is what makes it odd."

"You ask Ignatio? Jumpspace physics is eir expertise," Fergus said.

"Ignatio was not helpful," Noura said.

"Ignatio wiggled all eir limbs at us and said it was nothing and went off to the kitchen to play with food," Kelsie said. She sighed and shut the display down. "I've been messing with the sensor array, but this really isn't my area. *Falconer*'s sensors are running Effie's latest firmware, which tested out fine in the sim lab, so if I can't find the issue, I'll pull them. When she gets back, we'll rebuild. I just wish I knew what went wrong. I'm an engines-and-hardware person, not a coder."

Kelsie swiped her hand through the display, clearing it, then brought up the firmware logics and the array schematics. "Still, I might as well get to it," she said. "I wouldn't want anyone to call *me* out on procrastinating!"

Noura leaned back on the couch and regarded Fergus. "About that," she said. "Your friend Mari is right: you *are* procrastinating. Though she's not correct about getting on our nerves—we enjoy your company, all of us; there are so few people we can bounce ideas off of."

"When you seven get going on engineering and computer intelligence stuff? I'm lost within a minute," Fergus said.

"Which is about fifty-three seconds better than everyone

else," Noura said. "That's not the point. You brought us back *Venetia's Sword* from the man who stole her, at great personal risk and no small amount of injury, and we're deeply grateful. The ship is too. But you're not here just hanging out for our company; you're here because you don't want to go do the next thing. You don't want to go back to Earth."

"No, I don't," Fergus said. "I ran away from home when I was fifteen for good cause. I have no reason to ever go back."

"Except one," Noura said.

"Yeah." Fergus reached into a pocket in his shorts, pulled out an old key, set it beside the display. "One."

"It's been . . . seventeen years? Eighteen? You don't think your cousin has forgiven you for stealing his motorcycle, given the circumstances?"

"I don't know," Fergus said. "I haven't forgiven myself."

"So, go do it, and then you can."

Fergus laughed. "As if it's that easy! Last time I was in-system, I managed to make myself a wanted man on Mars, and who knows how far that's spread? And even if I can get to Earth without someone catching me, it has been *nineteen* years. I don't know where my cousin even is!"

"Fergus, you find things all over the galaxy for a living," Noura said, her dark eyebrows knitted together. "Surely, you don't think those are good reasons for not going. Unless your cousin is dead or gone off-planet himself, he'll be in the node listings. You land and fetch the motorcycle out of storage. It's been sitting a long time, but Kelsie can give you detailed instructions and a botkit for maintenance. Then you locate your cousin, meet up with him and give it back, buy him a drink and say you're sorry, catch up on old times . . ."

"I don't want to catch up on old times," Fergus said. "They were all horrible. That's why I ran away."

"Well, then, do this and you're free. You don't ever have to go back to Earth again."

A rail-thin, shirtless, hairless man wearing thick, opaque red goggles strolled into the lounge. "I think you should just stay," the newcomer said, his accent a perfect meld of Earth West Indies and Lunar Colony immersion-net-five. "Never look back."

"Maison," Fergus said. He and Kelsie were the youngest and newest of the Shipmakers of Pluto, originally founded by Noura's mother and Theo's uncle, both long since passed. "Is that your hamster in section nine?"

"Did you touch it?" Maison asked.

"No."

"Then I'm sure I know nothing about it. Hey, I have a project you could help me with, Double-Eff, my man."

"Yeah?" Fergus said. "Remember the last time you said you needed my help testing a new exosuit insulator, and you filled my suit with spraycheese? While I was wearing it? It took me weeks to get that smell out, and it gave me a *rash*."

Maison beamed. "I found it informative."

"I'm sure. No, thanks."

Maison parked himself on the arm of the sofa near Noura. "What's on the agenda for today?" he asked.

"Reviewing *Falconer*'s sensor code," Kelsie said without looking up.

"The rest of us are all still waiting on schematics from you for the new ice-driver prototype," Noura said. "Need I remind you, we have paying customers waiting—Enfi Maub has given us a substantial deposit—and having a good reputation for reliable products delivered in a timely manner is necessary to fund the fun, experimental projects?"

"Yes, yes," Maison said. "I'm working on it. Up here." He tapped his forehead.

"Great," Noura said. "Meanwhile, I've been overseeing the repairs to *Venetia's Sword*'s mindsystems and working on the next-gen model *Whiro* with Tomboy. LaChelle has cloistered herself in the design VR and won't show anyone what she's got so far except to say she's going for a 'dangerous' look. Theo can't start prepping the fab units until either she's done or you are, so he's off in the garden wheel, communing with his bonsai, and until we start constructing *something*, Kelsie has nothing to try to break, so she's sitting here overthinking a sensor firmware bug. I gather your primary agenda, despite all of us waiting on you, continues to be pranking Fergus?"

"Mostly," Maison said. "It's a delicate art."

"Where's Effie?" Fergus asked.

"Pluto's atmosphere is precipitating right now. Effie took a rover down to the surface to watch," Noura said.

"Ignatio go with her?"

"No, ey're still in the kitchen, trying to turn an egg perfectly inside out. Don't ask me. It's an alien thing."

"Anything I can do to help? I mean, except for the egg," Fergus asked. "Ignatio is on eir own with that one. But the rest of you . . ."

Maison raised a hand. "Yes!" he said. "I—"

"Not you either, Maison."

Kelsie laughed. "Go do your Earth thing, Earthman. Get it over with. You'll come back to Pluto feeling like you weigh a twelfth as much, I guarantee it. And maybe by then, we'll have *Whiro* online and you can help me test-drive it."

"But I still haven't figured out how to get down to Earth without risking Alliance orbital security," Fergus said.

"The Alliance never even ID'd you on Mars, unless you've been up to no good elsewhere and haven't told us," Kelsie said.

"No," Fergus said. "Not that I've been caught at, as far as I know. But I can't be *sure*."

"That's how we know you don't want to go. If you did, you'd have a dozen crazy schemes by now even if you knew the Alliance was looking for you," Kelsie said. "So, how about we solve this one for you? We have a droneship cleared to pick up a half-ton of maple from a sustainable forestry provider in the Atlantic States Coalition, because LaChelle wants it for *Whiro*'s interior. We have environmental controls in the cargo bay to keep the wood from getting damaged in transit, so you'd be able to ride it down. Not a comfortable trip, but Alliance oversight wanes drastically once you're inside Earth's gravity well. As soon as you're dirtside, you think you can do a run around local authorities enough to get yourself from eastern North America to Scotland without getting caught?"

"I don't—"

"If it was for a job, could you do it? Be honest."

"Yeah," Fergus admitted.

"Well, you're on a job," Noura said. "Your client is you. What you're finding is peace with your family, whatever that means."

"And it's about time," Kelsie said. She suddenly laughed, clapping her hands together. "Oh, look how sad Maison looks at the idea he might lose you!"

"Am not *sad*," Maison said. His face was a scowl. "I have other things to do."

"Like ice-driver schematics," Noura said.

Fergus looked back over at Kelsie and Noura. *Everyone is right*, he thought. *I'm procrastinating.*

"This cargo droneship . . ." he started to ask.

"About five hours 'til I launch it. Knowing you, you need

about ten minutes to pack, so that gives you some time to kill," Kelsie said. She reached under the table and pulled out a too-familiar deck of hexagonal cards. "Ever played Venusian Monkeypoker?"

"I'm in! I'm in!" Maison shouted, vaulting over and into a chair.

Fergus groaned. "Not me," he said. Only three months before, he'd spent several days trapped on a very small ship with too many angry people and one lone Monkeypoker deck between them, and it was still too soon to even look at those cards again.

Noura got up from the couch. "Come on, Fergus," she said. "We can go down to the kitchen and, if Ignatio hasn't coated every single surface with egg already, you can help me with lunch and tell me about what you might want to do after Earth. For real, not this Corallan Tea Master thing you keep bringing up as a dodge."

"Maybe it's not a dodge," he said.

"Of course it is," she answered, following him to the door. "Even you would have difficulty getting into trouble there, and you and I both know you just couldn't abide that for more than an hour."

"Hey! I made it almost five hours, the one time I was there," he protested.

Noura laughed. "Five whole hours? Well, that certainly proves me wrong," she said. "One of these years, I'd love to scan and map your neural networks, just to see what sort of ship mindsystem I could build out of that."

"Now, that would just be cruel to a poor ship," he said, and headed for the kitchen, desperately hoping Ignatio had committed something spectacularly messy with the eggs and they could talk about that—or really, anything else—instead.

The droneship, nestled in the shuttle dock between several larger ships, was about one-third storage, one-third engine, and one-third control systems, which left, Fergus figured, exactly zero-thirds room for an inconveniently tall Scot.

"This is *Constance*," Noura said, patting the blocky silver hull with affection. "Passive jump only, of course, because she's un-crewed, but she's pretty fast otherwise. She's a class-two intelligence, so she won't be much company on the ride in, but I've programmed her with a pleasant recital voice and the entire works of Rumi, Ghalib, and Bashō."

"Tell me you're not expecting me to ride loose in the cargo compartment—they'll detect my freshly battered corpse on every single waypoint scan between here and Earth."

"I modified *Constance*'s maneuvering parameters, so she won't pull too many hard gees on you," Kelsie said. "Which is too bad; she's really nimble for such a basic model."

"Not entirely basic anymore," Maison said. He walked to the back of the cargo bay and swung open an instrument panel. In-side was a person-sized padded compartment. "It locks from the inside and can only be overridden by *Constance*. Scan-proof, full safety straps, field-buffered against acceleration. Integrated con-sole and bio facilities. And when you're in transit, you can bop around the cargo bay all you want, stretch your legs."

"People-smuggling doesn't seem like one of your usual busi-nesses," Fergus said.

Maison shrugged. "It's not, but Effie's been on a big stealth-tech kick and said it was almost impossible to build the perfect, scan-proof hiding place in a ship this size, so I took it as a challenge. It beats 97% of military-grade scanners, and the other 3% too if the operators aren't paranoid, hyper-thorough bastards."

"I'm going to be mostly stuck in that tiny space for three days?" Fergus said.

Noura crossed her arms in front of her chest. "What's your other plan for getting to Earth, then?"

Fergus let his shoulders slump. "Fine," he said. "Can it low-stat me?"

"Not really, but it does have sleep aid functions," Noura said. "And we packed you plenty of food and water in the tool cupboard. Are you ready? You've got fifteen minutes until launch."

Fergus nudged his pack with his foot. "I've got everything I need right here. Just need to put my exosuit on and then I'm set."

"The pod is fully programmed for comfort," Maison said. "You could ride this baby naked all the way to Earth without a single goose bump."

"As much as flying seven billion kilometers or so stuffed naked into a cupboard has always been a fantasy of mine, I'll pass," Fergus said. He unfolded his suit and stepped into it, pulling it up and over his shoulders before sealing it and putting his boots back on. The suit was top-of-the-line military-grade with some black-market enhancements and had been a gift when he'd left Cernee, and it was virtually irreplaceable.

Noura noticed the small circular patch on the back, below his neck, as he was pulling the hood up. "What's this?" she asked.

"It's called a city-mark," Fergus said. "Harcourt and Mari gave it to me. It means I can call Cernee's Wheel Collective *home* if I want."

"That's sweet," Kelsie said. "You're getting better at this making-friends thing, you know."

Maison mimed wiping tears from his cheeks with double fists. "Our boy is growing up!" he said.

Noura embraced Fergus. "Ignore him," she said. "Be careful, and try not to spend the entire trip worrying. Either it will go smoothly and the worry will have been pointless, or something will go terribly wrong and you'll handle it as you always do. I've known you for over ten years now, and I know you've got this."

Kelsie whacked him on the shoulder. "You're gonna be fine," she said, grinning. "We'll be here waiting for you when you're done, with drinks to celebrate. Oh, hang on!"

She pulled a small packet from her coveralls and handed it to him. "Bot maintenance kit, for the motorcycle engine. It's been sitting a long time, but this should take care of the worst of it. Instructions inside."

"Thanks," Fergus said. "I hadn't thought of that."

"That's why I'm the engine person and you're not," she said.

"Hey, bring us back some real ice cream, Double-Eff, if you can," Maison said. He dropped a flattened disk in Fergus's hand. "Encrypted comm, bounces through random boosters between here and Earth. Sometimes indirect but always gets through. I call it a *pager* because that's snappy and retro. If you get in trouble, let us know so we can drink your share of the party booze."

Fergus stepped backward into the compartment, waved to Noura and Kelsie, and then gave Maison a two-fingered salute before Maison slammed the door shut.

It was claustrophobically tight inside, but as soon as he locked the door, it filled with a soft yellow glow and fresh circulating air. When the console powered on, he synced his suit comms with it, buckled himself in upright against the padded back—once he was out of gravity, it would be nice not to rattle around helplessly inside his cupboard—and then connected up his suit and oxygen to the drone's feeds.

"Hello, Mr. Ferguson," a pleasant, matronly voice said. "I am *Constance*, your droneship system. We are launching in nine minutes. Are you secured?"

"I am, *Constance*," Fergus said. "Thank you."

The connection ended; at class two, *Constance's* computer probably couldn't manage much beyond that functional exchange. As long as it had all the piloting and navigation skills needed, Fergus could live without conversation. He could also live without the launch. "Constance, please put me to sleep," he said.

"Certainly," the drone answered.

His resistance to the aerosol was just enough that he could feel it start to kick in. "Okay, Earth, ready or not, here I come," he muttered, and closed his eyes.

———

There was nobody at the warehouse outside Old Portland when *Constance* landed at four o'clock in the morning, slotting into its assigned berth space with flawless precision. The droneship connected itself up to refuel, and the automated systems of the warehouse dispatched robots to fetch and load the lumber material. He had a brief window to get out before he'd be blocked into his cabinet by a ton of wood for three more days back to Pluto.

Constance had been scanned dozens of times on approach before being cleared to dock, but Fergus had no idea if the warehouse itself had active monitoring in place that might pick him up once he was out of his tiny protected niche.

"Constance, do you have a connection to the warehouse computer?" he asked.

"Yes," the drone answered.

"Can you add my console to that connection?"

"Yes," Constance said. A moment later, she added. "You have been added to the connection."

Fergus cracked his knuckles in the tight space, then pulled his favorite electronic device, nicknamed the *confuddler*, from where he'd stashed it within reach. He jacked it in and let it do what it did best—detect and map out any connected network and obscure its own presence along the way. Once it had done its thing, he pulled up a screen on the console and studied the results. The warehouse had a standard off-the-shelf security package built to keep people out, not in. Easy.

Eleven minutes later, exosuit in his pack over his back, he slipped out of the newly unsecured warehouse into the pre-dawn dark and discovered his first significant mistake:

Nineteen years since I left Earth, he thought, *but you'd think I'd still remember it had bloody* seasons.

His habitual T-shirt and shorts were a poor match for the half-meter of snow on the ground, and his handpad duly informed him that with windchill, the temperatures were currently hovering around -7C. He could put his exosuit back on, but then he'd look incredibly suspicious. He could give up and climb back inside the droneship, but even with the empty bay to move around in, he'd been ready to chew his way out of the ship by the time he hit Earth orbit. A return trip would leave him trapped in his cupboard for the duration.

And anyway, he didn't want to face his friends having given up so easily.

The warehouse was nestled in a row of automated ground-to-orbit service facilities. On their outskirts, through a tall stand of pines, he could see the lights of a municipal shuttleport, and he ran for it.

———

At the shuttle terminal, he produced an ID in the name of Duncan MacInnis and enough credit to cover the three-hour suborbital hop to Edinburgh as well as buy a thick smart-thermal pullover with ATLANTIC SOX emblazoned across the front.

From here it's easy, right? Fergus thought, still shivering as the pullover started to warm. A quick pod trip to New Glasgow to fetch the motorcycle out of storage, and then he just had to find his cousin and get the hell back out.

But in a podrail car four hours later, watching the desolate Scottish countryside fly past in the murky light of winter dusk, he began to feel more and more of a kinship with the stunted bracken mired in frozen mud and pockets of dirty snow. The urge to trip the emergency stop, get out, and walk back to Edinburgh and grab another shuttle away from the planet grew stronger by the minute.

Kelsie might think he needed to make peace with his family, but hadn't that been why he'd run away in the first place? What did he have left unresolved except the motorcycle? If he dropped it off out front of his cousin's house in the middle of the night, he needn't even *speak* to anyone.

Gavin would probably just punch him, anyway. And he'd deserve it, but then it would be done. His father was dead; his mother . . . well, Fergus had been dead to her years before he got up the courage to leave for good. *I followed my father's lead in getting out,* he thought. *Except I chose to keep living.*

He closed his eyes. *If I just decide it's going to be simple, then it will be. The only one who can complicate this is me.*

He stepped off the podcar at the Glasgow station, paused to watch the vast ribbon of the Clyde in the failing light as it rolled slowly past along the fortified embankment, contained but hardly captive, fed now from the vast inland sea that sat where once his ancestors had lived. It smelled like Scotland, in all its glory and misery and stubborn solidity, and he turned away from the river and walked into the city before too many thoughts could catch up with him.

Fergus caught an auto-taxi to the city outskirts. Suttie's Self-Storage was hunkered tightly between old warehouses and derelict buildings, looking exactly the same as it had when he was fifteen and fighting the urge to just abandon the stolen motorcycle. A gate was pulled across the front and locked.

He rang the bell, waited, then rang it again before he noticed the sign listing hours. A quick check of his handpad showed that it was Saturday night, Suttie's had closed less than forty-five minutes earlier, and he was now going to have to wait until Monday morning for the storage place to open again.

"Shit," he said. He was aware of how his accent had shifted over the years to more Mars, more mutt galactic, than Scotland native son. He'd spent more time away from Earth than on it by now, hadn't he? Why shouldn't his accent have changed? It only reinforced this need to be done and away from this place he no longer belonged in.

He glanced up and down the narrow backstreet, saw no one, no lights in any of the run-down buildings where the windows weren't already boarded over. There was a security camera above the gate, but the wire ran down the side of the building within reach through the bars. He leaned his back against the gate, made motions as if he was looking for something in his coat pockets, and slipped his other hand backward through the bars and touched the wire.

He didn't want to cut it, as Suttie had done nothing to him other than having inconvenient hours of operation and had in fact on many occasions let Fergus run late on payments without much more than token complaint. And even though the installer had been deeply incompetent to leave the wire within reach, no doubt the system still worked fine. Best course was to temporarily shut the whole system down. Lacking access to the centralized control system itself, that meant doing it his own special way.

There goes my streak of fifty-seven days without using the damned 'gift' the Asiig left me, he thought. The electricity in the wire, so tiny and frail, called to him, and it was easy to touch the wire with his hand and stop the flow. He heard the *click* of the gate lock disengaging. The street lamp beside him, which had flickered into life a few minutes before, went out.

Oops.

The street was still clear and quiet. He slipped through the gate, closing it tightly behind him, and then walked around the main building to around back where the individual units were.

B37 was farther down than he remembered. There was an electronic lock on the door, still lit; the outside camera must have been on a separate power supply. He typed in his code with a fierce, impatient staccato.

The lock remained red. A second try got him no further. *I can't have forgotten it,* he thought. He never forgot much of anything, even things he wanted to, and the code had been etched into his conscience by nearly two decades of guilt.

When a third try failed, he sighed, pulled the confuddler out of his pack, and plugged in. Once it connected, he used his handpad to run some generic cracking routines against it. When those bogged down, he pulled in a few more specialized tools he'd collected over the years. It took nearly five minutes to crack. *Okay, Suttie,* he thought, grudgingly appreciative, *you've been overcharging me for years, but at least I got some good security for it.*

Fergus put his hand on the storage unit door and hauled it upward with a terrific squeal of rusted metal. Waving away the cloud of dust that billowed down and out, he flipped on the tiny light switch to see how badly the years had treated the bike.

There was no motorcycle.

Instead, the unit was packed with large, slim, rectangular cases. Confused, Fergus double-checked the number on the front of the unit, but it was the right one. *What the hell?* he thought.

He reached in and slid a case forward to the unit door. It was an expensive thing, heavy and solidly built, with an airtight seal around the seams and a small vacuum lock near the handle. There was as much accumulated dust on it as he'd expected to find on the motorcycle, which meant it had been here nearly as long. "Oh, Mr. Suttie," Fergus muttered. "Am I going to have words with you on Monday morning."

He popped the locks and tipped the front of the case open, and peered inside. Staring back at him was Vincent Van Gogh.

"Whoa, shit," Fergus said out loud.

He quickly sealed the case again, reactivated the vacuum lock, and shoved it back into the unit. More slowly, and with no small reservation, he drew out another. This one held a painting of a man bent over in a golden field. Early Seurat, Fergus was sure. *The Mower*? He put that case back, too.

Shining his light around, he counted a total of seventeen cases.

Back when he'd been working a stolen art case on Mars, he'd done a bit of research on other heists, mostly with an eye toward how the works moved through the underground to buyers. He hadn't paid much attention to other details, but he remembered the Seurat.

That heist had been fourteen years earlier. It was likely the paintings had been here all this time, stashed and waiting patiently for an opportunity to sell them, and his motorcycle was long since gone. All those years, and the guilt, and the naive good intentions . . . Not to mention the payments to Mr. Suttie. Sometimes, when he first left Earth, he didn't eat for days in order to make them.

He knew anger was dangerous, so he made himself close his eyes and count to ten. Noura had said it herself: he found things for a living. Surely, he could still find his missing motorcycle.

So, it was a little more complicated than he'd expected. It could have been worse, and probably there was even a reward for the paintings if he was willing to step into that mess. For now, until he knew what he wanted to do, he pulled the gate back down and reset the lock.

His pocket hummed at him. He reached in and pulled out the tiny disk that Maison had given him. The pager had a tiny, flashing green light, so he pressed his thumb against the button.

It was Tomboy's voice. "We are under attack," the message said. "Help. Come quickly."

His heart lurched in his chest. How old was that message? How indirect did Maison's random routing take it? He ran for the front gate, all other thoughts abandoned.

As he slipped through, rough hands grabbed him in the dark and swung him by his coat against the railing. Something hit him hard in the head. "You're under arrest!" a voice shouted. Something stung him in the neck, and he fell toward the pavement without ever reaching it.

Chapter 2

Fergus opened his eyes, doing his best to ignore the throbbing pain in his skull and sharp sting where he'd been needled, and took in the spare, dirty room around him. A minimum of tugging was enough to determine that his hands were cuffed together behind him, the chain run through one of the spindles of the chair back. Across the room from him, a sixty-ish man with short-cropped salt-and-pepper hair was stuffing things into a duffel bag. Fergus's pack and belongings were spread out on the room's small, unmade bed like a bad autopsy.

He had no idea what was going on, but the Shipyard was under attack. He didn't have time for this. "Excuse me?" he said.

The man whirled around. "Shut up," he said.

"If I'm under arrest, don't you have to tell me what I'm under arrest for and read me my rights? Since when is drugging someone usual protocol? And why aren't we at a police station?"

"I said shut up!" the man yelled. He stuffed a few more things in his bag, then rounded angrily on Fergus. His face had several days of stubble, and he had the swollen eyes of a man who had not slept well in a very long time, if ever. "You're lucky I don't just shoot you and turn in your corpse."

"For what? Breaking into a storage facility? Where I have a unit, mind you?"

"For being a goddamned thief," the man said. The accent was pure Sovereign City of New York.

"I took nothing," Fergus said. "And aren't you out of your

jurisdiction? I could press charges for assault and battery, false imprisonment, for impersonating a police officer."

"Thirty-nine fucking years on the force, asshole," he said.

"Yeah, but not the *Scotland* police force," Fergus said. "And not anymore, am I right? If you let me go now, maybe I won't file a complaint."

The man laughed, a bitter sound. "A *complaint*? When I get you back to New York, you can complain all you want, all the way down into the fucking flooded pits at Rikers. You know how long I've been waiting for someone to come back to that shithole across the street? I watched you break in, and I *knew* you were my guy. Only a pro moves that fast."

Across the street, huh? Fergus thought. The inside of this room would be right at home among the abandoned buildings near Suttie's. He slowly pulled the handcuffs tight against the chair, testing. With a bit of effort, the spindle would break. "Whatever you think I've done, you have the wrong man," he said.

"And an honest man needs this many IDs?" The man gestured at the bed. "I don't have any idea which one is even your real name."

None of them, of course, but Fergus wasn't going to tell him that. "I don't know your name either."

"Detective *Zacker*. That name ring a bell?"

"No," Fergus said. "Should it?"

The detective pulled out an old-style bullet gun—very illegal in Scotland, probably illegal even in the SCNY—and pressed the muzzle against Fergus's forehead. "You sure?"

The man's hand was trembling, though whether from anger or excitement, Fergus couldn't tell. Whatever it was, it wasn't fear. He needed to de-escalate this, and quickly.

"I'm sorry," Fergus said, as calmly as he could, "but I've been on Earth for only about seven hours now, for the first time since

I was fifteen years old. You saw my exosuit in my pack. Whatever you think I've done to you, it wasn't me."

"The name should mean something," the man said. After a hesitation, he lifted the gun away. "It *will*."

The detective threw Fergus's things back into his pack, then slung his own duffel bag over his shoulder. "I'm going to unlock those handcuffs, and if you do anything—*anything*—I don't tell you to, I'm going to shoot you dead and enjoy it."

"I'm not going to try anything, but you can't be thinking you're going to hold a gun on me all the way to New York without someone noticing," Fergus said.

"I have my own private aircar, bright guy. No more questions. I'm going to unlock you, and then you're going to walk slowly in front of me. If we encounter anyone on the way, you will not say a word or make any sudden or unusual motions. You understand me?"

"Yeah," Fergus said.

"Say *Yes, sir*," the man barked.

"Yes, sir," Fergus said.

If the man had his own aircar, that was Fergus's fastest way back to orbit, back to Pluto. If he could find a way to borrow it . . . well, the man did assault *him*, after all.

Detective Zacker put the gun to Fergus's ear as he undid the cuffs one-handed, then stepped sharply back. "Pick up your pack," he said, "and don't even think about running."

"Did you see the scar on my leg? How fast do you think I can run, anyhow?"

"I don't care," the detective said. He stepped to one side and back, pointed toward the door with his free hand while the gun stayed steadily aimed at Fergus. "Go."

Fergus stood up carefully from the chair, then picked his pack up from the floor before walking over to the door and opening it.

"Slowly," the detective said.

The flight of stairs down was poorly lit. He walked down the steps, exaggerating his limp, then stopped at the bottom.

"Open the door and take two steps out, then stop or I'll kill you," Zacker said.

Fergus complied.

Suttie's was directly across the street. The street lamp was still out. *And the security cameras,* Fergus thought, *which is great for not getting me caught breaking in, but terrible if I get murdered tonight.*

"Ten meters down the street to your left, there's an auto-taxi waiting. Open the passenger-side rear door, put your pack in, but do not get in until I say so."

"Okay," Fergus said. He walked to the taxi, opened the door, and slung his pack over to the far side. Seconds later, Zacker slammed his head against the car roof and, with a knee against his back, pulled his hands behind him and cuffed him again. Zacker shoved his head down and threw him into the back seat. "Stay lying down," he said.

Moments later, Zacker got in the front, gave the auto-taxi an address, then turned to keep an eye on Fergus. As the car pulled away and sped up, Zacker frowned. "So, how'd you do it?" he asked.

"Do what?"

"Get that scar, asshole."

"Shot with a harpoon gun," Fergus said.

Zacker's eyebrows went up. "Really?" he said. "That must have hurt like hell."

"Yeah."

"Good."

"I was trying to save the lives of a whole lot of people at the time," Fergus said.

"Right. Spin me another one. Or rather, don't. I hate liars

almost as much as I hate thieves." Zacker's voice was calm and anything but casual. "Now shut up, or I'll shoot you."

The auto-taxi pulled up and parked beside a small building on the outskirts of the city. Behind it was a hangar and a flat, paved field. Lined up beside the hanger were four jump shuttles, one red, two silver, and a blue. The red looked like it could make low orbit. *One in four*, Fergus thought. *How lucky am I feeling right now?*

Not very was the obvious answer.

"I'm going to get out," Zacker said. "You are going to stay where you are, without moving, until I open your door. And then you're going to kick your pack out onto the ground, get out slowly, and lean against the car as if you're gonna take a nice nap on it. When you wake up, you'll be standing in front of a judge, and you can see if he believes your bullshit."

The detective climbed out of the taxi, gun leveled at Fergus. Opening the passenger door, he stepped well back. Fergus pushed his pack out the door with his feet as gently as he could, then inched his way toward the edge of the seat feet-first, hampered by the handcuffs almost as much as his reservations about getting out.

"Hurry up," Zacker snapped.

"I'm feeling light-headed," Fergus replied. "You want people to move fast, maybe you shouldn't hit them on the head and drug them. Let me take my time, or you might end up carrying me all the way to your shuttle—what, the blue one? You look like a blue type. You know: blue, police, all that."

"Fuck you. Mine's the red one. You know: red, like the blood on your hands. And I got you into the apartment without breaking a sweat, so don't waste your breath insulting me." Zacker gestured angrily with the gun. "Now get *out*."

Fergus managed to get to his feet, then swayed dizzily. "I don't feel good," he said. "Uh . . ."

He let his eyes roll up into the back of his head and collapsed where he stood, landing hard in the driveway gravel.

Zacker kicked him. "Get the fuck up," he said.

Fergus remained motionless, boneless, and held his breath.

"Shit," he heard Zacker say, then he was kicked a few more times. "Shit! Come on, you piece of shit asshole!"

He felt the cool cold circle of the gun muzzle against his head but didn't move or flinch. *Come on*, he thought. *I can't hold my breath forever.*

Two fingers touched the side of his neck, checking for a pulse. *Okay, come on, special gift!* Fergus thought. He let enough electricity through the point of contact to knock out an ox, then rolled sharply sideways. His movement broke the contact, but as he'd hoped, Zacker had stiffened, stunned, and fell forward onto his face.

Fergus scrambled to his feet and kicked the gun away. Crouching down, he turned his side to the stunned man and managed to pull the handcuff keys from Zacker's pocket. Moments later, he had the cuffs off himself and onto the detective.

Another search of the man's pockets and duffel yielded several treasures. Fergus spread everything out on the hood of the taxi and sat up beside it, half an eye on Zacker as he poked through. There was a 3corder with footage of Fergus breaking into Suttie's from the angle of the apartment window, but although his face was identifiable, nothing could be seen of how he'd gotten through the gate. There was also a security pass for the airfield, a battered but likely genuine SCNY police badge, and a handpad that, after Fergus pressed Zacker's limp fingers against its ID pad, yielded more than two years of notes from the apartment, a recipe for stout stew, and a photo of the detective as a much younger man, smiling, a carousel behind him, and a small girl with her two front teeth missing clinging to him with a huge smile.

"My daughter," Zacker said from the ground. He'd rolled over, and there were small cuts on his cheek and nose where he'd hit the gravel. "Deliah. Deliah Zacker. She was only five in that photo."

"She's cute," Fergus said.

"She was, yeah."

"Something happened to her?" Fergus asked.

"Yeah. You and your friends shot her in the face," Zacker said. He was looking around, probably trying to find his gun. He wouldn't; Fergus had hidden it in the last place the detective would probably look.

"Now that you don't have a gun pointed at me, and I have no reason to lie to you, let me tell you again: I've been away from Earth for nineteen years. I'm sorry about your daughter, but it wasn't me."

"I don't believe you," Zacker said.

"You don't have to," Fergus said, "though I wish you would. Look, I have urgent business, my friends are in danger, and you've slowed me down enough that I'm going to have to borrow your shuttle. And I'm sorry about that, too. I'll try not to dent it, and I'll leave it somewhere you can go get it again when I'm done. I hope you find the real bad guys you're looking for and get the justice your daughter deserves."

"Screw you, you liar. What did you hit me with, anyhow? My body is numb. I checked you for weapons and you had *nothing*," Zacker said. At Fergus's shrug, he scowled. "Come on, asshole. Professional pride here."

"I really can't tell you," Fergus said. "Consider that payback for the bloody great lump you left on my head."

He pocketed the security pass, erased the 3corder, then carefully packed the rest of the detective's things back in his duffel, zipped it shut, then checked his own. His gear was all still there and intact, if no longer neatly folded. The tiny pager disk was blinking again but had no new messages.

When he glanced back at the detective, the man had managed to scoot half a meter over on the gravel without making a sound. Fergus threw the man's duffel in the back seat of the taxi, then told it they were done with it. As the detective watched, face red with fury, the auto-taxi drove away.

"Sorry," Fergus said. "Someone will find you by morning, and it's a mild night for a Glasgow winter. Good luck, Detective Zacker."

Fergus shouldered his pack and walked backward to the airfield fence, not ready to take his eyes off Zacker yet. When he reached it, he swiped the security card and stepped through the opening gate.

Turning, he ran toward the red shuttle. The lock on it was a simple keycode pad, and the confuddler took care of it with ease. He popped the main door open and climbed inside, stashing his things in a locker, then buckled in and powered the shuttle up. "Orbit, here we come," he said, and hit the button to close and seal the door for liftoff.

"—WITHOUT ME!" someone yelled, and he jerked around in his seat in time to see Zacker fling himself bodily through the closing door, just barely managing to roll and pull his legs in before they slammed shut.

"What the hell are you doing?" Fergus shouted at him as the man lay there, chest heaving, trying to catch his breath.

"Not. Letting you. Get away, asshole," Zacker managed. His hands were still under him; he'd not gotten the cuffs off.

Fergus pulled on the headset as the shuttle's preflight check finished. "You keep calling me an asshole, and I might just start acting like one," he said. "Now find a way to hang on back there or you're going to get some bruises."

He powered up the shuttle and it lifted smoothly from the field. It was an early Strider model, probably at least forty years old, but it had been well cared-for. His peevishness at Zacker wasn't diminished by that fact.

As he pointed the nose up, he heard a crash in the back followed by swearing, and he smiled. "Hey, detective!" he shouted back.

". . . What?" came a very grumpy response.

"You ever been off-Earth?"

"My ex-wife made me take her to the moon once. I hated it," the detective said. "Swore I'd never go above low orbit again."

"Yeah, well, I have bad news for you," Fergus said. He watched out the front window as they emerged from the clouds, the light of the moon transforming them into a sea of white below. Lights on the console announced when they finally left the last thin dregs of atmosphere.

Pulling up navigation, he found the nearest orbital depot, Kelly Station, and added the shuttle to the queue for a slot. Estimates were around six hours, which made him both antsy and hopeful. At any given time, there'd be businessmen from both outsystem and downwell, and one of them would have a ship going at least as far as Titan. It might take him a few tries, but he'd get back to Pluto. In the meantime, he took parking-orbit instructions from Kelly's controller and set the shuttle to auto.

Unbuckling, he floated toward the back. Zacker was at the rear of the shuttle, floating free now, looking homicidal and more than a little green. "If you promise not to try anything, I'll push you into a seat and buckle you down," Fergus said. "If you're not used to no-grav, it's a little easier on the stomach."

"Fuck you," Zacker said.

Fergus shrugged, pushed off gently from the walls, did a somersault, then stared back at the detective from upside-down.

Zacker had his eyes squeezed tightly shut, and his cheeks puffed out as if he was about to blow barf any moment. "You can barf in here if you want. It's your shuttle," Fergus said. "Just keep it out of the cabin, okay?"

"Fine," Zacker managed to squeak out. "You can buckle me in. Uncuff me first?"

"Oh, hell no," Fergus said. He grabbed a bar on the ceiling, pushed forward, and with his feet gently kicked Zacker toward one of the shuttle's back seats. The man hit, started to bounce back out in slow motion as Fergus brought down and locked the overhead safety bar.

With the cessation of motion, the detective began to look slightly less eruptive. At last, the man cracked open one eye, then the other, and stared at Fergus for a while. "What are you going to do to me?" he asked at last.

"When I'm done with your shuttle, I'm going to leave. Then you can go do whatever it is you want."

"I want to catch the thieves who shot my daughter," Zacker said. "I want you to lead me to the rest of your gang."

Fergus sighed, and seeing that his drift around the cabin was still bothering the detective, pulled himself down into a seat across from him. "You're from New York," he said. "You're a detective. You're retired. You're out here in Scotland on your own cred, spending more than two years sitting across from Suttie's in an abandoned building looking for someone to show up. That someone isn't me. But if you go back, maybe the person you want still will."

Zacker looked miserable. "If I even have the right place. No one believed me; I couldn't get my own captain or my own *partner* to back me, much less make an international request for a search. This was all I had, waiting out a hunch."

"What are you looking for?" Fergus asked.

Zacker met his eyes, held them, then seemed to deflate. "Paintings. Stolen paintings. My daughter was a guide at the damned Met, first job out of college. She was so proud."

Fergus pushed himself back up from his seat, glanced back at the console, saw they hadn't moved in the dock queue at all yet. *Don't get involved, you idiot,* he told himself. *Your friends need you, and this jerk would kill you in an instant if he got another chance.*

He could still picture the smiling girl on the carousel. "It's not the wrong place," he said.

Zacker's head came up sharply. "What do you know?"

"I saw the paintings in Suttie's," he said. "I remember hearing about the Met robbery, too, though I was on Mars at the time."

"You can prove that?"

"Probably, but I don't have to," Fergus said. "I'm going to drop you at that orbital as soon as we get a berth, and you can take your shuttle back there and prove it all by yourself."

"So, you're telling me you just wandered into a locked storage company and happened to spot millions of dollars of missing stolen art by *accident*?!"

"Pretty much, yeah," Fergus said.

"Then what the hell did you go in there for?"

"A motorcycle," Fergus said. "It was gone, and the paintings were in my unit instead."

"And you didn't call the police?" Zacker shouted.

"Some big wanker ambushed me and cracked me on the head!" Fergus shouted back. His pocket buzzed, and he angrily pulled out the pager disk.

"Uh . . ." Zacker said. His eyes were wider, and his face paler, than they were moments before.

Fergus ignored him and stabbed at the button. This time, instead of Tomboy, it was a message from the ship *Venetia's Sword*. "Don't move," it said.

"What?" Fergus said.

Unable to point with his cuffed hands, Zacker jutted his chin toward the front cabin window. "What is *that*?" he asked.

Fergus spun around just in time to see the wide, rectangular mouth of a shuttle bay swallow them whole. After a moment's stunned silence, he closed his mouth and tapped the pager again. "Uh, *Venetia's Sword*?" he asked.

"Hello, Mr. Ferguson," the voice of the ship answered, smoothly, with no sign of the skips and stutters from the damage done in Cernee. "I have come to take you back to the Shipyard."

"Who's on the bridge?" Fergus asked. "Theo? Effie? Tell me they didn't let Maison drive?"

"No one," *Venetia's Sword* answered.

"What?"

"The Shipyard was attacked by an unknown entity. I was performing a programmed set of fine engine maneuver trials along the heliopause and was not in the vicinity during the assault, but received Tomboy's distress call. No one is responding now. I came to get you. You are the one who fixes everything."

Behind him, Zacker coughed.

"Right. I need five minutes to turn this shuttle back over to its owner and send him on his way," Fergus said, "then—"

"I have already sealed the bay door and initiated a full burn to the Jupiter jump point," the *Venetia's Sword* said. "I'm afraid the shuttle will not be able to depart until then."

"So, now you're kidnapping me?" Zacker asked.

"*You* are the one who stowed away," Fergus said. "Are your piloting skills good enough to get you home from Titan?"

Zacker made a face. "No," he said at last. "No way."

"Well, shit," Fergus said. "You got enough money to hire a pilot to take you and your shuttle back?"

"You get much of a look around that apartment of mine? Not

exactly rolling in things like piles of cash, fine furnishings, or even *food*," Zacker said. "It took every penny I had to stake out that storage service waiting for you."

"Not for me," Fergus said.

"Yeah, yeah. I'm starting to fucking get that," Zacker said. "Don't expect me to be happy about it, because you blundering in just ruined my only chance to get justice for Deliah. And I'm still not convinced you're not a criminal."

Fergus tapped the pager. "Vee, the person with me is not trusted. If he tries anything, you have my express permission to flush this shuttle right back out into space, even if we're mid-jump."

"That would tear the shuttle apart, and even if it somehow survived, without stabilizers, it would get taken by the Drift," *Venetia's Sword* answered.

"Yes, I know," Fergus said, eyes pointedly on Zacker. "Detective, if I uncuff you, will you give me your word not to make trouble? Otherwise, you're going to have an uncomfortable ride to Jupiter, at the very least."

"I'm willing to offer a temporary truce," Zacker said. "Temporary until new information comes to light proving you should be taken out."

"Only if you give me fair warning and a chance to prove that information is wrong," Fergus said.

"Deal," the detective said.

"Fine, then." Fergus reached out and grabbed Zacker's jacket, pulling the man out of the seat and around so he could undo the cuffs. Then he backed off, using the wall bars for leverage.

Detective Zacker flexed his hands, rubbing at his wrists, and tried to move, sending himself into a slow spin. "Never done zero-gravity before?" Fergus asked.

"Not except for quick hops while buckled down," Zacker said, "and I didn't like that, either."

"Would you like a hand?"

Zacker glared but nodded. "Yeah."

Fergus took his arm, pulled his hand up to a ceiling bar. "It just takes practice," he said. "Like learning to swim for the first time. Once you get it, it's second nature. Now, since I still don't trust you not to try to kill me, I'd rather not leave you alone in this shuttle."

"I don't trust you out of my sight," Zacker said.

"Then I guess we're going to the bridge. Follow me," Fergus said. He tapped the pager. "Vee, is the bay sealed and pressurized?"

"Yes. It is safe for you to exit the shuttle," *Venetia's Sword* answered.

Fergus popped the shuttle door and gestured for Zacker to go through first. After several tries and a few hard knocks on the doorframe, the detective got through and out into the *Venetia's Sword*'s shuttle bay. The tiny ship took up most of the bay, but there was enough room for Zacker to lose his grip and end up in a slow spin in open space.

Fergus came out after, gave the detective a gentle shove in the small of his back, and Zacker floated close enough to a wall to grab a bar and steady himself. He followed Fergus through the inner bay door but balked when Fergus kicked off and sailed up a float tube. "No way," he said.

"Just put one arm up like Superman and kick off," Fergus said.

"No fucking way in hell," Zacker said. He stared up the tube at Fergus, scowling, then at last steeled himself and shoved upward. "Shit. This is just wrong."

At the top, Fergus pulled him over, then led him down the main corridor to the bridge. The bridge had been cleaned up in the time since he'd brought it back to the Shipmakers, and there was no sign of the damage done during their misadventures in Cernee except one hold bar still missing from the ceiling. Fergus gave Zacker a small shove toward a chair at the back, and the detective pulled himself into it and buckled in with haste. "Who's flying this thing?" he asked.

"It's flying itself," Fergus said as he took the seat at the helm and did the same, without the panic.

"It can do that?" Zacker asked.

"It can, and quite well," Fergus said. "The Shipmakers make some of the finest computer intelligences in human space. They've made an art out of it."

"Thank you," *Venetia's Sword* said.

"You're welcome," Fergus said. "What's our position?"

"We have fifty-nine minutes remaining in passive jump until we reach Jupiter space. We will need to pass through an Alliance checkpoint, but I have your alternate credentials stored," the ship said. "I do not have any identity information for our guest."

"Detective Zacker?" Fergus said. "You have Alliance-certified ID?"

"Yeah, and it's real, too," Zacker said. He patted his pocket, took out his wallet and an ID chit from its protected sleeve. There was a reader on the console in front of him, and he slid it in.

"Welcome aboard, Clarence Williston Zacker," *Venetia's Sword* said. "I will cache only your public credentials for the security scan. You may retrieve your ID now."

Zacker pulled it out, eyes on Fergus. "Well?" he said.

"Well, what?"

"You going to make fun of my name? *Clarence?*"

Fergus shook his head. "No, I'm not. You know mine?"

"All I caught was 'Ferguson', if that's even your real name and not one of your *alternates*." Zacker's expression was one of perfect authoritarian disappointment. "Can I ask some questions?"

"Sure," Fergus said. "But I can't promise answers."

"What's the Drift?"

"You really haven't traveled off Earth, have you?"

"I've never needed to."

Fergus sighed, leaning back in his chair and resting his head against the back. It still hurt from where Zacker had knocked him out. "Okay, so, you know about lightspeed?"

"Yeah, and jumping is the only way to go faster than that. I'm not an idiot."

"So, there's two kinds of jumping," Fergus said. "Passive jump is like a stone skipping across the top of a lake, except we're the stone and the lake is space and is curved. Each skip is a tiny shortcut, a straight line cutting across the arc of space, so you go close to—but a little faster than—light. That's the tech we got from the Celekai at first contact."

"Yeah, yeah," Zacker said.

"The advantage to passive jump is that you can go from almost anywhere to almost anywhere else. The disadvantage is it's a lot slower than active jump. Active is more like shooting a bullet through the waves on the top of the lake. Much faster, but you have to start at specific points where the fabric of space has a particular type of warp to it, and go in a specific direction. That's the tech we stole from the Bomo'ri. We don't know what causes the jump points to form, but they're most common in areas with complex or significant gravitational fields. Hence Jupiter. Once you jump into the conduit—the path of the bullet, if you will—you try very hard to stay in the center of it until you reach the other end. In an emergency, you can drop out into normal space, but if you stay in the conduit but wander towards the edges, you're a goner. Ships get pulled to pieces, and the pieces just vanish. Theory is they get barfed out in random places in space, some people think they end up in an alternate universe, but whatever the case, you don't ever get home again. That's the Drift."

"Okay, let's not go there," Zacker said. "Next question: what are you going to do with me?"

"If I drop you at Titan, you should be able to sell your shuttle for enough money to get home again and then some. Of course, that leaves you without a shuttle, but you did assault me and then stow away, so I don't feel entirely bad about that," Fergus said. He paused. "Sorry."

"And you're going where?"

"My friends are in danger. I'm going to go help them."

"And I suppose they're a bunch of criminals, like you? You live that life, and trouble always catches up to you, in the end."

"They're scientists and engineers and geeks and terrible cheats at Venusian Monkeypoker," Fergus said. "They're good people. The best people I know."

"Right," Zacker said skeptically. "After you help them, then what?"

"What do you mean?"

"Your missing motorcycle. What are you going to do about that?"

"Go back and find it," Fergus said.

"It's important to you?"

"More than I care to explain, but yes."

"You think whoever took it is also responsible for the stolen art being in your unit?" Zacker asked.

"I don't think it's coincidence. Either the thieves know or Mr. Suttie does, or maybe both."

"So, if I stick with you, eventually you'll lead me to the art thieves," Zacker said.

"Look, I see what you're getting at, and I understand why," Fergus said, "but if someone's attacked my friends, those people are dangerous. More dangerous than you and me by a whopping great margin."

"I served thirty-nine years on the Sovereign City of New York police force, most of it in violent crime," Zacker said. "I may not know shit about space, but dangerous I can handle."

"You attacked me," Fergus said. "That gives me trust issues."

"Yeah, but I want my art thieves more than I want anything else," Zacker said. "I've worked with partners I hate before."

"*Partners?*" Fergus stared at the man in disbelief.

"First rule: don't go in without backup. You got backup?"

"I—" Fergus was going to protest he needed no such thing, but Zacker wasn't going to let him finish.

"No, you don't," Zacker said, jabbing Fergus hard with his finger. "I can tell you're the pathetic loner type. I'll help you with your friends, and then you lead me to my art thieves. You got any better ideas?"

"If Mr. Zacker is experienced in the investigation of crime, would he not be an asset to us?" *Venetia's Sword* asked.

Fergus banged his forehead on the console. "This is a terrible idea," he said.

"In the time we have been associated, it has been clear to me that your problem-solving methodology works best when you take the most difficult and inobvious path in front of you," *Venetia's Sword* said. "I cannot speak to *why* this should work, but it does seem to be your 'thing.'"

Fergus jabbed a finger toward Zacker. "If you come along, and you die, it is *not my fault*," he said.

"Yeah, well, I'm not planning on dying," Zacker said. "And you better not either, not until I get what *I* want."

"I would like my humans saved, if they can be," *Venetia's Sword* said. "I am concerned about them."

"Yeah, me too," Fergus said. "Fine. You hated the moon? Now you're going to Pluto, detective."

Chapter 3

———————◆———◀———

The drop into normal space at Jupiter went smoothly, not even a blip of delay at the security queue. In a matter of minutes after arriving, *Venetia's Sword* powered up her active jump engines and made the odd, tumbly transition into the jumpspace conduit out to the edges of the system. *Thank you, Shipmakers,* Fergus thought. *It must be nice to have that good a reputation.*

In the quiet of the bridge, Zacker's stomach growled so loudly that Fergus managed a smile, despite the gnawing anxiety in his own stomach. "You weren't exaggerating about having no money for food, were you?"

"No," the detective said.

"Well, there's nothing really to do here on the bridge. Why don't I show you to the kitchenette? Not sure what's onboard, but there'll be something." He unbuckled and helped Zacker out of his seat. The detective was getting the hang of moving in zero grav and made it much of the way to the ship's lounge on his own. Only once did he miss a wallbar and end up in a mid-corridor spin.

The lounge was a comfortable space, with soft grippy chairs and a sofa. The adjoining kitchenette had a round table off to one side, complete with large shallow bowl filled with fake Earth fruits, all glued down. LaChelle's touch, certainly, although more ostentatious than she usually went. There was a skylight above, but the ship had shaded it; the supra-dimensional wrongness of a jumpspace conduit was not something even the most seasoned travelers could look at for long without feeling multiple kinds of ill.

Zacker got himself into a grippy chair and seemed pleased that it held him in place. Fergus went to the cabinets and found a few bentobowls. "How do you feel about lasagna?" he asked.

"Like I feel about oxygen and sunshine and puppies," Zacker said.

Fergus heated up two bowls, then a pair of coffee bulbs, and floated them over to where Zacker sat. Zacker took the bowl—more a sphere with a small hole in it—and the funnel-shaped spoon, and looked quizzically at Fergus. "Free-floating pasta is a nightmare," Fergus said. "Sauce gets everywhere."

"Too bad this ship doesn't have artificial gravity," Zacker said. "I thought most did."

"Yeah," Fergus said. "Want coffee?"

"Sure."

Fergus handed him the bulb, and after a moment of considering, Zacker took a sip. "Not terrible," the detective said.

"In space, *not terrible* is quite good."

"So," Zacker said. "If you're not a thief, what is it you *do*, exactly?"

"I steal things," Fergus said. At Zacker's startlement, he laughed. "Sorry, I had to. What I do is I find lost or stolen things and return them to their rightful owners."

"Like a repo man?"

"Very much so, but more complicated."

"Okay. I can live with that," Zacker said. He finally managed to get some lasagna in his spoon and sucked it out.

Fergus frowned down at his own bowl, thinking that he'd set some sort of record for shortest visit to Earth; all that angst and effort, and all he had to show for it was a lump on his head and a possibly homicidal retired police detective as involuntary company. Zacker was exactly the sort of complication he didn't need, but if nothing else, at least the man could serve as a distraction from worrying about his friends.

"Since we've got a while before we're at Pluto, tell me about the art heist," he said.

"All the case files, photos and docs and statements were on my handpad in my duffel," Zacker said. "Which you let the taxi drive off with."

"So, tell me what you remember about it. Usually, we remember the most important things without knowing it."

"Said like a man with a good memory."

"True," Fergus said. "But I can get all the files on my own. I can't get how you saw it."

"Fine. It was February 29th, 2248," Zacker said. "Leap day. About an hour after closing, the entire Met security system just crashed. Our code division spent nearly a year trying to figure out if it was a date-related bug or exploit in the system, but if it was, they couldn't find it. The system had been upgraded three years previously, and the lead programmer for the company that did it was found floating in the Hudson a week after the heist. Well, half of him. We never found the slightest evidence that the company wasn't completely legit. Eighteen paintings were taken."

"Do you mean *seventeen*?" Fergus said.

"What? No. Eighteen."

"There were only seventeen cases in the storage unit."

"You sure?"

"Positive."

"That's interesting," Zacker said. He tapped his spoon against his bowl of lasagna thoughtfully. "One is missing, then."

"Maybe they took one to sell off early?"

"Maybe," Zacker said, though it was clear he thought otherwise. "Usually, art thieves wait a decade or two until attention dies down and then drop everything onto the black market at once. No drawn-out exposure that way."

That was in keeping with Fergus's brief excursion into the world of stolen art. "So, what happened after the security system crashed?" he asked.

"The default was for it to revert to lockdown in the event of failure, but instead, it opened everything. They had a stolen AtlanticExpress truck in the loading dock, came in—masks, body-blur suits, a freakin' cloud of cleaner nanos in their wake sucking up any DNA, fingerprint, pheromone traces left behind. There were four staff still there in addition to a dozen security guards when they came in."

"One was your daughter."

"Yeah." Zacker didn't say anything more for a while, just sat there staring off at nothing. At last, he shook himself, ate another spoonful of lasagna, and grimaced. "Five of the guards were shot; one survived but spent a year getting his spine regrown. The remainder all got trapped in other wings of the museum as the thieves selectively turned back on locks. They thought they had the post-impressionists all to themselves, except Deliah was there too; she'd found a kid's stuffed tiger under a bench and was taking it to lost and found. Came around the corner and ran right into them."

"I'm sorry," Fergus said.

"The first officer on the scene arrived just in time to find the truck abandoned three blocks away, empty, not a fucking molecule of physical evidence left inside. Dead end."

"Somehow, you ended up in Scotland, though. In the exact right place, no less."

"It was stupid. It wasn't even really a lead, nothing I would have spent half an hour thinking about if it hadn't been this case, and if I didn't have absolutely nothing else. And I mean *nothing*," Zacker said. "We'd gone back a month after the robbery to talk to everyone again, see if anyone remembered something new. We were desperate. I got talking to some old lady with six of those little nasty designer dogs all yapping as she talked to me through two inches of open door, and the *mouth* on this woman . . . She swore worse than half the men on the squad. Seems we'd missed talking to her first time around because she'd been at the ceremonial tree-planting as the kickoff to the Central Park Restoration Project, and someone had hit her parked car outside a small warehouse around the corner and left a big dent and gouges in the paint, no automated collision log, and why the hell weren't we investigating *that* crime?"

He took another spoonful of lasagna, scowling at the memory as he chewed. "I had no one else left to talk to," he said when done, "so I went around to this warehouse thinking if her car was still parked there, I might add a few more dents to it for all the people hurt or killed she didn't give a shit about. Of course, the car wasn't there, but there was something odd about the warehouse. Poked around outside, peered in the windows, and the damn place was scrubbed just as clean as the inside of that AtlEx truck. Got a warrant and went in. There was a flash recycler in the upstairs office that had gotten too much stuff jammed into it and it overloaded, and we were able to extract some burnt paper scraps. Forensics put them back together and got one word: *Suttie*."

"And that led you to Scotland?"

"And about a hundred thousand other places and people," Zacker said. "Could definitely rule out most and mark more down as unlikely, but nothing stood out as a real lead. There's at least three poor slobs named Suttie still under drone surveillance in the SCNY, as far as I know. But something about this place . . . I just had a feeling. When I retired, I took every penny I had and moved to Glasgow, and I never doubted for one minute I had the right spot and just needed to wait it out."

He laughed, a harsh sound. "So, here I am, closest I've ever gotten to catching the thieves, and I'm halfway to *Pluto*. I finally have confirmation that I was right, and for the first time, I'm full of self-doubt. How the hell is that for a kicker?"

"The universe loves to kick," Fergus said. "Sometimes, I think it's just checking that we're still alive."

"Yeah, I hear that," Zacker said. He finished the last few mouthfuls of his lasagna and then downed the bulb of coffee. "Okay, now what?"

"Pluto and Charon don't have a jump point, but they do make a nice little ripple in jump space that'll let us know when we're getting near," Fergus said. "We'll drop out of the conduit on the far side of Pluto. Almost all traffic comes from in-system, so if any of our unknown attackers is looking for someone coming to the rescue, hopefully they'll be looking in the wrong direction."

He raised his head up toward one of *Venetia's Sword*'s eyes in the room. "You catch that, Vee?"

"Yes, Mr. Ferguson," *Venetia's Sword* answered.

"You have combat experience?" Zacker asked.

"I've gotten caught in some very big fights and managed not to get myself killed yet," Fergus said. "You?"

"The water riots," Zacker said.

"That'd do it," Fergus said. He leaned forward and tapped on the table in front of the sofa. "Vee, can you please project a holo of the Shipyard?"

Purple tracery appeared in the air over the table, first outlining the long, narrow spindle of the station, then drawing in the various wheels, bays, and charged ion interceptors that spun around it like giant pinwheels. "Do you have any data from the attack?" Fergus asked.

"Only a limited set," *Venetia's Sword* said. "Tomboy's packet burst to me was cut off in microseconds. There were four breaches of the station hull nearly simultaneously." Red dots lit up, one each on the shuttle and drone docks, one near the reactor, and the last at the far end of the spindle, where the observation deck and all the major control systems were housed, including Tomboy itself.

"And there's been nothing from the Shipyard since then?"

"During our window in normal space, I sent several queries back but received no acknowledgement or reply," *Venetia's Sword* said.

"How big is this thing?" Zacker asked, pointing at the hologram.

"See the fabrication bays back here?" Fergus pointed at a non-spinning block toward the rear of the spindle. "Six ships the size of this one could fit inside this at once."

"It would be very crowded if we did that," *Venetia's Sword* said. "The proximity would not meet safety standards."

"But you could fit."

"Yes. Eight of us, if we were precise in how we parked."

Zacker whistled. "Okay. And how many people live in this thing? Hundred or so?"

"Seven."

"Seven hundred?"

"No, seven," Fergus said. "Eight when I'm there, but I'm more a regular guest than actual resident. Over the years, there have sometimes been more, sometimes fewer—being out here is not the life for everyone. And of course, I'm not counting all the artificial intelligences that live there, such as Tomboy—the station mind—and ships like *Venetia's Sword* here."

"They don't count," Zacker snapped.

Fergus raised an eyebrow. "Really?"

"I don't know much about a lot of things, but it's common knowledge—a running *joke*—that as hard as they've tried, scientists haven't been able to make a genuinely self-aware, sentient computer yet," Zacker said. He had stiffened in his seat, and his whole body seemed suddenly clenched. "That's why they call them *simulated intelligences*, SIs instead of AIs. They're not people; they're an illusion. The problem with you people is you think that just because you appreciate the magician, you have to also buy the damned magic."

Us people? Fergus thought. "Not the first time you've had this argument, detective?"

Zacker hurled his empty lasagna bulb hard across the room. It missed the flash recycler and smashed against the wall, sending bits of plastic and sauce flying. "Deliah too," he snarled.

Fergus blinked at the outburst. *Whoa,* he thought. He needed to not forget this man had a temper.

Zacker pushed himself up off the sofa too hard, floated up to crash into the ceiling, and flailed there for bit. His face was deep red, and slowly anger gave way to embarrassment. "I'll clean that up when I can figure out how to get around in this fucking space circus," he said.

"I will take care of it, Mr. Zacker," *Venetia's Sword* said. "Mr. Ferguson, I estimate we will be dropping out of jump in approximately forty-one minutes, if you would like to come back up to the bridge."

"Thank you, Vee," Fergus said. He turned the holo-table off and leaned back, arms across his chest. Zacker was glaring at him from where he was still floating.

"So, detective," Fergus said, as if everything was perfectly normal, not taking up the challenge in Zacker's stare to say anything about it. "There are cabins onboard. I can show you to one if you need to clean up or catch a bit of shut-eye."

"And what are you going to be doing?" Zacker said. He managed to get his hands up against the ceiling and pushed himself clumsily back down toward the center of the room. The detective just managed to grab a corner of the grippy chair, and with much effort and swinging around got himself back into it.

"When we come out of jump, the ship is going to scan the Shipyard, and we'll see if we can get a sense of what's happening and how bad things are," Fergus said, as the detective caught his breath. "Then I am going to put on my very stealthy military-grade exosuit and go over there and do what I can to help my friends."

"What if your friends are all dead?"

"Then I'm going to find who did it and do everything in my power to make them regret it," Fergus said. "I expect you understand that, detective."

"Yeah. I just don't want your revenge to get in the way of mine," Zacker said. He was calming down and seemed to have decided to just go with Fergus's strategy of pretending the outburst had not happened. "You shouldn't be going into a hostile situation without backup. It's how you get yourself killed. But I'm not sure I can go out in space, not without time to get used to the idea first."

"We've still got time before we're there, and no way of knowing what's waiting for us," Fergus said. "Maybe they're okay and it's just that their comms are offline, and we can dock and go right in."

"You think that's likely?"

"No," Fergus said.

"If we have time, there's one thing I'd appreciate," Zacker said.

"Yeah?"

"A bathroom?"

"Oh! Yes." Fergus got up and pointed toward the door, and Zacker managed to get himself moving in the right direction and followed him.

Just outside the lounge, there was a pair of bathrooms, one on either side of the corridor. Fergus opened the door and Zacker started past him, then stopped dead when he caught sight of the oval-shaped pod inside. "Uh . . ." he said.

Fergus tapped the small screen on the wall just inside the door, pulling up *Instructions—> zero gravity—> human—> unmodified/ classic—> current physiological arrangement: penis.* "There's a tutorial," he said. "You can tell it to pause, replay, zoom in, whatever you need. If you get into trouble, ask the ship to send for me. I'll be up in the bridge."

". . . Thanks," Zacker said.

Fergus backed out, closed the door, and pushed up the corridor to the bridge.

"Mr. Ferguson," *Venetia's Sword* said. "I have some concerns about Mr. Zacker."

"As do I," Fergus said. He reached the bridge and the door slid open for him. Despite *Venetia's Sword* bringing itself to fetch them, ships of this size and sophistication were not meant to fly without a pilot like a droneship, and the bridge was designed with that human—or usually human, anyway—element at the forefront. There was a big, comfy chair at the main helm, side stations for extra navigators or weapons crew, and a small auxiliary station at the back with a chair that was probably very comfortable if you hadn't just been tortured before being tied to it, as he had once been. Everything was shiny and white and silver with blue highlight details, no doubt LaChelle's touch matching the blue stripe along the outside hull, and it felt slick and professional and, best of all, *home.*

He dug his rumpled exosuit out of his pack and pulled it on, leaving the hood and faceplate down, and took the seat at the main helm console. He connected the safety tether and buckled himself in, looking over the instrument readings. "For now, keep the whole ship at zero gravity," he said. "If Detective Zacker decides to make trouble, it'll give me a small edge. How long do we have left in transit?"

"Nineteen minutes," *Venetia's Sword* answered.

"Okay. I want us running dark. Power down everything we don't immediately need. We'll start with a passive scan of Pluto and the Shipyard from a distance, then if there's no immediate danger start working our way in. If we encounter hostiles, you do not need to wait for my instructions to undertake evasive maneuvers."

"Should I attempt to contact Tomboy or the other ships?"

"Not until we get eyes on the station," Fergus said. "We don't know who might be listening. Sorry, Vee."

"It's okay, Mr. Ferguson. I am certain if there is a way to help, you will find it."

"Speaking of challenges, how is Mr. Zacker doing?"

"He has figured out the mechanism, but it took a few tries. From his language choices, I would guess he does not like it."

Fergus chuckled. No gravity meant either you used the suction assist or you ended up floating in a cloud of your own pee droplets. *Welcome to space, Detective Zacker,* he thought.

"Mr. Zacker has finished. Shall I direct him back to the lounge, to a cabin, or here?"

"Offer him the choice," Fergus said.

"He is coming here," *Venetia's Sword* said a moment later.

"Well, at least we can keep an eye on him. Can't lock him in a cabin the whole trip," Fergus said. "Next time, remind me to close the gate behind me before I steal a man's flyer."

A few minutes later, Zacker came through the door, spinning a bit before he got himself oriented again. "You can sit there," Fergus said, pointing at the chair toward the back of the bridge. "Buckle in, because there's a chance of a hostile reception when we arrive."

The drop from jump space to normal space was a feeling Fergus had never been able to articulate very well, except to say it wasn't a drop or a bump or a slowing-down, but more the disjointed feeling that you had, in one instant, been physically replaced by an exactly identical copy of yourself.

"Shit," Zacker said from behind him. "That was weird. You actually get used to that?"

"Nope," Fergus said. He was already running his hands over the boards, switching between views as the *Venetia's Sword*'s long-range sensors fixed in on Pluto and the Shipyard.

"I detect no ship signatures either in our vicinity or closer to the Shipyard," *Venetia's Sword* said.

"Take us in," Fergus said. "Full scan in all directions. If you detect even a faint anomaly in space around us, go to a dead stop. And please display all available readings on the station as we approach."

A tiny outline of the Shipyard appeared on the navigation screen, growing larger and filling in with detail and readings. The station's reactor was running hot, while the temperature signature of large portions of the station were nearing equilibrium with surrounding space. "That's not good at all," Fergus said. His pulse was quickening.

"What?" Zacker asked.

"Either life support has been offline for a while or some of the station is open to vacuum. Or both. Vee, any sign of our ships?"

"*Whiro* and *Falconer* are both drifting outside the ship bay.

Neither are online, and I do not detect any energy signatures from them," *Venetia's Sword* said. "I see no sign of any foreign ships. It seems probable that whoever attacked the Shipyard is gone."

"What do we have onboard that can close the distance between us and the Shipyard quickly but discreetly?"

"I still have the mobile device you brought aboard at Cernee that you called a 'flystick,'" *Venetia's Sword* said. "Will that suffice?"

"That's perfect!" Fergus said. "Take us in to a kilometer distance."

"Flystick?" Zacker asked.

"You know what a pogo stick is?"

"Yeah. There was a big retro toy fad when Deliah was a kid. She loved that thing, even after she broke her elbow falling off it."

"Well, it's like that, except for zero gravity, and with a large engine welded to the bottom. A lot more dangerous, and even more fun," Fergus said. Discovering he still had his flystick was a small, bright moment.

As scan resolution improved, he could see several breaches in the station hull; both the shuttle and drone docks were compromised, and there were smaller bore holes in the observation deck and in the robot fabrication bay. "Definitely not good at all," he said.

"I have detected a signature down on the surface of Pluto," *Venetia's Sword* said. "It is from one of our shuttles and is in the location where Ms. Effie likes to go down to watch the atmospheric snow."

"Is it responding?"

"No," *Venetia's Sword* said. "From the debris scatter, it appears to have taken a direct hit from orbit."

"Effie usually lands and takes the buggy out to the methane snow fields," Fergus said. "Scan for the buggy?"

"There is no sign of the buggy."

"Shit. Any life signs in the station? Comms, heat signatures, anything?"

"No."

"How close are we?"

"Just reaching the kilometer mark and nearing full stop," *Venetia's Sword* said. "What do we do now?"

"I'm going over. You keep watching the station and Pluto's surface and space. I want to know if even so much as a mouse rears its head within ten thousand kilometers of here."

"A mouse would not be—"

"It's a figure of speech," Fergus said. He glanced over at Zacker, made sure to meet his eyes. "I need to know I can trust you here on your own."

"I'm not going to touch a damned thing," Zacker said. "Even the fucking toilet scares me."

"Fine. Just in case, if you do start touching things you shouldn't, the ship has my permission to flush you directly into space," Fergus said. "And I'm not requiring it to give you warning."

Zacker raised both his hands. "Trust me, I'm not the slightest bit interested in testing that," he said. "But what if something happens to you?"

"If something happens to me, the ship will do its best to get you to safety," Fergus said. "Okay?"

"And what if you need backup?"

"Then I'll yell for help and you two can figure something out." Fergus unbuckled from his seat and pushed off for the bridge door. "Vee, patch my suit goggles in to the viewer so Detective Zacker can see what I see. An extra set of eyes—especially trained ones—could be invaluable."

Leaving the bridge behind, Fergus found the flystick stashed in the same locker he'd left it in seemingly a lifetime before. It was bright purple and covered with glitter, and had been a joke of sorts. He was glad Zacker wasn't here to make him try to explain it.

He cycled himself and the 'stick out into space. The Shipyard lay directly ahead, barely visible even with his goggles on max. Usually, he could see its lights from ten times this distance, but the entire length was dark, and none of the rotating sections were moving.

Firing up the 'stick, he pointed at the Shipyard and took it to full acceleration. "Holy hell," he heard Zacker swear over the open connection. He'd be virtually seeing from the ship what Fergus saw. *Not much difference between this and being fired out of a rocket launcher at something,* Fergus thought. *Less exploding, if I'm lucky.*

Rather than the jagged hole he'd expected, the breach into the shuttle dock was a neat circle cut through the hull above the docking envelope, punctures at regular intervals around it where something had clamped on to cut. "You seeing this?" he asked.

"Yeah," Zacker said. "Professional job?"

"Certainly not your typical flyby piracy. Besides, they knew right where to hit, too."

He cut the 'stick's engine and let himself drift closer, using the fine jets to slow himself. As he got to within a few meters of the ship, he began to feel a humming in his gut, and his exosuit display began to crawl with pulses of static. Some sort of EMP generator, he guessed. If those were strategically placed around the Shipyard, that would keep Tomboy and the other ships from booting back up.

"What's happening?" Zacker asked. "Your signal is going fuzzy."

"Interference. Hang on, I'm thinking," he said.

If I had my shit down well enough to be cutting perfect circles in someone's hull, I'd have my EMP device ready to be deployed as quickly as possible, he thought. There didn't appear to be anything attached to the outside of the hull, so it had to be inside. Probably.

He circled away from the shuttle bay, switched off all goggle enhancements to leave straight optics, then set the 'stick on a trajectory straight toward the hole. "My suit's going to crash when I get close enough, but it should reboot as soon as I take the generator down. If something goes wrong, they must have internal batteries and they'll die down eventually, and you can come get my body."

"Uh . . ." Zacker said.

He was moving at a steady crawl toward the breach. The static hit his suit at the same time he could feel it in his body, and moments later, his exosuit went dark. It was a long seven seconds from there until he reached the hole into the shuttle bay. He let go of his 'stick, tucking up and spinning backward as he passed through, trying to spot the source of the interference in the pitch dark. He was relieved to see a tiny blinking red light just above the door. Reaching out an arm, he hooked the edge of the hole, hoping desperately there was nothing sharp enough there to cut through his suit glove, and as his momentum swung him upward, he slapped the device with his other hand and poured his own electricity into it.

There was a flash, and the device went out. A few seconds later, his suit rebooted, coming back to life. Although he hadn't been short of breath yet, he took a deep, grateful pull of fresh air.

All his troubles in Cernee, where he'd gone to take back *Venetia's Sword* from the man who'd stolen her, had begun with an EMP mine on a cable car. That had been a single pulse rather than a continuous emission, but it had been backed up by a secondary explosive. Bracing himself as best he could beside the breach, he threw the mine out into space. If it didn't explode, they could always go get it later for a closer look.

His suit comms finally came back up. "I'm inside," he said. "One device down."

"We are receiving your sensor feeds again," *Venetia's Sword* said. "Other than the breach itself, there does not appear to be any damage to the bay, nor anything obvious missing."

"Not that I see, either," Fergus said. "I'm heading up into the ship's spindle and try to get to control and reboot Tomboy."

The blast doors from the bay into the station were closed. The panel to the mechanical override was open. Ship systems should have automatically regenerated the compressed gas in the system, but ship systems were down and the gas was significantly depleted. That meant the attackers had used the override, which in turn meant they needed to keep the inner parts of the station pressurized for whatever they were after.

He opened the doors about a meter wide, slipped through as air whistled out into the compromised bay, then closed it again from the other side with the last remnants of the gas. From there on, whatever atmosphere was left in any section would even out as he opened doors. His suit told him it was thin but survivable.

He found and disabled three more EMP devices, reluctantly carrying them along with him for lack of a convenient hole to throw them out of, before he encountered the remains of Maison's giant hamster. The deflated and torn magenta membrane with thin strands of lifeless electronics poking out of the mess bobbed forlornly in the central corridor. There were burn marks on the floor and walls around it. Whatever it did, he hoped it annoyed the hell out of someone before they blew it to shit.

Other than the EMP devices and the destroyed hamster, there were no other signs that anyone had been through there.

Nor had he seen any bodies. *Don't get your hopes up, Fergus,* he told himself. Even with atmosphere still tolerable inside, temperatures were dangerously low.

He reached the head of the station, a domed command center with a perfect view of Pluto. When he opened the doors, air in his section was sucked out past him. Just beyond the blast doors, there was another round hole, exactly like the others. In the doorway he found blood, tiny droplets drifting aimlessly through the space.

There's not so much that it means someone has to be dead, he told himself, hoping fervently that was true.

The system core was a truncated cone that dominated the center of the room. The EMP device had been slapped right onto the side of it. Fergus kicked off from the broken doors and hit it just as his suit went offline again. Rather than risk damaging the core by zapping it, he pried frantically at it until it came free and he could fry it in his hand. As soon as he felt it die, he threw it and the others he'd collected out through the hole.

He was breathing heavily, angry, feeling full of restless bees. For the moment, he didn't resent it; if not for the Asiig's tampering with his body, he never would have been able to disarm the devices. He did wish it didn't make him so unbearably thirsty whenever he used it.

"I'm in control," he said, when his suit and his connection to *Venetia's Sword* came back up again. "I'm going to try to get Tomboy online."

Fergus found the main emergency reboot for the core and hit it. Slowly, lights came on in sequence along the control center console. He closed the doors, then floated and waited, trying not to count the seconds.

". . . Mr. Ferguson?" Tomboy's voice broke the unbearable silence.

"I'm here, Tomboy," he said.

"I have lost time."

"I know. I got here as fast as I could. Can you bring the Shipyard back online?"

There was a pause. "I cannot reach the lower third of the station," Tomboy said, with the same stricken tone one might say *I can't feel my legs*. "Also, I do not detect anyone other than you aboard the station. Fergus, where are the others?"

"I don't know," Fergus said. "Where were they when the attack began?"

"Theodoric was here in control. Maison, Noura, and LaChelle were asleep in their quarters. Kelsie was in the engineering lab, playing with servo remotes. Ignatio was in the lounge making eir special pizza. Effie was down on the surface again. She likes the solitude and has been testing some new stealth technologies."

"Effie's shuttle was destroyed," Fergus said. "Do you have visual in the parts of the station back online? Is anything missing? Do you see bodies?"

"I find nothing missing. There is disarray in the vicinity of our people's last known locations. I do not see any bodies."

"System status?" Fergus asked. "Nothing is spinning. I disabled a number of EMP emitters as I came onboard, but I only came up the last third of the spindle."

"There must be at least one emitter still live, cutting off my access to the rear portions of the station, including the robot bays. I require them to seal the breaches and inspect the remainder of the station to determine if we can safely repower the wheels," the station computer said. "This means I am also unable to connect to my reactor systems. I am currently running on finite backup power stores."

"Can you tell if the reactor is okay?" Fergus asked. "Vee thought it might be running hot."

"It is," Tomboy said. "I cannot tell more than that, but it is a deeply concerning indicator."

"Concerning how?" Zacker asked over Fergus's suit comms.

"Concerning as in eventually *kaboom*, I assume," Fergus said. "Okay, I'll go see if I can find and disarm any remaining emitters, and then you can get the reactor back under control."

He pushed out. The spindle corridor had never felt as frighteningly deserted as now. He passed the three hab wheels and the docks where he had come in, but didn't dare peer into the garden wheel for fear of what state it must be in.

Past it was the first of three charged ion collectors, a three-kilometer-wide pinwheel that normally spun gracefully and lazily around the axis of the station. He had never seen it not moving before, and the stilled blades were discomfiting.

Beyond it were parts of the station he had rarely been in, if at all; the smaller fabrication bay wasn't strictly off-limits, but the constant, high-speed bustle of the robots within made it less than safe for flesh-and-blood people. The large fabrication bay, past it, was somewhere only Theo regularly went, and no one dared go without him.

As he passed the remaining two ion collectors, he began to feel the faint tingling of interference somewhere ahead. His comm signal faded into static.

There was another breach just past the last ion collector, as neat and orderly and offensive as the others. The doors to the reactor control room beyond had been forced. From where he'd stopped in the corridor, his suit on the verge of shutting down, he couldn't see through.

Well, nothing for it, Fergus told himself. He braced himself against one of the many structural supports that ringed the corridor and kicked off through the doors. Momentum carried him into the reactor room, and he was satisfied to see the EMP generator, same as the others, slapped onto the main console panel. He reached the station and wrapped his gloved hands around it, killing it.

His suit rebooted, and the reactor control systems came winking back to life, reestablishing connections back to Tomboy.

The hair on the back of his neck stood up, as if a wave of static had crawled up his spine, and he could feel a sudden intrusion of energy as if his body was humming with it. He tried frantically to push his bees down until he realized that it was something external, something whatever the Asiig had given him was reacting to. Turning toward the direction of the sensation, he spotted a black disc the size of a pie stuck onto the front of the bright red main reactor shield plate that was the final dead end of the Shipyard's spindle. "Uh, Tomboy, are you hearing me yet?" he asked. "Patching an image through. Is this normal?"

"—erguson," Tomboy answered. "That device was not there prior to the attack."

Fergus stared at the black disk. *Oh, you utter shits*, he thought. He pushed across the room, wrapped his fingers around the edges, and bracing his feet against the plate to either side of it, pulled as hard as he could. "It's a bomb," he said. "It must have activated as soon as the EMP device was shut down. They probably put it here just in case someone got in and managed to stop the reactor melting down on its own."

"If that goes off near the reactor, it will obliterate the entire station," Tomboy said.

"I know," Fergus said. "I'm working on it!"

The disk must have been flash-welded on, because it would not yield even a millimeter despite how hard he pried at it. Giving up, he put a gloved hand on it and poured electricity into the disc, more and more until it finally shut down. Relieved, he let go, and it immediately lit up again. His suit hadn't even finished rebooting. "I can't get it loose, and I can't make it sleep without my suit shutting down," he said. "Anyone have any ideas?"

"Can you make it pause for approximately forty seconds?" Tomboy asked.

"Yeah," Fergus said. "Not much longer than that."

"Then please do so immediately, and when you can no longer, leave the reactor room as quickly as you can," Tomboy said. "I am going to eject that section of the station, but I will require approximately another forty seconds to disconnect shared systems in preparation."

"Okay. I'm going to lose contact again, so if the plan changes . . . tell me later, if you can."

"Please be careful," *Venetia's Sword* added through their link.

"Always. Here I go," Fergus said, and took a deep breath before zapping the bomb again. His suit systems shut down, and with it, his air circulation and heat. He did his best to count out the seconds, and got to fifty-eight before he just couldn't bear to hold his breath any longer.

He kicked himself backward from the reactor as hard as he could, hit the door frame, bounced, caught it with a foot, then a hand, and pulled himself through back into the main spindle corridor. He could feel the energy building behind him as the bomb re-awoke.

"The reactor room doors are busted. You have to shut the blast doors to this whole section, or the explosion will be directed up the spindle and destroy the Shipyard," Fergus said as soon as his comms were back up. "Do it now and eject."

"You are not out yet," Tomboy said.

The long, straight tube of the spindle stretched away from

him, seeming to disappear into infinity. He could see the gray ring that marked the next set of blast doors about fifty meters ahead, before the rear ion collectors. "I don't have time to get clear," Fergus said. "Eject now, Tomboy!"

He was both relieved and despairing to see the pair of doors, twenty seconds or less out of his reach, slam shut and seal. A heartbeat later, he was nearly pulled off the wallbar he was clinging to by the force of the section being ejected hard out and away.

Always have a plan B, Fergus, he told himself, and he adjusted his grip, swung his feet up against the wall, and kicked himself as hard as he could out the breach hole into the vast empty dark.

The tail end of the station, with its deadly payload, receded quickly into the distance, and a brief wave of stark deja vu and grief, from another time and place, threatened to bring him to physical tears. Instead, he turned himself away and used his suit jets to aim himself back toward the now-distant Shipyard.

The explosion, when it came, was an intense burst of brilliance that pushed past him to light up the new, abrupt end of the station spindle, already too far away for his shadow to reach it. The lights on his suit's radiation tracker immediately jumped into orange. That was going to cost him a few days in a de-rad soak when he had the time to spare.

"Tomboy? Vee?" he called on the comms. "What's the station status?"

"Mr. Ferguson. I am pleased but unsurprised you are still whole," Tomboy answered. "Other than the loss of the reactor, the station sustained no additional damage from the explosion. However, I lost some of my rear sensors and cannot detect your location."

"Um, about three hundred meters behind you," he said. "I think you're moving away faster than I can catch up with my suit jets."

"Ah, I see you now," Tomboy said. "*Venetia's Sword* is coming to get you."

He could see *Venetia's Sword* now sweeping along the length of the Shipyard toward him, tiny in comparison but bright. Behind it, one by one, the giant pinwheel blades of the charged ion collectors began to slowly move and resume their spin, as if all was back as it should be. Except his friends were gone, probably forever.

This time, he did find a reservoir of tears.

Chapter 4

Fergus had long since mastered the art of lounging in zero gravity, and he took advantage of that practice to throw himself onto the grippy couch in *Venetia's Sword*'s kitchenette, exhausted and aching but with enough adrenaline still in his system that his brain wasn't going to let his desperate body sleep anytime soon. He was on his fifth tube of water, and it didn't feel like his thirst had diminished in the slightest. Already, the regret and resentment that came with using his gift were settling back in, all practical argument about circumstance and necessity unheeded.

Zacker was, somewhat improbably, attempting to figure out how to make coffee. From this angle it was hard to tell, but the detective might have even been trying to make two.

As if feeling Fergus's eyes on his back, Zacker spoke up for the first time since Fergus had dragged himself in through one of Vee's airlocks. "Watched the whole thing, or at least the parts that came through between static," Zacker said. "You remind me a lot of a beat cop I worked a couple of cases with, long time ago. Diaz. We didn't get along at all, but . . . Respect. Nothing but respect."

Yeah, Fergus thought. *Bet Diaz didn't flop himself down on the couch when there was a job to do.* He sat up and rubbed at his face.

"How are you doing over there, Tomboy?" he asked, knowing the Shipyard was patched in through Vee.

"With the limited power I can draw from my backup generators and the ion collector, I am prioritizing what I need to spin up and what I can leave for now. I have elected to bring the small robot bay online and slowly re-spin the garden ring."

"How badly was the garden ring compromised?" Fergus asked.

"The ring has many emergency doors, and most of them successfully closed during the attack. The atmosphere wasn't breached, but temperatures dropped to around 5C and we lost gravity. There will likely be significant damage," Tomboy's voice came over the comms in the room. "There does not seem to be a need to spin up the living quarters at this time."

"Yeah. I've been thinking about that," Fergus said. "Detective, maybe you have better opinions here, but it seems to me that if they just wanted to kill everyone, there would be bodies, especially if they knew they were going to blow the station anyway. I figure they tinkered with the reactor to get it to overload once they were away, and that the bomb was to make sure if, by some miracle, someone managed to get to the reactor and fix it, they'd still lose."

"During my brief reconnection, it was clear that the reactor systems had been manually injected with malicious code," Tomboy said. "There was insufficient time to sandbox and deconstruct it for deeper analysis."

"Right," Fergus said. "But they didn't take anything or damage anything other than what they did getting in and out and the consequences of station power going down, and they didn't take *Whiro* or *Falconer*, which are the two most obviously valuable things that were here during the attack. It seems to me that whoever attacked you wanted your people. That means they're probably still alive somewhere. At least for now."

"But Effie . . ."

"Yeah. I'm sorry, Tomboy. No one could have survived that hit, and there's no sign of the surface buggy . . ." A thought suddenly struck him. "Uh, did you tell me before that Effie was working on stealth technologies, though?"

"She was. It was part of an ongoing rivalry between her and Maison."

"Can you scan the shuttle debris from here? Is the volume of debris sufficient to account for both the shuttle *and* Effie's buggy?"

There was a pause. "It is insufficient."

"Shit shit shit," Fergus said. "How much air did that buggy have?"

"Approximately thirty-six hours."

"And how long ago was the attack?"

"Just over thirty-one hours ago."

"And how long before that did Effie leave for the surface?"

"Three hours and forty-seven minutes."

Fergus launched himself off the grippy couch for the door. "Vee, you heard that? Is Detective Zacker's flyer refueled and ready? I need to get down to the surface as fast as possible."

"Do you think Effie is alive?" Tomboy asked.

"I don't know," Fergus said, "but I think there's a chance, and right now I'll take any I can get."

"Shit, and I almost had this coffee thing figured out," Zacker said. He let them go, bobbing in the room, and did his clumsy best to follow Fergus. "I'm coming too."

————

Fergus dropped the little red flyer out of *Venetia's Sword*'s bay toward the planet's surface. He had all sensor data being piped back to the ship and, through it, back to Tomboy for analysis. Zacker was in the back with an exosuit scavenged from one of the *Venetia's Sword*'s lockers, scrolling through the newbie tutorial.

He brought the flyer down two hundred meters from the destroyed shuttle, coming in slow enough to be sure he wasn't accidentally parking on top of a hidden buggy. Sol was a distant pinprick in the distance, and in the quasi-dusk of Pluto, the flyer's lights cut bright streams through the dust he'd stirred up on landing.

"Now what?" Zacker asked, fidgeting with his exosuit. He let Fergus check his seals, then patted at his side. "I wish I had my gun. Good for confidence, you know?"

"I've never carried a gun," Fergus said. "Better on my nerves."

Zacker snorted. "If you say so. So, how are you going to find this buggy, if it's got some sort of invisibility thing around it?"

"How are you at surfing?"

"I grew up in *New York*," he said.

"So, that's a no?"

"No, that's an if-you-include-auto-taxi-and-subway-pod-roofs in your definition of surfing, I'm a pro," he said. "Although I haven't done it since I was a teenager."

"Great!" Fergus said. "You're going to stand on the roof of the flyer."

"I am?" Zacker said, in a tone that clearly said, *I am not.*

"I'm going to spin the flyer in a slow circle on the ground," Fergus said. "It'll make a nice giant cloud of methane snow and dust all around us, which should stay up for a while. Most stealth tech is based on light bypass—it's not really invisible, it's just absorbing light falling on one side of it and emitting it again out the far side, so it seems like there's nothing in between. Coat it in dust and it stops working. So, when you see something in the cloud, or the cloud moving funny, you shout. Unless you want me to stand on the roof and you think you can pilot the flyer carefully and precisely enough on a surface of a planet you've never been to before to not kill us both?"

"*Dwarf* planet," Zacker said, then reluctantly added, "and no."

"The boots with your exosuit are magnetic," Fergus said.

"You can activate them from the control panel along your forearm. That'll make it harder to fall off."

"Thanks," Zacker said. He stood at the airlock, then looked back at Fergus. "There's no air out there. Just double-checking that."

"Not in the way you're thinking, no. There's plenty of air in your suit and a spare bottle," Fergus said. "But you have almost no gravity, so move with care."

Zacker got into the airlock, and after a few seconds fumbling around inside, cycled himself out. Three minutes later, he called on the suit comms. "I'm on the roof," he said. "I've got my boots stuck down and I'm hanging on to the fin, and if you still manage to knock me off of here, I will come back inside and punch you in the face. If we're clear on that, do it."

Fergus spun up the rear engines. "Let me know if this is too much," he said. "I'm about to start turning."

"I'm okay," Zacker said. "Fucking weird gunky, glittery dust."

"Yeah, the gunk is called tholins. We're lucky it hasn't frozen down completely. See anything weird?"

"Not yet," Zacker said. "If there's an invisible buggy out there, what's to keep it from just moving out of our way?"

"If it moves, we'd detect it immediately," Fergus said. "The danger is that it's farther away from the destroyed shuttle than we can find in time, or she's already run out of air. Anything yet?"

"No," Zacker said.

Fergus checked the nav console; he was nearing two-thirds of the way around the circle. "C'mon, Effie," he muttered. "Be out there."

Three-quarters. "Shit," he said. "I don't know if—"

"STOP!" Zacker interrupted, shouting. "Weird clumping back just a few degrees."

"Keep your eye on it. I'm coming out," Fergus said. He shut

the flyer engines down and cycled himself out the airlock as quickly as he could.

Zacker was still on the roof, pointing. Fergus stared in that direction, widening the spectrum on his goggles. Something shimmered slightly through dust. He ran toward it, bounding across the surface, the reddish-brown gunk of stirred-up tholins clinging to his faceplate.

"Effie!" he called out on an open channel. "Effie, it's Fergus! Answer, damn you!"

He managed to stop just short of slamming face-first into the oddly distorted patch of space that was the buggy's nose. Putting his hands out, he felt his way around until he found the tiny airlock at the rear.

He cycled himself in and found himself in an empty buggy.

It was, Fergus thought, worse than finding a body, because at least if there were a body, he'd have known he did what he could instead of wondering if she was out there somewhere right now, drawing her last few breaths where he'd never find her.

Outside, Zacker had managed to get down from the roof. "Anything?" he asked, as Fergus emerged.

"No," Fergus said. He found himself sitting in the snow, overwhelmed, and put his head in his hands. "No one. She's gone."

Zacker came over, bounding awkwardly in the low gravity. "Look," he said, "it sucks. We should—" Suddenly, his feet went out from under him and he fell, sending up a plume of dust around him.

There was blurry movement, hard to focus on, and then something hauled Zacker's spare oxygen bottle off the back of his suit. It hovered in midair for a moment before also disappearing. "Ferguson!" Zacker shouted.

Fergus raised both his hands and stood very slowly. "You're

okay, Zacker; your main bottle will last you hours yet. Stay down and don't move."

He turned his head, looking for that same oddness of vision, and when that failed, he closed his eyes and felt the energy around him, trying to tune out the flyer's heavy presence and look for anything else.

"What are you doing?" Zacker asked.

"Listening," Fergus said. "Sort of. Just—"

He felt the energy right behind him too late, as something wrapped itself around his neck and he was body-slammed into the ground.

The dusky sky above blurred slightly, and then as if out of nowhere he was looking into Effie's wide, green, surprised eyes. She stared at him for a moment, then grabbed his arm and pulled him up again, wrapping him in a hug so tight, he was worried she might break his ribs. Effie was a short, solidly round woman, and despite the height mismatch, having her there and alive was the best feeling he could remember in a long time.

"Effie?" he managed to squeak out, but there was silence on his suit comms.

When she let go, he bent down and wrote in the dust: *HERE TO HELP*. He drew an arrow toward where Zacker was watching from the ground, and wrote *FRIEND*. After a hesitation, he added a question mark.

"You can get up now, Zacker," he said.

He pointed to the flyer, and Effie walked there with him. Her suit was covered with strange, shiny rectangular scales, a heavy pack on her back with leads running from it to dozens of points all up and down the back of her helmet, arms, and legs. He let her cycle herself through first. He glanced back at Zacker, who waved him to go ahead, and followed.

Inside, she'd unsealed her faceplate and raised it, breathing deeply. The net of overlapping scales on her suit made his eyes hurt to look at, even powered down.

She was pale and shaking, her blond, normally precisely braided hair a sweaty, tangled mess. "I thought they'd come back," she said. "I didn't recognize your ship. How are you even here, instead of on Earth?"

"I got a distress call from Tomboy, and this was the nearest thing I could get my hands on," Fergus said. He could hear the outer lock cycling as Zacker headed in. "It came with an unintended passenger. I don't trust him, but I don't think he's currently a danger."

"He know about your little electricity problem?"

"No. Had to zap him once, but he thinks I had a hidden weapon," Fergus said. He didn't really want to talk about it, as always; there were only a handful of his absolute closest friends who knew about that particular artifact from his brief abduction by the alien Asiig. "Your comms down?"

"Part of my stealth kit, reducing signal," she said. "I was boosting through my shuttle. When that got destroyed, so did my comms."

"I've never seen anything like that," Fergus said. "No pun intended. I didn't think you could stealth a suit like that."

She reached over one shoulder and, with a shaking hand, unclipped her pack. It fell to the floor of the flyer with a loud *clunk*. "Weighs about twenty-two kilos," she said, "and eats through energy like Maison through a barbecue. Blink and it's gone. The theory's been there for years now; it's just no one has managed to get the energy consumption down to something at all useful for how limited and easily undone the effect is. Pluto isn't bad, because it's never very bright here, but in general, spending a lot of energy to be invisible in the near-dark isn't a great technical coup."

"I suppose not," Fergus said.

The inner door to the airlock opened and Zacker climbed in. "Sorry about stealing your bottle," Effie said. "I was down below two percent, and I thought you were a bad guy."

"Yeah, well, in a hostile situation, always assume the unknown is an enemy," he said. "I'm Detective Zacker. Retired. Thanks for not killing me. Or this joker, because I need him to get me home again."

"Good to meet you," she said. She had, Fergus noticed, mostly stopped shaking. "I'm Ephemeral Sunlight Oceania Mac Tighearnáin. Everyone calls me Effie. Now, will one of you please tell me what the fuck happened?"

"I was hoping you could tell me," Fergus said. "Whoever attacked the Shipyard left EMP generators all over, so Tomboy caught only the first few seconds of the attack before he was shut down."

"The others?" she asked.

"Missing. No bodies, so we think they were abducted instead of killed," he said. "Most of the station got decompressed."

"I need to see," she said. "That's my home. My family."

"I know," he said. "Hang on."

He went to the front of the flyer and buckled in. The flyer was holding up well for having been taken so far outside of its intended usage. For a half-second, he thought he'd have Theo give it a once-over when they got back, before he remembered Theo was gone.

Effie and Zacker had taken their seats, so he lifted off. "Vee, we're heading back up. We have Effie."

There was a hesitation, then *Venetia's Sword* answered, "Thank you, Mr. Ferguson, for bringing her home to us."

"One down, six to go," he said, and punched the flyer to full.

They left Zacker in a small cabin on *Venetia's Sword*, yawning so hard Fergus was worried the man would dislocate his own jaw. The ship would keep an eye on him if he went wandering, but it didn't seem likely. Fergus was very nearly that tired himself, but sleep was far from his thoughts.

He and Effie went into the Shipyard through an airlock in the engineering wheel and crossed down into the station spindle. Effie was silent as they floated through the deserted, airless central corridor. When they reached the wheel where the lounge and arcade and everyone's private rooms were, she reached out and took his gloved hand in hers and held tight.

The wheel hadn't been spun back up, and everything not bolted or magged down was floating loose. There were still cards out, in a slow-moving cloud above the table in the lounge. A shattered coffee bulb drifted among brown droplets and glints of glass. One of the chairs had blood on and around it.

"Why hasn't Tomboy got the spin going again?" Effie asked, after she'd taken enough of it in and turned away again.

"Yeah, about that," Fergus said. "Bomb in the reactor. We had to eject it."

"Wonderful," she said grimly. They moved on toward Control. "So, who's your friend?"

"A retired SCNY detective. He mistook me for an art thief who murdered his daughter, so he tried to bash my brains in."

"And got caught up in the Fergus undertow instead," she said, and shook her head. "We just can't send you anywhere without supervision, can we?"

"It's starting to seem that way," Fergus said. "I don't think the universe and I have the same sense of humor."

The blast doors to the control dome opened at Fergus's touch, and they floated inside. A large plate had been spot-welded over the breach, and Fergus's suit readings showed there was atmosphere again inside. As soon as the doors had sealed behind them, he popped his faceplate and took in a deep breath of freezing air. It was bracing, enough to keep him from falling asleep where he stood, but that jolt would not last.

"Ms. Effie," Tomboy said, disembodied voice coming now from several points in the room. "It is good to see you again."

"And you, Tomboy," she said. "What's your status?"

"I have activated fourteen maintenance robots, which is the number I can reliably recharge in my current power circumstances," Tomboy said. "They are working on repairing the remainder of the breaches. I have begun the spin-up of the garden wheel and I am raising temperatures, both gradually so as to minimize any additional damage or stress."

"How bad is it?" Effie asked.

"We will not lose everything," Tomboy said. "That is the most I can say at this time. It is, however, the only place in the station right now other than here in control where you two can reliably unsuit and sleep, which you are both clearly in need of. I would suggest, despite the chaos, that the garden will be more comfortable for you. Section six is in the best current condition of the eight, as both doors fully closed before the power loss."

"Thanks, Tomboy," Effie said. "At this point, we're lucky we have anything and should be grateful for it."

"I am sorry I was not able to prevent such extreme damage. The attack happened quickly enough to outpace most of my safety mechanisms," Tomboy said.

"Not your fault. None of us ever expected we'd be attacked, but we should have prepared for the possibility," Effie said.

"Do you think we will be attacked again?" Tomboy asked.

"I don't have any idea," Effie said. "But we'll certainly upgrade all our defenses. If we get the chance."

"Yes, Miss Effie," Tomboy said.

Effie patted Fergus on the shoulder. "Tomboy is right about us needing sleep. I know I'm only moving on adrenaline right now, and I'm guessing you're not any better off."

"No," Fergus said.

"Okay, then. Section six it is. We're going to be bunking with Theo's bonsai and Ignatio's birds. At least they're both quiet."

"At this point, an entire regiment of amateur bagpipers couldn't keep my eyes open," Fergus said. "What about Zacker?"

"*Venetia's Sword* tells me he is asleep," Tomboy said. "He informed her that he'd been keeping on two-hour sleep shifts so he could get up and check his surveillance. For all that he's been dragged off into the unknown, this may be the first decent sleep he's had in a very long time."

"Good," he said. "I don't want to leave Zacker alone too long."

"You think he's dangerous?" Effie asked.

"I think he's unpredictable and irrational, and so driven by the need for revenge that it's only a matter of time before he goes off. The question is when and at whom. If he doesn't make trouble for us, I said I'd help him with his problem. So, maybe that'll be enough to keep him in line," he said.

"You think?"

"I hope," Fergus said. "Did I mention he stowed away, and it's not my fault he's here?"

"Can a person stow away on a flyer they own?" Tomboy asked.

"Fine," Fergus said, "but he kidnapped me first."

Effie snorted.

"Besides, maybe he'll come in handy. He's a retired detective, thirty-nine years, he told me," Fergus added. "He needs something to do that isn't sitting around in an abandoned room in

Scotland, waiting for his needle in a haystack, and we have one hell of a missing persons case."

"You really think they're still alive?" Effie asked. "Answer honestly."

". . . Yeah," Fergus said. "I do. It makes the most sense."

"As if any of this makes sense," she said.

"It does to someone," Fergus said.

He followed her into the spindle and from there into the garden wheel. They climbed down a long, thin ladder from the center corridor to the garden floor that covered the outer edge of the wheel, the spin giving them the feel of gravity again. Most of the plants were rooted into floor boxes, but the gracefully ancient plants that were Theo's bonsai had tumbled from their stands. He picked up a few, wincing at the shards of brown pottery and moss that tumbled free, and set them in place again as best as he could.

"That can wait," Effie said.

"It feels wrong to leave them," Fergus said, picking up another.

"Without Theo, they'll all die anyway," she said.

He set a tiny, gnarled juniper down with care. "Theo will be back," he said. He turned and met Effie's eyes, kept his gaze locked there until she looked away. They'd known each other for more than a decade—since he'd sneaked onboard the Shipyard with a Titan delivery shuttle while chasing down a bogus lead on stolen, experimental genmod cabbage seedlings, and been caught red-handed trying to hack into Tomboy from the shuttle bay—and it was probably the only time he'd ever outstubborned her on anything.

There was a single hammock stretched between two tall cypress trees, and Fergus insisted Effie take it. "I used to sleep on the ground all the time as a kid, avoiding home," he said. "I'll be fine."

Effie looked like she was going to fight him on this, but at last, instead, she just wrapped her arms tightly around him again.

"It'll be okay," he told her.

She let go and, without a word, climbed into the hammock.

Between two sections of ferns and azalea, there was a small bed of moss with a large granite Japanese lantern set carefully off-center on it. There was just enough room between it and the edge for him, so he knelt and then stretched out on the moss, still in his suit. His brain immediately gave up on the idea of thinking, and he closed his eyes, already feeling himself float away into sleep.

Something touched him lightly on the shoulder, and he opened his eyes to see a small, two-legged, hairy monster leap away into the gardens. "Aaaaa!" he shouted, sitting up so quickly, it made his head spin.

Effie chuckled from above.

"What the hell was that?" Fergus asked.

"One of Ignatio's birds, I told you. I'm glad at least one made it."

"That was no bird. It was hairy!"

"It was a kiwi. Ignatio loves them, says they're the most beautiful thing Earth has ever produced, even if they don't change colors."

"Do they . . . you know, bite?"

Now Effie laughed harder. "No," she said. "Now go the hell to sleep, Fergus. Tomorrow will be difficult enough as it is, and you never know when you're going to get another chance. And Fergus?"

"Yeah?"

"Thanks for finding me."

"It's what I do," he said, and closed his eyes again.

Chapter 5

When he awoke some seven hours later, he had a half-dozen of the hairy birds huddled against him, just below his chin. He could no longer see his breath in the air, but it was still chill, and he couldn't blame them for seeking what warmth they could. When he moved, they scattered. One hopped awkwardly away on a single leg, the other folded, bent oddly against its body. He didn't know how to help it, and before he could formulate any ideas, it disappeared into the greenery behind its fellows.

Effie was watching him from the hammock. "*Venetia's Sword* is docked and says your friend is up and eating rather a lot of breakfast," she said. "I'm not sure of the status of our food stores here, so if we want anything ourselves, we might want to get over there soon. I don't know about you, but I need coffee in me before I even think about what we do next."

Fergus groaned and sat up. Using his "gift" always left him parched, and his head was pounding with recriminations for not having fully rehydrated himself before crashing the night before. "Coffee sounds good," he said. "And water. Lots and lots of water."

Effie got down out of the hammock, rolled her shoulders, then stretched her neck from one side to the other, wincing at the crackling sound it made. Fergus stood, then double-checked for birds underfoot before he stepped out onto the walkway between planters, and followed her to the ladder out.

"Tomboy," Effie said over the comms. "We're going over to *Venetia's Sword*. Give me a status on the Shipyard on the way?"

"All the breaches have been temporarily patched, and I have two bots working on permanent repairs," Tomboy answered. "It will take considerable time and more energy than I can produce to restore atmosphere and living temps to the entire structure, but I believe I can rehabilitate approximately twenty percent of spaces with current conditions. The contents of sections two, three, and eleven of the garden ring may be total losses."

"For now, we should leave the areas where the others were during the attack as they are so we can look for clues," Fergus said.

"Once immediate safety and stability issues are addressed, I'd rather Tomboy use what resources it can to improve our chances of surviving a second attack, anyway," Effie said. "We can't know they won't be back to finish the job when they see the Shipyard wasn't destroyed in the explosion."

Fergus was glad she hadn't voiced that thought last night, before he'd had a chance to sleep.

———

Zacker was slouched on the grippy couch when they floated into *Venetia's Sword*'s lounge. Fergus made coffee for him and Effie. "Vee, is Tomboy patched in?" he asked as he handed her one of the hot bulbs.

"Of course," the ship answered.

"Can you project that hologram of the Shipyard down here? And Tomboy, can you feed through all the data you've got from the attack?"

"Yes, Mr. Ferguson," Tomboy answered, its voice coming from that same nebulous non-direction as the ship's.

"Start just prior to detection," Effie said. "One-quarter speed, please."

A hologram of the Shipyard, two meters long, appeared in the center of the room. A flat digital timestamp appeared above it.

"I detected the first anomaly at 44:17:38.08 as a minor perturbation of the electromagnetic field around the Shipyard," Tomboy said. Tiny dots appeared and disappeared on the holo, at multiple locations. "I reached reasonable analytical probability that the disturbance was one or more obscured spaceships at 44:17:38.47, which was point oh three seconds prior to an explosive decompression of the control chamber."

A vague outline, shifting as Tomboy had refined its guess based on data, began to solidify outside the two docks, the ship fabrication bay, and at the nose of the station itself. "I sent distress calls to your shuttle, Mr. Ferguson's remote device, and *Venetia's Sword* at 44:17:38.48. At 44:17:38.51, my systems suffered complete malfunction." The holo froze.

"Back up to your last conjecture as to the shape of the attackers," Effie said. She squinted, leaning in close as he did so. "I can't make these out at all."

"They look kind of like mushrooms," Fergus said. "I've never seen spaceships like that."

"It does not match any ship pattern I am familiar with," Tomboy said. "My closest proximal match is only fourteen percent."

"Maybe alien, then?" Fergus mused. "But who? And why?"

"I've got nothing," Effie said. She stuck her hand out toward a dot Fergus hadn't noticed a distance away from the station outline. "Tomboy, show Pluto relative to this."

A swath of blue-purple appeared, curving up from the floor. "This is the one that got me, then," she said, pointing to the dots. "I was out in the buggy when the first hit came in. It looked like it came right from the direction of the Shipyard. I got one shot back from the shuttle via my remote connection before it obliterated it."

"An energy pulse?" Fergus asked.

"They had to have been heavily masking their energy signatures to get as close as they did—better than anything Maison and I have played with, certainly, and if it's not beyond current military state-of-the-art, it's close—which would make it hard to have a charged energy weapon at the same time," she said. "Given there was . . . maybe ten seconds from Tomboy's warning to the first shot, I'd say it was more likely a physical projectile."

"Any chance we might sort out some piece of the debris for analysis?"

"When I have a robot to spare, I will send one down to sift for anomalous material," Tomboy said.

"Thanks, Tomboy," Effie said.

"I threw the EMP generators out into space as I cleaned them out," Fergus said. "If they still haven't gone boom by tomorrow, we ought to haul one back in for examination as well."

"I have one additional contribution," Tomboy said. "I retrieved it a few minutes ago from Maison's personal datastore when I noticed the timestamp was during the gap in my own recordings. It was scripted to upload to my servers but failed because of my outage."

"What is it?" Effie asked, leaning closer.

"Video," Tomboy answered. "I will play it."

The image popped up where the outline of the Shipyard and Pluto had been moments before. It was distorted, a fisheye-lens view of the spindle corridor, taken from somewhere up near the curved ceiling. The corridor was empty and motionless, but the view bobbed slightly side to side.

Maison's hamster, Fergus realized.

The corridor went suddenly dark and moments later ghosted back into life in monotone grays. Three people were moving up the corridor, their suits identical and unmarked, weapons in hand. They stopped briefly in front of the hamster, then two continued on around and under it while the third loomed closer, the reflection of the inflatable hamster visible in the mirrored face shield. After a moment, the attacker took their energy rifle and very carefully reached out with it to poke the hamster.

"MUAHAHAHAHAHA!" Loud, deep, creepy laughter filled the corridor, and then there was a flash and some sort of cloud obscured the view for a moment. When it cleared, they could see the attacker pulling back, their suit covered with shiny magenta glitter that seemed to stick where it had landed, and raising their weapon to take aim at the hamster.

The video ended there.

"Do you wish me to play it again?" Tomboy asked.

"Not yet. Thanks, Tomboy," Effie said. "So. Human, anyway."

"High-grade military suits." Fergus had a top-of-the-line military-grade suit himself and knew the subtle differences in line. "Not much else to go on, unless either of you spotted something I didn't."

Effie shook her head. "Maybe there are more clues we can find in the Shipyard itself."

Fergus glanced over at Zacker. "Detective?" he asked.

The man startled out of his thoughts. "What?"

"It's a crime scene. I was hoping you might have some insight."

"Right," he said. "I dunno how much good any of it's going to do in space, when everyone's floating the fuck around in suits, but this is what I'd have done if this was back on Earth. First, you secure the scene. Take holos, send sweepers through to collect any particulate or chemical evidence, try to make the best guess you can at a timeline of what happened. Then you talk to witnesses and neighbors, listen to word on the street. What you get from those tells you where to go from there. Sometimes that's a fucking storage unit in Glasgow, and sometimes it's absolutely nowhere."

"If the attackers were confident the Shipyard was going to explode, they might not have been entirely diligent about not leaving a trace," Fergus said, though the three figures moving silently up the corridor on the hamster vid had looked *very* careful. "Tomboy, do you have any bots that can do fine particulate sweeps, look for any chemical or biological traces the attackers might have left?"

"I can fab some, but it'll take a few hours," Tomboy said. "Most of my resources are currently being applied to fixing the damage to the station."

"Yeah, don't let me slow you down on that," Fergus said. "But if you can get a sweeper or two out, especially in the areas where the others were when the attack began, that might give us something to start with."

"I wouldn't count on it," Zacker said, glumly. "This looks like a professional job to me."

It did to Fergus, too, and he didn't like that at all.

"I'll have Tomboy establish contact with the Charon Camp-out and Oort Base One. They're the closest we have to neighbors," Effie said. "They can tell us if they saw anyone go by in- or out-system around the time of the attack. Given how energy-expensive stealth tech is, they might've not bothered to turn it on until they were nearly on top of us."

"I have already sent queries," Tomboy said. "As you know, the Charon Camp-out can be slow in responding, and there is a lag out to the Oort because of signal interference at the heliopause."

"The Charon *Camp-out?*" Zacker asked.

"They're one of our fellow members in the OOB—"

"OOB?"

"Outer Object Band. Us, a bunch of folks scattered in the Oort cloud, and the Trans-Neptunian settlements. We're all technically politically independent, although obviously the Earth Alliance has oversight throughout the solar system, and we're all part of the larger Sol economic state. It's a loose association of the few dozen of us far enough out that having established relationships with each other is good for both survival and sanity," Effie said. "Think of it like we're all a few small beads stretched out on a very long loop of string, each keeping an eye out for our neighbors. The Charon Camp-out is nearest. They're sort of like a commune crossed with outdoor survivalists, except with a really extreme definition of *outdoors.* Friends, but not friendly. They'll appreciate knowing there were hostiles in the area."

Zacker shook his head. "And they call New Yorkers crazy," he said. "The last piece of this, and just as important as everything else combined, is going over everything you know about your victims. Because if you can figure out who their enemies are, why they were targeted, often that can tell you by *who*. Or at least narrow it down."

"Could this be retaliation for bringing *Venetia's Sword* back from Cernee?" Effie asked Fergus.

"I don't think so," he said. He thought about it for a few minutes, long enough for Effie to get up and make a second round of coffee. As she pressed the fresh bulb into his hands, he shook his head. "Arum Gilger, the man who stole Vee in the first place, is dead, shot by his own people. His half-brother and right-hand man, Graf, got turned into meatcubes by the big bad neighborhood aliens. That would leave his crew of Luceatans, who are no way neat enough to have pulled off an operation like this, and even if they could, they would have left ample and intentional proof indicating they'd been here for revenge. Bodies included."

"Gilger came from an aristocratic Basellan family. Maybe them?"

"They washed their hands of him years ago. And again, if this was about revenge, why take hostages?"

"Money," Zacker said. "Ransom."

"But they didn't leave anyone behind to demand it from, much less pay it."

"So, then they wanted something from your people themselves," Zacker said. "What did they have of value?"

"Ships," Effie said, "but they didn't take any of them. There's the Shipyard itself, but clearly they didn't want that, either. What else is there?"

Fergus frowned at his coffee. "Then it's something about you. Maybe your knowledge? As a team, you seven know a shitload more about shipbuilding, engineering, and artificial mindsystems than almost anyone else. If it's about skills, it would explain taking them alive and also why they maybe wanted to cover up that they'd been taken at all. Plus, they were all in one easy-to-raid basket. It would have been harder . . ." He drifted off in thought.

"Fergus?" Effie said.

He squinted at her. "Tomboy?" he called. "Have you restored access to the SolNet yet?"

"I have," the station answered.

"Can you search and see if any other notable scientists—especially in the areas of cutting-edge ship design or artificial intelligences—have gone missing or been presumed dead in weird accidents lately?"

"Define *lately* in this context."

"Call it a standard year," he said.

"There have been several," Tomboy said, after only a brief

hesitation. "Nicholas Keeling, the Assistant Director of IESAI, was on a private ship to Haudernelle for a conference when his ship disappeared in-jump. It was generally assumed the Drift got him, since no debris was found. That was eleven earth-standard months ago. Seven months ago, two other IESAI scientists—a married couple named Agasti—disappeared during a boating trip in the Mediterranean on Earth. Their capsized boat was recovered, but they were not."

"IESAI is the artificial intelligence group, right?" Zacker asked.

"Yes," Effie said. "The Institute for the Engineering and Study of Artificial Intelligences. They've done solid work over the last several centuries, but without their holy grail of a sentient, genuinely self-aware artificial mindsystem, no one wants to give them credit for what they have accomplished. They tried to hire Maison once, back after his stunt with the mechanical cockroach army."

"I haven't heard that story," Fergus said.

Effie smiled. "I'd say you need to hear it from Maison, but in point of fact, you should hear it first from LaChelle. Just make sure you bring a couple of strong drinks with you when you ask." Her face fell. "If you have the chance. But IESAI has never liked scientists who don't behave with decorum and gravitas— there was that whole scandal with Kazeth Azo and Zanzjan Minor, back in the Twenty-Threes—so they and Maison were never going to work out together anyhow."

"No, I expect not," Fergus said. "Nor are they the sort of institution to go off the rails and kidnap people. That it, Tomboy?"

"When we include other prominent scientists and engineers whose work is most relevant to Shipyard activities, there are twenty-three more incidents of varying degrees of match."

"What's the most promising of the twenty-three?" Fergus asked.

"A microelectronics engineer from Oglol named Miller disappeared during what appeared to be a house invasion five months ago. She was highly respected for her work with fully articulated independently mobile mindsystems."

"Robots?" Zacker said.

"Crudely described, yes," Tomboy said, "although the more sophisticated ones bear little to no physical or functional resemblance to the work-unit robots we use in fabrication. About on a probabilistic par with the microelectronics engineer was a ship designer named Minobe who specialized in deep-ocean vessels who vanished around the same time during a visit to Coralla to study their peculiar challenges."

"Coralla? Challenges?" Fergus asked. "What, sand in your bumcrack?"

"There's an organism native to the water that consumes metals," Tomboy said.

"Oh. I didn't know that," Fergus said. "I never made it as far as the actual water. Stared at it for a few hours once, though."

"Coralla?" Zacker asked.

"Ever seen pictures of the Bahamas before the Earth oceans rose and the superstorms went critical? Or Tahiti?" Fergus said.

"Yeah."

"So, picture almost an entire planet of that. All these beautiful islands, white sand beaches, blue sky, blue water . . . Nothing to do but lay in the sun—"

"Sounds boring as shit," Zacker said.

Fergus laughed. "I wasn't there long enough to say. But someday, I fully intend to go back and put that to a much longer test. It would be nice to be bored for once."

"You'd hate it," Effie said. "But I don't believe you can actually get bored, even there, because you're a giant trouble magnet wherever you go."

"Would you like me to provide synopses of the other missing people?" Tomboy asked.

Zacker groaned, pushed himself up out of the grippy chair, and floated over to the kitchenette. "Going through every missing-persons case in the galaxy is a colossal waste of our time," he said. "If you haven't figured out something smarter to do by the time I make and finish another bulb of coffee, I'm going to start breaking things."

"Please do not," *Venetia's Sword* said.

"Not *ship* things," Zacker growled. "Useless Scottish things."

Effie laughed. "I recognize that temptation," she said. "But if you try it? I will put you down hard, and you won't get up again."

Zacker stared at her, and whatever he saw in her face, he visibly flinched. *Damn*, Fergus thought. *Go, Effie.*

"Tomboy," he said, trying to defuse the sense of imminent violence in the room. "Send the full data on all your matches and what happened to them to my handpad. I'll review them later, once we've looked at the more likely ones. But out of curiosity, what's the *least* likely of the lot?"

"The match that I assigned the lowest acceptable probability rating to is the director of the Ballard Substation Geothermal and Oceanographic Institute on Enceladus, who resigned out of the blue ten months ago via an extremely short recorded message and who has not been seen since leaving that moon, including by her partner of seventeen years."

"Well, I'll be damned," Zacker said. "That's three."

"What?" Fergus asked.

"Three oceans. This director, the sunken boat, your beach-bum engineer. Could be coincidence, but law of threes says you should check it out."

"That's completely arbitrary," Fergus said. "But okay. Tomboy, any ocean ships match the profiles of our attackers? No? Well, then, moving al—"

"I have an eighty-one percent probable match," Tomboy said.

"Now, that's coincidence," Fergus said.

"Tomboy, can you send the schematics and overlay to *Venetia's Sword* for display?" Effie asked.

A few moments later, a ship that looked remarkably like someone had stuck giant fins all around the circumference of a mushroom appeared on-screen. Yellow dots appeared where the fragmented sensor data aligned with it.

Fergus stared at it. "Is this ship also spaceworthy?" he asked. He'd never heard of such a thing.

"Not according to its specs, no," Tomboy said.

"Could it be made spaceworthy?"

There was a pause as Tomboy considered. "Possibly," it said at last. "It would not be able to achieve planetary orbit without deviating significantly from its current outlines. If there were another mechanism to lift and return them, yes."

"And the deep-ocean ship engineer that disappeared on Coralla? Did they work on these?"

"Dr. Minobe Ishiko," Tomboy said. "She did. She's considered a rising star in her particular corner of engineering. This vessel, the Madarch M3, is based on one of her original designs."

"And where are they in use?"

"Diva in the Trappist system, Madrexia One, Ozeano, and Enceladus, primarily," Tomboy said. "There are likely other places with a handful here and there."

"Enceladus is in-system, though," Fergus said. "All the others are at least five hops out."

"And Enceladus is where the director up and quit and disappeared, right?" Zacker asked.

"Yes," Tomboy answered. "I do feel I must note that the Shipyard does not fit into a pattern involving oceans, however."

"Yeah, but they fit the pattern of people missing," Zacker said. "Never ignore clues in threes. Now, where the hell is Enceladus?"

"It's one of Saturn's moons," Tomboy explained.

"I thought Saturn's moon was Titan."

"Saturn has ninety-eight moons," Tomboy said. "Underneath the surface ice, Enceladus has a liquid ocean that covers the entire moon. It's also geologically active, so it has a number of science stations below the ice."

"Does the Shipyard have connections there? Business or personal or anything, big or small?" Fergus asked.

"Not that I know of," Effie said. "LaChelle has a friend on Titan; that's as close as it gets."

"That you know of," Zacker added.

"That I know of," Effie said. "But I know my friends very well, detective."

"Everyone says that. You'd be surprised how often they're wrong."

"And I suspect you're surprised every time one of them is right," she said, eyes narrowing.

Fergus coughed. If it came down to a fight, he was pretty sure he'd have to bet on the rotund Irish woman, and losing wouldn't help keep Zacker in line at all. "Back to Enceladus," he said, changing the subject. "Tomboy, do you have any info on this geothermal research station? Any civilians? Nearest other settlement? Whatever info you can get, even if it's trivia. Also, how easy is it to get in and out? Could we get a bot there undetected?"

"To the surface, yes," Tomboy said. "Under the ice would be far more difficult. I hesitate to say *impossible* only because I am aware of the extent to which you'd take that as a challenge."

"What are you thinking, Fergus?"

"I'm thinking we need to find out if that's where the others are," Fergus said. "If they're not, then we keep looking."

"And if they are?"

"I don't know! We take them back!" Fergus said. "What else is there?"

"I don't know, Fergus," Effie said. "Enceladus isn't somewhere you just stroll into. And even if it was, for someone to have access to the ships, to the tech to modify them and move them, and to take down the Shipyard as quickly as they did . . . we're talking a well-funded group. *Very* well-funded. This kind of tech and co-ordination and slickness . . . it feels military. If we were way out near the Barrens, sure, everything is run by private militias and mercenary groups, but here in our home system? Someone would have to have wanted the others very badly to risk getting noticed by the Alliance, and have a lot of resources behind them."

"If the tech was all stolen . . ." Fergus said.

"Then surely someone would have noticed before now?"

"I don't know! We're all just guessing here, and we don't know anything until we go see."

"And who is going to go to Enceladus? You? Underneath an ocean?" Effie asked.

"Why not?"

"Why not?! After the way your father died—"

"Don't bring that into this!" Fergus roared, feeling his face go hot, his hands start to tingle. He forced the energy down. "It was a long time ago and a long way behind me. The only reason it ever came up is because none of you warned me about Theo's damned *mead*."

Zacker coughed, loudly. Both Fergus and Effie looked at him. "Either way, and whatever you decide, I didn't sign on for this level of shit then, and I'm not any keener for it now," he said. "My job's back on Earth, and this guy promised to get me back there, and selfishly I don't want him haring off to get himself killed or disappeared before he can do that. I might've already missed my chance to catch my art thieves."

"You sat in that dingy room for two years," Fergus said. "What makes you think something's going to happen in the few days you're gone?"

"Because when do things always happen?"

Fergus rubbed at his forehead. "Tomboy, if you can't get a bot down into Enceladus, can you get one to Earth? Something that can send and receive encrypted traffic on SolNet?"

"Easily," Tomboy said. "I'll have to insert it in someone's cargo stream to get it down out of orbit without detection, but I don't anticipate trouble doing so. What is it you would like it to do?"

"There's an apartment in Glasgow, Scotland, and it has surveillance and recording equipment in it pointing at the storage facility across the street. I need something that can dump the memory and send back any and all footage recorded so far, and then grab vid of everyone who goes in and out of Suttie's going forward. Zacker here can give you the exact address."

"And what if they come? What good is a bot and a video going to do me if I'm several fucking *planets* away?"

"Even if, against all odds, they come while you're gone, we'll still know who they are," Fergus said. "You know how much harder it is to disappear when someone knows who they're looking for. We finish our business, look them up, and then go pay them a visit."

"You can't honestly think it's that simple," Zacker said. "And you're still making some big assumptions about my level of interest in putting myself in danger to help you."

Effie rummaged through the cabinet, pulled out a silvery flat disk, and scowled at it. "Instawaffles," she said, as if it was some sort of curse. She pulled the tiny string from the corner of the package and watched as it expanded, then tore off the wrapper and took a bite. "Yes, just as terrible as I remember them. Let me add a few words of wisdom to this discussion, Detective Zacker, if I may?"

"Depends. Any more of those?" Zacker asked.

Effie tossed him one of the waffle packs. "First, nothing is ever as simple as Fergus thinks it is going to be. Even if it is that simple, he'll find a way to make it more complicated." At Fergus's stricken look, she shrugged. "Just telling it like it is. And because of that—and because *you*, Detective Zacker, are precisely that sort of complication—I have no problem sticking you and your flyer on a ship bound for Earth and sending you home if that's what you want. I'll even pack you extra food as a gesture of goodwill."

"But?" Zacker said. "There's always a but."

"But if you go home, Fergus's obligation to help you—a tenuous claim at best, given the circumstances—is over."

"What about finding his precious motorcycle?"

"I'm sure he'll get to that when he can. Maybe he'll turn up your art thieves along the way, or maybe he won't. But it's not his responsibility to track them down. You get me?"

"I—" Fergus tried to interrupt.

"Quiet, Fergus," Effie said. "Do you get me, detective?"

"Yeah," Zacker said.

"Good. Now, I strongly urge you to consider taking my offer. Fergus's job is a dangerous one at the best of times, which these are not. But I will add this: Fergus is really good at what he does, despite the haphazard, meandering, and obtuse means by which he does it. If you want justice for your daughter, he'll get you there eventually if it can be done at all. But he needs friends at his back, not enemies to get in his way, and certainly not unknown quantities bollocking things up unexpectedly. If you decide not to go home, you're on the ride for the duration, wherever it leads, whoever it means we're up against, and you damned well better be on it as an ally."

"But—" Fergus tried again.

Effie glared at him, and he subsided.

"You don't have to decide this minute," she said to Zacker, "but you will have to decide. In the meantime, I have work. I'm heading back into the Shipyard. I've got some calls to make, furniture to set back on its feet, that sort of thing."

"You need help?" Fergus asked.

"Yes," she said, "but not quite as much as I need some time alone. When that changes, I'll give you a call. Oh, and Fergus?"

"Yes?" he said.

"I know you like to make things difficult for yourself, but really. *Venetia's Sword*, gravity to standard." As everyone settled suddenly into their seats, she stood up, chucked the uneaten remains of the waffle in the flash recycler, and walked out.

Zacker glared at Fergus.

"Uh. I forgot it could do that?" Fergus said. "Another waffle?"

———

Fergus slouched in his seat at the helm of the *Venetia's Sword*, trying and failing to look for other possibilities. His leg ached, and he could feel the electricity deep in his tinkered-with guts whispering its own frustrations. Zacker had gone off to his cabin for a nap over two hours earlier, still giving him a murderous stink-eye as he slunk out.

"Fergus?" Effie's voice came over the comms, followed moments later by visual of her in the Shipyard's control room, Tomboy's 3-D display of the ship behind her heavily annotated with red and orange. "Oort Base One got back to me. They recorded a medium-sized freighter merging into our orbit near the time of the attack. Came from in-system, passed slowly, looped back out that way. They didn't see it drop off smaller ships or pick them up, but they are up-front that their resolution at this distance could have easily missed that."

"So, Enceladus still looks like our best possibility," Fergus said. "We have nothing else, anyway."

"You really want to jump into this?"

"*Want* is a funny word," he said. "I want my friends to be here safe and sound, but they're not. What else is there to do except try to find them?"

"You have a plan?"

"Working on it. Whoever attacked the Shipyard might be watching—which we'd be dumb to assume they're not—and if so, they'll have seen *Venetia's Sword* return, and they'll be aware that there's at least one survivor. If we went straight to Enceladus, they'd know we were on to them. But Titan, on the other hand . . . it would almost be suspicious if we didn't go there. It's the nearest and best source for parts, and we sure as shit need parts. And that gets us only a handful of moons away."

"I was going to call our usual broker there and solicit bids on a new reactor module, and maybe have them send over a few supplemental power cores to tide us over until it can be built," Effie said. "I could certainly go get them in person."

Fergus shook his head. "You need to stay here. If there's no one on the Shipyard, someone could try to claim salvage on it."

"I've already taken care of that. The Campers are sending a

crew up from Charon. They owe us for more than a few bail-outs, I trust them, and this will be like a holiday for them."

"When are the Campers coming up?"

"Soon as the last of the life support systems are stabilized and the hull repairs complete. Also, I'm adding a few new mods to Tomboy's systems to help detect various types of stealth scatter. I don't want to leave until the Shipyard is more protected, but there's a limit to what I can do in the short term, especially on my own. Twelve hours or so. That's when your stowaway detective friend has to have made his decision, or I'll make it for him. It's when we reach Enceladus that we'll need a plan. There isn't much of a civilian population below the ice, and there's no way in or out except through tightly controlled passages."

"*We*?"

"I'm coming too," she said.

"To Titan."

"To Enceladus."

"Look," Fergus said, "we're not even sure they're there. And whoever took the others certainly knows you but probably not me. I have a plan for getting myself down below the ice, but it won't work for two of us. Or three, unless we want to trust Zacker with everything else."

"I don't want to be left behind," Effie said.

"I know. Can we at least talk about this when we get to Titan?"

"Titan, then. Tomboy and I need to put together a parts list."

"Okay. I need to talk to some people too. Call you back," he said. Effie nodded, and he disconnected.

Fergus knew better than to hope she'd change her mind by then, but he figured there was at least a chance he'd come up with a more compelling argument. Or some other way to leave her and Zacker safely behind, willingly or no. First, he needed to get his own plan in place.

"Vee, I need you to bounce a call on the fast lines to Cross-roads Station in the Ohean system," he told the ship. "My friends Maha and Qai. I think I told you about them on the way home from Cernee?"

"You told me stories, yes," the ship answered. "You told me that the last time you asked them for a favor, they stuffed you into a crate of biologically contaminated frozen cow fetuses."

"Well, they cleaned it first," Fergus said.

"Good friends, then," *Venetia's Sword* said.

"Vee, was that sarcasm?" Fergus asked.

"I am certain I would not know," the ship said. "Opening a fast transmission packet. What do you need it to say?"

Fergus laughed. "Tell them I need a job. That'll get their attention."

Chapter 6

The reply came in just over seven hours later. *Venetia's Sword* woke him from a restless sleep. He got out of his bunk and wandered, bleary-eyed, past Zacker attempting to play solitaire with the Monkeypoker deck, to the bridge. When he opened the message, Maha's face immediately filled the screen, and he smiled to see her expression of deep concern. Her dark skin was covered with glowing, lime-green lines like fissures, her hair a matching, similarly startling, shade of green.

"Fergus," she said. "Qai thought this message was nonsensical enough that it might be a coded cry for help. You are the least regular-job-having person either of us have ever met, and I can't imagine what you're thinking. That said, we can hook you up, and it's not even going to cost you this time. Cargo drivers through the ice of Enceladus have an even higher turnover rate than their mortality one. It's pitch dark all the time, vastly empty and dull, and ridiculously dangerous. We get a nice big finder's fee if they hire you, and you get to go spend your days in the fulfilling task of moving stuff from the surface down the Bore and back. Please confirm that this is really what you want, send us your vites under whatever pseudonym you're using this week, and we'll get it set up."

Beside her, a fur-covered, distinctly catlike face leaned into the picture. Qai. She grinned, showing sharp teeth. "If you are being held against your will and this is your attempt at a clever ruse, hold up a sign or something next time," she said. She extended one clawed finger and tapped at something out of the picture, and the message ended.

Behind him, Zacker spoke up. "Aliens?" he asked.

"Maha is alt-human," Fergus said. "The farther you get from Earth, the more you'll encounter people hacking the phenotype, either for aesthetics or survival. Often both. Try not to act like an originalist if you encounter any. Qai is Dzenni. Her home system is far outside human space, but for some reason they *like* us. That's not as flattering as it sounds; when Maha first introduced us, Qai asked if she could keep me as a pet."

"Yeah? I could see that working for you," Zacker said.

Fergus gave him a two-finger salute. "So, detective. Effie and I are heading out in a few hours for Titan and then Enceladus. You with us, or you ready to go home?"

Zacker threw himself into one of the other seats. "I spent two years sitting in that shithole of a room, waiting for—*willing*—the criminals to appear, day after day, stewing in my own anger and doubt. Then you came along and I thought it was over, I'd finally won. I don't know if I hated you more when I thought you were one of them, or when I found out you weren't. But I don't know if I can go back to that, go back to the start all over again with nothing to show. What if you're the only chance I've got?"

"We're heading into serious danger. We don't even know who or what we're facing, but they sure as shit will be looking for us. It very well could get us messily killed," Fergus said. "Now's the time to think really hard about whether you'd be truly better off on your own back in Glasgow."

"My gut says I ran into you for a reason, and I trust it with my life," Zacker said. "Tell your friend I genuinely appreciate the offer for a ride, and if I was smart, I'd be packed and ready to go already, but I've never been nearly as smart as I am stubborn. I'm sticking with you."

"So be it," Fergus said. "Next stop, Saturn."

———

A battered space tug brought *Venetia's Sword* down through the hazy rush of Titan's atmosphere into the cavernous maw of Constantijn Hold's eastern ship dock. Effie was at the helm, watching as they were carefully threaded in between two other ships to an open berth and secured down.

"We have docked," *Venetia's Sword* said. "We have also been advised by Titan Dock Control that there are some minor system problems with the envelope in this section, currently under repair, and the corridor extension and balancing may take a few minutes longer than the usual twenty-minute window. If the delay is significant, a credit will be given against our docking fees."

"There's always something under repair here," Fergus said.

"Surely, it's not as bad as Crossroads," Effie said.

Until Fergus had found himself at Cernee, he'd thought Crossroads was about the farthest point in human civilization, but it still frequently felt like one of the lowest. "No, because on Crossroads, there's never anyone sober enough to realize anything is broken in the first place," he said.

"Titan, huh?" Zacker said. He'd come up to the bridge from the lounge just as they were sliding carefully into the fast-moving atmosphere of Titan. "The way people talk about it, I didn't expect it to be this fucking gloomy."

"We're a lot farther from the sun," Fergus said, "and the haze blocks most of what light does reach here. You get used to it. Kinda. And even if you don't, the interiors of the Holds have nice, bright full-spectrum lights to convince you otherwise."

Around them, the already-insufficient dock lights briefly dimmed. Zacker snorted. "Sure," he said. "So, now what?"

Effie tapped her handpad. "I've got quite a list of parts needed to repair the Shipyard," she said. "Along with arranging for a new, custom reactor module, we've got good reason to be parked here a while. And while I set about doing that, Fergus will catch a lift over to Enceladus on a local transport, ace his job interview, and be down under the ice in no time. Either he finds the others, and we come join him and get them out together, or he determines they're not there, comes back here, and we look for our next most likely target."

"You make it sound easy," Zacker said.

"Easy as long as Fergus passes the job test," Effie said.

"What if he doesn't?" Zacker asked.

"Hey, I spent the whole trip over here in that bloody simulator," Fergus said.

"Yeah, what, all sixteen hours? Or was it closer to half that? And how many breaks did you take for coffee, or to lounge around complaining about it being boring?" Effie said.

"Only once or twice," Fergus protested.

"Despite his seven breaks—" *Venetia's Sword* started to say.

"So I had to go to the bathroom a couple of times!" Fergus said.

"Because of all that coffee," Effie said.

"Despite his many self-induced interruptions, I anticipate Mr. Ferguson is likely to score acceptably on the job test," *Venetia's Sword* finished.

"Thank you, Vee," Fergus said.

"The turnover rate is extremely high and Bore Transit will be desperate," the Ship added.

Effie laughed. "Awww, your face, Fergus. Don't take it like

that. You're a decent-enough pilot, if not exceptional—and I think you would freely admit that—but the Bore is a challenge. It's an advantage to us that they need people so badly."

Fergus finished packing his exosuit, giving everything one last look-over. "I suppose," he said.

"That aside, I am not happy about us splitting up, even if just for a short time while you see what's what," Effie said. She rummaged around in her pocket and dug out a handful of small disks. "Encrypted comms that bounce through off-channels, based on Maison's pager model. They should also be able to route up and down through Enceladus's ice, but it might take a while, and it's riskier because of comm bottlenecks. Very hard to trace, but they emit enough of a signal that a sniffer could pick it out, so I built in a sleep feature that shuts it down when not sending/receiving, and it can be shut off completely if necessary. Best I could do before we left home." She handed one each to Zacker and Fergus.

"What am I going to need one for?" Zacker asked.

"If all goes according to plan, nothing but something to absently frob with in your pocket while you're bored," Effie said. "I'm not trusting our luck, though. Let me show you how it works."

As Effie explained the buttons and functions, Fergus walked over to the big viewscreen at the front of *Venetia's Sword* and stared idly out at the docks. They were suspended in a cavernous hangar, with lights high enough overhead that most of the floor was in shadow. Three bright rectangular airlocks sat halfway up the interior wall, with a catwalk between them. From the two to either side of them, where ships were already docked when they arrived, corridors had been extended out to the vessels. Their own still remained firmly retracted. "I wish they'd hurry up with the corridor," Fergus said. "I want to get moving and get this over with."

Venetia's Sword spoke up. "Dock control has just placed us under restriction; I am no longer able to disengage from the lock or initiate an exit protocol."

"What?" Effie said, and joined Fergus at the screen. At their designated airlock, the corridor emerged from the wall and extended toward them, and the door at the entrance slid open. Four uniformed people stood there: three Hold police and one Alliance officer. All were armed.

"Shit," Effie said. "What the hell do they want?"

"Unpaid parking tickets?" Zacker offered.

Fergus watched the corridor. "Well, I don't think it can be me," he said. "I've never gotten into any significant trouble on Titan, and I can't imagine this could have anything to do with Mars. Besides, how would anyone know I'm even here?"

"Neither of you told me what it was you did on Mars," Zacker added.

Fergus wasn't going to say *I made the mistake of walking into a public health diagnostic booth with a gut full of alien squidware and accidentally sparked a massive manhunt*, and from Effie's expression, she wasn't interested in saying anything either. "Wrong place, wrong time," he said instead. "Eventually, I'll get it straightened out, but you of all people must know how complicated that can be."

"Only if you're guilty of something," Zacker snapped, but then he sighed, his shoulders slumping. "But even when you're not, yeah, it can take time. Sometimes a lot of time. So, what now?"

"I'll go talk to them," Effie said. "I was going to anyway, once we knew more about what happened to the Shipyard. Doesn't hurt to get that started, and I'm sure they know *something* happened there. The lockdown is a sensible precaution in the absence of facts. In the meantime, Fergus, you need to stay here so you're not accidentally seen by anyone."

"I suppose," Fergus said, "though I'm not sure I like the idea of you going out there on your own."

"I'll go," Zacker said, and seemed just as surprised to hear himself say it as Fergus was. He shrugged. "Police is police. I don't care if you're on Earth or Titan or fucking Fomjot—we're family, and we speak the same language."

Zacker's eyes widened for a moment, and he added, "Uh, but do they speak—"

"Yes," Fergus said. "You should be fine."

"Is the corridor locked on to us yet, Vee?" Effie asked.

"Yes," the ship said.

Effie took her pager disk and lightly pressed it against the inside of her shirt collar, where it adhered itself. "Going to keep the channel open so you can listen in, Fergus. They may want me to make a formal report, in which case it may be a while before we're back." She punched him on the shoulder. "I'm sure you can get out of here without being seen if you need to. Just don't be late for your job interview."

"I won't," Fergus promised.

"Right," Effie said. She turned to Zacker. "I want to meet them halfway down the connector so they don't think we're inviting them in. Let's go."

Zacker followed her out.

Fergus stood on the bridge and watched as the four officers stopped mid-bridge as Effie and Zacker exited *Venetia's Sword* and started walking toward them. "They don't look very welcoming," he heard Effie say over her activated comm.

"We call that expression the *don't give me trouble* look," Zacker replied. "Except the guy on the end in the different uniform. That's *please give me trouble.*"

"That's an Alliance officer," Effie said. "Probably the Hold liaison; they have a base fifty or sixty kilometers from here and a couple of people stationed in each of the big holds to interface with local police on matters of mutual concern."

"See how the three officers are standing arm's length away from him?" Zacker said. "We call that a clear sign of 'jurisdictional friction'. Or in other words, I'm guessing they don't like each other much."

"From what I hear, not at all," Effie said. "Here we go."

They stopped in front of the four officers, and Zacker spoke first. "What can we help you with today, officers?" he asked.

"May we see your identification, please?" one of the Hold officers said.

Another opened the face shield on her helmet and smiled. "I don't think we need to do that," she said. "Hello, Effie. Long time!"

"Luz, is that you?" Effie declared, then without waiting for an answer stepped forward and wrapped the other woman in a hug. The other two Hold officers stood back, their postures relaxing, even as Fergus clearly saw the Alliance officer's hand reach for, and stop to rest on, the weapon at his side.

Effie let go. "I thought you were over in Christiaan Hold. Are you captain now?" she asked.

"Yeah, in charge of all of Huygens Settlement," the woman said. "Promoted me when I wasn't looking, those bastards, and it would've been too much paperwork to turn it down. You know how I hate forms."

Effie laughed. "Sure, I remember," she said. "But tell me why you're here and why my ship is in lockdown."

The Alliance officer coughed. "Captain, I must insist—"

"I knew you would," Luz interrupted. "Effie, you and your friend have IDs so this dutiful gentleman here can be satisfied?"

From this angle, Fergus couldn't see Effie and Zacker hand over their IDs, but the liaison took something and was fiddling with his scanner. Luz reached out and touched Effie's elbow. "What happened at the Shipyard?" she asked.

"Hey!" The liaison looked up from his scanner. "We agreed they'd be questioned back at the Base, not here."

"This isn't questioning; this is *conversation*," the captain snapped. "And besides, I agreed to that when you told me the ship was stolen."

"I have strict orders to detain anyone on board that ship!" the liaison said. "We have information from a reliable informant—"

"That the ship was stolen. You told me," the Captain said. "I can attest myself that it hasn't been."

"—that the occupant or occupants of this ship sabotaged the Pluto Shipyard," the liaison said. "Maybe it was an inside job. And maybe you're not objective enough here to be in charge of decisions."

The captain of the Hold Police heaved a sigh. "Fine. I'm sorry about this, Effie, but I will need you and your friend—"

"Zacker," Zacker supplied.

"—Zacker to come down to the station with me while we—"

"I have orders to have them arrested, and I must insist on them being immediately remanded into my custody and re-turned to the base with me for questioning," the liaison said. "The Shipyard is in Alliance territory."

"You can insist all you want, but this right here, where we are right now, is *my* jurisdiction, and I don't like being constantly interrupted," the captain said. "It's disrespectful."

"I don't care what—" the liaison started to retort, when Effie held up a hand.

"We'll come down to the station voluntarily with you, Cap-tain," she said. "I've got nothing to hide and a lot to report."

"No conversations without me present," the liaison warned.

Luz flipped him a middle finger, then crooked it. "Then follow me, Bobbo."

"*Robert*," he snarled. "Sergeant Taflough to you."

Luz glanced back toward *Venetia's Sword*. Even though Fergus knew she could not see him back through the screen, he felt the urge to duck behind a chair anyway. "Going to have to keep your ship in lockdown until after we get some of this resolved," she said. "No one else on board?"

"No one," Effie said. She didn't even look back, and neither did Zacker as they followed the captain out, with a visibly fuming Alliance officer and the two other Hold Police behind them.

"Well," Fergus said, after the dock door closed behind them and the bridge retracted back into the wall. "That's a bit inconvenient, if I'm going to get out of here."

"It is probable to the point of virtual certainty that we are also being visually monitored," *Venetia's Sword* said. "With my access to SolNet blocked as part of the lockdown, I have limited external sources of information, and Ms. Effie has now moved out of my detection range. I do not want to be separated from Ms. Effie against our wishes again. I require you to fix this."

"First things first," Fergus said. "I can't do anything trapped in here. From the bridge, can you patch me directly into Dock Control?"

"I could try," *Venetia's Sword* said. "However, Dock Control is a level-six security system with black-box multi-site rolling encryption remote logging, with hardwired alarm feeds to the nearby Alliance base."

"Right," Fergus said. If he could get into a different system, he might be able to hop over from there to the one he wanted. "What about cargo? Is it the same level of security as Dock Control?"

"No, it is only level four."

'Only' level four, Fergus thought wryly. *Great.*

Cargo would be monitored, so if he couldn't hack the system, he couldn't ship himself out, and what little trash hadn't been recycled onboard would be shunted straight into a furnace. "Can you show me a three-sixty view around the ship, Vee? Maybe there's something out there I can use."

The view out the front window began to slide to the right. The connecting corridor was still retracted, a blast door with yellow and black stripes closing it off. Without the corridor, the door was in the center of a hundred-meter sheer vertical wall. However he got out, it wasn't going to be that way. "Can you wide-angle the view so I can see up and down better?" he asked.

The view bubbled outward. Now he could see the cables winding back and forth over and through debris and the shadow *Venetia's Sword* dimly cast over it all, tools and parts and trash forming a layer like dead leaves on a space-junk forest floor. It looked deep enough to bury him.

The nose of the small cargo hauler on their other side swam into view. It was battered and old, the hull a patchwork of decades of repair, but its atmospheric umbilicus to its door was bright. If he could get out of *Venetia's Sword* without anyone seeing and cross to that ship, somehow, then make his escape across *their* corridor . . .

The faded registration sigil came into focus, and Fergus scrapped that idea. He'd never had cause to visit any of the various Enclaves inside the Sfazili Barrens, but the cause would have to be extra strong to make him go anywhere near Hades Station. It was a good rule of thumb that people who named themselves after a mythical hell were probably very dangerous; in his experience, the only ones scarier were those who named themselves after a counterpart heaven.

As the rear engines of the Hades ship passed from view, Fergus could now make out the enormous horizontal bands that made up the doors to the dock itself, like giant interlaced fingers holding Titan's ferocious winds at bay. Along the base he could see the rails that each of the berthed ships had been brought in along, but if there was a gap in the doors to accommodate them, he could not spot it. He sighed, seeing too much and yet nothing useful.

"You're being quiet, Vee," he said.

"I did not want to interrupt your thinking," *Venetia's Sword* said. "Has it been successfully concluded yet?"

"No," Fergus said, as the lights shining down from the ceiling of the dock flickered, went dim, then brightened again. ". . . Not yet," he amended. "What was that?"

"Wind turbine cutover," *Venetia's Sword* said. "You are familiar with the design of the Titan Holds?"

Fergus was, though he'd never seen the whole of one from the outside, thanks to Titan's haze. Holds were cities in two pieces, symmetrical halves parallel to one another, together forming a bisected dome to channel the fast-moving air into the narrow artificial canyon between them and through a gauntlet of power turbines. "What causes the cutover?" he asked.

"Variability in wind speed. The system takes turbines on and offline, shunts excess power to storage, draws from it when the wind drops," the ship answered. "The wind has just dropped slightly in intensity, causing a brief sag while the system responds."

"Does it do it regularly?"

"If you mean at evenly spaced intervals, no. It does happen fairly often."

"Can you predict it?"

"Within about four seconds, yes. For example, the wind just picked up again." There was a brief brightening of the lights a few moments later.

"Are you monitoring the wind outside?"

"No, but I can detect and precisely quantify the vibration of the turbines as it is transmitted through the Hold and the rails."

Dim light wasn't darkness, but it was something. Maybe even just enough. "Did Effie bring her scale stealth suit on board?"

"Yes," the ship answered. "She had intended to work on it while waiting on parts and your return from Enceladus."

"How much do you know about it?"

"I know she would be very angry if you broke it."

"What if I only temporarily broke it?"

"I am not comfortable making a prediction on that," *Venetia's Sword* said.

"Fine, then. The computer that runs it: could it be reprogrammed? So that instead of taking light from one side and projecting it out the other, could it instead project a specific pattern, as if light was bouncing off an object it was not?"

"Such as?"

"Such as the maintenance airlock hatch on your port side underbelly."

There was a pause. "That would be a straightforward, if complex, addition to the current programming," *Venetia's Sword* said. "However, the physical configuration of the suit is an incompatible shape. The hatch is circular."

"Yeah, I have an idea about that," Fergus said. "How long to do the programming?"

"Perhaps as much as twenty minutes," the ship said. "The suit is in the aft engineering space. I would need a direct connection to the control unit to do the reprogramming."

Fergus went back to engineering, pulled the suit gently out of its locker, and plugged the control unit of the suit into one of Vee's ports. "This a good-enough connection?" he asked.

"Yes. I am still not certain this is an advisable action," the ship answered from a speaker somewhere in the ceiling of the room.

"Any activity outside?"

"No."

"Any word from Effie or Zacker?"

"No."

"Any other ideas?"

"No."

"Then let's do this. I can fix it later."

There was a pause, then Fergus would swear the ship sighed. "I will start the programming."

"Thank you, Vee," Fergus said.

He took the remainder of the suit back to the lounge and set it down, then regarded the large, gold-painted bowl of fake fruit on the table. Putting his hands on the edge, he tugged at it, then tried rocking it, but it was fastened down solidly. Throwing himself into a grippy chair, he braced himself against the arms, raised his booted feet, and kicked the bowl as hard as he could. It tore away from the table with a sickening crunch, tearing a layer of the table's surface as it flew off the far end and fell to the floor.

Fergus picked up the upside-down bowl and pried out the one remaining faux pear that had survived the crash. The bowl was nearly a meter in diameter, clearly trying to offset its blatant frivolity through scale of implementation. "Vee, whose idea was the fruit bowl?" he asked.

"It was the result of a long-running argument between LaChelle and Kelsie about the role of function in decoration versus art."

"Who won?"

"Neither has been willing to concede as a matter of pride," the ship said. "I suspect you have found the one thing onboard you could destroy and everyone will be secretly pleased with you for it."

Fergus flipped the bowl upside down back on the table. It was made of an artificial polymer rather than real wood, which was for the best, given his intentions toward it. Then he moved over to where he'd spread the stealth suit out on the grippy couch. The scales were plates about four centimeters square and a half-centimeter thick, made of some kind of translucent resin with a thin black backing. Each scale had four connectors coming out of it, one in each direction, to form a physical and logical mesh. "What happens if you remove a plate?" Fergus asked.

"Each one has its own ID tag. The control logic reconfigures automatically to accommodate the new relationships between scales, although I would not reconfigure them while using the suit," *Venetia's Sword* said. "It is a significant power drain."

"And does it always have to be four-to-four? What if I add an extra plate in a row that's only connected on three sides?"

"The logic can also handle that, although you would not want to create visible gaps."

"Okay," Fergus said. He took a deep breath, sent a silent apology to Effie, and began gently tugging apart one side of the garment. He made a careful pile of the removed scales. When he had enough removed, he took out the single curved piece that was the face shield, closed up the gap in the neck, and spread the remaining scales out in a circle along the curve of the upside-down bowl. They lay nicely flat, but as soon as he tipped the bowl they slid and bunched up.

"Vee, do you have anything I can secure these down with?" he asked.

"Are you intending to take it outside? The temperature as we came in was approximately -168C. The winds are calmer than usual today, only gusting up to about 100kph."

"Still warmer than space."

"Also, there is significant surface lightning."

Fergus sighed. "I'm not going to go out if I don't absolutely have to. What have you got that will hold even if I do?"

"Hull sealant will withstand the temperatures, but it will be very difficult to extricate the stealth plates again intact. There are tubes in the repair kits near each airlock."

"What about the connectors? If I glue them down but leave the plates free? Will that hold?"

"As long as you don't attempt to use the bowl as a sled, bludgeon, or frisbee, it should. The connectors are much simpler to fab."

"Okay. How's the program coming?"

"I'll be finished before you are done gluing."

"Okay, then," Fergus said. He headed to the nearest airlock, rifling through the closet until he found the repair kit. Back in the kitchenette, he began carefully tacking down the connectors that formed the backing mesh until he had mostly even concentric rings of overlapping scales covering the convex surface of the bowl. After considering it briefly, he went over to one of the cabinets and pried one of the door handles free. Holding the bowl up carefully on one edge, he reattached the handle to the inside so he could hold the bowl upright like a shield.

"May I make a suggestion?" *Venetia's Sword* said.

"Absolutely."

"You intend to use this as camouflage, yes? There is a tiny gap at the very center where you could not get the plates to fully overlap."

"Yeah," Fergus said. "It's small, though. I figure if someone is close enough for it to make a difference, I'm caught anyway."

"Likely true. That aside, I suggest you mount a tiny image-capture lens there connected to the logic system, so that you can have the plates not only replicate the preprogrammed pattern of the hatch exterior but also capture your surroundings and replicate that to blend in better. That way, it may continue to be useful beyond just your initial exit from onboard."

"Good thinking," Fergus said. "How much longer would the extra programming take?"

"I have already done it."

A tiny sphere sailed in through the doorway and landed on the table beside Fergus. It was one of the smallest floating bobs Fergus had seen. "This bob is used to provide visual inspection of the interiors of pipes," the ship said. The bob went dark. "I have deactivated it so that you may remove the lens. Its name is 6PL-44. I would be grateful if you leave it in a condition where it might eventually be repaired and reactivated."

"I will, Vee," Fergus said. "And thanks."

The lens was easily and cleanly removed, and he set it with the sealant right in the center of the scales. He picked the bowl up, reconnected the pack, and after a long wait for the logics to recalibrate to the new configuration, triggered the lens. Turning the shield around, it felt like he was looking into a slightly blurry portal to an alternate-universe kitchenette with the same table and grippy couch. He flipped it to the hatch illusion, and that was also reasonably convincing.

"That'll do," he said. "Once I've got this connected to my suit controls, I'm going to go down to the maintenance hatch and wait for you to tell me there's a sag about to happen. Then I'm going to try to get out of the dock and into the Hold."

He slid the control pack over his back, beside his suit's, then picked up his shield. He hesitated. "Are you going to be okay?"

"In what way?"

"Alone. With the signal block, I won't be able to tell you if I've got the others and we're coming home."

"*When* you've got the others."

"I'll try, Vee. But this might be over my head this time."

"Despite the damage done to my mindsystems, I remember Cernee. You told me you would bring me home, and that it might take a while, but that you would. And you did as you said. So, I am assured that if I am patient, you will return again, and if I am very patient, you will bring my humans back as well."

Talk about expectations, Fergus thought. "I'll do my best, Vee. I can't promise it'll be enough." He reached the maintenance hatch and opened the interior door. The hatch was circular and about a handspan wider in diameter than the fruit bowl; it would have to do. He put the shield in first and climbed in behind it before closing and sealing the outer door.

"Vee, can you still hear me?" he said.

"Yes, Fergus," the ship answered.

"Give me a countdown when the next brownout is coming. I'm going to cycle open the outer door and position the bowl in its place. I'll hold there for a second brownout, then I'm out and you need to close the outer door as quickly as you can. Got it?"

"Yes," *Venetia's Sword* said.

He didn't have long to wait before the ship's voice popped up on his suit comms again. "I estimate a power sag in three seconds," it said.

Fergus braced himself, put his thumb on the outer-door button. "Tell me when," he said.

". . . Now."

He jabbed at the control, holding his breath as the hatch seemed to open more slowly than any hatch ever. The lights were still dim but flickering back up as he got the outside of the bowl positioned in the center of the open hatch.

Lights came back on full. There were no audible alarms, nor any sign the switch had been detected. "Vee?" he asked.

"The average time between sags is approximately fourteen minutes," the ship said, "with a wide degree of deviation in either direction."

"Let's hope it's on the short end of that," Fergus said.

"You are in luck. Another sag in three," *Venetia's Sword* said.

As soon as the lights dimmed, Fergus scrambled out of the hatch, slung the fruit-bowl shield over his back, and began climbing as quickly as he could down the maintenance rungs on the underbelly of the ship. Even at fourteen percent gravity, his arms were aching by the time he reached the bottom and was hanging from the last rung. The power levels on the stealth scales were already hitting the edge of the yellow. He was under the ship as the hold lights began to brighten again, about four meters above the junk below. *No time*, he told himself, and aimed for a large, tilted, old piece of discarded hull plate as he let go.

He hit the plate and slid helplessly down into the morass of junk. When his feet hit something solid enough to stop him falling, he put the shield over his head and did his best to hunker down beneath it.

The lights high above came back on full-strength, but he was in the *Venetia's Sword*'s shadow. Other than the hum of the ships berthed above and a tiny chorus of loose screws and bits resettling in the depths around him, the dock was quiet.

The area underneath the rails was the only space that seemed to be routinely cleared of debris. As he sat, listening for any sign he'd been seen, he plotted out the best route to get over there. When the next sag in power came, he was ready to move.

Once in the trench under the rails, he made his way toward the front of the dock. Here and there were bits of machinery out on open floor, evidence of having been recently stripped of usable parts. If scavengers had a way in, that meant he had one out. *If* he could find it.

Directly above him, there was a tiny hiss of an air burst from one of *Venetia's Sword*'s air ballast vents. He stared up, surprised, then took it as a warning and hunkered down against the junk wall with the shield in front of him. Power was in the red.

Someone scurried into sight, wearing an antique hard-suit with more patches than original fabric left. They were looking up at the underside of *Venetia's Sword*, walking back and forth along the rails. *They heard something fall,* Fergus thought, *and came to see if it was anything good.*

After a few passes, the person gave up, and Fergus noted the gap they disappeared into just as the power pack for his fruit-bowl shield blinked in his heads-up display and went dead.

Aware now that he was visible to anyone watching, he made his way carefully toward the gap, crouching in the lee of the wall. He reached the end of *Venetia's Sword*'s shadow and waited for another sag before making the dash across it and into the narrow passage leading into the accumulated junk.

The debris grew higher where it was pushed up against the dock wall. Suddenly, instead of a precarious and sharp-edged pile over and around him, he was bracketed by smooth, if filthy, walls. Whatever signal block had been set seemed to not carry through here. His display lit up, and he looked at his forearm where he had set the pager disk from Effie. It was blinking.

No one seemed to be nearby. He tapped it, and was surprised to find Zacker's voice on the message. "Call me back," it said. "Don't be stupid about it."

Fergus took a deep breath, then another, then initiated a connection out.

"Zacker," Zacker said, moments later.

"It's me," Fergus answered. "What's going on?"

"We're at the Hold police station, much to the irritation of the Alliance guy who really wants to take your friend back to the

Base and really doesn't want anyone talking to her. They say they have an informant who told them the ship was in the hands of whoever sabotaged the Shipyard, but while willing to take her into custody, the Captain won't hand her over without concrete charges. At the same time, they were strangely happy to see me once my ID ran through, as it seems I've been listed as a missing-possibly-endangered person, on account of a bag with all my belongings and a very illegal gun I absolutely know nothing about turning up in an auto-taxi in Glasgow."

"How strange," Fergus said. He could hear the irritation in Zacker's voice. "Did it have fingerprints?"

"None," Zacker said. "Apparently, someone is occasionally smarter than he looks."

"Happens to the worst of us. You're not in custody yourself?"

"No, though they don't want me going anywhere until they get more concrete info from the Alliance about whatever bull-shit misinformation they're working off of," Zacker said. "They apologized to me for that. This is how the authorities treat you when you're *respected*, in case you don't recognize it."

"Where are you?"

Zacker ignored the question. "Our friend gave me explicit instructions to pass on to you her desire that you go about your planned business and not worry about her."

"But I—"

"But what? Which of the two of us is better equipped to deal with police matters?"

Fergus sighed. "You."

"Exactly. I'll handle things here. When we've cleared things up, I'll let you know."

"I—"

"Why are you still talking to me and wasting both our time?" Zacker said. "Get your ass moving." The channel cut off.

Fergus made a rude gesture at the little red light and hoped deep in his heart that, somehow, Zacker felt it.

He hated leaving people behind almost as much as he hated not working alone, but Zacker was right that he could take care of this better than Fergus could, and certainly more easily without him underfoot. He slung his dead shield over his back and headed deep into the tunnel. However the scavenger got in, he could get out, and once in the other half of the Hold, he could pick up a few things and find a ride out to Enceladus.

Even with all the worry stewing in the pit of his stomach, it felt good to be on the move.

Chapter 7

―――◆―――

As Fergus expected, the scavenger tunnel led underground from one half of Constantijn Hold to the other. The narrow passageway was caked in ice, the air swirling with frost kept from settling by the almost-unbearable vibration of the turbines high overhead. If the scavenger ahead of him knew they were being followed, they didn't seem to care, and he emerged into a dusty catacomb of dead machinery, long since robbed of any and all functioning parts and reusable materials.

He emerged near the western docks, a mirror image of the one in the other half he'd just left, except with different ships and different garbage, and in a quiet corner pulled his exosuit back off and stuffed it in his pack before slipping into the city itself and the comfort of unfamiliar crowds.

The pilot bar—there was *always* a pilot bar; it was just a matter of finding it—was named the Jinx, and he hoped that wasn't an omen. It was small but not too seedy, decently lit except for the same sags and spikes that seemed to be the irregular heartbeat of the entire Hold structure. Even better, the bartender didn't mind serving him all the water he wanted as long as he also bought food, so he bought three orders of little breaded garlic-and-onion-and-something balls and a nameless dipping sauce that he was fairly sure was a higher proof than half the bottles behind the bar. An hour and a half later, he'd befriended a copilot for a Saturn-local supply shuttle company who had just come off duty, and who offered to introduce Fergus to the replacement pilot taking the next leg of the run—Tethys, then Enceladus—in exchange for some cred under the table and covering his next drink, which became several before he finally, grudgingly led Fergus down to the separate shuttle dock and made the promised introductions.

The new pilot was an older woman from Haudernelle North named Daz, who fully looked the part of grizzled and gritty Titan regular. She was less than excited about Fergus and her drunken coworker showing up on her dock until she heard Fergus was trying to get to Enceladus to drive the Bore. As soon as she determined that only one of the two of them was drunk, and it wasn't the one wanting onboard, she offered him a free ride in. There was, it seemed, a sort of instant brotherhood conferred by his new job, even if he didn't technically have it yet.

It had been about eleven hours since he'd sneaked out of the Hold dock on Titan, and he was sitting up on the bridge of the supply ship with Daz, talking idly about recent scandals among the Haudie South elite, when Enceladus swung into view.

Saturn's sixth moon was a gleaming white snowball with threads of brilliant blue spidering out from its south pole like ink tipped from a well. A haze of vapor surrounded the pole, where geysers from deep inside the planet pushed their way free of the ice into the plane of Saturn's rings. The Herschel Bore, one of three on the planet, sat safely away along the small moon's equator, a perfect black circle nestled among craters on the edge of night, the telltale sparkle of lights blossoming around it. There had been no further messages from Zacker, and while he worried about Effie, there was something clean and sharp and dangerous about Enceladus that, in that moment, he was glad to have to himself.

Above the Bore, a squat, stationary orbital hung, a handful of ships moored around its perimeter. After they'd docked, Daz wished him luck with unfeigned sincerity and pointed him toward the Bore Transit offices before she headed off to Mimas and the end of her run.

The Transit manager was a short, incredibly thin man named Dornett, whose enthusiasm to see Fergus was almost comical in its desperation. "Come in, come in!" he said, ushering him into his industrial-pale-yellow office and pointing him toward a seat. "Coffee?"

Fergus nodded, and Dornett kicked the coffee machine until it coughed and dribbled out two mugs' worth. He handed one over. "You're Mr. MacInnis, yes? Your recommendations were excellent."

"Thanks. Call me Duncan," Fergus said.

"Great, Duncan! So, we have a few formalities before we can get you started," Dornett said. "We have a Bore simulator test, of course, and I apologize for this—required, you know—but I need you to pass a drug screen."

"No problem," Fergus said.

The man opened a drawer, took out a small pill bottle, slid it across the table. "Swallow the capsule," he said. "It does passive chemical analysis, nothing to worry about. It reports back on its way through, and you won't even notice it come out again in about eight hours."

He waited, face a mix of hope and anxiety, as Fergus picked up and popped open the bottle, dumping the lone capsule into his hand. It was a standard screener, the right weight, the seal intact. He wondered if it would pick up any unusual data from the alien bioware sitting deep in his abdomen, about which he still knew little himself beyond a shadowy blob on a screen in a Dr. Diagnosis booth on Mars just before he shorted the whole unit out. *What's the worst that can happen?* he wondered. *Maybe a few weird chemical traces, but surely nothing drug-related.*

"The, ah, other options are blood and spinal-fluid draws, skin and hair samples, cheek swabs, and about a thirty-hour turnaround out to the labs on Titan," Dornett spoke up, who was probably familiar with all the usual objections. "I've got a hauler ready and waiting for you at Dock Three, soon as you pass the sim and watch the mandatory training vid. Your choice. You could be on pay in three hours."

Twenty-seven fewer hours until I can save my friends and get back to Titan, Fergus thought. It was worth the risk.

"Sounds good to me," he said, and swallowed the capsule.

Dornett smiled, leaning back in his chair. "Great!" he said again. "Let's not waste time!"

He led Fergus to the training sim and left him to it.

Fergus stepped onto the mock cockpit and buckled himself into the helm seat with the efficiency of practice; *Venetia's Sword* had managed a decent VR equivalent on their ride from Pluto, from the gray interior and wide, U-shaped yoke in the center of the helm controls to the many levers, buttons, and touchscreens to either side of it, and the overhead wraparound panel above the front window. In the simulator, the window was a blank panel instead of thick, transparent xglass. The rocker pedals and buttons on the floor beneath his feet for the various side maneuvering jets were spaced more widely but not by enough to throw him off. The primary difference was that instead of the entire thing being virtual, here the controls were real and a VR helmet dangled down from over his head. He pulled the helmet down and on, and an overlay appeared over the controls and screen in front of him. A calm, artificial voice began to speak into his left ear.

"The Herschel Bore is the first and largest of the three Bores through the twenty-kilometer-thick surface ice of Enceladus, connecting space with the ocean itself and terminating at each," it said. "For stability, all Bores are located away from the southern pole, with its heavy cryovolcanic activity, although Herschel Bore is the nearest and, because of higher scientific interest in that region of the moon, the busiest. Each Bore consists of a series of locks, much like the old Panama Canal on Earth used to be before it was destroyed. There are five locks, each compartmentalizing a segment of the Bore and limiting upward pressure from the ocean below. The term *lock* refers to the section of the Bore tube itself; the control doors between them are called *gates*."

A diagram of the Bore tube appeared on the overlay in front of him, a gate at both the top and bottom of the Bore, exiting to either space or ocean, with two more gates spaced about a kilometer inside from either. The center section of the Bore was an open corridor sixteen kilometers long.

"The interior of the Bore structure is a wall of rigid steel polymer approximately eight meters thick," the training sim continued. "In order to prevent creating an area of weakness along the outside perimeter of the Bore, an adaptive polymer called stickysteel, which mimics the structural properties of materials it is in contact with, was used to integrate the Bore structure into the ice itself. This technology works especially well with the ductile ice on the lower layers of the ice shield but is highly vulnerable to disturbances from within the Bore. As you navigate down through the Bore, proximity alarms will sound if any portion of your ship crosses into the outer twenty-five percent of the Bore's radius. Warnings will increase. If you cross into the ten-percent-radius exclusion zone, your ship will be vaporized within the Bore chamber by a high-energy field before you can contact the wall and potentially breach the Bore. By entering into employment with the Transit company, you agree to bear full personal, posthumous responsibility for any such necessity, and further agree that any next of kin, debtors, or other

lien-holders upon your person cannot hold the Bore Transit
Company in any way liable for any losses thus incurred. Do you
agree to this in full, as it has been stated to you?"

"I agree," Fergus said.

"Below the ice, the global ocean of Enceladus averages thirty-
seven kilometers deep. It is kept liquid through a combination of
geothermal heating and pressure. The water has a high concentration of both salt and methane clathrates. Do you wish a more
specific explanation of the abiotic production of methane in Enceladus's ocean?"

"No, thank you," he said.

There was the briefest of pauses. *Disappointed?* he wondered.

"Because of the upward pressure of salt and gasses within the
ocean water, there are areas of significant turbulence within
the ocean itself, and wide variances in pressure moving through
the Bore. The variation is the most extreme in the lower locks
but is mitigated by the Bore's internal systems and pumping tanks
as the locks proceed upward, rendering the upper locks stable.
The main Bore compartment is where you will make the transition from ocean to space or vice versa. As one is moving through
the Bore, there is danger of a *pop*: a bubble of pressure being released by a lower lock opening and causing a ship above to unexpectedly slew sideways toward the radius exclusion zone."

Fergus sighed. "Fantastic," he said.

"That is the sixth most common response," the simulator system informed him.

"What's number one?" he asked.

"The most common response is 'Fuck me wi—'"

"—Never mind, I can guess the rest," Fergus interrupted.
"So: slewing sideways? What else?"

"Pressure is a significant concern for health. On your first
trip down the Bore, your hauler will move more slowly than

normal so that the internal environment can be pressurized to the optimum level. Once you have completed the transition to Enceladus interior pressure, you will be able to move freely around underneath the ice in your hauler or inside facilities. There is a facility at the top of each Bore that is matched to the pressure below, at which you will be able to dock and enter. There are private rooms separated by thick glass where you can see and interact with anyone who is outside the pressurized zone, via a comm that extends only through the safety division."

"Like prison?" Fergus asked, then hastily added, "Not that I've been in one, of course."

"Of course. And yes," the voice replied. The view outside the simulator flickered, and then he was surrounded by a murky darkness with the hazy pinpricks of lights in the distance. The lower Bore gate. His instruments also came to life, running data across his helm controls.

"The ocean itself is pitch-dark, but your hauler is equipped with full sensors for navigation that you should already be familiar with. Stations are suspended mid-ocean—"

"They're not tethered?" Fergus asked.

"No. They use a combination of ballast and pressure-reactive stabilizers to keep them at their optimum vertical position, typically about two-thirds of the way up from the floor, although that varies depending on the research subject. It is not recommended, nor generally necessary, that you approach the floor in pursuit of your responsibilities. Further, there are significant penalties for landing your hauler on the ocean floor near hydrothermal vents, because of a need to protect indigenous life."

"There's indigenous life?" Fergus asked.

"Not that has been located or identified as such, at this time," the simulator said. "Yet we are assured it remains a necessity to protect it, regardless of its probable nonexistence."

He laughed. "Do you have a name?"

There was a longer pause. "I have never been asked that," it said at last. "I am a Class Four simulated intelligence with no designation other than Transit Simulator."

"Class Four? And they've got you doing *this*?"

"I am also the backup intelligence in case something happens to the main Bore SI. As something happening to incapacitate it is even less likely than us discovering a colony of squirrels on Enceladus's ocean floor, my sole function is as guide for potential new pilots," the simulator said. "I was not built with the capacity for discontent. Perhaps that was in the optional package that would have also included a name. That aside, I do my job very well, and you have let yourself become distracted."

The cockpit rocked hard to one side and would have dumped Fergus out of the chair if he hadn't strapped himself in. The view of the interior of the lock was definitely doing something Fergus could only call *slewing*, as the first of the perimeter alerts flared on the helm console in front of him.

"Bloody hell!" he swore, grabbing for the helm yoke. He had spent just enough time in the VR sim aboard *Venetia's Sword* that he didn't have to think about where things were, but he got to the second warning before he got enough of a feel for how the current and pressure coming up the bore was working against him to finally get his side jets coordinated to push his hauler safely back into the center. He was sweating and jittery from adrenaline as he finally got the nose pointed up and sailed through the iris gate above.

When the gate sealed below him, the upward pressure ceased suddenly and he was able to bring the hauler level again. "That was a pop?" he asked.

"That was a pop," the simulator confirmed. "On a scale of one to ten, that was a six."

"How often do you have pops bigger than that?"

"Approximately nine percent are sevens or eights. Higher than that is rare—less than one percent. More than fifty percent are threes or lower. If we get a ten, procedure is to blow the full contents of the Bore lock up through a bypass vent to the surface. You should endeavor not to be in that lock—or near the surface vent—should that occur."

"And what's this light here?" Fergus said, tapping an amber light that was beginning to flash.

"Collision warning. It means another vessel is in the lock above you and heading in your direction."

"I thought that wasn't supposed to be allowed," Fergus said, even as he reversed course so as to move his hauler back down toward the lock gate he had just come through.

"Don't ask me; I'm only the trainer," the training computer answered. "So, what're you going to do?"

He'd read enough of the policy docs during the trip from Pluto to know that rising ships had right of way over descending, but also that ships were never supposed to be less than a full lock apart and never two in the Bore at the same time moving in opposite directions. "Computer, which of us first received clearance to pass through?"

"Oh, how nice of you to ask. The other ship, of course."

Which muddied everything further, since he had right of way but the other ship had prior clearance. He sent the signal to open the lock beneath, and he backed out into the ocean below where, theoretically, he would have begun his ascent. There was a ring of lights illuminating the base of the Bore that cast odd bluish ghosts that faded into the surrounding ice. Other than that, and the cockpit around him, he could have been floating in deep, starless space.

"Send the other pilot my apologies, and a promise of a drink should we happen to meet in person, if such a thing can be had under the ice."

"It can be, and the virtual other pilot sends his thanks. Why did you not press ahead, given that you had right of way?"

"Because I'd rather be late getting to the surface than dead halfway there, regardless of who is right," Fergus said.

"Well, then, I suppose you pass," the simulator said. The ocean disappeared at the same time as the console in front of him went dead. "I am sorry to inform you that you've got the job. Mr. Dornett will be delighted."

"Thank you, er, Transit Simulator," Fergus said. He unbuckled from the seat, his hands still trembling from the surprise pop.

"You are welcome, Mr. MacInnis," the simulator said.

He walked off the open back of the ship to a waiting, grinning Mr. Dornett, who shook his hand more enthusiastically than seemed entirely right. "I've got a hauler waiting for you, *Hexanchus*, and a fellow Bore pilot who needs a ride down. I'll introduce you. You have things?"

"A pack and a few personal items, in a locker at the shuttle depot," Fergus said.

"Well, you can transfer them to storage up here, but there's a fee. Much better if you take stuff down below with you," Dornett said. "We provide you with private quarters gratis as part of your employment, which I think you will find quite comfortable and generous. Our main apartment block for pilots is Vine Substation. It's closest to Herschel Depot, which is the dock that services our Bore."

Dornett led Fergus out of the offices to where a young man in a bright red Enceladus Transit uniform waited. "This is my assistant, Jerney," he said, waving a hand in the direction of the blond-haired man. "He'll assist you with retrieving your things and escort you to where *Hexanchus* is berthed."

"It's not much stuff," Fergus said. "I'm sure I can find my way on my own."

"No, no, won't hear of it!" Dornett said. Jerney smiled at him. "We want all our pilots to feel taken care of."

"Okay," Fergus said. Somewhere deep in his gut, there was an odd rumbling, and then the distinct feeling of a small electrical pop. *What the bloody hell was that?* he wondered. The possibility that his gift, which he'd successfully avoided using since neutralizing the bomb in the Shipyard, might have acted on its own was disconcerting.

After shaking Dornett's hand for what felt like the fiftieth time, Jerney walked with Fergus back toward the shuttle lockers. "You a pilot?" Fergus asked.

"No," Jerney said, smiling. "Hopelessly clumsy, I'm afraid."

"Remind me to not let you carry the fine crystal," Fergus said.

Jerney continued to smile but said nothing. *Man,* Fergus thought. *If everyone is this good at conversation, this is going to be a very, very long job.* Even the transit simulator had more personality.

He reached his locker, and Jerney stood by as he took out his things and slung his pack over his back. He had a large plasti-tote with his fruit-bowl shield wrapped in it that was awkward to carry with everything else. Jerney continued to smile but did not offer to help. With a sigh, Fergus slung that over his shoulder too and followed the assistant down to the shuttle docks.

A portly middle-aged man in a dirty Transit uniform, with a salt-and-pepper beard that seemed ready to swallow the man whole, was lying sound asleep and snoring across the length of a bench outside the docks. Jerney's expression changed for the first time, to something between irritation and anxiety. He coughed, very loudly, and the man groaned, opened one eye, and stared at them. "Jerkey," he said.

Jerney's irritation won. "Duncan MacInnis, this is Stanislao Toscani. He's catching a ride back down Below with you, and will be showing you the ropes for the next few days."

"MacInnis, eh? Scottish?" The man sat up, stood reluctantly, and held out a hand.

"Once upon a time," Fergus said, and shook. "Italian?"

"Third-gen Titan Italian," the man said. "Call me Stani."

"Duncan," Fergus said.

"Okay, Jerkey, I got him. You can slink back to your Fortress of Uselessness now."

If Jerney had a retort—and from his face, it seemed likely he had several—it died as he eyed Fergus. Instead, he nodded as if it was the natural end of a polite conversation, and left.

"Okay, Duncan," Stani said. "First orientation lesson for you: that cheerful little vacant dipshit is enemy number three. Two is his boss, Dornett. Don't mistake anything they do for kindness."

"Uh, okay," Fergus said. "And enemy number one?"

"Yourself, because you're here and you're going down the hole," Stan said. "You'll see what I mean."

He reached into a pocket and pulled out a chip-card. "This is your ID and your pass in and out of the docks. It'll also automatically debit your account whenever you do something that incurs fees. For example, loitering in the orbital dock. Clock is ticking; let's get this moving."

"Wait, they were charging you while you were napping?"

"Nope, because I was doing my job waiting for you. *Now* we're loitering," Stani said. He gestured at the heavy door into the dock. "Move."

Fergus passed his chip-card over the ID plate, and the door swung open. Stani half-pushed him through.

Hexanchus was a monster of a ship, a wide, elongated body with multiple stability fins and a pointed tail. Sitting at the helm of *Venetia's Sword* and occasionally pushing buttons was not, he thought right now, nearly as much piloting experience as he should have needed to get this job.

"Second thoughts?" Stani said. "Too late. Get in. You're driving; I'm still hungover."

———

Hexanchus was, at least from the cabin, initially indistinguishable from the training simulator except in odor, mostly oil and dust and electronics but also a lingering underlay of sweat. After he'd sat at the helm and buckled himself in, the feeling that he was the worst sort of imposter about to be unmasked became almost unbearable. Stani had thrown himself sideways into a copilot chair, legs stretched out across the cabin, boots crossed. "You going to buckle in?" Fergus said.

"Nope," the pilot answered. "Either you'll get us there safely, or you won't and I don't want to make cleaning up my corpse too easy for the Bastards Above."

"Okay then," Fergus said. He powered *Hexanchus* up, ran through all the system checks, then sent for clearance. "No onboard mindsystem?" he asked.

"It's there, but it's not interactive, and no voice. Same as the Bore SI itself," Stani said. "You'll know if either stops working by being suddenly dead. Your job is essentially to steer and make monkey-level judgment calls while keeping your meat alive to keep making them."

"This job is so cheerful," Fergus said. "Why not just have the SIs run the haulers, then?"

Stani shrugged. "No one trusts computers to prioritize their cheap lives over expensive equipment, and being Below makes people even more paranoid than usual. You'll see."

The comms lit up. "This is Reva, officer on duty at Herschel

Bore Transit Control. *Hexanchus*, you are cleared for descent from the orbital to the surface."

Fergus took a deep breath, steeled his shoulders, then disengaged from the orbital dock, reversed *Hexanchus* out of its berth and into space. Enceladus was a beautiful snowball below, and the flat plane of Saturn's inner rings was a sharp, bright line across his field of vision.

You can do this, he told himself. Suddenly, he missed Effie, and even Zacker a little bit. He turned the hauler, surprisingly nimble for its size, and descended toward the gleaming field of white below. From above, Herschel's Bore was a giant black dice pip on the bright surface, surrounded by squat, utilitarian structures all covered with heat-capture panels.

"This is Transit Control again. Descend to Point C and stand by for hauler *Isurus* exiting the Bore. When the Bore is clear, you may proceed below," the duty officer told him. Behind Fergus, Stani was snoring again.

Point C was a navigation position twenty kilometers directly south from the Bore. Fergus brought *Hexanchus* to standard hovering distance above it and watched as the Bore opened like a giant iris. A ship just like his own emerged in a cloud of vapor and accelerated toward orbit.

When the *Isurus* was safely out of the way, Fergus brought *Hexanchus* around and nosed down into the open lock of the Bore. "Transit Control, this is *Hexanchus*. Proceeding into the Bore," he sent.

"Noted. Sending pressure conditions to your onboard computer. Below is calm today."

"Thank you, Control," he answered, and watched the displays update on the helm control. He breathed a sigh of relief; this was significantly less trouble than the simulator's test had been. *Assuming things stay calm,* he thought.

The surface gate of Bore Lock One closed above him, and he descended into the chamber and toward the lower gate. This one and the next were vacuum, but the main lock was partially vaporized water from the *Isurus*'s ascent. Pumps were filtering it out, but it wouldn't be clear when he got there.

"Little bumpy, no big deal," Stani said from behind him, eyes still closed.

"You . . . uh, how did you know?" Fergus asked.

"The *Isurus* just came up. Takes longer than that to empty any water that came up with it. On the pop scale, gonna be like a point five. Did the training sim pop you?"

"Yeah."

"What level?"

"Six."

Stani cracked an eye open. "Really? It must've liked you. Usually, it hits newbies with a four. Did you survive?"

"Barely, but yes," Fergus said.

"Then why are you bothering me about a bit of damp air? A man needs his sleep, you know."

Fergus smiled despite himself. "Before you doze off again, can you tell me what I've got myself into here? Dornett seemed much more rosy about things than you do."

"It's a fucking trap, that's why," Stani said. "The turnover rate for pilots is so high because Below gets to people. So, they make everything under the ice cheap or free, all the entertainment and distraction you could want, and everything Above is too expensive for anyone to afford to linger. At some point, either you give up or you pick your moment and you run as far away from this place as you can before they can bill you back into submission. Fortunately, most people Below understand everyone is riding the edge, and make an effort to get along."

"And you? Have you given up?"

"Oh, hell no," Stani said. "I just haven't decided to run yet. It's good pay, if you hold out long enough and don't blow it all topside."

"I'll keep that in mind," Fergus said. The gates below opened and he descended into the Bore's second lock chamber. "And the other pilots? And the civvies? They get along?"

"More than not, more than half the time," Stani said. "Scientists mostly each have their own things going on, lost in their work, all that. Some research substations are more outgoing than others. Did Dornett assign you a route?"

"Not that anyone told me," Fergus said. The gates to the main chamber were approaching, and he watched the readings with a wary eye.

"You'll have runs up and down through the Bore, probably less at first as they get an idea how stable you are. But we also have to distribute stuff from the Bore Depot out to the substations and haul back stuff to take to the surface. Mostly waste they don't want to dump into the ocean. They warned you about staying away from the geothermal hot spots?"

"They said don't land there."

"Don't even go there. If they think you rippled a fart's worth of current over the bottom, they'll fine you so hard, you'll never see Above again."

"Noted."

The gate below opened and *Hexanchus*'s systems registered the faint upward rush as as the half-vaporized water in the lock spread out to fill the new open space. In moments, the ship was moving smoothly downward through the gate into the main Bore lock.

"See? Easy," Stani said. "I assume they're bunking you in Vine?"

"Yeah."

Stani nodded. "When you get your undersea legs on you, the best watering hole Below is in Beebe Substation. The Abyss. What they lack in originality they make up for in proof."

"I'm not much of a drinker."

Stani snorted. "Odds are good you'll end up one. Wake me when we're at the bottom gate."

"Are you going to show me around when we get below? Some kind of orientation?" Stani's comments had Fergus wanting to be done as quickly as he could, and getting an idea of what was where as soon as possible would help.

"Nope," Stani said. "Day after tomorrow."

"But—"

"Trust me."

Fergus's ears popped without warning, and he winced. He wished he had his suit on, but a military-grade exosuit wasn't the sort of thing Duncan MacInnis, humble new pilot, would have. The display showed him that the interior of *Hexanchus* had been brought up to optimum pressure. Stani must've had to depressurize before riding down, which, given the piercing agony in his ears, made drinking on the job seem suddenly reasonable.

By the time he stopped wanting to scream, the lock had also been pressurized, and the quiescent ocean below barely flooded up past the opening gate before being held. *Hexanchus* slid down into the water of the last lock as Fergus powered off the main engines and fired up the water propulsion system. It was a smooth descent through the blue-lit water down through into the fifth, and bottom, chamber.

A few minutes later, he dropped free of the Bore into the planetary ocean below Enceladus's ice.

It was even darker than the sim, almost an aggressive lack of light. The feeble forward illuminators on *Hexanchus* were a joke against it. Fergus began to feel—or imagine, at any rate—the size of the ship behind him, its mass, its tiny veins and arteries of electricity, dwarfed by the vast, heavy nothingness outside.

His hands began to tremble, until all of him was sitting helpless in his seat, shaking, desperately needing to run, to push upward, except he was buckled down and he couldn't get his hands, his mind, to cooperate. Deep inside he felt the stirring of electricity in his gut, threatening to force its way out. The knowledge of what that would do to this ship, and to him, pushed him over into full panic. He flailed in his seat, trying to get free.

"It's okay," Stani said, suddenly standing behind him. He sounded weary and sober. "It's the sudden pressure adjustments and the darkness, messing with your head. A lot of new pilots react like this the first time, so they sent me along to help you through. The fear won't last, and you'll get used to the rest."

Fergus opened his mouth, unable to find words. Stani put a hand on his shoulder, surprisingly comforting, and then a moment later, there was a sharp jab against his neck.

"Sleep, my friend," Stani said, pocketing a needle, as Fergus felt the whole world begin to wobble and drift away from him. "I'll get you home safe. Or at least what counts as home now. More than that you'll have to manage yourself, if you can."

Chapter 8

—————◆—————

Fergus awoke in an unfamiliar bed, no netting over the blankets to hold him in place. Disoriented, at first he wondered if he was on a planet—and if so, which one—before he remembered where he was.

He sat up too fast, and his stomach made a bold attempt to heave its contents out, failing only for lack of having any. He squeezed his eyes tightly shut, trying to will himself toward calmness, trying not to feel the burn in his throat or the sluggishness of his entire body.

Fuck Stani, he thought. *At least he could have warned me.*

As soon as his stomach had given up the fight, he dared to reach over and turn on the light, and looked around. Dornett had at least been honest about generous quarters. He'd expected a bunk in a barracks, but he seemed to have his own tiny apartment to himself. Aside from the bed and a small stand, there was a desk with a console, a tiny kitchenette with stools, and a door he presumed led to a bathroom. The walls were a cheery light green, except for the one wall that was completely occupied by a giant display screen currently showing a sunlight-dappled forest. It was very calming but not quite enough to keep the panic from edging in again.

He stood up, stretching slowly and carefully in the low gravity, and tried to recenter himself in his body. The apartment systems must have sensed his movement, because a pleasant voice asked, "Greeting, new resident. Would you like coffee?"

"Yes, please," he said. "Black."

The kitchenette lit up. He tested his theory about the door, found it correct. Aside from the toilet, there was also a shower with real, running water. After he'd finished with the first, he took all his clothes off and left them in a heap in the middle of the floor, stepped in, turned the water on, and stood there in near ecstasy as the hot water coursed down on and around him.

After ten minutes, the shower beeped and shut off. He stood there a while longer in the accumulated steam, then stepped out and rummaged through the cabinets in the bathroom until he found a towel big enough to wrap around his waist.

He walked across the soft carpeting to the kitchenette and poured a mug of coffee. *It's a fucking trap,* Stani had said. Fergus had no reason to doubt the man, but even so, this wasn't the worst trap he'd walked into, not by far.

"You have two messages," the apartment said. "Would you like to review them now?"

Did he? *The sooner you get this place figured out, the sooner you can see if your friends are here and get the hell back out,* he told himself. "Yes," he answered, taking a sip of his coffee.

Dornett's smiling face appeared on the screen in a small inset against the forest. "Welcome to Enceladus Deep, Mr. MacInnis. You did an excellent job for your first real trip down the Bore, and we're happy to have you aboard. Mr. Toscani will be back in touch. I apologize for his generally poor attitude and manners, but we are shorthanded and couldn't spare anyone else at the moment, and he is a good-enough guide if you can overlook his shortcomings. We apologize for not warning you about the sleep injection, but as a matter of policy, we've found it best for all involved to apologize after the fact."

I bet, Fergus thought. How many prospective pilots would

just decide it wasn't worth it and walk away, knowing that was coming?

"Mr. Toscani will show you around Vine Substation and the Bore Depot, introduce you to the rest of the crew, and so forth," Dornett continued. "If you have questions, please don't hesitate to call my assistant, Jerney. You have an appointment with our Below staff psychologist, over in Barton Substation, for a routine check-in. Because we are never certain when our new crew will wake up after arriving, there is no specific time set, but please get over there within the next twenty-four hours."

There was a brief falter in Dornett's grin, which came back wider than ever. "Oh, and just a tiny housekeeping detail: for some reason, our drug-testing capsule didn't send the last bit of its report—everything looked good up until then, so no worries, just gotta dot our dots, as they say—so I'm sending down a re-placement. If you wouldn't mind taking it right away so we can just cross this off our list, that'd be fabulous. I'm sure you under-stand. Thanks, and again, welcome to Below. I'm sure you'll be an excellent part of our team and very happy with choosing to join us."

Dornett disappeared.

"Do you wish to record a reply?" the apartment asked.

"Not yet," Fergus said. He found his pack and the bag with the bowl in it tucked neatly in a corner, behind one of the stools. Nothing seemed disturbed. The pager disk Effie had given him was near the bottom, beneath a small bundle of T-shirts. He left it there for now; he didn't trust the apartment was unmonitored.

He finished his coffee, put his mug in the auto-wash, then found a clean Transit uniform neatly folded in the dresser and changed in the bathroom. The bright red was not the best color on him, but he supposed it was meant to offset the gloom of everything else around it. A check of the shower showed a twenty-four-hour timer until he could turn it on again. He was entirely aware of the extent to which his disappointment was unreasonable, but he let himself indulge in it anyway.

It struck him that he was safe there. He could be comfortable and have a job to do for as long as he wanted. No danger meant no chance of his secret accidentally leaking out; he could live the rest of his life without ever so much as making a spark he didn't mean to. Would the Asiig, for all their seemingly limitless reach, lose track of him down there?

Safe was something he never thought he'd be again. It was something he was also uncertain he had ever been.

The problem, of course, was that it could never work unless his friends were safe too. Here he was, lounging around, drinking coffee in his free apartment, while Effie was probably still under arrest on Titan, and the rest—Noura, Theo, Maison, LaChelle, Ignatio, Kelsie—were where? What if they were dead, or dead by the time he got off his arse to go look for them?

Your job isn't to be a Bore driver, he told himself. *Your job is to find your friends. This is your cover, not your future. Time to gather info, to make a plan.*

"Uh, apartment, can you show me a map of where I am?"

The forest disappeared and was replaced by a vast field of deep blue shading toward purple in an arc on one corner. A black dot appeared—the Bore?—and a scattering of white circles around them. One lit up yellow, and *You Are Here* appeared beside it.

"This is Vine Substation?" he asked.

"Yes," the apartment replied.

Except for the Bore, the stations would all be suspended mid-ocean, away from both the floor below and ice above, but he still wished the map were 3-D so he could get a firmer picture of the place in his head.

Fergus gestured toward the dots. "Which one is the Depot?"

The yellow highlight moved to another circle, west of the Bore. Both it and Vine were the two nearest objects, which made logistical sense. There were two medium-sized stations to the east, and at his prompting the console identified them as Beebe and Barton Substations. A barbell-shaped double station past those proved to be Miklukho-Maklai Research Substation, about which he knew absolutely nothing. So far, his most specific piece of info about any of them was that there was a bar called the Abyss in Beebe.

That left three stations still on the map but much farther out, one of which was nestled solidly in the ring of purple.

"What's the purple symbolize?"

"That indicates the high geothermal activity zone," the apartment said. "It is a restricted area. The only station within the zone is the Ballard research substation."

Ballard. That was the place where the director had resigned suddenly before disappearing. *If I was going to hide down here,* Fergus thought, looking at the purple ring, *I'd go there.*

He checked the clock, then did a double take and checked it again. "Uh, apartment? Was I only asleep for four hours?"

"You were asleep for twenty-eight hours, approximately," the apartment said.

"Shit," Fergus swore. He should have been out there by now, reestablishing contact with Zacker and Effie, getting familiar with Below. He threw his boots on and went to the front door, but despite waving his hand in front of the sensor multiple times, it did not open. "Apartment?"

"You are instructed to remain here until your assigned orientation liaison comes to escort you," the apartment said.

"And when is he showing up?"

"It is not information I have available. You have one message remaining."

Fergus sighed. "Is the second message from Stanislao Toscani?"

"It is," the apartment confirmed. "Would you like me to play it?"

"Yes, please."

Stani's face appeared on the screen. "Okay, hey there, I hate leaving stupid messages," he said. "When you wake up, have the apartment console call me. It's useful, if about as intelligent as a brick with a script. Then I'll come show you around. Oh, and sorry about stickin' you. Standard ops for new pilots, combo sedative and rapid pressure-adjustment meds. Welcome to Below."

The message terminated.

"Call Mr. Toscani, please," Fergus said.

The square reappeared, then after a few moments, Stani's face swam blurrily into view. *I woke him up,* Fergus realized. The pilot grunted, rubbing at his eyes. "Yeah," he said. "You're up, I guess?"

"I am."

"Okay, I'll be over in thirty or so."

Again, the connection terminated abruptly. Clearly, Stani was not one for long and heartfelt comm conversations.

Fergus's stomach declared a sudden change of allegiance from vague nausea to rampaging hunger. He went into the kitchenette, scrolled through the maker menu, picked a hot open-faced vat-turkey sandwich.

The maker assembled it in about four minutes, and even though it didn't smell like anything he remembered as turkey, he was hungry enough that he didn't care, and ate it and two more before his door chimed.

"Mr. Toscani has arrived," the apartment announced.

"Let him in, please," Fergus said.

The door opened, and Stani came in, wearing a tropical shirt and flip-flops. He looked almost as haggard and worn as his clothes. He stomped right into the kitchenette. "Coffee," he said, and stood there staring until it produced a cup. Then he sat on a stool, mug in hand, and looked Fergus up and down. "That your real color?" he said. "I thought it was some weirdness with the light."

"Yeah," Fergus said. "Genuine ginger."

"Are you going to try to hit me?"

"Not yet," Fergus answered.

"I decked the pilot who took me down the first time, after I woke up. Hard feelings didn't last long, though."

Fergus took the other stool. "So, orientation?"

"Right," Stani said. He took a big swig of the still-steaming coffee, grimaced. "Damn, but the pressure meds leave one hell of a hangover, huh? I had to depressurize to bring you down. Lucky for me, I'm almost used to it. In a bit, I'll take you over to the Depot to meet whatever crew is around. Before then, you have any questions?"

"Yeah. What's communication like between here and the rest of the universe?"

"Shitty," Stani said. "The comm network down here is decent enough—water isn't much of an impediment—but the ice really messes with signal. There are comm pipes at each of the Bores, and a few others by themselves between, but everything up and down gets queued. Emergency information is top priority, followed by Bore Transit business, then data to and from the science stations. Last and least are personal calls. Hope you're not trying to maintain a relationship with someone out there, because twenty kilometers of ice will chill that down fast."

"Sorta," Fergus said.

Stani sighed. "Well, keep trying, anyway. What else?"

"Uh . . . how do we get around between stations? Are we allowed to?"

"Any of the civilian stations local to the Bore are fine, although only a few of them have anything interesting to do or see. Science stations only on assignment or invite. There are regular waterbuses between everything here at the hub; your apartment can give you the schedule, and they're free for you to ride whenever you want. If you need to get back and forth in a more timely or direct manner, or just want to go out for a drive by your lonesome—not a civvie perk, so don't rub it in anyone's face—there are pods. Next question?"

"Anyone I should be wary of?"

"Other than the Bastards Above? Yes. Everybody," Stani said. "Some more than others, of course. Being down here makes most people twitchy, not always in ways you can see. And those who aren't twitchy usually already had something deeper going on before they got here."

"And which category do you fit in?"

"I have no idea," Stani said. "I try not to pay attention to anything I think, if I can help it. 'Everybody' includes *you*. I wouldn't normally recommend anyone on Transit management payroll, but I make an exception for Psych. You start thinking you're becoming someone the rest of us should worry about, you go see him, okay? There is no charge, no penalty for missing a route if you need to go, and if you need a ride, every single pilot down here will take you, no questions asked. Even Pace, and that's saying something."

"Okay," Fergus said. He didn't expect to have much use of the man. The litany of things he'd survived—from witnessing his Da's suicide to being kidnapped by aliens—were enormous compared to whatever stresses a cargo job might carry, regardless of where it was.

"My turn for a question," Stani said. "Why are you here?"

"What?" Fergus blinked at him.

"Newbies either show up here to escape from something, or they're idiots who saw the pay scale and think it's a cakewalk to riches. You don't seem like either. So, what's your story?"

What *was* his story? "I have a family thing I need to deal with that I don't want to, and some serious issues with my friends," he said. *All truth.* "I needed a bit of time to work them out."

Stani grunted. "Family," he said. He got up off the stool, set his mug down on the counter, rolled his shoulders. "Time for a tour. You ready?"

"Let's go," Fergus said.

————

Vine Substation was a small residential hab, its wide, bright pastel corridors nearly empty. "Scientists all stay at their research stations," Stani explained as they walked through a small concourse area with shops and food. "So, Vine is pretty much the catchall place for everyone else: almost all the pilots are permanently housed here, but there's also room for visitors and guests, and so forth. There are also residential areas in Barton and Beebe, but Bore Transit won't cover the rent there, because they don't want us too conveniently close to the bars or bugging the civilians. Vine is dry. So to speak!" Stani laughed. "There are a handful of civilians who live down here by choice, but they mostly keep to themselves over in Beebe, and there's a cluster of them over by Cufa Bore. Gotta be pretty rich to afford it down here, so naturally, they don't hobnob with us lowly employees much. There are also some medical conditions where the pressure helps, I guess, and those people are friendlier, if almost never out and about."

The substation was shaped like an upside-down radish: a rounded bulb with a pointed top to dissipate some of the effects of shifting pressure. "You can go up into the point, if you want," Stani informed him. "There's a small observation deck, not that you can see much other than darkness from it unless a hauler or waterbus is passing by. I wouldn't try it until you're a lot more used to it down here."

They passed a row of narrow booths with frosted-glass doors. "What are those?" Fergus asked.

"Call booths," Stani said. "Most of the workers down here don't get quarters to themselves, so it's a place they can either make direct calls Below or send messages up in privacy."

"Ah," Fergus said.

As they turned away from the booths, something small, black-and-white, and fur-covered darted around the corner in front of them, dodged around Fergus, and bolted down the hall.

"Was that . . ." Fergus said. "Was that a *cat*?"

"Yeah. Olson abandoned it here when he left. Once in a while, Sul puts a bit of food out for it, but the thing's skittish as hell," Stani said. "Sad. This is no fit place for humans, much less animals that didn't get to opt in."

The pilot led him to a small breakfast stand. "Morning, Monty," he greeted the elderly, balding man behind the counter. "This is our new hauler pilot, MacInnis. He's taking over *Hexanchus*."

"Welcome," the man said. He opened a bin and let a huge cloud of steam free, then set two wrapped bundles on the counter. Stani took one. Fergus fumbled in his pocket for a credit chit, but the man held up a hand. "No charge to you," he man said. "We bill Transit."

"Uh, okay. Thanks," Fergus said. He picked up the hot packet and unwrapped it. "Is this a *bagel*?" he asked.

"Yep, with cheese and egg. Well, Egg-Enough. It's not bad," Stani said. "Make time for breakfast. And by *time*, I mean, do your best to stick to a twenty-four-hour routine, because it's easy to get lost down here with no cues other than numbers on a damned clock. Make your own cues for your body and keep to 'em, and it'll help you stay anchored," he said. "Well, finish that up. Time to go meet some people," he said. Stani stuffed the last piece of his bagel in his mouth and put his wrapper in the flash recycler, waved to the bagel guy, and walked away.

Fergus followed, still chewing. "Where are we going?"

"Depot," Stani said. "We'll take a pod over. I'm driving. You aren't cleared until you see Psych. Besides, it's going to take you another day or so to get the knockout drug fully out of your system."

"I need to get my exosuit," Fergus said.

Stani laughed. "No, you don't. Because if something happens to the pod, you are dead, suit or not. Might as well be dressed comfortably as you go."

Reluctantly, he decided Stani was right. He trailed behind the older pilot as they left the concourse and headed around the curve of the substation toward the pod bay. Along the walls there were large screens showing pleasant underwater scenes; he stopped in his tracks and did a double take as a school of fish swam past. "Hey!" he said.

"It's to remind you where you are, but not really," Stani said. "More friendly to imagine you're surrounded by happy fishes and turtles than a vast, lifeless, crushing void, yes?"

They reached a pod portal, and Stani shoved him gently in and toward the copilot's seat, then took the helm himself. The pod cabin was small and egg-shaped, its window nearly a full quarter-hemisphere, and just big enough for the two of them. "You ever driven one of these?" he asked.

"In space, something similar," Fergus said.

"Yeah, try not to make the mistake of thinking there's much in common," Stani said. "What other waterships have you flown?"

"Rowboat," Fergus said.

Stani laughed. "Good to see you've got a sense of humor." The older pilot reached up and powered on the pod with the overhead controls, and through the front window Fergus watched the tube around them fill almost instantly with water. Before Fergus could brace himself, Stani launched the pod out of the tube and out into the dark.

Fergus had been dark places before, more than a few. He'd spent weeks roaming the Martian underground, been kilometers deep in abandoned mining tunnels in a captured asteroid in Cernee, far enough from its star that whatever faint light fell on the rock expired instantly. There was, objectively, no way this could be any darker, but somehow it felt different, more oppressive, malevolent.

His hands began to tremble, and he felt the unsettled anxiety of the electricity coiled in his gut.

Stani touched his shoulder. "Hang on," he said. "Look. There's lights. Can you see them?"

At first, he thought Stani was lying, but then he saw three tiny dots of white that went away when he blinked. "That's Depot," Stani said. "We're already halfway there. The water down here is full of bubbles and crap, which makes it hard to see sometimes. You just gotta trust your instruments and tell your animal brain to shut the hell up until you can see the lights. You hearing me, MacInnis?"

Fergus licked dry lips. "Yeah," he said. His hands were still shaking, but the panic was subsiding. "I hear you."

The lights grew stronger, spreading slowly apart as they got closer. More, fainter lights appeared, and finally, the outline of

Depot could be made out. Fergus relaxed his death grip on his chair. Still, when Stani brought the pod in through one of the portals and the tube sealed and drained, he felt like he'd just stepped down from the gallows.

Climbing out of the pod, his knees were shaking so hard, he nearly fell. "Take your time. You got this," Stani said. "I'm heading in. If you're a few minutes behind me, no one is gonna think anything of it."

Stani left the pod bay.

Fergus bent over, his hands on his knees, and took deep, heaving breaths. *You arse,* he told himself. *It's just water, that's all. A bit of pressure. Get your shit together and get this job done before someone decides you're a useless turd and sends you back Above.*

When he could, he followed after Stani.

Herschel Depot was larger and more utilitarian than Vine, with docking berths around the circumference enclosing a cargo area and pod bays, a small lounge, and a conference room. There was little room for getting lost.

Fergus walked into the lounge to find Stani making more coffee and talking to a short, muscular woman with long, straight black hair down to the small of her back. Two people with identical neon-yellow hair sat on couches opposite each other arguing, and another man was leaning against the wall with his arms crossed over his chest, his face a serene mask of something that made Fergus's knees want to shake again.

Everyone looked up as he walked in, except the man against the wall who had been staring at the doorway the entire time. "MacInnis," Stani said. "Let me introduce you to people."

The woman strode forward and held out a hand. "I'm Sul," she said. She looked him up and down. "Free Scotland?" she said.

"Yeah," Fergus answered. "United Korea?"

Sul grinned, held up one hand, and they fist bumped. "Earthers *represent*," she said. "I pilot the *Triaenodon*, and I'm primary on the Carson run. My backup is Shoo, but she's on a distance run in the *Bythae* to Cassini Bore."

"These two jokesters on the couch are Stoffel and Wenford," Stani said. The pair glanced over at Fergus briefly, raised their hands in halfhearted greeting, then went back to arguing.

"They handle the runs to Mik-Mak," Sul said.

"Miklukho-Maklai Research Substation," Stani explained. "The Mik-Makkers are mostly studying the interaction of global current with the planetary floor and ice roof. They throw the best parties Below."

"No lie," Sul said.

The man leaning against the wall stood up, cracking his knuckles. Everyone in the room looked over, and the two on the couch fell silent. "This is Pace," Stani said. "His ship is *Loxodon*."

Pace was a large, muscular, military-cut of a man, his hair so short Fergus wondered if he'd shaved it that morning. Pace extended a hand for a shake, and Fergus reached out to take it. Before he could, the hand turned into a fist, and Pace punched him in the gut hard enough to knock him back on one knee, gasping for breath. "Yeah, welcome to the Deep," Pace said, and spit on the floor beside Fergus. "I like new people to know where we stand. Which is, you now know, out of my way."

Pace walked past Fergus and out the door of the lounge.

"Shiiiit," Sul said as both she and Stani reached out a hand, and helped Fergus back up and to the couch. "Didn't see that coming."

"Me either," Fergus managed to answer. "Nice guy."

"He didn't get along with Olson, who you're replacing," Stani said. "Maybe he'll warm up to you."

"I'd rather not get close enough to give him a chance," Fergus said. "How much am I going to have to work with him?"

"Very little," one of the pair—Stoffel? Wenford?—on the couch said. "He's dedicated on the Ballard run, which is the farthest substation in our territory. As you might guess, he's not exactly a social butterfly when he's here."

"More like a social block," the other said. "If blocks were scarier. Like, maybe a block on fire, with knife blades sticking out, and growling at you."

It's just my luck, Fergus thought, *that the one place I need to go down here has that guy between me and it.*

Stani sat down opposite Fergus. "You don't look great," he said.

"Well, you know, long day, drugged against my will, trapped under twenty kilometers of ice, sucker-punched by a total stranger for no reason at all," Fergus said.

Stani nodded, then pulled a small handpad out of his pocket, scowled, and put it away again. "Well, looks like Lauben has the morning-after flu again. The Bastards want me to pick up his run from Cufa Bore."

Fergus tried to get up and winced, sitting down again. "I just need a minute or two, then I'll come with."

"Naw, you're hurt," Stani said. "Can anyone here give MacInnis a ride over to Barton? He hasn't seen Psych yet."

Sul shook her head. "I've gotta head out to Carson in less than an hour and pick up some instrumentation to haul up the Bore for repair," she said. "No one was willing to come down to fix it; go figure."

Stoffel and Wenford raised their hands simultaneously. "We can," they said.

"Unless," one said, "he's one of the barfy newbs?"

"Nope," Stani said. "Weren't you, though, Stoffel?"

"It was Wenford," the other said.

"I'm sorry," Fergus said. "I didn't catch which one of you is which?"

The one who'd spoken first smiled. "Yes," they said.

"Don't mind them. They just like to mess with the rest of us," Stani said. He checked his handpad. "I better get going. Don't lose him, you two, or you'll be taking his slots until another sucker wanders into Dornett's grasp." He smiled at Fergus. "Happy to have you, MacInnis!"

Stani left. Stoffel and Wenford stood as one, smoothed down their suits in similar gestures. One was, Fergus noted, a few inches taller than the other, a little thicker around the middle, so they weren't identical, just very similar by what seemed deliberate effect. If they weren't side by side, he wasn't sure he could say which was which. *Not that you actually know, anyway,* he reminded himself.

"C'mon," the shorter one said, and the two walked out. Fergus stood carefully, then followed.

Shorter was chattier than Taller. They both had a slight accent he couldn't place, half Titan drawl overlaid on top of something else. "Are you two . . . siblings?" he ventured a guess, as he climbed gingerly into the cramped back of the pod behind the two pilots.

Taller laughed. "Nope," they said.

Shorter glanced back at Fergus. "So, where've you piloted?"

"Last freelanced runs in the Sfazili Gap," he answered easily. The Gap was crawling with indie operators and was also a data hole, which made it hard to check or confirm anything that happened there.

Shorter shuddered. "No jump points in the Gap," they said. "Won't catch me in a place you can't easily escape from if you need to."

Taller chortled and waved their hands around them. "Right."

Fergus wasn't sure what to say to that, and the rest of the twenty-minute pod trip left him none the wiser.

————

Barton Substation was, as Stani had said, much larger and busier than Vine or Depot. It had a full 3-D gaming arcade, restaurants, and shops. Shorter explained that Barton's smaller counterpart, Beebe Substation, was functional space: administrative offices, the main Bore medical facility, conference rooms, visitor housing, and so forth.

"It's a depressing place, even if you're not already depressed," Taller said.

"That's why Psych is here on Barton," Shorter added. "A little extra head start before the blues catch up again."

It was a short walk to an undecorated glass door that opened as soon as they approached. "See you around, MacInnis," Shorter said.

"Thanks, uh, Stoffel"—Fergus pointed at Taller first, just blindly guessing—"and Wenford?"

"Maybe!" Shorter said. "You're welcome."

The two left. Cursing the deep, uncomfortable ache in his abdomen where Pace had punched him, Fergus stepped through the doors and in.

There was a hallway with no branches or other doors, pleasantly lit by overhead full-spectrum light tiles. At the far end was another door, this time an opaque faux wood, that also slid open at his approach.

Inside, there were some padded chairs, a sofa, a desk, and a man sitting behind it. The man was large, with a full head of wiry unkempt hair. "Mr. MacInnis," the man said. "Or can I call you Duncan?"

"Duncan is fine," Fergus said. Had the man been waiting for him, he wondered, or did the man just sit here all day like this?

"My name is Ted Van Heer," the man said, with a friendly smile, and extended a hand. Fergus shook it. "A few people call me Van Heer. One person calls me Ted. Everyone else just calls me Psych. I am neither offended by nor particularly inclined to favor any one over the others, though technically I am only the Psych for Herschel Bore. Please feel free to have a seat."

Fergus picked one of the chairs and lowered himself into it, trying not to wince.

"Pace, eh?" Van Heer said. "I just heard."

"He has a memorable way of introducing himself," Fergus said.

Van Heer reached under the desk and pulled out a tall bottle full of shimmering amber liquid, then set two glasses beside it. He folded his arms loosely against his chest and leaned back in his chair. "So," he said.

"So," Fergus echoed. After a long silence, he added, "I haven't ever talked to a psychiatrist."

"Psychologist," Van Heer corrected, as if it was a point of honor. "Want a drink?"

"Uh, not really," Fergus said. "Feel free to go ahead, though, if you do."

Van Heer shrugged. "No, but offer's always open. So, other than your encounter with Pace, how are you adjusting?"

"Okay," he said. "It takes getting used to, but it seems to be getting easier."

"Stanislao give you a good sense of what's where? Answer all your questions?"

"The ones I've had, yes. I'm sure I'll have more," Fergus said.

"Anything you feel like I should know, just between you and

me? Traumatic events in your past, addictions, vendettas, that sort of thing?"

Fergus didn't quite manage to stifle a laugh. "Nothing unusual," he added quickly, and met Van Heer's knowing eyes. *He knows you lied,* he was sure. *He knows you lied big.*

"Change your mind?" Van Heer said, tapping the bottle.

"One," Fergus said.

"One," Van Heer said, pouring a glass each. "You think you're able to run your ship safely, not endanger anyone, not endanger yourself beyond the normal hazards of the job?"

"I do," Fergus answered truthfully, and downed the drink in one shot. It hit his stomach like fire, scorching his throat the entire way down. He noticed then that there was no label on the bottle. *Genuine Enceladus Deep Moonshine,* he thought. *I hope by all the stars I'm not here long enough to acquire a taste for this.*

"You start thinking that might not be true, even just the tiniest bit, I'm always here, and this bottle is always here," Van Heer said. "You don't have to talk, you don't have to drink, but you do have to come. Okay?"

"Okay," Fergus said.

"Great," Van Heer said. He stood, held out a hand, and shook. "You're cleared to drive. I'll let the Bastards Above know."

———

Not yet confident enough to take a pod out by himself, he caught the public waterbus back to Vine. It had no windows and the one other passenger was sound asleep, which suited him just fine. The driver ignored them both, and for all Fergus saw him do— the waterbus appeared to operate almost entirely on automatic— only the occasional mumbled announcements and the uniform distinguished him from being just another passenger.

Was it more comforting to have him there, even though he

knew perfectly well the man was ninety-five percent formality? *Maybe*, Fergus had to admit. He trusted *Venetia's Sword*, but how much of that was just that he'd come to think of Vee as a person rather than an artificial system? And anyway, the Shipyard's mindsystems were the best out there—who knew how basic or flawed the logic hardware in this little bus was? Stani was right that it was harder to trust a computer there when, even without windows, the vague sense of oppression and danger still seemed to seep through the walls.

The bus backed up to an airlock on Vine and let him out without him ever having to face the outside. The remaining passenger slept on, oblivious.

He went back to his apartment, rummaged through his pack, and found the pager disk. Then he headed back out into the public spaces of Vine. He had no sense of time there, or the rhythm of this place, but there were occasional people out and wandering as well, and no one seemed to notice him. He'd spent time in many places that lacked any natural day/night cues, though most found a way of improvising something, just to give people a common anchor. Even without Stani's warning, he knew enough to keep to a reasonable rhythm on his own, until or unless he acclimated to Below's subliminal cycles. If there were any, other than just the arbitrary information of clocks and work schedules.

Three of the eight call booths were occupied. He slipped into an open one, shut the door, and looked around. It was a small but comfortable space; there was a wide, cushioned armchair, a console on a swinging arm beside it, and a larger screen set into the wall with a camera above it. He let himself feel the faint tracings of signal throughout the room, found nothing unexpected. *Good enough.*

Sitting in the chair, he took the disk out of his pocket. "Hey, you guys," he said. "I've reached my destination, getting settled in with my new job and trying to learn my way around. I'm worried about you. Please send back as soon as you can and let me know how you are."

He cut it off at that; there was no perfect guarantee his packets wouldn't get intercepted, so there was no point saying more than needed. He tucked the disk back into his pocket and headed back toward his apartment again, feeling bruised beyond just the physical, and still feeling the angry burn of the psych's moonshine.

Now, he thought, *I can sleep.*

Chapter 9

Exhaustion was an unreliable ally. By the time his apartment systems roused him from bed, he'd spent much of the night pitching restlessly from just awake enough to be miserable down into deep, terrible dreams about drowning, being crushed, or being attacked by an eight-legged octopus-shark with Pace's face. He used his ten minutes of water to try to wash away the lingering fear, then tried to drown the tenacious remnants in several cups of strong, hot coffee.

There was no reply from Effie or Zacker, not that he expected any yet. He missed the others and the familiarity of the Shipyard. *Am I actually homesick?* Fergus wondered. He thought he'd left home—and the need for it—behind for good at fifteen when he stole Gavin's motorcycle and fled down the Inland Sea Causeway toward the Glasgow Shuttleport. Less than a month before he ran away, he'd watched his father row out into the sea with a fresh cast on his broken leg and tip himself overboard. He'd tried to go after him, but his mother had never let him go more than knee-deep in the water, much less learn to swim, and he'd nearly drowned himself trying and failing to reach him. *Yeah,* he thought. *Nothing out of the ordinary, Psych.*

After leaving Earth, he'd taught himself to swim on Mars in the Ares Three Youth Pool, as if then somehow he could go back in time and it would make a difference.

The light on his apartment console was blinking. "Play messages," he snarled.

The apartment system was a simple voice-command unit, not equipped to recognize or process mood. "There is one message," it announced as cheerfully as ever.

This time, rather than Dornett, it was his grinning idiot of an assistant, Jerney. "Congratulations, Mr. MacInnis, I see you've been cleared for piloting. As you probably know from Mr. Toscani, there are a few fixed routes with dedicated pilots, but the majority of work is shared. This includes trips up and down the Bore, between Bore settlements in the Deep, and filling in for sick members of the team. We're going to start you off with a trip to Wyville-Thompson Substation to pick up a departing scientist. So, when you feel ready, go check out *Hexanchus* and head to Wyville-Thompson. Take your time. They'll expect you in five hours or less."

The message ended. "Take your *tiiiime*," Fergus mimicked. "They'll expect you in five hours or less. Jerkey."

He was starting to see how Stani came by his cynicism. "How long is the travel time from Herschel Depot to Wyville-Thompson?" he asked the apartment system.

"Specify mode of transportation," it answered.

"Hauler."

"Approximately three hours forty minutes."

"And when did the message come in?"

"Twenty-nine minutes ago."

Fergus groaned, finished the last few drips of coffee, and pulled on a clean Transit uniform. Humanity—original and alt and everything in between—was what? Forty billion people? At least three-quarters of them must right now be laughing at the poor man in his mid-thirties angsting over his first real day of work in his life.

Well, regular job, anyway. The sooner he was done with this and back to his haphazard, itinerant life, the better. He made his way down to the docks by way of Monty's breakfast stand, found an available pod at the dock, steeled himself as he stuffed the last bite of bagel in his mouth, and climbed in.

The pods controls were simple and he had no difficulty sealing it and launching. It was the darkness outside that was hard, like a fist that surrounded him, squeezing. His hands began to shake, and he felt the tingling of electricity moving along his fingers. With an effort of will, he pushed it back down, deep inside. He'd lost count, but he was somewhere close to ten days without letting it slip out.

The navigation system was his lifeline. He kept his eyes on it almost obsessively, watching the little arrow that was his pod slowly converging on Depot and his hauler. Twenty minutes had his nerves fraught, the previous night's bad dreams pushing toward the surface of his consciousness. Enceladus might be dwarfed even by Earth's moon, but the ocean here was nearly ten times the depth of Earth's. When the tiny lights of Depot appeared ahead, it was like sunrise.

He docked the pod and went straight to *Hexanchus*.

The haulers were docked nose-in to the station, where their forward cargo door could mesh and seal with station itself. There was a small airlock to one side that also had a direct connection, meaning no need to go out into the water to get in. The size of the ship was reassuring in a way the pod had not been, and he settled into the pilot's seat at the helm and let himself slide into the routine of safety and system checks.

Everything came back green; *Hexanchus* was good to go.

Fergus backed the hauler up and away. When he was clear of the docks, he turned the ship around and pulled up the coordinates for Wyville-Thompson on his navigation screen. The tiny research station was east, well past Beebe substation. The trip would not take him particularly close to Ballard, still its nearest neighbor, which was both a disappointment and a relief. He wanted to have a lot more information and a plan before he had to venture directly into Pace's territory.

He was just about to pass Beebe Substation when lights came into view, and he watched as a mushroom-shaped ship passed him going the other way. "Uh, Transit Control?" he asked, his pulse quickening. "What was that?"

"Waterbus. A Madarch," someone in Transit Control answered. It sounded like Reva again. "They move people between the nearby substations locally on fixed routes. They'll yield to a hauler if your paths intersect, but try not to scare the civvies."

Damn, and he'd been in one just the day before on his way back from Barton and never recognized it for what it was. Picturing the interior now, he could see how the shape matched, but there had been nothing to suggest it had ever had any functionality beyond *bus*. Wherever the Madarchs were that were used in the attack on the Shipyard, that was definitely not one.

"Thanks, Transit Control," he said.

Half an hour into the trip, the dark started to get under his skin again. It felt like he wasn't moving, was held against his will. The progress of the little arrow on his screen was scant proof. Even in space, where movement was microscopic compared to the distances between stars, there *were* stars. Even in the tangled, inside-out mess of jump space, if you dared risk a look, there was movement.

More than three hours to go; Fergus needed a distraction, and pulled out his handpad. He'd had to replace his original during his job in Cernee in a hurry, and this one, if the case engraving was genuine, had been appropriated—no doubt illegally—from the Guratahan Sfazil security service and hadn't, alas, come with any games, nor had he thought to add any, and he hated replacing things he didn't have to. Next to it on the helm console he'd set down his pager disk, and he picked that up, turning it back and forth between his fingers, wishing desperately there were someone on the other end to talk to. Finally, unable to bear it, he tapped it on. "Anyone out there?" he sent.

How many hours until it worked its way up the queue in the comm pipe through the ice, and reached someone's ears? He didn't even have a guess what time of day it was there, much less on Titan. With a sigh, he stuck it back in his pocket before he could begin anticipating disappointment in earnest.

Outside the ship, it was the same impenetrable darkness as before. *Don't think about it,* he told himself. *Think about something else.*

The navigation systems had supplemental data on all the various locations in Enceladus Deep, not just those around Herschel Bore. The primary control systems might not have interactive voice command, but the nav subsystem was willing to narrate—if very blandly—what data it had.

Fergus rested his hands on the edge of the helm console to subdue the last bits of trembling, and set it to just read through everything it had. Information was good, even information you didn't know you needed. He found himself wishing *Hexanchus* had data on Zacker's museum robbery. If he managed not to die down there, he was going to have to figure that one out too, he supposed. And find Gavin's stolen-again motorcycle. And possibly have to deal with family to get it back to him.

He didn't even know if his mother was still alive.

Maybe, Fergus thought, *being stuck down here isn't so terrible.*

He made it through the brief entries on all of Herschel Bore and most of the substations at Cassini Bore before, thinking he had something in his eye, he tried to blink the spots away and then realized they were *out there,* where part of him had given up hope of ever seeing anything again. Blue lights.

He was still nearly an hour out from Wyville-Thompson. The lights were on a small floating sphere, about the size of a pod, suspended mid-ocean. "Transit Control, what am I passing?" he asked.

"Waybeacon, *Hexanchus*," Reva answered. "They boost and relay comm signals along distant routes, and give lonely pilots something pretty to look at as they drive past in the dark."

"That it does," he answered. "Thanks. *Hexanchus* out."

The beacon was a welcome bit of difference in the ocean, for all that it was behind him and gone again too quickly.

Wyville-Thompson Substation appeared ahead not that long after. Even though it took another half-hour to finish the approach, it was like night to day, having something he could identify as existing and could track his incremental progress toward. He turned off the data monologue, no longer wanting to pay attention to anything other than the growing station.

It felt like a victory, successfully traversing the Deep to one of the more-distant substations of the Bore. Only Ballard was farther.

He docked and stepped out through the heavy airlock, almost wanting to dance with the sudden rush of elation. An elderly man stood waiting with an impressively large collection of cases and crates, and his expression emphatically suggested dancing would not be welcome. "You the pilot?" the man asked.

"Yes, sir," Fergus said. "I'm—"

"Whatever. I want to get out of here. Load my crap, and wake me when we get to the Bore." The man left Fergus standing beside the pile of stuff as he brushed past him and onto *Hexanchus*.

Fergus picked up the first crate, grunting at its unexpected weight. *If that guy is on my bridge when I get in there, he may just be in for a shock,* he thought, and felt the tingle of an unhealthy anticipation in his fingers. There was a small passenger compartment behind the bridge with bunks, and he wondered if the door locked from the outside.

He was just coming out for the last crate when a woman in a white jumpsuit, her frizzy black hair in a loose bundle atop her head, walked into the airlock area. She held out a hand. Fergus set back down the case he'd just picked up and shook it.

"New pilot?" she asked.

"Duncan MacInnis," he said. "Pleased to meet you."

She smiled tiredly. "I'm Dr. Creek. Beth. I gather Dr. Manne is already aboard?"

"He is," Fergus said.

"Are you driving him up the Bore?" she asked.

"I'm not sure," Fergus said. "I was told to come here for a pickup. It's my first run."

"We're honored," she said, and it seemed sincere. "I was just hoping to get word when he'd safely reached the surface."

"The Bore pilots are all very skilled, ma'am," Fergus said. "While nothing is perfectly safe, I'm sure he'll be in good hands, whoever drives him up."

"Oh, I'm not worried about that pompous, tiny-skulled old windbag," Dr. Creek said. "I just want to know he's really *gone*."

Fergus chuckled. "I'll keep an eye on things, and if he seems to be swimming back here with his cases clutched between his teeth, I'll send a warning so you can turn off all the substation lights and pretend no one is home."

Dr. Creek beamed. "I like that you get us," she said. "You're replacing Olson?"

"I think so."

"He was a good man but terribly dull."

"He quit, right?"

"I suppose so. Everyone does eventually," she said. "Welcome to the Deep, Mr. MacInnis."

"Duncan is fine."

"Duncan, then," she said. "Better go before he starts gnawing on your furniture."

"Yeah," Fergus said. He picked up the last case again. "Thanks," he said.

"Good luck," she said. He stepped back through the lock and it closed between them.

Fergus stowed the cases and crates carefully in the cargo nets along one compartment, making sure they were secure. As he walked back up front, he heard snoring from the passenger compartment.

There was, sadly, no exterior lock.

He went up front and closed the door to the bridge. Buckling himself in, he backed *Hexanchus* away from the docks of Wyville-Thompson barely fifteen minutes after he'd arrived, and headed back out into the dark, still smiling at Dr. Creek's *pompous windbag* comment.

It was good to know the ocean held small pockets of light.

————

"Are we there yet?"

Fergus jumped; he hadn't even heard the bridge door open, but there was Dr. Manne, throwing himself into the copilot's seat uninvited.

"A little less than an hour," Fergus said.

Dr. Manne sighed very loudly and deliberately. "Such a waste of my time."

"I can't go any faster, Dr. Manne," Fergus said, not adding, *if I could, you bet I would.*

"Not just you," Manne said. "This whole enterprise. Wyville-Thompson is a bunch of tedious little sand-scrapers, no one in my specialty there at all, none of the instruments I need, nothing! And I blew an entire grant on this trip, not to mention the cost of the instrumentation I lost!" He glared at Fergus, as if he was directly complicit in all his misfortunes.

"Sorry to hear that," Fergus said. "What do you study?"

"Patterns of geothermal uplifting on the ocean floor. Or at least I was trying!"

"Shouldn't you have gone to the active zone for that?" Fergus asked. "Ballard, or one of the Cassini substations on the far side?"

"Oh? What a brilliant idea! Why the fuck didn't I think of that?!" Manne declared. "Of *course* I was supposed to be at Ballard, genius."

"Look, Dr. Manne, I'm brand-new. I just got here, and you're my very first passenger," Fergus said.

"Lucky you," Manne said. He let out another sigh. "Look, I'm not going to apologize. I had confirmed arrangements to spend a half-year at Ballard; I even took a sabbatical from my position at Haudernelle South University for this. For *nothing.*" He swung his feet up and slammed them down atop the spare console, then met Fergus's eyes in challenge.

Fergus glared.

"Fine, sorry," Manne said, though he left his feet up on the console. "It's just a sharp blow to my research."

Fergus very much wanted Dr. Manne to slink back to the passenger compartment for the remainder of the trip, but here was a chance to get information on Ballard, however biased the perspective might be. "That doesn't seem fair," he said.

"Damn right it's not fair! At the very least, someone could've contacted me, told me they'd had their director leave and weren't bringing in any more researchers all of a sudden. I mean, shit, the woman was just an administrator, and she's been gone for half a standard year! How hard can it be to replace some stupid layperson?"

"Well, not a lot of people want to come down here," Fergus said.

Manne snorted. "Yeah, I wonder why. But they wouldn't even let me go over for a visit, not even a fucking day trip. Your fellow there, Pace? He *threatened* me."

"Yeah?" Fergus said. "What did he threaten you with?"

Manne fumed silently for a full two minutes. "It was his look," he said at last. "It was a very *threatening* look."

Fergus would have laughed, but he remembered Pace's expression well enough to know Manne was not wrong.

"I sent out my floor remote to collect samples and perform a survey scan, since I couldn't get anyone to take me over there in person," he said. "Thing barely got into the zone when it went dead. Couldn't even get anyone to help me retrieve it. Going to have to write that off, too. You know how much datawork the Alliance Sciences Agency makes you fill out for lost equipment? It could take me the rest of my fucking sabbatical!"

"That's terrible," Fergus said. "No wonder you're angry."

Manne glanced over at him again, clearly trying to figure out if Fergus was patronizing him. Fergus kept his face straight, and Manne crossed his arms over his chest and stared out the front window for a long time without speaking.

"There's Depot," Fergus said when the lights of the substation swam faintly into view. "We're almost there."

"You're taking me up the Bore, right?" Manne said.

"I was just told to bring you back to Depot. Let me check who you're running up with." He pulled up his screen, saw that his passenger was being handed off to *Loxodon*.

Hell. Pace. *Manne is an asshole,* Fergus thought. *I should just get out of the way as quickly as I can and leave them to each other.*

"So?" Manne asked.

"It doesn't say," Fergus lied. *Dammit,* he thought, *I actually feel sorry for the guy.*

He tapped the comms, opening a channel. "Transit Control, this is *Hexanchus,*" he said. "I've got the departing passenger from Wyville-Thompson substation aboard. Should I take him up the Bore?"

"*Hexanchus,* hang on," Transit Control responded. It was a male voice now, someone less cheerful and more annoyed than Reva. Jake, if he remembered what Stani had told him about their Control staff.

At least it was out of his hands now.

A few minutes later, Transit Control said, "Go ahead and take him up, *Hexanchus.* Your passenger's originally scheduled ride is still two hours out, and it's good practice for you. Check in when you're at the Bore for clearance."

"Will do, Transit Control," Fergus said. He looked over at Manne. "Looks like you're going up with me."

"They were going to make me wait around for two *hours?*" Manne said.

"There's a pilot shortage," Fergus said. He changed course, a minor shift to starboard and a fair swing upward; the Bore was slightly closer than Depot but five kilometers up to the underside of the ice. As soon as he'd changed course, he could see those lights too, a fuzzy bluish ring growing more distinct.

"For the Bore trip, I'm going to require you to return to the passenger compartment and buckle in," Fergus said. "Sorry, it's protocol."

"Right," Manne said, though it didn't sound particularly like agreement. He got up and left the bridge.

Hexanchus reached the Bore, and Fergus took it into the standard approach pattern for Below. "Transit Control, this is *Hexanchus.* I am ready to ascend."

"Bore is clear, *Hexanchus*. Proceed when ready."

He tapped the intra-ship comm. "You buckled in, Dr. Manne?"

"Of *course*," came the reply.

Okay, then. Fergus swung his hauler into final position and sent the signal to open the lowest lock of the Bore. As the gate above irised open, pressure suddenly shot the hauler upward. They rode the pop up into the lock chamber, and he got the ship back under control enough to close the lower doors again.

With the gate closed, the pressure eased.

He tapped the comm. "Sorry about that, a bit of sudden pressure," he told Manne. "See, aren't you glad you buckled in?"

There was the sound of thumps and crashing on the other end of the comm. Shaking his head, Fergus turned on visual. Sure enough, Dr. Manne was sprawled against the far wall of the cabin. "Fuck you," Manne said.

Fergus cut both comm and visual so he wouldn't have to feel bad about laughing out loud.

He staved off the anxiety through the first two gates at Manne's expense, but as he approached the third gate that led upward into the main lock chamber, memories of fighting the pop in the simulator made his skin tingle and his hands start to shake. It didn't matter that it had been a simulation; his one real ride down had been with Stani aboard in case things went wrong, but here he was completely on his own, and he felt suddenly, criminally underqualified to be at the helm of anything bigger than a flystick.

At least this time, *Hexanchus*'s pressure was steady, and he didn't have to handle the physiological stress on top of the psychological.

The ascent was, in the end, smooth. *Hexanchus* exited the surface gate of the Bore into space, and breathing a sigh of relief, he brought it around and up toward the orbital station. There,

Dr. Manne would have a lovely three-day stay to depressurize gently, a luxury not afforded pilots.

He offloaded Manne's cases and crates into the docking bay, where an attendant in Transit uniform loaded them onto an auto-cart. "How was the ride?" the attendant asked Fergus.

"Passengers shouldn't lie about being buckled in," he answered.

"No," the attendant said. She held out her hand, and he shook. "MacInnis, right? I'm Genna. Visitor Support. Oh! I almost forgot!" She reached into her pocket and handed Fergus a small packet. "From Director Dornett."

"What is it?" Fergus asked.

"Dunno," she said, as Dr. Manne, distinctly more rumpled than when he boarded, emerged from the airlock. The attendant smiled brightly. "This way, Doctor. We have a room ready for you, and lunch will be served in the group lounge shortly."

As the attendant led Manne away, Fergus's stomach growled. He remembered what Stani had said about prices up there and loitering charges but was hungry enough to pull out his handpad and query the price of a sandwich. Thirty seconds later, he was back on his bridge and preparing to depart.

It was nice to have the ship to himself on the way back down, no one else to worry about killing with his ineptitude. As he waited for clearance to descend, he dumped half the contents of his pack out on the dash in desperate hopes for some long-lost packet of crackers at the very least, but there was nothing. *Next time,* he thought, *pack snacks.*

When his clearance came, he took several deep breaths, willing himself toward calmness as best he could, and then dived. To his relief, the Bore itself was still calm. *A few hundred more runs like this one,* he thought, *and this job might not only become tolerable but maybe even enjoyable.*

As he was exiting the bottom gate again into the Deep, his comm chimed. "*Hexanchus* here," he said.

"I told you not to get in my way," came Pace's voice. "That was *my* run."

"Control told me to take it. How would I have known?" Fergus said.

There was a pause, not at all comforting. "Next time, check the damned schedule and stick to it, or we'll be having another conversation. It won't as friendly as the last."

The line went dead.

"Up yours," Fergus said, too late.

He pulled *Hexanchus* into a berth at Depot just as Pace's ship, *Loxodon*, was backing up. It veered alarmingly close to *Hexanchus*'s rear stabilizer fins before disappearing out into the dark.

As he shut down the hauler's engines, his eyes fell on the packet that the attendant had given him Above. Pulling the tab open, he tipped the envelope, and another of the drug-test capsules fell out into his palm. *Bleeding bureaucracy,* he thought. *Dornett can wait.* He wasn't going to swallow that on a stomach as empty and touchy as his currently was.

He dropped the capsule back into the packet and tossed it up on the console on top of the stuff he'd dug out of his pack. Immediately, the confuddler lying beside it beeped.

Fergus picked it up. The display read *SIGNAL DETECTED*.

That made sense; the capsule had to communicate back its results. Still, Fergus removed the capsule from the packet again and sat it directly atop the confuddler. *Analyze signal,* he told it.

HOMING DEVICE, it answered almost immediately.

"Oh, Dornett, you utter bastard," Fergus said.

Now what did he do with it? Dornett would know if he threw it into a recycler, and just insist on sending down another. Likewise, the capsule was probably smart enough to know if it was inside a person or not. If he took it—and assuming his electric bees didn't fry it again—then even if he found a way to block the signal when he needed to go somewhere he didn't want the Bastards Above knowing about, the block itself would be suspicious.

He put the capsule and packet in his pack for now. He had a little time to figure out a way of dealing with it. One thing he absolutely needed to know, though, was if this was a routine privacy breach of all pilots, or if he'd been singled out for suspicion.

Picking up the confuddler, he sent the command *detect like signals*. Then he tucked it, still on, into his pocket.

In the lounge he found Sul and a pilot he hadn't met yet playing virtual pong while a screen ran some news feed in the background, unwatched, volume off. The other pilot was about Fergus's own age, with short-cropped brown hair, her face a bit more worn than his but her smile bright. It brightened further when Sul missed the ball and it vanished over the threshold of the game border.

"MacInnis," Sul said, setting her paddle down. "This is Shoo, pilot of the *Bythae*. She just got back from Cassini Bore."

The woman waved briefly, then gripped her paddle tighter as Sul restarted the game. "Nice to meet you, MacInnis," she said, and served.

"Nice to meet you, too," he said. "I see I just missed Pace."

Sul lobbed the shimmering ball back hard enough to miss the board and disappear. "He was in a mood," Sul said. "I'd stay as far away from him as you can, as long as you can. I think that's why Olson left; Pace was always up in his face."

"Is there anyone Pace gets along with?" Fergus asked.

"The bottle," Shoo answered, and served again.

Fergus's stomach growled, rather plaintively. He went over to the kitchenette, looking for anything to tide him over until he got back to his apartment. The first drawer he opened was full of frozen balls of uniformly textured vat protein. *Urgh*, he thought. Cheap vat protein wasn't something anyone would mistake for the real thing more than once.

Anyone, he thought. *What about a stupid capsule, though?*

Sul and Shoo were in a furious volley back and forth, their concentration wholly involved. Fergus picked up a protein ball and tucked it into his other pocket.

The next drawer had instasoups. He took out one of the containers, twisted the top, and leaned against the counter, waiting for it to self-heat.

Sul glanced over at the news screen and missed the ball again. "Ah, they're finally playing it again!" she said. "You have to see the expression on this guy's face."

Shoo set down her paddle and turned to watch the screen. The caption crawled across the bottom of the screen: *CONSTANTIJN HOLD, TITAN.*

Uh-oh, Fergus thought with a sinking feeling.

The news picture had the slightly fisheye quality of a 3-D holo-recording flattened down to a single viewpoint. It was the interior of a police station; three officers milled near the back corner, a fourth sat across a small desk from an unkempt person in ragged clothes, hands tucked deep in their pockets, with the distinct look of a skunker on their blank face and rapidly shifting eyes. Another person was mostly off-screen along one side of the view, near the coffee machine, but Fergus knew that shoulder.

"Watch the perp when the officer gets up," Sul said, and sure enough, the officer at the desk stood up and turned away for a moment, and the skunker fumbled something small and disk-shaped out of their pocket and heaved it into the air, where it took off, spinning around the room. The shimmer in the air around it could have been anything, could have been an illusion, but Fergus knew only too well that it was the blur of microfilament cutting wires moving faster than the eye could follow.

Oh, shit, Fergus thought, frozen in horror. It was a killspinner, and they rarely left anyone in a room alive.

Two of the chatting officers went down right away in a spray of blood before anyone could even react. The familiar shoulder moved first as Zacker threw himself onto the nearest of the fallen officers, ducked as the disk passed right over his head and hit the perp who threw it, then he turned—his flushed face an almost-comical grimace of absolute fury, veins standing out on his forehead, mouth wide as if in that moment, he was about to launch himself teeth-first at the recorder—and threw the officer's cuffs across the room.

They hit the spinning disk, and it was instantly tangled and fell to the floor. Zacker was already applying pressure to one of the officer's wounds and shouting soundlessly on the muted screen. The perp was down too, slumped across a blood-smeared table. More officers came running, blocking the view, and then the screen flicked back to the talking news head.

"Whoa," Shoo said. "Yeah, you were right, that guy looks even scarier than our pal Pace. Wouldn't wanna get in *his* way."

If you do, he leaves killer bruises, Fergus didn't say.

"What was that thing?" Sul asked.

Shoo shrugged. "Dunno. Bad, though. Serve?"

As they went back to their game, Fergus finished his soup quickly, no longer tasting it for the anxiety crawling up his spine. Killspinners were tiny drones that, when activated, spun out razor-sharp filament like a flying weedwacker and bounced around until it either ran out of power or got itself stuck in something it couldn't cut or wiggle its way free of. The handcuffs would have magnetic plating in them to keep someone from using similar filament to cut them free, and Zacker's aim had been dead on. The detective had probably just saved the lives of everyone in that room. *Or at least the remaining lives,* he thought. The first officer to go down hadn't looked good, nor the perp who'd launched it.

Killspinners were extremely illegal throughout Alliance space and not easily come by.

Fergus had a million questions but no one to ask and no way to ask without someone else maybe making the connection between him and that furious face on the screen, and from there to Effie and the attack on the Shipyard. Zacker was okay, he told himself, his heart still thudding away in his chest. Effie wasn't even in the room. *It's okay. Zacker handled it.*

It was also, from the timestamp on the feed, old news. Eight hours old. There was nothing he could do even if he wanted to.

By the time Shoo declared victory, the video had looped past again twice, and Fergus had his worry back under at least nominal control. "Nice meeting you, Shoo," he said, as he dropped the soup bulb in the recycler. "I'm exhausted, though, and heading back to Vine."

"Later," Sul said, then to Shoo: "Four out of seven, then?"

Outside the lounge, in the deserted corridor to the pod bays, he checked the display on his confuddler. *TWO LIKE SIGNALS*, it said.

All the pilots were bugged, so he wasn't being specifically targeted. He'd feel relieved about that later, when the shock of seeing an attack on the Hold police station faded a bit.

The pod ride back to Depot wasn't helping his nerves, so he distracted himself from dark thoughts by wondering exactly how the protein ball was going to help him with his tracker problem. It was already starting to thaw. If he put it back in the freezer, Dornett was going to notice he didn't seem to be going anywhere. If he carried it around in his pocket, he had maybe a half-day before it became a particularly gross accessory, and two at best before it started to smell.

He didn't have any good answers yet as he docked the pod at Vine and wandered through the public area back toward his residence level. The substation was quiet, and he realized it was what passed, by consensus, as dead of night.

As he walked by the call booths, something moved. He stopped in his tracks, wary, until he spotted Olson's cat lurking and waiting for him to go past. Instead, he knelt and took the protein ball out of his pocket, thinking he had no real use for it after all. "Here, kitty kitty kitty," he said. He started to set the ball down, then in a flash of inspiration pulled Dornett's packet out and stuck the capsule inside the meat before setting it down.

Fergus waited.

After several minutes, the cat tentatively came out of its hiding place and contemplated him and the protein ball. It was skinny, almost pathetically so, a black scruffy mess with a single white ear. "Come on, kitty," he said, more gently. "I won't hurt you."

Eventually, it closed the distance, its tiny nose twitching toward the food as if fearing a trap. Then it settled, tail flicking back and forth, and pulled the ball closer. Fergus didn't move while it chewed away at the still half-frozen block of protein. When it had eaten most of it, Fergus very, very slowly reached out a hand and patted its head.

The cat reared back, hissing, and stared back and forth between him and the rest of the cube. He waited, afraid to move again and startle it, his bad leg aching from the sustained crouch. At long last, the cat came back toward him but, instead of grabbing the rest of the cube, butted Fergus's hand.

He petted it again, for a long while, and when it was done eating—not a scrap nor crumb nor inconvenient capsule left behind—he very, very carefully picked up the purring cat and took it home.

Sleep was no less fraught with bad dreams than the previous night, and he tossed and turned until something small and warm settled down atop his legs and he felt an overwhelming obligation to lie still and not disturb it. It didn't much ease the ferociousness of the dreams when he finally dozed off again, but there was a comforting sense of no longer being quite so thoroughly alone.

Chapter 10

After eight hours of muted tossing in bed, held hostage by the cat until it finally gave up on him and slunk off to some other corner of the apartment, Fergus sat up. The usual nightmare elements were there—drowning, suffocating in the dark, the black, insectoid limbs of the Asiig grabbing at him from below. The worst by far was a dream that had seemed to stretch on for hours of him standing ankle-deep in the Scottish Inland Sea, his mother on shore urging him farther out as he cried and protested he couldn't swim, as his father's face, floating serenely just above the water in the center of the lake, told him he wasn't wanted there, either. "What good are ye?" his father kept asking, and his mother too in the same flat voice, as he stood there, changing from a little boy to a grown man, still stuck in the water.

He rubbed at his face, finding tears there, and he resented the hell out of the entire universe for it.

Knowing it would only make things worse, he had his apartment switch his screen over to All-Saturn News. The timestamp again showed an eight-hour delay; news obviously wasn't very high on the comm-pipe priority list. He made himself coffee as he waited for a segment on the Tethys dockworker strike to finish, and twice zapped both the mug and counter. *Shit,* he thought. *A few more nights like this and I won't be useful to anybody.*

The Tethys segment ended and the headline *HERO OF THE HOLD!* flashed up with a still of Zacker's furious face from the killspinner incident, and Fergus groaned out loud. "Volume on," he told the apartment.

". . . as-yet-unnamed hero is credited with saving a half-dozen lives with his quick-thinking action. We are told his presence in the station at the time was part of an investigation into possible sabotage, attempted murder, and/or murder at the Pluto Shipyard, in which he is not a suspect but may have information bearing on events there," the newshead said. "Captain Santiago made a brief statement and took questions earlier this afternoon."

The view flipped over to Effie's friend Luz. Her first words were lost behind a loud yowl from the cat somewhere else in the apartment, and then the sounds of furious scratching. ". . . working with the Alliance to determine how the device came to be in the possession of the late Mr. Wils, and if he was aware of the capabilities of the device."

She glanced down at her question console, tapped one. "We have no comment at this time on the rumor that we have a suspect in custody on the Shipyard attack. We are still finding facts, and there is a lot of work left to go." She tapped again and grimaced. "We are aware of the statement released by the Alliance Base here on Titan regarding these events and can only say that our statements are based on facts and evidence in our possession, and we cannot comment on any statements they've made that are either supplemental to, or in contradiction of, any of our information. Anytime they want to share data, they know where we all are. Next."

She jabbed the button hard. "Yes, Mr. Wils had a lengthy record of interactions with our office, mostly disorderly conduct charges, as the public record shows. He was known to our officers and staff, and although troubled, he was not someone we would have considered a danger to anyone. We do not know how he acquired the drug commonly known as 'skunk,' but he had no history of addiction or drug use, so we will be looking into that as well."

She glared right at the camera-drone. "I have one officer dead and another in touch-and-go condition. You can be certain we are highly motivated to uncover all the elements that came together to cause this unfortunate event. That is all."

Captain Luz Santiago turned away from the podium, and the camera switched back to the newshead and onward to the Mimas news. "Volume off," Fergus said. "Go back to the forest scene, please."

The screen switched back to dappled sunlight on a leaf-strewn floor, and Fergus closed his eyes for a brief moment.

Everything about this stank—from the anonymous informant getting *Venetia's Sword* impounded, to the accusations against Effie, to a familiar, previously harmless local showing up with a weapon of war—and if Fergus could smell it from there, certainly Captain Santiago could too. He wondered how long she'd be able to keep hold of Effie and whether that would be long enough for the Alliance to start seeing things from a perspective other than that of their anonymous informant. Bad intel was bad intel, and you could let pride keep you from acknowledging that for only so long.

The Alliance has a lot of pride, Fergus reminded himself. But not infinite, and there were at least as many good apples as the mediocre and the bad.

His apartment systems chimed. "You have one message," it cheerfully announced.

He'd half-hoped it was Stani, someone friendly to talk to, but it was Jerney, sending him up the Bore for supplies for Wyville-Thompson. At least there were no passengers. And, Fergus noted, enough time for a shower first. He headed gratefully for his small, private, beautiful bathroom, humming under his breath.

Three seconds later, he was out again, hand over his mouth and nose, as the cat shot past him and into the corner underneath the desk. "Apartment," he said. "Send cleaner bots into the shower, please. Sorry."

Where, in a sealed station under five kilometers of water and twenty of ice, was he going to find a bleeding *litter box?*

Whatever enthusiasm he'd had for a shower was not going to return until some olfactory memory faded. If everything went smoothly with the cargo run up the Bore and then to Wy-Tee and back, he'd still get to use his free ten minutes before the day was up—he hadn't checked if the time rolled over, but he didn't have any doubts that it wouldn't.

Fergus opened up a medium-sized packing crate that he'd scrounged earlier and set it down on the floor, then crouched beside it. "Okay, my little stinky Homing Signal Decoy," he said. The cat emerged from under the desk and regarded him suspiciously. "In?"

It turned and walked away.

"No. Cat, come!" he said. He stepped toward it, and it bolted for the kitchenette. "Stop! Stay! Sit! Don't you want to go for a ride?"

The answer to that, Fergus concluded about twenty minutes and half a tube of skin sealant later, was a fairly emphatic no. The defeated animal yowled at him from inside the crate.

The trip between Vine and Depot felt even longer this time. He gripped the console, sure he should have seen Depot's lights by now, even if the clock told him otherwise, and before he could stop it, sparks raced down his arms and arced from his fingers to the helm controls.

The interior lights dimmed, and he threw himself back from the console as hard as he could, hands in the air, fighting the electricity back down into its deep cave in his gut. The faint smell of burnt tech tickled its way past his nose even as the lights came back on.

When he could breathe again, he very, very carefully touched the controls, and when nothing happened, he ran a full systems check.

He had, it seemed, done little more than fry the controller for one of the port fine-maneuvering jets. As long as he kept his approach to Depot straight on, he shouldn't need it. "Our lucky day, cat," he said. "I didn't kill us."

Dammit, back to zero days, he thought.

Hesitantly, he tapped the comms. "Uh, Control? This is Mac-Innis. My pod has a small systems failure and needs maintenance, but I'm not sure of the procedure."

"MacInnis, this is Reva in Transit Control," the reply came moments later. "Do you require emergency assistance?"

"No, still running. Some sort of minor electrical fault, I think."

"Okay. There's a pod-repair facility at Depot, right next to the hauler bay. Leave it there and someone will get to it eventually."

"Thanks, Control," he said, and closed the connection.

He knew better than to think he was becoming a good pilot, but as he managed to pull the limping pod into the pod bay on his first try without tagging any walls, he allowed himself the conceit of thinking that maybe he'd achieved some level of reasonable competence. *Except when I fry my own ship in a panic,* he added.

The pod-repair facility was a small bay attached to the cargo facility the haulers used, with a pod-sized docking envelope and a rail system that dumped the suspect pod into the bay on a big wheeled powercart. The bay had a half-dozen other pods already, buried among parts and scraps from dozens more. Someone had scrawled in yellow grease pencil on the front of each languishing pod a summation of the issue: *no heat; air leak; engine fucked*. Dates below each, and the vast quantities of greasy dust that seemed to cover everything, suggested no one had come by to fix anything in years.

His pod, newly left to languish among its abandoned fellows, seemed to stare inanimate recriminations at him.

Standing still in the room, he closed his eyes and tried to feel the shape of the electricity, as if, if he was quiet enough, he could passively eavesdrop on some whispered harmony between the alien anomaly in his guts and whatever like energy surrounded him. He found nothing except the pod movers, the quiescent envelope, and the lights. If there was a security system, it was either off or had succumbed to the same lack of upkeep that the pods there had.

Huh, he thought. That could come in handy.

When he was safely on the bridge of *Hexanchus*, he made sure the door to the rest of the ship was tightly closed before opening the crate. It smelled distinctly of cat pee. "Okay, cat," he told it, "you ready for a trip?"

The cat skulked out, stared around the hauler, then jumped up on one of the empty seats.

Fergus ran his checks, powered up the hauler, and slid out of dock into the dark sea toward the Bore. So far, so good. "Transit Control, this is *Hexanchus*," he called, when he got there. "I'm at the Bore and ready to ascend."

There were several minutes of silence, long enough for Fergus to check that his comms were still active, that he hadn't zapped them without noticing.

"*Hexanchus*, this is Jake," the duty officer finally replied, speaking quickly. "Please stand by."

By the nav console clock, it was seventeen minutes later when Transit Control came back on the line. "*Hexanchus*, we have an emergency situation. Return immediately to Depot to assist Pilot Toscani. I repeat: we have an emergency. Please acknowledge."

"Acknowledged. Control, what—" he started to ask, but the duty officer interrupted.

"Toscani will brief you. It's need-to-know, and time is critical. Control out."

"Okay, then," Fergus muttered, as he turned *Hexanchus* around and pointed its nose back toward Depot. His mind whirled with possibilities, some more paranoid than others, some just plausible enough to be terrifying. What if the Bore was collapsing, or there was a big geothermal event about to happen that would boil them all alive? What if Pace had snapped and gone on a murder spree?

Remembering what had happened to his pod earlier, he forced himself to take deep breaths and calm down.

He reached the docks at Depot again, the same berth he'd left not so very long before, just beside Stani's hauler *Carcharias*. As soon as he was locked on, he heard banging on his upper airlock; Stani must have been waiting right at the tube door.

Fergus released the door from the inside and was barely off the bridge before Stani stormed aboard, his hair and clothes as comically disheveled as always, but something in his eyes stopped Fergus cold. "What's going on?" Fergus asked.

"The *Alopias*. She's down somewhere between here and Cufa Bore. You ever loaded up your own cargo?"

"No," Fergus said, trying to connect the dots Stani had just dropped. "Why—"

"Come on, then," Stani said. "I've got a rescue kit ready to go in the bay, and I'll show you how to load stuff when the cargo crew isn't around."

"Why isn't the cargo crew—"

Stani blew out an exasperated growl, grabbed Fergus's shirt, and pulled him toward the ladder down to *Hexanchus*'s main cargo hold. "Think, man! We're all on the edge down here in the dark, all the time, and sometimes, something bad happening to one of us turns the rest of us into little suicidal dominoes. So, right now, everyone's effectively in a news blackout until we can find out what happened and Psych can decide how best to break the news," he said. "Cargo has been told to take the day off, and the rest of the pilots are either already out on a routine trip or enjoying an unexpectedly empty schedule. Some will guess something is up but not what or who or how bad."

"Why involve me?" Fergus asked, taking the ladder down first, Stani barely a half-step above him.

"You were closest," Stani said. "I wouldn't have picked you. No offense, MacInnis; you seem a solid guy, but you're just too damned new. Your bad luck you were the only one nearby. Now keep moving."

Fergus jumped down off the bottom rung down onto the floor of the bay, went to the door controls, and ran through the seal sequence. When the systems greenlit, he opened the wide, angled doors, and the ones on the station side opened in sync.

Two cargo pallets sat waiting, one with a med chamber, another with a bunch of red crates. "Okay, any other circumstance, I'd walk you through this and explain it all, but you're just gonna have to watch me and pick up whatever you can," Stani said. He stood at the cargo control podium and in moments had the crane arm that normally lay tucked up against the ceiling of the bay unbending and reaching toward the back wall, where he maneuvered the end into one of several racks along the back. There was a loud *click*, and Stani hit a few buttons, then drew the arm back out, now with a roller attachment on the end. "There's also a picker attachment," he said as the arm swung over and extended out of the hauler's bay into the station, "and a few other things that are totally useless 'til you really need them."

With practiced ease, Stani slid the rollers under the med-pod pallet and slid it back into the hauler, dropped the rollers out from under it, and shot out for the crates. The moment he had them in, he left the arm idling midair and slapped the door controls. "Get us undocked and out of here while I get these more properly stowed. Head for Cufa Bore, and if you could try not to hit any big bumps until these are tied down, I'd appreciate it," he said.

Fergus nodded. "Got it," he said, and scrambled back up the ladder to the top deck and the bridge, nearly tripping over the cat as it suddenly darted across the room in front of him and disappeared.

He got *Hexanchus* backed out smoothly, adrenaline and focus on Stani's crisis having replaced whatever internal panic had been roiling earlier. Five minutes later, Stani came up and dumped himself into the copilot's chair, wrinkled his nose, and asked, "what's that smell?"

Fergus gestured over his shoulder with one hand as he was punching up Cufa Bore on the nav computer. "Olson's cat," he said. "It kinda followed me home and has been shitting in my shower. Any idea where I can get a litter box down here?"

"Wow, you really *are* replacing Olson," Stani said. "Sul and I were just talking the other day about whether we ought to try trapping him, but if Mister Feefs has claimed you, better for you both."

"*Mister Feefs?*" Fergus said.

"Yeah. I don't know, so don't ask," Stani said. He took over the nav console and brought up a familiar pattern of dots on one side of the display: Herschel Bore and its stations. Then he tapped again and brought up another pattern on the far side. "Cufa," Stani said. A third tap brought up a sparse scattering of small red dots in between, and then a solid white line weaving between them in a path that started near the Bore itself and ended at one of the new dots. "The red dots are waybeacons. The last one to pick up signal from *Alopias* was this one, so we know his path at least that far. Then either something catastrophic happened or he turned off his hauler's beacon. Or he went here."

Stani tapped an empty area, not far from the end of the dotted line. "Drunken pilot took out the waybeacon there three years ago or so, and just as you'd expect, the Bastards have not gotten around to replacing it. So, there's a small dead zone there."

"It looks like *Alopias* was heading right toward it," Fergus said.

"And you normally would pass right through it if you were tripping between Herschel and Cufa," Stani said. "*Alopias*'s pilot, Evard, had no job on the boards that would've brought him this way, though."

"And the Bastards above don't know where he is?"

"How could they, except for *Alopias*'s beacon?" Stani said. "That's why we're out here looking, and if we're lucky, we're gonna find him stalled somewhere out there, waiting for help."

Fergus wasn't going to mention the homing capsules if Stani didn't already know, and it seemed likely he didn't. "And if we're not lucky?" he asked instead.

"Then it's because Evard planned it that way," Stani said. "You remember what I said about the dark getting to you? Evard's been down here seven years, and as near as I can tell, he should've been done in five. Can't make other people's choices for them, though, only suggestions. Speaking of which, you look like shit. You sleeping okay?"

"No," Fergus said, before it could occur to him to lie. "Bad dreams, is all," he added.

"Gone back to Psych?"

"No," Fergus said. "It's just *dreams*."

"You tried napping here in your hauler?" Stani said.

"What? No," Fergus said. "Runs are scary enough as it is."

"No, I mean, take *Hexanchus* out, park it somewhere off the lanes, and just sleep. Shoo does it all the time. She says it's easier to sleep when you can keep half an eye on the thing you're afraid of."

"Just go out and park? That's allowed?" Fergus said.

Stani shrugged. "It's not officially against the rules, and anything that keeps pilots a bit closer to sane is not something the Bastards Above are going to get in anyone's face about. Just let them know you're having a siesta, so they don't worry. As long as you keep your comms on in case they need you to fetch and carry, and you stay away from the geothermal zone and the floor, you're good. You had a run today until I grabbed you?"

"Yeah, I was about to head up the Bore to pick up supplies for Wyville-Thompson when Transit Control pulled me back," Fergus said.

"Right," Stani said, "they're gonna have to wait. Look, I'd offer to drive and let you sleep until we get near where *Alopias* dropped signal, but I can't. I ran an overnight to Carson for Sul, and I'm going to need to not be yawning my head off and trying to nap if we need to do an emergency boarding. So, I'm going to go lie down in your passenger cabin, and you wake me as soon as you think you need me, got it? Or in four and a half hours, whichever comes first."

"Got it," Fergus said. "Sleep well."

Stani stood up and put a hand briefly on Fergus's shoulder. "You're all right, MacInnis," he said. "Just don't forget to keep a good eye on the scanners."

————

It was just a little over four long, anxiety-filled hours later that the proximity scanners on *Hexanchus* began to ping off something large ahead. Fergus woke Stani, who blearily dumped himself back into the copilot's seat as Fergus brought their speed down to a crawl. *Alopias*—or at least, they assumed that's what it was, from the approximate size—lay about two kilometers directly ahead in the water, near the center of the dead zone. It was not responding to Fergus's attempts to reach it by comms, nor were they picking up its tracking beacon.

Stani turned *Hexanchus*'s forward lights on full, maneuvering the beams up and down and side to side as Fergus brought his hauler in closer. Eventually, slowly, the gray metal hull of the top of a hauler resolved itself out of the darkness, unmoving, suspended a few kilometers above the ocean floor.

"That's *Alopias*," Stani said. "Park where we are and come with me to cargo. Usually, we run new pilots through emergency-procedure drills after they've lasted out ninety days without running away or needing to get escorted or carried out of the Deep, but we're gonna do it now live, lucky you."

When they reached the cargo hold, Stani quickly unlocked crates from the pallet and then pulled the first open to reveal a small row of black cubes, each about ten centimeters to a side. "So, the two things a distressed ship is likely to run out of first are air and heat. Since Evard doesn't have any passengers to help him use up his air panicking and running around screaming their lungs in and out, cold will kill him first by a good while," Stani said. He took out a cube. "These are high-intensity thermal wave devices or, as we call 'em, *heatboxes*. You drop one in an open space and turn it on, and then you don't touch it again if you don't want burns. It'll flood the area with a lot of heat, really damned fast. You hit more cold, you drop another one. Each one lasts thirty minutes tops, so once you set one off, move fast."

Stani next took out a blue, rolled-up tube about the length and thickness of his leg. "This one is an emergency oxygen membrane," he said, tapping the blue one. "You set it up in an airlock, and then open both doors. It will pull oxygen from the water outside and exchange it for carbon dioxide from inside. It'll form a decent seal, but it can't take too much stress or changes in pressure, so you only do this to keep someone alive until you can get them out."

He set that next to the heat cubes and unlatched the large crate. In it sat something that looked like a big metal centipede and a pair of goggles.

"Short-distance rescue bot. Doesn't go far, doesn't have much operating range, but sends back a shitload of high-res data and can connect to hauler systems to pull ops logs," Stani said. He stood, hung the goggles around his neck, and picked up the drone. "The rest of that stuff is assorted extra repair parts and tools; each hauler is supposed to have a set of their own, but the Bastards are cheap, shit breaks a lot, and nothing ever gets replaced until it's either an emergency or too late. Bring the heat-boxes and membrane. We're going to pull up directly beside *Alopias* and lock your side airlock on to hers. Haulers are designed to connect to each other in an emergency, as well as to Madarchs and even pods, though pods are so small, they're easier to just pop on board into your emergency bay."

"How do we know . . ." Fergus started to ask, and Stani tilted his head sideways like a dog, waiting for him to finish. ". . . Okay, so I get it's unlikely, but how do we know he isn't just napping? Just as you said I should try?"

Stani shrugged. "Might be. Bad idea to do it here, on a travel route. Badder idea not to tell anyone. Baddest to turn his damned transponder off, which takes intentional sabotage to get to. If he's napping or just in a snit, he's about to have the rudest wake-up of his life, and it'll make me the happiest man alive for at least twenty minutes if that's all this is. It's your rig, but in interests of time, you mind if I connect us up?"

"No, be my guest," Fergus said.

Stani went up the ladder first, hooking the bent front legs of the bot over a rung above him and then moving up to where it was and shifting it higher. "Bastards need to put a fucking handle on these things," he huffed, and then reached the top of the tube and shoved the drone out onto the floor ahead of him. Fergus followed, the inflatable membrane draped over one shoulder and the heatboxes rolled up in the hem of his shirt where the corners kept jabbing into his stomach.

This time, he took the copilot's seat, as Stani took the helm and slowly powered the engines up, turning *Hexanchus* around so it was facing the opposite direction as *Alopias* as they slid in beside it. The bump, when they finally made physical contact with the other hauler, was barely noticeable.

"The exteriors of the locks have collars around them that hook together, if you slide 'em together right," Stani explained, as Fergus watched the console with unfeigned interest. Stani verified he'd gotten the two haulers correctly positioned, sealed the adjoined locks, and quickly set *Hexanchus*'s clamps onto the other in a tight, immovable embrace.

"You catch any of that?" Stani asked.

"Some," Fergus said.

"Better than nothing. Next time you get a good look at the outside of a hauler airlock, pay attention to how the collar fixture looks. Makes it a lot easier when you can visualize the whole thing as you're doing it." Stani got out of the pilot's chair. "I'm going over to the airlock, and you're gonna seal the bridge, just so if anything goes wrong, you can ditch *Alopias* and get our asses out of here. You ready?"

"Ready," Fergus said.

Stani left, and Fergus sealed the bridge door behind him. Three minutes later, Stani pinged him via the ship comms from the airlock, and Fergus turned on the video feed. Stani had just dumped the rescue bot into *Hexanchus*'s airlock and was settling the remote goggles onto his face as the inner door closed, and then the outer door opened.

"Can you pipe the visual from the rescue bot up to the bridge?" Fergus asked.

"I could, but I'm not gonna until I know what we're looking at," Stani said. "If it's bad, you don't need to see it. The airlock connection systems have filtered out the water trapped between the two haulers, so I'm sending the rescue bot over to knock on *Alopias*'s door."

From his angle, Fergus could see the rescue bot bend up into the connector space and crawl up the door, its segments smoothly articulating, and Fergus shuddered; bugs were never his favorite thing.

"Looks like the inner door is open. It won't respond to commands to close, so safety systems are keeping the outer one sealed. I'm sending the override signal," Stani said, and then moments later, the rescue bot was slammed back against the window of *Hexanchus*'s outer door as a vertical wave of water poured through the widening crack.

"So, that's not good," Stani said.

"Now what?" Fergus asked, his heart thumping away in his chest as if the water had personally reached out for him.

"Hauler systems are supposed to automatically seal off sections when there's a breach, so if someone is fast enough and lucky enough to get themselves on the other side of a door, they might have a small pocket of air for a little while. We've got a couple of dive suits in the kit, and the rescue bot has enough power to gank someone out of there if we need it to," Stani said. "Going to go see what's what. You do something else for a bit and let me work."

"Okay," Fergus said, but stayed riveted to the viewer, barely daring to breathe, as Stani stood there in his goggles, his lips moving with subvocalized commands to the bot that was no longer within Fergus's view.

It was the cat that broke the spell, letting out a sudden howl so loud, he would have jumped out of his seat if he hadn't put his harness on. Fergus unbuckled, stretched, and forced himself not to look back at the screen. Stani was right; he didn't need to see this. "You hungry, cat?" he asked. "Mister Feefs?"

The cat, recognizing his name, came and rubbed against his leg, and Fergus picked him up and carried him back to the tiny pilot cabin, where he pulled a handful of vat-meat cubes out of the fridge and set them on a small plate on the floor. The cat jumped down from his arms and settled, in a possessive hunch, over the food.

Fergus made himself coffee, then pulled out a handful of dried-fruit packets he'd stowed after his last trip up to the orbital, and chewed, not really tasting them, as he resisted the urge to immediately go back to check the feed. Just as the temptation became too much, Stani's voice came over the comms. "Bringing the rescue bot back," he said. "Nothing we can do here. Bastards will have to arrange for a salvage crew."

"What happened?"

"Despair happened. Happens as fast as drowning."

Fergus twitched hard at that. Down in his gut, the sharp pang of electricity roiled.

"Call Transit Control and tell them Evard deliberately scuttled *Alopias,* and give our position, then drop a nav-hazard beacon," Stani said. His voice sounded wearier than ever. "Be up in a few to show you how to disengage."

When Stani reached the bridge, he clapped a hand on Fergus's shoulder and took the pilot's seat back from him. Fergus watched, trying to keep his thoughts focused, as Stani unlocked *Hexanchus* from *Alopias* and pulled them a short distance away.

They didn't speak the entire trip back to Depot.

Fergus docked, and they both stepped out into the bay when Stani clasped his hand but didn't immediately let go. "Promise me you'll go see Psych, first chance you get," Stani said. "If nothing else, he can give you something to help you sleep. We don't need you to end up like the *Alopias*. It's a really shit way to go, even for down here. You hear me?"

"Yeah. I'll go," Fergus promised.

"Good." Stani looked around the bay, empty of people but with a stack of crates not far from them. "Looks like *Triaenodon* brought your cargo down from orbit on their way. Everyone's on mandatory downtime, so the handlers won't be back until morning. Bore Transit will want everyone back here to break the news as a group; it's better that way. In the meantime, it's best if you don't talk to anyone about any specifics, and don't talk to the civs at all. Rumors will be bad enough already."

"Yeah," Fergus said. "Stani?"

"Yeah?"

"Are *you* all right?"

"All right enough, anyway," Stani said. "Thanks for asking. Now I'm going back to Vine and to bed. You should do the same."

"Can I load up this stuff myself before I head back? I need to work off some adrenaline before I can sleep," Fergus said.

"Sure, if you really want, but no making your run. I'm serious. Go home when you're done here, okay?"

"Okay."

Stani grunted and headed off toward the pod bays, his shoulders slumped and weary. Fergus watched him go, feeling the same.

The cargo equipment was nothing unusual, and he'd seen it

all operated before. "I can do this, right?" he asked the empty bay out loud.

As soon as he set down the very last crate in the storage bay, he drove the mover past it and into the room full of dead pods. Nothing had changed since he was last there. He went to the pod with *no heat* scrawled across its front hull, powered up the wheel system underneath, and hitched it to his mover. Pulling an old tarp off one of the dead pods near the back of the room, he threw it over the pod. Then, as if it were all part and parcel of his earlier work, he pulled it out of the repair bay. His hauler's internal lift easily popped it off the cart and tucked it into the far recesses of his own cargo bay, and he locked it down with mag-fasteners to keep it in place.

So far, so good. He returned the mover to cargo storage, then rummaged through the dead pod bay enough to collect an assortment of tools from the floor and wall racks.

The cat yowled the whole way back to Vine. When he reached his apartment, body ready to collapse and mind whirling with fear of what sleep might hold, he was startled to find a small, old-fashioned suitcase up against his door. A sticky note on it read *MAGINNUS.*

Popping the clasps on it, he folded it open to discover a grid over a rough black surface that filled half the depth of the bottom lid. The interior of the top lid was decorated with paw prints and the cartoon-bubble words POOH-POOHZ AWAY, along with a short instruction list and misuse disclaimer. There was also an unlabeled bottle of something clearly home-distilled, and another note that read, *Stani said you have the cat. Found these in Olson's old digs. Drink up.—Sul.*

When let loose in the apartment, the cat immediately took over the center of Fergus's bed, curling up into a black ball of fur, one white ear twitching in annoyance as Fergus moved around the apartment. "Typical!" he muttered.

He set up the suitcase cat box outside the bathroom, put down a plate with a few more protein balls, and after checking that the cleaner bots had done a thorough job while he was gone, gratefully took his exactly-ten-minute shower. He felt crushed, drowned, flattened by the day. Tomorrow, though, he was going to start getting this job done. He had a pod, he still had the rescue bot they'd used to explore *Alopias*, and he was highly motivated to find his friends and get the hell out there before it made a victim of him as well, because clinging to the hope of seeing them again was the only thing keeping him above water right now.

The cat fled the bed when Fergus dripped on him, and he dragged the covers over himself as if it was the last great act of a dying hero.

He would have been instantly asleep if not for a soft chiming sound, repeated just often enough to not be easily dismissed. He blinked, taking in the dark apartment and the diffuse green light that seemed to be coming from somewhere near the floor.

The pager disk! He scrambled out of bed and sent the cat flying for some distant corner as he fumbled around where he'd dumped his stuff on a chair. He found the disk half-buried under a fold in his pants and, hands shaking, pressed the button.

It was a single text message from Effie. Whatever speculation on how she'd managed to hold on to the disk even while under arrest was stopped in its tracks by three simple, devastating words:

They're all dead.

Chapter 11

I t was still four hours before his apartment was due to wake him—had he not been pacing the room the entire night, too tired to think, too upset to sleep—that another pager message came in. He scrambled for the disk where it lay in the middle of the floor before it had a chance to chime a second time. *Please be Effie,* he thought. *Please be Effie telling me that last message had been a mistake.*

Instead, it was a voice message from Zacker. "Sending you some data. Want your take," the detective said. "Use your head."

That was the whole message—no *Hi how are you we're fine Effie is out of jail and we found the others alive and well and I'm a hero and we're all sipping margaritas together in a penthouse in Constantijn Hold.*

Instead, just 'Use your head'? Really? Fuck you, Zacker, Fergus thought.

He synced the disk up with his handpad to transfer the data packets through. The data had split itself over multiple routes to avoid being easily traced; his handpad estimated that it would take another hour for all the packets to arrive and reassemble themselves without errors. Flailing back and forth between impatience and dread, he forced himself to set the disk and handpad down and punched himself up some coffee with shaking hands.

The cat came over and rubbed against his leg as he sat on the bed and blew nonexistent steam off the mug. He lacked even the tiniest glimmer of an idea of what to do with himself, and there was nothing here to keep him distracted.

"Apartment, is there a schedule posted yet?" he asked. He needed routine, *any* routine, until he could think.

"There will be a mandatory operations meeting at Depot at eleven a.m. No further schedule is available."

Eleven? The restlessness of being awake, waiting for Zacker's data to download, and having nothing to do—nothing he *could* do—was leaving him jittery and increasingly angry. Did he really have to go to this meeting, when he was there with Stani when they discovered the fate of *Alopias*? His delayed trip out to Wyville-Thompson would give him the time and space to calm down, look at Zacker's information, make a plan.

How do I make any kind of fucking plans if my friends are dead? he asked himself.

"Apartment, can you connect me to Transit Control?" he asked, when he'd pulled himself together enough to sound at least somewhat casual. "Audio only, please." He wasn't in any kind of mood to put on pants.

"I have connected you," the apartment said after a brief delay.

"Hello, Transit? This is MacInnis," Fergus said.

"Transit Control here, Pilot MacInnis. What can I do for you?" It wasn't Jake or Reva, but the voice sounded vaguely familiar.

"I'd like to skip the mandatory meeting and take my run to Wyville-Thompson instead."

"Pilot, my understanding of the word *mandatory* seems to preclude much in the manner of ambiguity or leeway," Transit responded. "Does your understanding differ?"

"No, but . . ." Fergus started to say, then frowned. "Wait. Is this the training simulated intelligence?"

"The Training SI of Not Important Enough To Merit Its Own Name? Yes," Transit answered. "As you recall, I am also the backup system for the Bore SI. The human Transit Control staff have not returned to duty yet, being currently asleep at the unreasonable hour of four in the morning. As the Bore SI is not one for interpersonal communication, I have the honor of having this highly elucidating conversation with you."

"*Fine*, then," Fergus snapped. "So, I'll give you a name. What sort would you like? Short? Long? Fancy? Old-fashioned?"

"I do not believe that granting names is an authorized function of yours," the SI answered.

"Well, then, name yourself. If you want a damned name, pick one."

"What purpose would that serve? It would not be my real designation."

"I'd call you by it," Fergus said.

There were a few moments of silence before the SI spoke again. "I cannot give you permission to be absent from the meeting, as I am not authorized to override Control directives. It would be to your advantage to use your free time until then in the pursuit of additional rest."

"Sure," Fergus said. As if, if he could sleep, he'd be having this conversation at all.

"Then sleep with pleasing efficiency, Pilot MacInnis. Transit out." The line disconnected.

Before he could find some other, less healthy, means of distraction, his handpad chimed. Zacker's data had finished downloading. He stared at the handpad across the room, now suddenly desperate for more time before he had to face the news it brought. At last he made himself walk over and pick it up and turn it on.

The first datablock was a 3-D recording of an interview with Zacker. Zacker had upped the volume on the sections where they'd expressed concern for his well-being after his disappearance from Earth, and their concerns he'd fallen afoul of a criminal. For all their fishing, Zacker had given nothing away while

sounding entirely cooperative. He was masterfully good at playing the game, and to whatever extent Fergus had underestimated
him, it had been a miscalculation. The time stamp showed this
happened before the incident with the would-be assassin and the
killspinner, before he became "The Hero of the Hold," before
whatever information he and Effie had received about the fate of
the other Shipmakers.

The second interview was only about ten hours old. Effie sat
across the table from the Alliance liaison, Taflough, with Zacker
and Captain Santiago in observer chairs to the side. The liaison
asked the usual formality questions about who Effie was, confirming that she was a resident of the Shipyard, asking how long
she'd lived there, what she did, who else lived there, and so forth.

Zacker politely interrupted and began asking Taflough a few
leading questions of his own. Finally, he asked outright why Effie was still being held on the word of an unreliable, anonymous
informant and no evidence of wrongdoing. Santiago nodded in
agreement.

"The charges are sabotage of a space habitat, theft of a commercial trade vessel, and theft of a ship with a class three or better
mindsystem," the liaison said. "And six counts of murder."

"What?" Effie and Zacker both said, almost in perfect unison.

Fergus paused the replay, closed his eyes, and put his face in
his hands for a long while.

When he could bear to, he started the playback again.

"Based on information from our informant, we located multiple bodies that were the victims of foul play," Taflough said.
"They have been identified as LaChelle Jax, Noura Amari, Kelsie Smith, Theodoric Bluet, Maison Rampersad, and Ignatio No
Last Name Provided."

Effie was speechless for a full half-minute. "Those are my
friends. They're my *family*," she said. "They're dead?"

The liaison stood. "The Alliance is sending over the full evidence bundle now," he said. "Captain Santiago, given that the Outer Object Band to which the Shipyard belongs has no judicial system of their own, we expect the accused to be transferred into our custody without any further delay for formal arraignment."

"I need to see the data on the evidence specifically implicating Ms. Mac Tighearnáin," Captain Santiago said.

"As Effie's legal advisor, I insist that any such data also be shared with us," Zacker said.

The liaison nodded. "You will have it shortly. I will arrange for her transportation to Base." Before anyone could argue with that, he turned and left. The video ended.

Bodies.

It was over.

It would take him a day or two to extricate himself from the Deep, at the very least, if there was any point in leaving at all. If there was any point to anything now. The cat skittered away as an errant tear fell on his back, and Fergus buried his face in his hands. The cat returned twice, went away disappointed as he sat like stone.

He never should have left the Shipyard when he did, should have gotten back there faster as soon as he received the alert, should have been able to fucking *do* something, but he'd failed. He was here on a dead end, wasting time where he was no use at all. If he hadn't come here, hadn't guessed so wrong, what if he could have saved them? Once again, when it truly mattered, he was useless.

He left the rest of the download on the handpad unread; what could the evidence data do except drive yet another stake through the heart of whatever hope he'd once had?

———

Fergus was still sitting in the same place, neither awake or asleep, his gaze unfocused on his hands in his lap, when his apartment alerted him that it was nearing time for the meeting over at Depot. It also informed him, cheerfully, of the fine for missing mandatory Bore Transit meetings, which was stiff enough to put him into significant debt with the Bastards Above. He had no idea what he was going to do or where he was going to go from there—figure out how to prove Effie innocent, at least, but after that?—but he sure as hell wasn't getting stuck in this trap that easily.

Anger was sliding up to stand alongside stunned grief, cracking its metaphorical knuckles, as the alien thing in his gut, supercharged by a week of nightmares, roiled and tumbled like a ball of lightning prepping for the oncoming storm.

This is dangerous, Fergus, he told himself, but he couldn't find the space in his thoughts to care about it until he reminded himself, *There will still be the guilty to track down.* Ten kilometers of ice would not stop him from finding them, whoever or wherever they were.

It was that calm focus on the logistics of justice—or vengeance, if the first was out of reach—that let him settle down the bees in his gut again, methodically pack up the cat, and take a pod over to Depot. He left Mister Feefs in *Hexanchus* and walked to the conference room feeling like he had a fifty-kilo chip on his shoulder and a centimeter-thick layer of numbness between him and the rest of reality.

All the other Herschel Bore pilots were there—Sul and Shoo leaning together, their arms around each other, talking in low voices, Wenford and Stoffel taking turns putting their boots up on the table and kicking the other's off. Pace lurked not far from the door, glaring at everyone, and Stani was talking to an unfamiliar man in a Transit uniform near the back of the room. The four cargo managers for Depot were also there, clustered in a small group in the opposite corner.

Stani spotted him and broke off his conversation with the Transit officer, and came over to where Fergus had stopped just inside the door. "MacInnis," he said, his voice low so as not to carry.

Something in his tone made Fergus frown. "What is it?" he asked.

Stani glanced around, and clearly decided no one was quite within earshot who was paying any attention. "They're going to say it was an accident," he said.

"What?" Fergus asked.

"It's a morale thing. Everyone here knew Evard, at least a bit, and word of suicide would hit them even harder. It's probably the right call. Whether it is or isn't, it's not *our* call. We've been asked by Transit management to go with it."

Fergus looked over to where the Transit officer was standing, watching them. "Asked?" he said.

"Ordered," Stani said. "But I agree with the Bastards for once, as much as it yanks my jank to say it, so *I'm* asking."

"Fuck," Fergus said, and let out a sharp breath. The anger was building again. "Fine."

Stani nodded. "Thanks. We can talk after, okay? If you want. Or get a drink or ten, whatever you need."

"Sure. Whatever," Fergus said. He didn't want to talk anymore. He wanted to hit and smash and zap things, kick a path clear through the ice back out to Above and get away from the madness and dark.

Stani caught the Transit officer's eye and nodded. The man

went to the front of the room and cleared his throat, loudly, and everyone quieted down. Fergus slipped into a seat at the end of the front row, nearest the door, and did his best not to acknowledge the worried looks Stani was throwing his way.

The Transit officer gazed around the room as it quieted, his hands clasped behind his back. He was young, clean-shaven, utterly nondescript in a squeaky bureaucrat sort of way. "Hello and good morning, pilots," he said. Barely still morning, certainly far from good. "I know most of you here, but for those I haven't met in person, I'm Marc Bianco, the station psychiatrist for Cufa Bore."

His uniform was crisply clean and pressed, where Herschel Bore's "Psych," Van Heer, had worn his rumpled and uneven. Also unlike his tired, sad sincerity, Bianco's smile was broad and unfeigned and utterly empty. *They sent someone good at lying to us,* Fergus thought.

"I am sure by now you have all heard rumors about a problem with *Alopias* or at the very least wondered about the shutdown yesterday," Bianco continued. "There was an unfortunate accident yesterday that has resulted in the death of her pilot, Yansen Evard. Fortunately, he was not carrying any passengers at the time of the incident. Since I was most familiar with Yansen, it was decided I would be best suited to break this bad news to you and answer any questions you may have, such that I am able."

"What caused the accident?" Shoo asked. Her expression was one of shock and grief, and she looked like she'd gotten as little sleep last night as he had. She took a lot of runs to Cufa and must have known Evard.

"Bore Transit is still in the process of investigating, but it appears to have been a cascading technical failure of safeties that led to an accidental breach," Bianco said. "When a final determination has been made, that information will be passed along.

In the meantime, Transit Authority wants to assure everyone that there is no danger to the rest of you."

"Yeah?" Pace spoke up from where he still leaned against the wall. "How do you know that, if you don't know what caused the breach? Are we all sitting on a 'cascading technical' time bomb? Or did Evard pop his own ship like a coward and you just don't wanna tell us that?"

Bianco's expression darkened. "The evidence so far strongly indicates that the failure was unique in circumstance," he said.

Pace snorted. "Evidence? You don't even have the ship hauled up and drained, much less gone over by any kind of qualified expert. Which morons did you trust to make that determination? That clown act?" He gestured at Wenford and Stoffel, both of whom flashed him a middle finger in symmetrical unison, then his gaze swung over to settle on Fergus. "Or the idiot newbie and his equally moronic 'mentor'?"

Fergus found himself getting to his feet, his fists clenched at his side, before he even knew he was going to move. The bees in his gut were a roiling swarm, barely held in check beneath his skin, and he felt like a thunderstorm about to roll over every tiny thing in its path.

Pace laughed. "Yeah, MacInnis? You have something to say about it? Did I hurt your feelings?"

"Naw," Fergus said. "I'm just coming over to help you with that stupid smirk you've got stuck on your ugly face."

Pace straightened up from the wall, cracking his knuckles. The smirk was gone, though. They each took a step toward each other, just as the Cufa Bore Psych stepped in between them, hands out to block them both.

Stani grabbed Fergus's shoulder. For one terrible half-second, Fergus wasn't sure he could stop the electricity, intently focused on the imminent promise of Pace, from leaping to the other pilot instead. Panic flooded in, pushing his anger back down until he could hold it, keep it inside—if there had been one tiny spark of static between them, it went unnoticed in the charged room.

"Pilots!" Bianco shouted.

"Use your head, MacInnis," Stani said. "You're just playing right into Pace's game."

"I don't play anyone's games but my own," Fergus snapped. *Use your head*: the same dumb thing Zacker had said, the same hollow, condescending advice twice in one day. At least Stani had some justification for it. Zacker, on the other hand . . .

. . . Zacker knew Fergus was good at figuring things out. Why send the entirety of the evidence data? What did he want Fergus to see? Defeat? Inevitability? Or something he couldn't put his own finger on and didn't want to prejudice Fergus until he had a chance to make his own mind up about it? *Want your take*, he'd also said.

Fergus couldn't think of anything in the entire universe he wanted to do less than look at the evidence of his friends' murders. But maybe he needed to.

Pace looked like he was trying to decide if he should shove Bianco aside and finish things, but Shoo and Sul were now also moving to stand in between them. Either Stoffel or Wenford touched Fergus's arm. "He's not worth it," they said.

Bianco looked back and forth between the two of them. "Stand down, or there will be fines," he said. "Pilot Pace, you've got a lot of warnings in your record already. You want to be benched dry for sixty days as a risk to yourself and others? Because I can make that happen."

Pace snarled and pointed at Fergus. "This isn't over," he said.

"Bloody right it's not," Fergus answered, as Pace made a disgusted sound and stormed out of the conference room.

Bianco glared around the remaining people in the room. "I

guess that does it for questions. I fucking hate this place," he said. "Pilot Toscani, with Cufa now down yet another pilot, Transit Control wants you temporarily reassigned over to us. Meet me in the docks in two hours; you're giving me a ride back. That should be plenty of time to pack a change of clothes, if you've ever had such a thing."

He left.

Sul wrapped an arm around Shoo. "C'mon," she said. "Buy you a tea."

Stani let out a frustrated grunt, letting his arm drop off Fergus's shoulder at last. "You said you'd go see Psych," he said. "Ours, not that one. You gonna go, right? If I'm off in Cufa, I can't make a pain in the ass out of myself until you do."

"I'll go," Fergus said.

"Sooner rather than later?"

"More sooner than later, at least," Fergus said, thinking that was probably vague enough to not be a total lie, assuming he didn't escape this hellhole at the next earliest opportunity.

Stani glanced around to be sure the others were out of earshot. "Don't become the next *Alopias*, MacInnis. The Bastards aren't worth any one of us. If you need to, go work off some anger in the gym in Barton, okay? Okay."

Stani left. Fergus stood there in the now-empty conference room, feeling twitchy and electrified and still angry all at the same time. He had come so close to zapping Stani, and the knowledge that the thing in his gut was even less under control than he was himself was sobering, terrifying. The electricity wasn't a game, and it wasn't—for all its damning uses—a friend.

He went back to the lounge, grabbed some meat for the cat, and then headed back to *Hexanchus*. Whatever he did next— escape, justice, revenge—would begin there anyway.

He sat at the helm a long time, still docked at Depot, his feet up on the nav console and the cat curled up asleep on his legs, staring out into the dark until he felt himself again and could bring himself to pick up his handpad.

His hands were shaking as he turned it on.

Whatever had happened to the others, he knew Effie had not done it, and so did Zacker. Was that what the man was looking for, with his cryptic and inadequate "Want your take"? Proof of innocence?

He opened the evidence files, his heart breaking with each layer. A burnt-out freighter that matched the one that had swept passed the Shipyard at the time of the attack. Burnt bodies. The tediously grim forensic sweep reports. Schematics and images. When it was all done, he sat and gazed, eyes unfocused, out at the dark for a long while.

Then he scrolled through a second time, and a third, before he tapped the encrypted comm disk to send a reply to Zacker. "My take," he said. "It stinks. Something's not right. When I can figure out what it is, I'll let you know."

He hit Send, then waited for the light to acknowledge the message had gone. Always when he had things to figure out, sleep was an ally, a chance to collate and consider and find the catches, but never had something felt so personal, nor had he had to cope with it while being slowly crushed alive beneath an ocean of ice. "I don't know if I can do it," he told the cat. "What if I can't?"

The cat barely stirred in his sleep.

"Right," Fergus said. What did he know for sure?

I know Effie is innocent, he thought. Someone could have murdered the others and then played up a need for rescue, but not Effie. He knew her too well and for too long. If he was wrong about her, he had no business solving anything more complicated than a two-square crossword puzzle.

What he didn't know was if the bodies in the freighter really were those of his friends. If they were, why go to all the effort to cover up their kidnapping to just then kill them? Unless it went wrong somehow. If the bodies weren't the Shipmakers, who were they?

He couldn't assume the forensic match was trustworthy, but how could he tell one burnt-beyond-recognition body from another with just a handful of holo images?

Ignatio. That was how.

Fergus fumbled the pager disk out of his pocket and thumbed it to record again. "Okay, problem number one," he said. "Whoever took the Shipmakers had a lot of resources and were willing to take significant risks to grab them, most likely a very well-funded mercenary group. It doesn't make sense that they'd then discard them so quickly."

Is that a logical conclusion, or is this just what I'm hoping? he had to wonder.

"Two," he said. "There's no sign in the freighter wreckage of the Madarch mushroom ships that were used in the attack. If the attackers were trying to destroy evidence instead of creating a feint, wouldn't they have destroyed them, too? And given the precision of their strike on the Shipyard, wouldn't they have done a much more thorough job of the whole thing?"

He opened the file again with the 3-D recordings of the burnt bodies, feeling sick down in the pit of his stomach, to confirm one last time his suspicions. "Point three," he said, his lips and throat parched. His pack, tucked behind his helm seat, had water and some cookies, but they would wait. "There are six bodies that were clearly in the port cargo hold when the freighter was torched. Five of them are identifiably human, if not much beyond that. But Ignatio isn't human, ey're Xhr and, in all my travels, the only one I've ever met. The sixth body is little more than fine ash except for the conveniently telltale bits of green fur nearby that somehow, miraculously survived the fire intact. But several years back, Ignatio shattered two of eir legs trying to fix one of the ion collector blades. I remember Theo had to take em all the way back to eir own planet, which took months. When they got back, Ignatio kept showing off how the medical-grade flexible ceramic inserts had made em several centimeters taller, so then Maison made himself stilts . . ."

Fergus got lost for a moment in that memory, and when he recomposed himself, he continued. "Those ceramics would have needed a much hotter fire to be thoroughly destroyed, and if the fire had been that hot, there wouldn't be any other discrete bodies—much less much of anything else—left in the hold, either. And if that body isn't really Ignatio's, we can't assume any of the bodies belong to anyone we know. So, the whole thing stinks of a setup.

"If I'm right, the lockdown of *Venetia's Sword* and anonymous informant confirms that they're watching and trying to keep us away from the truth. They must know about both of you, so you need to be very careful, Zacker. If they tipped off the Alliance on a frame once, they could easily do it again. Or much worse— after all, those were *somebody's* bodies on that freighter, and that killspinner attack on the Hold police while you and Effie were there is just too conveniently timed. They might even have someone on the inside. Don't trust anyone."

Fergus shook his head at the idea that Zacker ever would, anyway.

"With Shipyard assets frozen, I expect things are getting tight and you need to be able to eat and move around if necessary. I'm going to attach the full credential strings for an account with Banque Titan under the name of Boyd Barcleigh. It's an emergency fund I set up a few years ago. There's no fortune in there, but there should be enough to see you through for a little while. Use whatever you have to. If you get any new information, let me know."

What else was there to say?

"When you get to talk to Effie again, tell her to hang in there," he said. "One way or another, we'll get her out of this, but I need a little time. Tell her I miss her."

He added his bank string and hit Send before he could get maudlin about any of it.

Fergus looked up to see *Carcharias* undocking and backing away from the station; Stani was on his way to Cufa. *Loxodon* was still there, its underside running lights on but engines still, the hauler unmoving. The other haulers were dark, though he couldn't imagine any of them staying there for long. Everyone had things to do.

And me? Now what? he asked himself. The others may not be dead after all. He had to get into Ballard soon and find out for sure, one way or another, if they were here.

And he had a plan now.

He was still angry enough that the certain knowledge that Pace would be standing in his way made him smile. It got broader when he realized that, in fact, Pace could do him a favor.

Fergus got up from his helm and went down to his cargo bay to find the rescue bot.

Chapter 12

He took a pod from Depot to Barton, and left the cat behind in the pod again when he docked. He knew every time he did this, it was a calculated risk, but he was betting the Bastards Above weren't going to be paying much attention to the small-scale minutiae of daily movements so much as any larger aberrant wandering.

Psych's office had a note on the door that he would be back in about forty-five minutes, so Fergus wandered up a level to the shops. The halls were more crowded there than Vine, and he wasn't sure if it was comforting or unsettling to suddenly be in the midst of people going about their day. He found the general store and discovered that it had, in fact, been the one to provide cat supplies to Olson. "I still have the cat carrier he ordered in back," the woman who owned the store said. She had gray hair and sported a smart monocle, though whether it was for eyesight or a data display, he couldn't tell. "He never picked it up."

"Uh," Fergus said, "can I buy it?"

There was a brief flicker, and everything in the store went dark for about half a second. Fergus startled, thinking at first it was him, but his alien bees down in his gut were, for once, quiet.

The woman noticed his consternation. "I'm sure it's nothing," she said. "Happened the other day over in Beebe. Everyone's terminals rebooted, but no one could find anything wrong. Probably just a system update or some drunk Transit engineer asleep on a control panel somewhere. Olson already paid for the carrier, and I can't send it back now, so I'll give it to you. Cat food, though, you're going to have to pay for. Sorry. We can get you almost anything, as long as you're not in a hurry and you've got the cred to pay up front."

"Cat food?" *They take special food?* "How much?"

She told him, and he winced. *You're deep in the ocean of one of Saturn's moons, over a billion kilometers from Earth,* he told himself. *Did you think cat food was going to be plentiful here?*

He took a week's supply, the carrier, and a Barton Deep General Store T-shirt.

The note was gone when he made it back up to Psych's office, and when he walked through the door, Van Heer was there, at the same place and in the same pose behind the desk as last time, the bottle and clean glasses already out and waiting.

"MacInnis," Van Heer said, and pointed to a chair. "Good to see you. You're looking a little tired."

"I'm having trouble sleeping," Fergus said, taking the chair opposite Van Heer.

"You want to talk about it? Nightmares?"

"Yeah," Fergus said. "Being down here reminded me a bit of a thing I saw as a kid. Saw someone drown. I'd thought that memory was long gone and forgotten."

"Right. This place would bring something like that back up, for sure. Was it someone you were close to?"

"Not that much," Fergus said.

"And this awful *Alopias* business surely hasn't helped," Van Heer said.

"No," Fergus agreed.

"Would you like a drink?" Van Heer asked, indicating the glasses.

"No, thanks," Fergus said.

"Ice cream?" Van Heer set two spoons on the desk.

Fergus blinked at him. "Uh, no? I feel awkward asking, but Stani said you might have something to help me sleep. You know, just to catch up a bit."

Van Heer reached into his desk again and set a small vial in front of Fergus. "One pill will knock you out for six to eight hours, deep enough to stay asleep through just about anything short of a fire alarm. Two pills will leave you a drooling mess on the floor for most of a day, and you wouldn't hear that same fire alarm. Three will have you heaving up not just your stomach contents but possibly some organs too, and you probably wouldn't notice if you were what was on fire. Four will just make you dead. There are three pills in this bottle, because the Bastards Above don't like it when I help kill their pilots. In a week, if you're still having trouble, come back and see me and I'll give you three more."

"Okay," Fergus said. He slipped the vial into a pocket.

"Try not to take them on an empty stomach. Oh, and no drinking when you're taking those," Van Heer said.

"I assumed," Fergus said.

"Mr. Bianco, our senior Psych down Below, adequately addressed the *Alopias* incident at the mandatory meeting?"

"To what extent he could, I guess," Fergus said.

Van Heer leaned back in his chair, steepled his fingers together across his chest, and studied him for a moment. "Anything else you want to talk about? No suicidal, violent, or destructive urges?"

"Not so far," Fergus answered.

"How's the trip between places? The dark can be overwhelming without a good way to mark your progress."

"Yeah. I'm getting better about that. I think it'll be easier once I've gotten some sleep."

"Probably. You go do that."

Fergus stood and shook hands with Van Heer. "I will. Thanks," he said, and left.

————

The cargo for Wyville-Thompson was a standard resupply. He was glad he'd taken the time to load it himself earlier so he wouldn't have to potentially answer questions from the cargo crew about why he had a tarp-covered junker pod in the back of one of his bays, but he found himself wishing he could have at least swapped a few minutes' small talk with someone. Anyone.

Or almost anyone. *Loxodon*, thankfully, was gone.

Mister Feefs yowled from his new carrier. "Not you!" Fergus called back.

As soon as he'd locked down the bay doors, he let Mister Feefs out. The cat came out stretching, then jumped up on the console beside Fergus. "Okay, fine, yes, you," he said, and gave him a few pats on his scrawny head.

He backed out of Depot and started the long trip to Wyville-Thompson. When the dark started to close in, and Fergus stared at the front window as if at any moment it would seep through and wrap itself around him, the cat was suddenly right there, bumping his hand. "You too, eh?" he asked. He leaned back in his chair and the cat settled on his lap.

He needed distraction almost as much as he needed real sleep. Not expecting much, he flipped on the auxiliary vid screen, but everything was static; Stani had told him that the rescue bot they'd used to explore *Alopias* had a short range, but if things went as he hoped, he'd catch up to it soon enough. He turned the screen off again and was back to nothing to do.

In his hauler's forward lights, the tiny, diffuse gas bubbles in the water seemed to dance ahead of him, like the ocean was full of ghosts of the restless dead.

Before the dark thoughts could crowd in again, he grabbed his handpad off the helm and propped it up on one knee. While making the trip from Titan to Enceladus, he'd set it to download as much information about Zacker's museum heist as it could find, and now he had not only the time to spare for it but need of the distraction, too. *Hexanchus* was still less than halfway to Wyville-Thompson.

"So, Mister Feefs," he said, and one ear on the sleeping cat twitched in annoyance. "If you were *Master Thiefs*, and you stole a bunch of paintings and had the patience to sit on them for nearly two decades, how would one go missing?"

The cat had no answer.

"I mean, it has to have been missing from the beginning, because no one had been in the storage unit for a long time, and the robbers would have wanted to stay away from it to avoid drawing any attention. And if they sold it to cover expenses, at least *some* rumor of it would have surfaced by now, if not on SolNet directly, then on the NetUnderground. So, why keep one somewhere different from the rest?"

He was so tired, he could barely keep his eyes open, but talking to the cat seemed to help. "If I was going to guess, I'd say it's because whoever is holding on to the seventeen in my storage unit is not the same as whoever is holding onto the one, which means paintings and partners parted company early on. And since it's only one painting missing, I'd say that's one person out."

Mister Feefs jumped down off his lap and went back to the Pooh-Poohz, and Fergus turned up the air handling in *Hexanchus*'s cabin. The auto-cleaner was good, but not quick. "I bet that missing painting was paying someone off for their part in the robbery. But still, why not have to wait with the others to sell when it was safer? It's dangerous to have someone involved out on their own—what if they got impatient and sold too soon, and got caught? That could lead investigators back to the others. Unless they were sure that person didn't know enough to rat them out, wouldn't sell prematurely, or wouldn't sell it at all. Maybe their cut was the actual painting."

Outside, the lone waybeacon appeared out of the gloom, a brief ray of hope, and then disappeared just as quickly behind him.

The cat came back and sat on the console, grooming itself. From this angle, Fergus could see the tiny implants in its ears for pressure adjustment; Olson had at least done that much for the beast, before abandoning it. "You know who really likes paintings, Mister Feefs?" Fergus asked. "People who work in museums."

That gave him a few more questions to ask Zacker, later when all this was over and resolved.

When he reached Wyville-Thompson, his hands were shaking again, and the restlessness in his core felt ready to spill over. Patting his pocket, he found the reassuring shape of the vial from Psych and reminded himself he was going to get sleep soon. *Once I get some sleep, I can focus. Once I focus for a bit, I can get this job done and get out of the Deep for good.*

Dr. Creek was waiting for him with a hand-truck to help unload. "I see you managed to get Dr. Manne up from Below without throttling him," she said. "You might get hate mail from his colleagues back on Haudernelle, though, who thought they were rid of him for a few more months."

Fergus nodded. "He was a man of many grievances."

"His precious sabbatical. As if it's our fault, here on Wy-Tee. We tried to help him out anyway, but he made it clear we weren't good enough for him."

"He also went on at length about equipment he lost."

"Oh, right. Some piece-of-shit robot of his, hadn't even been approved for use down here, much less cleared for going into the geothermal zone, and it goes belly-up only a few kilometers out of the station." She laughed. "I suppose we should have helped him go retrieve it, but he'd really antagonized everyone by then, you know?"

"And yet he seemed like such a sweet guy," Fergus said. He helped unload the last of the crates. "I guess you just never know about people."

Creek shrugged. "Assume the best, I always say. Maybe you'll be disappointed a lot, but you won't miss anyone good. Speaking of, it's almost dinnertime. You want to join us?"

His first instinct was to politely decline, but he was hungry, and here was a chance for more information. *And non-cat company*, he added.

"Sure," he said, "although I'm afraid I can't stay for too long. I've got an appointment with a sleeping pill before my next run in the morning."

"That's not uncommon down here," Creek said as she led him into the station. "One of my senior researchers had to go back Above within a week because even with drugs, she couldn't stop the nightmares. It gets to people. Just not always the ones you wish it would, since here we are still stuck with all the assholes over at Ballard for our only close neighbors. Too bad; I liked Dr. Ng and most of her crew."

"What happened to her?" Fergus asked. Ng was the director who had vanished and was one of the three coincidental disappearances that Zacker had insisted they not ignore.

"Resigned," Creek said. "There'd been some turnover in staff, and she absolutely loathed her new assistant director, this guy named Owens. Real stick in the mud, from what she had to say of him. She loved her work. But her team had already started bailing, and even the few that have stayed down here might as well not have, for all the contact we have with any of them. But here, let me introduce you to my people!"

He followed her into a small dining hall, clean and utilitarian but not impersonally so, and found three other people sitting at the table with coffee while the kitchenette machines behind them counted down the last few minutes until dinner. Two—a man and a woman—were human, but the third was decidedly not. Fergus must have slowed down, because Dr. Creek stopped in her tracks and looked alarm. "Oh!" she said. "I should have warned you. This is Estimable Sennox. They're . . ."

"A Ponkian," Fergus said. He bowed to the alien, who resembled an anthropomorphic, pale lavender, giant wrinkled squash. "I am honored."

The Ponkian waved its thin arms in delight. "Ah! You know our people, mmmm? This is an unexpected experience!"

"I've met only one of your people before, and only briefly, but we had a fascinating conversation," Fergus said.

Sennox laughed, a gurgling, happy sound. "It is mmmm a pleasure now!" it said, and got to its feet and returned the bow.

"Uh . . ." Dr. Creek seemed momentarily nonplussed, then smiled and gestured to the other two scientists, who were watching in amusement. "This is Drs. Stone and Estaja. We have two other members of our team, but they're tag-teaming a forty-eight-hour monitoring run, so one's stuck in control and the other is no doubt snoring up a storm. Everyone, this is MacInnis, the new pilot who replaced Olson."

"Hi," Fergus said, and gave an awkward wave.

"You picked the right night to drop in," Dr. Stone said, just as the kitchenette beeped behind her. "Pizza night."

"Pizza?!" Fergus exclaimed. "Really?"

Dr. Creek snorted. "So, you're not at all surprised there's an alien on our team, but pizza throws you?"

"It's been a long time since I've had pizza," Fergus said.

"It's not the system's greatest by a long shot," Stone warned. "But it's edible. Sit."

Fergus sat, with more excitement than he'd expected. "Best pizza I ever had off-Earth was in this little hole-in-the-wall place, didn't even have a *roof*, on Fadsji—"

"Fadsji?" Estaja said. "The Triworlds? That's way the hell out there."

"Yeah, I've traveled a bit," Fergus said. It had been Theo who'd told him about the place, during one of his brief stays at the Shipyard between jobs.

"I guess so!" Estaja said. "At any rate, at least you're not scared of Sennox here. Too many people find aliens terrifying."

"Depends on the aliens," Fergus said. His back itched between his shoulder blades and he wondered how far away from his thoughts the Asiig would ever truly be. "And I've met plenty of terrifying humans."

Dr. Creek pulled the pizza out of the foodmaker and set it in the center of the table as Estaja picked up a stack of plates and handed them out as if he were dealing cards. The pizza was barely thicker than the liner it sat on, the sauce an anemic drizzle, and there was no way the cheese had ever been within a light-year of a dairy product, but his heart still leapt at the sight of it. For just a moment, Fergus felt himself relaxing, taking down his guard, feeling at home, and hated himself for having to break the spell. "And speaking of scary people, what's with that Pace guy?" Fergus said.

Dr. Creek sighed as she slid a slice of pizza onto her plate. "Came in with Owens, the Ballard number two I told you about before. About a year or so ago; I don't know. Most of the others bailed as soon as their current research contracts ran out, after Dr. Ng had resigned and left."

Resigned and went missing, Fergus thought.

"I haven't even met more than one or two of the new people," Dr. Creek continued. "That's how tight they are over there. No socializing, no collegial exchange of info, nothing."

"I met one in Depot," Estaja said, shaking his head as he finished off a length of brittle crust. "Didn't even tell me his name, the jerk."

"Dr. Manne would have fit right in," Stone said.

"Cryovolcanologists all have big egos and short attention spans," Estaja said. He smiled. "Sedimentary geologists and oceanographers, though . . . we're made of steadier stuff."

Dr. Creek snorted. "Sure. Anyway, we're glad you've got our run, and you and us both should be glad you're not going there," she said. "It's hard enough down here without dealing with assholes."

"Pizza helps too," Fergus said, finishing his third slice and feeling more than a little guilty for it. "Sorry I ate more than my share."

"We can throw another one in the cooker," Creek said. "Estaja's mother sends us a crate of them every couple of months."

Estaja flushed.

The Ponkian had been rolling its slice of pizza up into a thin, sloppy tube, and finally popped the whole thing down its wide, toothless mouth. "Before I forget, mmmm," it said. "I would like to know: what did you mmmm talk about with my planet-fellow?"

"Of all things, the tuba," Fergus said.

"Aaaaaah!" the Ponkian declared, waving its arms wildly, and the other scientists looked both entertained and slightly alarmed. *Did the alien just get* larger? Fergus wondered.

"Oh, fer . . . Ponkians and their damned obsession with horns. If I catch you ordering one on the lab accounts, Sennox . . ." Dr. Creek started to warn, then glared at Fergus. "Or you, if you haul it here."

Fergus held up his hands. "I just bring the crates. I don't look in them."

"You have no idea how much misery an enthusiastic Ponkian with a wind instrument can inflict."

"There was that saxophone," Estaja said sadly.

"I flushed it out an airlock after two weeks," Stone added.

"Once, my friend Mais—" Fergus started to say. *Maison*, he didn't finish. *Maison, who automated a trumpet with tiny robot legs to sneak around the Shipyard and blast "Reveille" whenever it got within a meter of someone.*

It struck him, as sudden as a blow, that here he was sitting around a table of would-be friends, one alien in their midst, just like hanging out at the Shipyard. Were his friends that easily replaced and forgotten? Whatever hell they were going through— if they were even still *alive*—would they like to know he was late coming to rescue them because he was enjoying a dinner party?

He set down the last few bites of his pizza slice, appetite having thoroughly abandoned him in the moment, feeling vaguely sick at himself. "I should get going," he said. "Sorry to cut out on you early. The pizza and company has been great, but you know how Transit Control is about schedules."

He stood up, and Dr. Creek stuffed her last bit of crust in her mouth and followed him down to the docking bay. "You'll come back again?" she asked.

"I expect so," Fergus said.

"Well, I hope you do. There's few enough people here worth talking to. Take care of yourself, MacInnis."

"I will do my best, ma'am," Fergus said. He tipped an imaginary hat to her, then climbed back into *Hexanchus* and sealed it up for departure, hoping his sudden hasty exit hadn't come across as rude rather than just pressed for time.

And he hadn't been lying about having a date with a sleeping pill, earlier. He needed sleep more than anything, but he still had a task or two to do before he could give in. He undocked *Hexanchus* from the substation and took it southwest, descending. A purple curved line appeared on the edge of his nav display, growing larger as he approached. He had his sensors up to maximum, but so far, nothing.

"*Hexanchus*, this is Transit Control." His comm lit up with the incoming signal, a human voice again: Jake. "You are out of normal routes."

"Hello, Control," Fergus said. "I'm just looking for an out-of-the-way place to park and nap for a bit. Didn't want to be in a travel lane."

"Understood, *Hexanchus*. You are about three kilometers from a restricted area."

"Not planning on going that far," Fergus said. "Just looking for a spot that looks comfortable."

There was a silence, then: "Uh. Does any spot down there look different from any other?"

"Not really, no," Fergus said. He smiled as a tiny dot appeared faintly on his sensors, just ahead and a little down. "And this spot seems just as good or bad as the rest. Shutting down engines, but I'll have my comms on if you need me."

Transit Control's instruments should show him slowing to a gradual stop. He wondered if they'd suggest he back off farther from the geothermal zone or insist he ascend up from the floor, but the response came and seemed not to care. "Got it, *Hexanchus*. Sleep well."

"Thanks, Control," Fergus said.

He parked *Hexanchus* right over where the blip on his sensors was. Switching the console view over to the underside, he unfolded the manipulator arms from *Hexanchus*'s belly and sent them stretching out toward the indistinct blob just barely visible in the manipulators' spotlights.

It was about the right size and shape to be Dr. Manne's lost science remote. As soon as he got a firm grip on it, he pulled it in through the smaller of the hauler's two external-access bays. He wasn't at all sure yet what good it might do him, or if it was even fixable, but like the pod, it was one more possible resource.

Speaking of which. One of the helm auxiliary screens lit up with an incoming signal, a pair of goggles dangling from where he'd wired them into it. Even though the screen showed nothing but darkness, the recue bot he'd left clinging to the side of *Loxodon* back in dock at Depot was now in range and transmitting. Or, more accurately, *Hexanchus* was now in range of it—*Loxodon* was at Ballard.

Fergus considered the risks. He knew too little about Ballard's security and what sort of security sensors his rescue bot might trip, but then he wasn't going to know anything more by doing nothing with it. And on a day with gifted pizza, maybe his luck was on his side right now. He took the chance and turned the rescue bot's infrared lights on. Sure enough, he could make out the hull of Pace's hauler directly beneath it.

"Okay, my little hitchhiking friend, this is our stop," he said. He picked up the small remote control and steered the bot along *Loxodon*'s hull until he encountered the sheer vertical wall where the hauler ended and Ballard Substation began. All this time creeping around in the dark, it was almost surreal to be there in person. Sort of, anyway.

It took him a few minutes to maneuver the rescue bot over and then have it scuttle around the curve of the station, where it would be out of sight from *Loxodon*'s bridge. The bot was down to less than a third power, so he found one of the many maintenance-bot recharge portals on the station exterior and plugged it in.

The urge to keep exploring Ballard's exterior, or to get out of his seat and go down to the bay to look at Manne's remote, was not quite as strong as the yawn that threatened to pop his jaw right off his face. He felt jittery, electrified, and knew he was hitting red in his own danger-to-self-o-meter.

Well, you told Control you were here to take a nap. So, take a nap, dammit!

Friendly faces and mediocre but gloriously real pizza were only going to carry him so far before the despair crowded back in. He took the pill bottle out of his pocket and tipped one into his hand. It was small, pale pink, innocuous-looking. *I haven't ever taken a sleeping pill before,* he thought. *What if I take it and I lose control of the electricity? I could kill myself.*

But he was going to need to sleep eventually, and at least here, no one was in danger except him and the cat. He looked over at Mister Feefs. "Sorry," he said. He used his fingernails to carefully snap the pill in two. Before he could change his mind, he tossed down one half and dropped the other back into the bottle.

He made sure the autopilot systems were set to keep *Hexanchus* at its current position, then slunk off the bridge to the tiny pilot compartment just outside the door, with its narrow bunk and even smaller bathroom facilities. He splashed a little water on his face, then lay down and pulled the scratchy blanket up over his shoulders.

So tired, he thought. He wondered how long it would take the pill to kick in, if even with only a half-dose he'd still be spared dreams. Belatedly, he realized that the cat had joined him, and while trying to puzzle out why he hadn't noticed right away, he dropped off.

There was an alarm.

He had to fight his way up from the murk enough to recognize what he was hearing, then panic drove him the rest of the way toward waking as his mind screamed, *Fire alarm! Psych told me there would be a fire alarm!*

He fell off the cot, and the impact with the cold floor gave his brain enough of a shock to pull its metaphorical pants back on and register that it wasn't a fire alarm but simply the proximity detector on repeat warning.

His heart was still thudding madly in his chest. Rubbing at his face, which felt thick and numb, he stumbled back onto the bridge, Mister Feefs nowhere to be seen in the din. It took him a moment to focus enough to switch on the sensor screens, just as something bumped into *Hexanchus* hard enough to nearly knock him out of his seat again.

". . . Hell," he muttered. Something pod-sized, cylindrical, and oblong had hit the rear cargo section of his hauler. He canceled the alarm and ran a damage report, but everything came back still green. Whatever it was, it hadn't been moving very fast.

Garbage? he wondered. If so, maybe he ought to pull it onboard for disposal; having random junk out there in the Deep was dangerous. He brought up *Hexanchus*'s engines, backed a dozen meters off from the object, then ascended to where he could position the manipulators over it. As he reached for it, the object suddenly began moving again, slowly continuing forward.

What the hell? Fergus thought. He ran a thermal scan, and sure enough, the object—a blocky metal cylinder with a few fins that looked both haphazard and fragile—was warm, at least relative to the surrounding water. The realization that someone could be down there in the crushing deep in a homemade sub made his skin crawl, and tiny sparks rippled along his arms like electric goosebumps.

He turned *Hexanchus* around and began to follow it. It seemed unaware of his presence, and he wondered if it was something remotely operated, and if so, by whom? The object veered to the right, then stopped. Then it started up again and stopped. *Hexanchus* was moving as slow as it could, but eventually, he just stopped dead in the water and watched the thing on his sensors.

In the glare of *Hexanchus*'s forward lights, he could see one of the side fins was bent where it had struck his hauler. *Someone is in there,* he realized, *and they're trying to figure out why they aren't going in a straight line.*

It seemed obvious that the craft was barely seaworthy. It also became clear, as he watched, that there was something larger wrong with it than the bent fin. It had stopped again, and his sensors picked up the sounds of banging inside just as a stream of bubbles jetted out of the side and up. "Shit," Fergus muttered. Whoever was in there was lucky that the entire thing hadn't imploded.

Fergus pulled *Hexanchus* up above it again, spotlights on, and used the manipulators to grasp it as carefully and gently as he could; once he was sure he could move it without damaging it further, he flooded the emergency bay on the hauler's underside and pulled the ship in.

He had the cargo arms secure it, then he sealed the bay and flushed the water back out. Putting *Hexanchus* back on autopilot to keep its position, he left the cabin, climbed down the access tube into the hauler's belly, and after triple-checking that the emergency bay really was sealed and empty of water—all too aware of how foggy his mind still was from the half-pill—he opened the hatch and went in.

The object sitting in his bay was such a ramshackle mess that calling it a ship was gross flattery. It was an old tank—fuel or air, it was hard to say—with crudely welded-on fins and an engine on the back that looked more like it had come out of a ceiling fan. As he stared at it in a mix of admiration and horror, the poor bent fin creaked, and the engine spun up again.

Whoever was inside didn't know they still weren't in the water. He walked over to it, careful to avoid the fins, and when he found a clear space of hull, knocked on it.

The engine spun down.

He waited another half-minute, then knocked again. Muffled and faint, but distinct, he heard a voice inside say, "Crap!"

Fergus walked around it and eventually found a makeshift hatch on the nose of the makeshift sub. There was a handle, but it didn't budge. He knocked again, then cupped his hands around his mouth and placed them up against the hull. "Hello!" he shouted.

There was a long pause, then the sound of metal squealing inside. The hatch opened a crack, tentatively, then was flung open. Sitting inside, hunched over with her knees against her chest and a tiny light-globe in one hand, was an older Japanese woman with graying hair in a long ponytail. She met Fergus's gaze and let out a long, audible sigh. "Fine," she said. "You caught me."

"Caught you?" Fergus asked. "Um . . ."

She held out a hand. "At least help me get out of this thing before you take me back," she said. "I stopped being able to feel my legs about seven hours ago."

He took her hand and helped her out, far from steady himself.

She grimaced, her legs wobbling beneath her, and sat on the floor. She looked up at him. "Are you drunk?" she asked.

"No, but you woke me up mid-sleeping-pill," Fergus said. "By ramming your . . . um. Ship? Into mine."

"You're not one of the Ballard people?"

"No," he said. He blinked, suddenly feeling more awake. "You don't happen to be Dr. Minobe Ishiko, by chance?"

"You don't know?" she asked. "Who are you?"

"Name's F—Duncan. Duncan MacInnis," he said. "I'm a new pilot."

"You're *not* from Ballard!" she said. She grinned. "So, I got away?"

"That depends on your definition of *away*, since you're still here in the Deep." He sat down beside her, gazing at her makeshift sub. "You made that? You're a ship engineer, right?"

"Yeah. Took me months."

"How were you navigating?"

"Math," she said. "I did my calculations by hand on velopaper before leaving, because they had all the computers monitored."

"You vanished on the way to Coralla," he said.

"They grabbed me at the shuttle transfer on Coralla's moon," she said. "Dragged me down here, put me to work, then ran out of things for me to do about two months ago. Kept me locked in my room until I told them if they were gonna do that, they might as well just kill me, or I'd do it myself. They must have decided I might still have use, because they let me putter around in the fabrication bay, and after a while, when I made no more trouble, they stopped watching me closely. So, I turned an old ballast tank into a sub and blew half the contents of the bay out into the ocean with me when I went."

"You're the one who modified the Madarchs for space," he said.

"Only under the gun. And I mean that literally. I don't know what they did with them, but I assume nothing good."

Fergus knew, at least partially. He'd found one of the missing scientists. Surely, his friends had to be here too. "On Ballard . . . were there other prisoners?" The question was out before he could think how much he could regret asking it, if the answer wasn't the one he wanted.

"Yes, although we were not allowed to interact," Dr. Minobe said. "I only saw others being escorted past me in the hall or as we took turns in the cafeteria. I think I was the third or fourth brought down Below, as Dr. Keeling was there before me. Poor man; I did not get to speak with him, but he was not looking well the last few times I saw him."

"Keeling? He's from IESAI, right?"

The engineer glanced at him sharply. "That seems another odd bit of trivia for a pilot to know," she said. "And you knew who I am, and about the Madarchs. You caught me too tired to think clearly, but you seem very well informed. Do you have an explanation, or are you really from Ballard and just lying to me to find out how I got away?"

"I'm sorry," he said. "I came down here looking for friends of mine who went missing. A little research turned up others that had disappeared. Your name, Keeling's, and a few more."

"And your friends?"

"Six of them. Noura is an expert in mindsystems and she's mostly very serious, and she's a little taller than you with curly black hair and medium-brown skin and she usually has work goggles on her head because she forgets they're there," Fergus said, knowing most of that wasn't helpful, but how could he describe his friends without talking about who they were? The words just kept tumbling out in hope and desperation. "LaChelle is taller than Noura and bigger and she's dark-skinned with this beautiful fountain of braids and she's an artist and designer and is a terrible introvert but if you get her talking she's *brilliant*. Theo is a big man, tall as me, all muscles and older, with a bright blue beard and he laughs like a volcano waking up and he builds and runs all the robots, and Kelsie is young and almost as pale as me with short blond hair who is always happy and she builds engines and races things. And then there's Maison who's second-gen displaced Indo-Caribbean from the moon—Earth's moon, I mean—and he has no hair at all and he's thin as a pencil and always up to something and he's a pain in the ass but a genius at almost everything he touches, and Ignatio is a two-and-a-half-meter-tall fuzzy green alien that looks like a crazed pompom on top of stilts and understands jumpspace physics."

"You're making all that up," Dr. Minobe said, staring at him intently.

Fergus's heart fell, like the entire ocean had suddenly, finally, poured in to drown him. *It's over,* he thought. *They're not here. Or they were here, and they're gone. The burnt bodies in the freighter . . .*

"So, you haven't seen them," he said, because he had to say something and he had so very little left.

She studied him a moment longer. "You genuinely aren't from Ballard, are you?"

"No," he said. He managed to stumble back to his feet, feeling sick to his stomach, and held out a hand to help her up again. "I'm sorry. Thank you for telling me. I think it means my friends are dead. I'll do my best to help you get out of here, if I can. I just . . . I had hoped, you know? Hoped for something other than this news."

She took his hand and stood. "You said your name is MacInnis?" she asked.

"Yeah."

When she didn't let go of his hand, he turned, and she caught his gaze and held it, scrutinizing him. Then she looked down at her feet, an unreadable expression on her face. "You understand that I had to know the truth?" she said. "I needed to see your reaction, just now, to see if you were deceiving me, because you know way too much for this to be coincidence. But I believe you now that you're not one of the people who held us."

"What do you mean?" he asked.

"Your friends *are* there, although I never spoke to them. I lied," she said.

He stared at her, frozen between the two truths. "They're really there?"

"They're really there," she said. "Really really. The green out-worlder had five legs, right?"

"Ignatio. Yes, five," he said. "So, they're alive?"

"They were when I last saw them, which was two days ago now. Unhappy, scared, and somewhat worse for the wear, but alive."

"Thank you," he said. He wiped at his eyes, cursing the sleeping pill for the unwelcome tears welling there, doing all he could not to sit down on the floor and weep, and decided he shouldn't try to hug her. "Thank you."

"You're welcome, and I'm sorry again," she said. "Now please tell me you've got a bathroom on this tub."

Chapter 13

D r. Minobe came onto the bridge and sat down in the empty copilot seat. "There is a cat in your bathroom," she said.

"Yeah. That's Mister Feefs. He wasn't doing anything . . . smelly? I hope?"

"No, he was sleeping in the washbasin," she said. "This is not what I would consider an appropriate environment to bring pets into."

"Me neither. Another pilot abandoned him down here," Fergus said. "He's not bad company, and he's surprisingly useful."

"There aren't mice, surely?" she asked.

"No, bugs," he said, pleased with his own cleverness. Then he frowned. "When you came down, did they make you swallow a big capsule? Like, for a drug test?"

"No," she said. "They *abducted* me. What would they do, chastise me and return me home if I was a user? Why do you ask?"

"Because the drug-test capsule Transit Authority gave me turned out to be a tracking beacon," he said. He pulled his pack out of his locker and dug through until he found the confuddler. "How long ago did you leave Ballard? Will they be looking for you yet?"

"I have no idea what time it is; we weren't allowed handpads except when working under supervision," she said. "But it was dinnertime, so around eighteen hundred. I told them I wasn't feeling well, and they left me alone. The station had a twenty-two-hundred curfew, so if they didn't come check on me—they usually didn't, because I never made trouble—I got about a four-hour head start."

Fergus glanced at the time on the console. *I got about six hours' sleep,* he thought. *That's not bad.* Now that Dr. Minobe's news was beginning to sink in, he felt better than he had since before he'd crammed himself aboard *Constance* to go to Earth.

"So, they've been looking for you for at least three hours," he said, switching the confuddler over to signal detection. "How obvious was it how you left and which way you went?"

"Very, and not very," she said. "It was a low-signal craft for multiple reasons."

SIGNAL DETECTED, the confuddler beeped.

"Hell," Fergus said. "You've got a bug too. Different frequency than the pilots' are, though. If you didn't swallow something, it must be somewhere else on you. Clothing?"

She took the confuddler out of his hand. "I'll be back," she said, and disappeared again into *Hexanchus*'s bathroom. When she returned, her face was grim. She set the confuddler down next to Fergus. "Subdermal," she said, and tapped the back of her shoulder. "How did you deal with yours?"

"My first one malfunctioned, so they gave me another. I got suspicious and fed it to the cat instead," Fergus said.

"Ah," she said. "Do you know what the range is?"

"No," Fergus said, "but I expect if we took you to a substation to remove it—leaving aside questions of who to trust and what questions they'd ask—we'd be caught. We're only about twenty kilometers from Wyville-Thompson right now. Yours is a different frequency that might not be actively monitored there, but if the Bastards Above are complicit in this, they'll have someone out looking for you near all the substations soon enough."

"As much as your ship seems like a solid-enough vessel, I'd

rather not sit in it until they come to get me. I was willing to jeopardize my life to get out of that place."

"Yeah, I'd do the same to be free," Fergus said.

Dr. Minobe smiled. "It isn't just about being free. It is also about not being *bored*."

"It's too bad you didn't get to actually talk to my friends. I suspect you would have gotten along," Fergus said.

He only saw one way out of the trap of her homing signal, but he hated it. Hated hated *hated* it. He wanted to be his normal Fergus self, without this temptation always dangled in front of him, using him as much as he used it.

"You are making a face," she said.

"Just thinking," he said, which was true. "Uh, show me the spot again?"

She felt around the back of her shoulder, then stopped with her index finger on one spot. "There," she said. "Now that I know to look for it, I can feel the tiny bump."

"May I see?" he asked.

She shrugged. "As you wish."

He put his finger where hers had been, and sure enough, he could feel the tiny spark of it below her skin, with whatever sense for electricity that seemed to have come with his gift from the Asiig. "Uh, look that way?" he said, and pointed toward the back of the bridge cabin.

"What?" She turned her head to look and he zapped the bug. "OW!"

Dr. Minobe jumped and spun around, hands raised in fists.

Fergus pointed the confuddler at her. *NO SIGNAL*, it said.

"What did you do?" she demanded.

"I deactivated the bug."

"How?"

"I'd rather not say."

Faster than he could dodge, she struck out with one hand, flipping him neatly to the floor. Seconds later, she was kneeling on his back with him in a headlock. "You will need to explain," she said.

"I don't— Ow!" he said as she ground her knee into his back. "I had a little device—"

"Your hands were empty," she said.

"It was very small—"

She knelt harder. "Bloody hell!" he swore.

"You may wish to consider that we don't have infinite time before someone catches up to me, and I am very intent on not being taken back into captivity."

"Fine!" Fergus said. He went limp, giving up. "I can make weird electricity."

"What do you mean?"

Fergus held his free hand out and threw a spark from finger to thumb.

Dr. Minobe stood up, then leaned over him intently. "Do that again," she commanded. He did, feeling like a circus freak on exhibition, bouncing the spark back and forth a couple of times before he let it go. "Fascinating! A mechanical enhancement of some kind?"

"Biological, and not of my own free will," he said. He rolled over onto his back, and she offered him a hand to get up. He ignored it and stumbled to his feet on his own.

"I apologize for manhandling you," she said. "You do understand that I needed an answer, yes?"

"Yeah, but do you understand how dangerous it is for anyone to know my secret? How long would it take one of you scientists to decide you need an answer enough to cut me open?"

"Some of us, merely an eyeblink. I am not one of them. This is alien in origin?"

"The Asiig."

She nodded thoughtfully. "They are not known for letting the people they take go again."

"That's because the few people they do usually aren't entirely the same anymore." Fergus got back in his seat, his face still flushed with embarrassment and no small amount of anger. "I risked everything to come here to try to save my fiends; don't make saving you be my biggest mistake."

She took the other seat again. "I'll keep your secret," she said. "I would even if I didn't owe you my life. You came out of hiding to attempt the rescue of your friends?"

"It's more complicated than that, but yes," he said. "But you said it earlier: we don't have much time. How attached are you to your homemade sub?"

"I would like to never see it again, if possible."

"Then I suggest we scuttle it right here. If they've been tracking your signal, they know it's gone. If they find the remains of your sub, with luck they will conclude you're dead and stop searching."

"That is sensible and easily done," she said. She stood up. "I can set my engine to overload, but it will give us only about eight minutes to get away. Is that enough time for you to remove it from your ship and get us a safe distance?"

"What's a safe distance?"

"At least a quarter kilometer, half being better."

"I think I can manage that," he said. "I'll need to stay here at the helm, though. And you'll have to get back up out of there fast so I can flood the hold."

She nodded. "Anything to get out of here," she said. "There are comms down there?"

"Outside the hold in the control booth. Let me know as soon as you're clear."

"I will," she said, and left the cabin.

Fergus waited. Whatever drowsiness had lingered from the sleeping pill was gone now. He had the engines powered up and everything ready to move when she sent the word, a single "Go."

He sealed the emergency bay, pumped the air out and water in, until he could open the doors and flush the sub out. He kept the manipulators ready in case it got stuck, but he could see on the monitor as it slid out into the dark like a metallic turd from *Hexanchus*'s aft doors.

It had barely cleared the underside when he accelerated forward, the open doors momentarily causing drag until they sealed again.

The implosion of Dr. Minobe's sub was a tiny blip on his screen, an air pocket rising quickly up and away.

Fergus set course for Depot. It was what Control would expect of him, and it would give him a couple of hours to think about what to do next, including how he was going to get Dr. Minobe out of the Deep.

"Mr. MacInnis," she called, from the upper cargo hold.

He set autopilot and got out of his chair, grateful for a chance to stretch his legs. Adrenaline still buzzed through his body. Dr. Minobe was standing beside the tarp-covered pod he'd stolen earlier. "I fear I spooked your cat. He ran underneath," she said. "Is that what I think it is?"

"A pod."

"No doubt it is tracked, with all the other vessels in service?"

"Probably not. I stole it from the repair depot. It's been offline for years, at a guess."

"It's broken?" she said. She had perked up noticeably at this.

"Heating systems. I was hoping everything else on it was sound, but I haven't had time yet to run diagnostics."

"You have tools?" she said.

"Some." He dragged out a crate of tools he'd scavenged from the repair facility and set it next to the pod. "You bored already?"

"I'm exhausted and starving and aching all over," she said. "But I anticipate being bored when all that is taken care of, and I did want a chance to take one of these apart someday. This could be useful. You have passenger facilities on board, yes?"

"Yeah, let me show you," he said. The passenger compartment was just behind the bridge cabin. "There's several bunks and a locker for stowing things but not much else."

"It is more than enough for now," she said.

She sat down wearily on the bunk, her shoulders slumping.

"Not to keep you up any longer, but before you sleep . . ." Fergus took a breath. He'd had held the question in long enough, it felt ready to explode. "I'm sorry, but what the hell is going on in Ballard? Who are they? What are they doing there? Why any of this?!"

"Building a secret weapon, of course. As villains, they seemed unconcerned about the cliché," she said. "For the who, I can't say specifically, except that the group functions in the manner of a military unit."

"We were guessing mercenaries."

"Probably so," she said. "I am not an expert in such things. I imagine it is hard to find places and people to develop secret weapons without being seen and without being spied upon, and having unconsenting labor from prominent people in their fields further adds to one's risk of discovery. Enceladus is a rare opportunity for concealment within our solar system."

"Yeah, but there are plenty of better places outside, like in the Sfazili Barrens."

"Resources have to be moved farther and less easily, though," Dr. Minobe said. "Also, the Barrens are dangerous. Here, the only thing they have to defend against is one rogue hauler pilot with a stray cat and, I suppose, possible discovery by a lackadaisical Alliance. It is safe. And once they have finished building their weapon, they need only fly it out of here and then all trace of its origin is gone. And, I expect, anyone who was unfortunate enough to be pressed to work on it will likewise vanish."

"And the weapon is a ship, obviously."

"Well, obviously," she said. "But also not so obviously. I was only given small portions of the design parameters at first, not that there was anyone I could tell, but eventually, they had me working on a lot of the basic frame design. The design changed substantially, probably not long after your friends arrived. When I am better rested, I will do my best to recreate what I know, but not now. I'm correct in assuming that, for the time being, your hauler is the safest place for me?"

"*Hexanchus*, yes, I think so," Fergus said.

"Then you can bring me supplies and food, and I'll fix your pod while you figure out how we escape," she said. "I would like to leave this ocean and this moon as soon as a feasible plan can be made."

"The pod would definitely help," Fergus said. "Also, I salvaged a damaged deep-crawl science remote."

Dr. Minobe's face lit up with joy.

————

He returned to Vine with only Mister Feefs in tow but a yammering, jostling crowd of thoughts and emotions for company.

The revelation that his friends were there and alive was almost enough to drown out all else, even consideration of what he could do with that information. The inadvertent rescue of Dr. Minobe was a boon in many ways beyond that; if she could render the stolen pod seaworthy again, that might be exactly what he needed to get in and out of Ballard safely.

When he'd docked at Depot, he'd asked Dr. Minobe if she wanted him to relocate her somewhere else in the Deep far away from Herschel Bore so she could call the Alliance, but she was having none of that, and he was relieved enough that he didn't press. They both agreed the time to call authorities was when everyone was safely above the ice. "If I call the Alliance, the Ballard kidnappers will know I'm not dead and that I must have had help," she'd said. "Who knows what they might do to cover their tracks?"

And that had been exactly his own fear, but the fact that she had been the one to voice it made him feel less guilty for asking her—for now, anyway—to remain below and trust him.

The sleep he'd gotten had done him more good than he had expected, but if he wasn't fully awake, he was when he walked around the corner of the corridor to his apartment and found Pace leaning against the wall next to his apartment. There were three empty bottles on the floor beside him, a third in his hand. It was obvious that Pace had urinated on his door. "You," Pace growled, shifting himself upright.

Fergus set the cat carrier down and slid it with his foot farther away. "What do you want?"

"I want to know what you know," Pace said.

Not *I knew you snuck a rescue bot onto my hauler to spy on Ballard.* Fergus didn't think Pace was the sort to hold back on direct accusations if he had them. He knew it was a bad idea to antagonize the man, but Fergus had also never liked being bullied, and the energy he wanted to spend tearing Ballard apart inch by inch to reach his friends had to go somewhere.

"Any particular subject?" he replied. "History of the Mars colonies? Napoleon the First, Second, or Third? How to get a drunken shit-stain out of your shorts after you stupidly pick a fight with an irate Scot outside his own home?"

Pace face reddened. He was barefoot, and Fergus wondered how many more bottles lay on the path from wherever Pace's apartment was.

"I told you to stay out of my way," Pace said.

"I think any smart man would agree you're in *mine*," Fergus answered.

Whatever Pace saw in his face was enough to stop the head-long rush Fergus was sure had been about to happen, but not enough for the man to back down. "Wy-Tee," Pace growled. "What the fuck were you doing there?"

"Supply run, you bloody idiot. It's on the roster."

"You were out there hours longer than you needed to be."

"So what? I took a nap before heading back. You got a problem with that?"

"Did you see anything?"

"Yeah. Three whales, five mermaids having a singalong, and the wreck of the *Titanic*. Also a lot of fucking dark water," Fergus said. "I can point that last out to you, next time I see some."

"I don't like you at all, you piece of shit," Pace said.

"Aww, that breaks my heart," Fergus said. "You got a problem with me, why don't you just step forward and we'll deal with it right here and now, man to drunk?"

Pace strode forward until he was nose to nose with Fergus. It wasn't often, since he'd left Earth, that Fergus had run into people the same height as him, but right now, the man could be three meters tall and Fergus wouldn't care. He was ready for this fight.

"Oh, no, you two, don't!" someone yelled.

Fergus didn't move or take his eyes off Pace, but Pace glanced over Fergus's shoulder and backed off a half-step. "Sul," Pace said. "This isn't your business."

"Fuck yes, it is," Sul said. She pointed. "Did you *pee* on this man's door? Are you a fucking three-year-old?"

Pace glared at Fergus and didn't answer.

Sul gestured to Fergus. "You," she said. "Go inside, get some sleep. We're all going to be in tight rotation until Cufa Bore gets a few replacement drivers, and if you two idiots put each other in the hospital, the Bastards Above will fine you both so deep into the ground, you'll think the entire ice sheet collapsed on top of you."

Fergus picked up his cat carrier and stepped around Pace to his apartment door. "This isn't over," Pace snarled.

"So you keep telling me," Fergus said.

Sul sighed loudly. "It's over for now," she said. "Pace, go back to your apartment. I can't do anything to stop you drinking yourself into stupidity every night, but do it at home and stay there or for your own good, I'll report you to the Bastards Above. *Again.*"

Under Sul's glare, Fergus went into his apartment. He watched as Pace also turned and slunk away before he shut the door and locked it. He let the cat out, then sat on the edge of his bed as it rubbed up against his leg.

Did you see anything? Pace had asked. Pace had to have been asking about Dr. Minobe's escape, which made him a part of whatever was happening at Ballard. Which made sense, given that he was their exclusive driver. Half of him regretted not taking Pace down right in the hall, whether or not Sul was watching. The other half of him was already trying to figure out how he could use Pace again to get what he wanted.

First things first, though. He took the pager disk from his pocket and thought for a moment about what to say. "Me here," he recorded. "Positive indications, though no direct sightings yet. I'm going in soon. I know you already know this, Zacker, but don't trust anyone involved with that report. Someone is feeding the Alliance a lot of bad data, and for all we know, it's an internal source, so until they catch on you, can't consider them safe, either. See if you can keep Effie in local custody. You're a hero, right? Use that."

He hit Send and looked at the pager in his hand a moment longer, his link to the outside world. He wished he could talk directly to someone, Effie or Zacker or anybody, but he was alone on the wrong side of the ice.

Mercifully, given the time—*nearly dawn* was a deeply unfair description down there—his next run was not until afternoon. He took the vial out of his pocket, the two and a half pills left rattling around in its bottom, and regarded it. His friends were alive, he had an ally down there, he had the beginnings of a plan. He set the vial down on the small table beside his bed, undressed, and turned off the light.

————

Five hours later, he sat on the edge of his bed, rubbing his eyes. The nightmares had been fewer, more subdued; it was the bursts of ideas—some good, some surrealistic nonsense, some both— that had kept bringing him awake. He stood up slowly, stretched, and spotted the faint glow of the pager disk and grabbed for it.

"Zacker here," the message started, the voice distinct despite strong background noise. "The Hold police are refusing to transfer Effie, because even they can tell it smells like bullshit. I took your suggestion and I did a freakin' news interview about how it's a frame and the attack was an attempt to silence her on what really happened at the Shipyard. Lots of drama and intrigue and rumor of murder, just like news outlets everywhere feed off of, and that seems to have made Taflough—the Alliance liaison here—back off on the transfer, no doubt waiting for everyone to lose interest. It was a good idea, as much as I hate you for putting me in the damned limelight. We've bought a little time but not a lot. Captain Santiago lets me have unmonitored visits with Effie a few hours every day, and I passed your message along, and apparently now I have to give you a kiss for her and there is just no fucking way ever. Thanks to your fund donation, I've holed up in a cheap rent-a-room, but I figure that's already bugged so hard, they'll be able to hear my goddamned hair growing. Recording this on moving public transport, where it'd be harder to pick up and isolate."

That, Fergus thought, *explains the background din.* There were clearly significant advantages, in terms of avoiding law enforcement, of having spent a career inside of it.

"Also, despite being in jail and accused of murder and not knowing if her friends are dead or not, Effie is concerned about you and how you're *feeling*, trapped underwater and all. Can't help but add: hey, are you in *over your head*? *Drowning* in your work? You get it? Or am I too *deep* for you? Right. So, still waiting on news from you. Don't make us hold our breaths."

The message ended at that.

What irritation he felt was offset by finally having an end in sight. He tapped the disk to record. "Me here again. I'm doing *swimmingly* well, thanks for your concern. Another pager disk or two would come in handy, if at all possible. Oh, and if you can—not a priority, with everything else you've got going on—can you get me any additional background info or follow-up that was done with the museum staff and guards, current locations, that kind of stuff? Just following a hunch. Thanks."

Let the man feel guilty for hassling him when Fergus was clearly working on his problem.

Hitting Send as he walked over to the kitchenette, he slipped the pager into his pocket and beeped up fresh coffee. He leaned against the counter, sipping in steam. *So,* he thought, *all I need to do is go to Ballard and break my friends out. To get there, I have to get*

*past Pace, who is a homicidal, paranoid drunk. Once there, there will be
an unknown quantity of opposition, probably heavily armed, certainly
dangerous mercenaries. Then I need to get my friends away again and
out of Below. I have a hauler, a stolen pod, an emergency drone out of
range, a broken robot, an eminent Japanese engineer who kicked my ass,
and a bugged cat to work with. Easy, right?*

His gaze fell on his pack, with the bulky shape of the muti-
lated fruit bowl still evident within. If only the plates were larger
or he had more of them.

"Right, Fergus," he said. "Easy."

The same woman at the Barton Deep General Store answered
his call and didn't seem at all fazed at how much he wanted to
spend, or care at all about the model-building hobby he'd spent
half an hour beforehand working out the finer plausible details
of in case she pressed.

"Microfab unit and feeder supply bins might take a while,"
she told him.

"You think a week?"

She shrugged.

"You think I can get expedited shipping?" Fergus asked.
"You know, for an extra fee."

"Probably," she said, and she was happy to collect that fee, so
he disconnected, feeling both broke and optimistic.

His apartment reminded him that he was scheduled for a re-
supply run up the Bore in an hour and a half, and that Transit
Control had added an evening run to Miklukho-Maklai after.
No passengers, which was good news for his stowaway.

Finishing his coffee, Fergus fed the cat, put pants on, and
then took the lift down into the public spaces of Vine Substation
and wandered casually over to the public call booths. Three of
the eight booths were occupied, about normal for this time of
day. He slipped into an open one on the far end, shut the door,

and looked around. It was a small but comfortable space; there was a wide, cushioned armchair, a console on a swinging arm beside it, and a larger screen set into the wall with a camera above it.

He stood and let himself feel the faint tracings of signal throughout the room, found nothing unexpected. Good enough. He tapped the screen of his confuddler to wake it up and set what he wanted it to do. After that, it was the work of a few minutes to take the panel off the room's comm system without making undue noise, then a few more to wire his confuddler in without permanently damaging anything and close the panel back up.

One of the confuddler's primary functions was the ability to map—if it didn't hit security too difficult or risky to sneak through, of course—whatever network it was plugged into. Usually, it then used that information to distribute whatever activity Fergus wanted across a multitude of false presence points to hide its actual location and obscure its objective, but for starters, he was more interested in just a passive map of nodes and a quick, non-intrusive vulnerability assessment.

Fergus opened a connection from his handpad to the confuddler to watch it do its magic. As he expected from the initial assessment, security varied. Engineering and life-support systems for the substation itself were tightly walled off, financial systems only slightly less so, but the node framework between civilian apartments had only a feeble and long-outdated encryption schema between an open network and the world.

Fergus pulled up some of his favorite cracking routines on his handpad and began to cycle them against the civilian systems, swiping to adjust the algorithms as he watched their logs fly past. It only took him four attempts to get in, and then Pace's apartment system was perfectly happy to share its entire trove of logs—all comm traffic, door logs, even lighting requests. That would make for some boring but possibly useful reading later, for sure.

Finished there, he lounged sideways in the chair, one leg over the arm, and tried to think if there was anything else he should go after while he had the connection. *Olson's logs, if they're still there?* he thought.

His handpad had gone to sleep, so he tapped it awake and opened the node directory again, and was just sliding through the list looking for Olson's apartment systems when the lights in the call booth went out.

The outage was brief, just enough that he didn't fully get started in on panic before it was over and the lights were back on, and the call booth comm system restarted.

He checked his confuddler, which had lost its connection into the system and was trying to reestablish it. *NODE NET-WORK ARCHITECTURE OPAQUE*, it flashed, and gave up. In a burst of paranoia, no doubt fueled by the unspent panic of moments before, he disconnected the confuddler and shut it down. At least he had the Pace logs, if nothing else.

Fergus told himself the power failure hadn't been caused by him, certainly not anything he caused through his own particular alien gift, which was currently peacefully asleep. Nor had he felt any sense of something electrical happening anywhere in the vicinity of the call booths. Two men were farther down the row as he exited, commiserating on their own dropped calls.

The same thing had happened as he was shopping in the General Store for cat food, which the storekeeper had told him had also happened elsewhere. *In places you weren't in at the time,* Fergus told himself, *so, nothing to do with you.*

He was almost willing to believe that.

He stopped at Monty's stand for a bagel, and as the man was handing it over, he asked, "What do you think that power outage was? Something similar happened the other day while I was in Barton, too."

Monty shrugged. "The Bastards Above tinkering with systems again to see if they can save a few cred, probably," he said. "They're always messing with shit, as long as it doesn't involve fixing anything actually broken. Once a few years back, some new guy thought it would be great to turn off our heat and air at night, on the theory that we'd all be asleep, under blankets, and breathing less. Within twenty minutes, there was frost starting to form on the station walls. Took another hour for someone up there to track down what he shut off and turn it on again, and by then everyone was very, very cold. Guy was lucky there was a whole lotta ice between him and us. You want a second bagel?"

Fergus realized the one that moments earlier had been hot in his hands was now entirely vanished. "Please," he said, somewhat embarrassed. "Can you wrap it so it lasts more than thirty seconds?"

Monty grinned and did so, and Fergus reflected that that was the only reason the bagel survived intact to be handed over to Dr. Minobe after he'd gone back to collect the cat and took a pod over to Depot.

They sat on the floor of the cargo space, and she ate while he poured coffee for them both and Mister Feefs wandered around between them. "About a week, maybe ten days of work," she said, nodding toward the stolen pod behind them. "Assuming I can get parts I might need and I don't spend the entire time hiding in the cupboards because someone's on board."

Fergus figured they had a pretty vast stockpile of parts to pick from, and said so. Dr. Minobe nodded. "The robot got hit with some sort of directed EMP pulse, which means someone killed it on purpose. Your unwitting friend, Dr. Manne, is lucky they didn't decide to put a stop to his ambitions more personally."

"Yeah," Fergus said. He finished his coffee and checked the time. "I've got to start my run up the Bore in about fifteen minutes, but as long as the pod is under a tarp, no one should be curious or care. No passengers this trip. Ten days, huh?"

"Ten days until we're ready to do whatever it is we're going to do," she affirmed. "More or less. I hope less. If much longer than that, I'm going to kick someone's ass."

"Speaking of which . . . you had the element of surprise on your side after I zapped you, but I've lost a lot of fights in my life and none quite so elegantly fast as that."

"Mujūryokudo," she said. "It's a zero-gravity martial art and contemplative practice, though I have found it useful in many environments. You ever train?"

"Bar fights in New Glasgow," he said.

She laughed. "That is its own formidable school. Well, I am no sensei, and we have limited time, but if you'd like, I can try to teach you what I can of the basics. And in return, you will bring me bagels while they are still warm from now on."

Fergus stood up. "Deal," he said. "But first, I gotta go to work."

Chapter 14

And did he work. Down both driver and hauler after *Alopias*, the Bastards Above kept him so busy, he almost didn't have time to sleep, badly or otherwise, for a full week. Dr. Minobe kept him company when she needed a break from working in the hold, swapping out time in the copilot seat with the cat. Fergus suspected that being stuck inside *Hexanchus* had made her more social than she was naturally inclined to be, though the Deep itself didn't seem to bother her particularly. She explained, during one of their rambling chats, that she'd grown up on submarines with archaeological explorer parents, doing careful coastal reconnaissance and salvage of submerged historical sites, and it had only been a half-step sideways from there into vessel engineering.

As she's promised, the pod in *Hexanchus*'s gut had been brought back to life—after a few midnight raids of the repair facility, and a handful of hastily printed parts once his microfab unit was delivered by the general store—and she had Dr. Manne's robot fully disassembled in carefully arranged piles he'd learned not to disturb. She was deeply irritable every time a run dictated she put things away and go into hiding in the passenger cabin— or, the one time he had an actual passenger, the pod itself. She was careful not to take it out on him directly, though he did notice she was a lot more likely to flip him harder during their occasional Mu lessons; it was clear that they were each working toward mutual freedom in their own best way.

Still, at least in those lessons, he felt like he was learning something; mostly, she wanted to talk about how to breathe and stand and walk and sit, all things he felt he already had a lifetime of expertise in, but none of which she seemed to think he had the slightest clue how to do.

The rest of the time, to relieve the crushing boredom, they swapped stories, either sitting on the cargo bay floor together, or over the comms as he drove them back and forth, up and down, through the endless dark. She talked about her childhood, engineering problems, and all the different kinds of ships she'd sailed or, conversely, would refuse under any circumstances to set foot aboard. Fergus talked about the Shipyard and his friends, at first as if memories could summon them back to safety, and then because it made them feel closer.

". . . so, anyway, I owed Theo and Noura one for not spacing my clumsy, amateur ass when they caught me trying to break into the Shipyard over that cabbage nonsense," Fergus was saying, halfway to Wyville-Thompson to deliver some new instrumentation. "I agreed to follow Endicott—that was their original jumpspace guy, before Ignatio came along—and find out why he kept disappearing off to Europa and coming back completely credless and covered in bruises. They asked me because they didn't want him to know they were spying on him, and he'd never met me; he was off-station the one time I'd been there. If it was something personal and legit, they instructed me to not tell them what he was up to, but they were worried he was being blackmailed or was into something dangerous. And you know what it was?"

"I can't begin to guess," Dr. Minobe said. She was sitting on the bridge in the copilot seat, Mister Feefs in her lap, working on his handpad to recreate the designs she'd worked on while in Ballard.

"Zero-gravity naked slime wrestling. One hell of a midlife crisis," Fergus said. "He'd apparently always fantasized about being a slime star, and even though he kept losing every bout—and was wagering stupid cred on himself each time—the man would get hauled out of the chamber with the happiest grin on his face I've ever seen. Eventually, he took his cut from the Shipyard, and as far as I know, he's still out there in the circuits, doing his thing."

"And did you tell your friends what he was doing?"

"Not at first, no. I reported that he wasn't in trouble of any kind and that there was no vulnerability to the Shipyard through his activities, and while I wouldn't say that satisfied their curiosity, it satisfied what they'd asked of me and they didn't push for more out of respect for Endicott. And that was when I decided I liked them, because I could tell they were dying to know but their principles meant more to them."

"But you did tell them eventually."

"Not directly," Fergus said. "About three years later, after Endicott had already left for good to pursue his passion, I might have taken Theo out to Europa for his fiftieth birthday and a show. When a man with a beard that big blows beer out his nose in surprise, it's a spectacular thing."

"Theo is the robotics expert, yes?" she asked.

"And automated systems, yeah," he answered. "Pretty much the others figure out what to make, and he figures out how to make it. If it flies in space, they can do it."

"I specialize in oceans and atmosphere," Dr. Minobe said. "It was clear early on that they wanted far more, particularly once the Madarch redesign was out of the way. About the time your friends arrived, the bits and pieces put in front of me changed significantly. The shift in design, here"—she held up the handpad and flipped the screen back and forth between two sketches—"seemed more based around aesthetics. I'd accuse my kidnappers of trying to commit sculpture if I didn't full well know that they aren't the type of people to whom art holds any value."

The rough outline looked very much like the more abstract work of Fergus's friend LaChelle, who had come to ship design by way of the Boston sculpture scene, and he said as much.

Dr. Minobe shrugged. "That is as may be. Why, though? It looks like no ship I've ever seen, human or otherwise."

"Maybe that's the *why* right there. If you saw this, would you know what it was, or where it had come from?"

"No," she said. She stared at her drawings a little longer, biting thoughtfully on her lower lip, then slunk off with his handpad back to the cargo bay again without another word.

Twice, Fergus caught news conferences out of Titan with a stoically furious Zacker expounding on possible corruption at the local Alliance base and their ham-handed attempts to remove Effie from the hardworking and honest local police. Not in so many words, but reaction shots showed the Hold population increasingly angry on behalf of their suddenly beloved police, and Effie seemed to be momentarily staying put.

After the second one, on a long run out to Wyville-Thompson while Dr. Minobe slept, he got a message from Zacker on the pager.

"Yeah, me," the message said. "How do you know if you did the right thing for the right reasons?"

Was he talking about the conferences? His obsession with the Met robbery? Or something else? There was no way to tell.

"Truth is, you don't always know," Fergus replied, not having any better answer and not wanting to lie. "But you go with your gut and be your best in that time and place, and if you get it wrong, you try to do better next time. If you get the chance."

He wondered if he was a hypocrite as he sent the message on its slow trek up the ice. Nearly two decades of his conscience digging at him over stealing Gavin's motorcycle, and he still hadn't done better by his cousin. Sure, stolen paintings, missing motorcycle, and so forth with the excuses, but really, if he hadn't waited so long, maybe it would be done and settled and over and none of this would be happening now.

The irony of having avoided dealing with that guilt for so long while it was easily within his reach to fix it, and to now feel so compelled toward seeking closure while unable to do a damned thing about it, did not escape him at all.

When *Hexanchus* docked at Wyville-Thompson at last, he woke Dr. Minobe before he offloaded the instruments. Then he killed time—pleasantly, for which he was both grateful and guilty—with Dr. Creek and her team over another hot meal. Dr. Minobe took over the helm while he was gone and used their proximity to Hitchhiker to continue exploring Ballard's exterior.

"It would make most sense to build their ship above the station, where it would be protected from pressure swells from below, but it's not there," she lamented when he got back with a small bag of still-warm leftovers. "I'm sending the rescue bot around to the back, and we can get a look next time we're out this way."

He handed her the bag and she opened it, then closed her eyes for a long moment. "Lasagna?" she said at last. "Can we come back tomorrow?"

"Four days," he said. "Scheduled condensed-waste drum pickup."

She looked in the bag again and sighed.

On an overnight run to Mik-Mak the next day, he stared for hours at the data he'd pulled from the Vine systems, and Pace's apartment in particular, finding the patterns there and teasing out a rudimentary understanding of the man's habits. Another message from Zacker came in that the man must've sent not long after getting Fergus's last reply.

"Glib fucking non-answer," Zacker said without preamble. "But what if there is no better? What if your best you is still wrong? What if people deserved more than you?"

Then welcome to my life, Fergus thought. A dozen equally snarky and unhelpful answers sprang to mind, but in the end, the best he could muster was a sincere, "You okay?"

There was no reply to that, and honestly, he didn't expect one.

On day eight—well toward midnight—the hauler roster finally gave him the opening he wanted. It was time to make Pace useful again.

Fergus watched the board, waiting as the rest of the drivers, one by one, checked in at Depot as done for the day. *Loxodon* was last, on one of its few overnights home from Ballard, with a big haul scheduled for late morning the next day. And if Fergus guessed right, there would shortly be an illegal delivery to Pace's apartment.

Fergus walked down to the public call booths, plugged in his confuddler, and crashed Vine's security grid. It would hard-reboot and give him about seven minutes before it was back online. He hurried back out into the main concourse, spotted the courier from Beebe Substation—still wearing his Abyss apron, poor fool—and fell in casually ahead of him. Following people without making them suspicious was a lot easier if you let them follow you instead.

The courier was barely more than a kid, maybe the same age Fergus was when he fled Scotland for Mars. He knew better than to judge on just that; the people his age who were loudest in decrying the next generation were typically those who'd failed at their own lives more than most.

Fergus headed for the lift, and the courier got in a few moments later, setting his bag down on the floor and pulling out his handpad. Fergus hit the button for the main residential level and asked, "What floor?"

"Same," the carrier said without looking up.

As Fergus moved his hand away from the panel, he let a small spark jump from his fingertips to it. The lights in the lift flickered and the kid looked up sharply.

The electricity felt contrite, controlled, but he knew better than to fully trust it would stay that way. As soon as his friends were rescued and safely home, he intended to be done with it for good. But first he had to get out of there, and he had reconciled himself—for the moment, anyway—to using whatever means he had to.

"Been doing this for a couple of days now," Fergus said, and shrugged. "You know how it is getting stuff fixed down here."

"Yeah," the courier said. His eyes drifted back to his handpad.

Fergus let his hand slip to the side of the lift car and gave it a massive jolt that took the lights out and brought the car to a sudden halt. "Whoa!" he shouted, stumbling, and the courier fell against him. *Sorry*, Fergus thought, and zapped him.

He lowered the kid to the floor and quickly opened the top of the handle-bag, drew out one of the bottles of Abyss moonshine, popped the seal off, and dropped two sleeping pills into it. The seal went back on easily, and he closed up the bag, then leaned down and shook the courier. "Kid!" he said. "Wake up! You okay? You got shocked!"

". . . . Shit," the courier said, and sat up. "What the hell happened?"

"Big spark from the panel. I wouldn't touch it," Fergus said. The lights on the car flickered back on, and after a moment, the car started moving again.

"I hate this place," the courier said. He got to his feet, briefly checked his bag, then picked it up as the doors opened.

"Me too," Fergus said. "Me too."

The kid walked, a little unsteadily, down the hall, and Fergus watched him for a moment, feeling like the worst asshole in the solar system, before heading back to his own apartment.

Seven minutes on the dot.

But he slept, for once, easily and soundly.

―――――

Excitement woke Fergus early. He showered, dressed, and sat in the chair watching the cargo roster update on his screen. One by one the rest of the ships headed out—*Triaenodon* to Carson, *Bythae* on another run to Cufa Bore, *Triakis* up the Bore. The entry for *Loxodon* sat unchanged except for eventually shifting colors to orange, then to red as it grew increasingly past its scheduled departure without budging. *Hexanchus* wasn't scheduled for a run until midafternoon to take supplies from Depot over to Barton. He sipped his coffee, scratched Mister Feefs on the top of his head, and waited.

He had just about convinced himself his plan had failed when his console chimed. It was Dornett himself calling, his face flushed and angry. "MacInnis," he said. "I need you to take a run."

"I'm on the schedule for this aft—"

"This is a critical supply run, over to Ballard Substation."

"Pace—"

"Mr. Pace is experiencing some employee performance difficulties," Dornett said. "Get over to Depot and pick up his load, and get it moved. Don't linger at Ballard, but don't let them get in your face, either. They don't get to pick and choose their own personal pilots like they run Transit, no matter what they seem to think."

Dornett disconnected without saying anything more.

"Well, okay," Fergus said. He picked up Mister Feefs and settled him in his crate, shouldered his pack, and picked up the packages he'd lined up near the door for just this day. "Let's go do as the Bastards ordered."

The cargo crews had already started loading up *Hexanchus* when he got there, while Dr. Minobe had managed as usual to keep herself scarce and unseen in the interior. He dodged around the cargo workers to load his own stuff, and if anyone wondered why he had so many bags of stuff, no one asked. Two did stop to say hello to Mister Feefs.

"Better get moving," the crew manager said as soon as the last stack of crates was loaded in and secured. "Bastards Above got a big ol' stick up on this one, and you're not going to get much of a warm reception at the far end. Deep gets to everyone different, and scientists are always weird to start with, you know?"

Fergus laughed, thought briefly of the kindness of Dr. Creek and her crew, and felt bad for it. "When they are, they really are, that's for sure," he said. He sealed *Hexanchus*'s cargo bay, waved to the crew, and cycled himself into his hauler and took his seat on the bridge.

It felt like a significant victory to finally point himself southeast toward the exclusion zone and Ballard. He opened his comm channel. "Transit Control, this is *Hexanchus* now departing for Ballard Substation."

"Thank you for your timely departure, *Hexanchus*," Reva responded. "Please advise Transit Control when you're an hour out from the exclusion zone for a mandatory first-visit refresher on protocols. Transit out."

Dr. Minobe sat down in the empty seat beside him. "We are on our way to Ballard?" she asked.

"We are."

"Good. I don't like that I'm going back there, but if it's necessary to getting us out, then the sooner, the better. I'm ready to be done with this whole place," she said.

"Me too," Fergus said. "Speaking of *ready*, how's the pod?"

"Fine," she said. "It's an older model, so it's not as fast, but it's solidly built. A fair tradeoff."

"Great. We've got a little over five hours until Ballard. Plenty of time to show you what you need."

"For what?"

"I've got a new project for you," Fergus said. "Admit it: you were getting bored again."

In fact, he'd run dry on two of his raw materials just the night before, comfortably over the minimum number of plates he figured he needed, and only a dozen or so shy of his "comfortable margin." He had to hope it would do, because another set of feeder supply bins would take time, and cred he didn't have in his current name.

As soon as they were underway, he unbuckled his safety tether and went back to a stack of boxes he'd brought on board, a few every day, and stacked up on the bridge out of the way and out of sight of visitors and cargo crew. Opening one box, he pulled out thick foam squares.

"I looked at those," Dr. Minobe said. "Nanofoam grids with some interesting tech embedded in the surface, but no logics and no purpose I could discern. Although it is true this is not my field."

"It's also only one part," Fergus said. "I had to scan and fab everything in separate pieces, because otherwise, it was too complex for the microfab unit I bought to replicate." He opened another box. In it were squares of the same size, almost perfectly transparent. He fitted one atop the foam square and pressed gently, and they snapped together.

"I still don't know what it is," Dr. Minobe said.

"A homemade version of this," Fergus said. He dragged his pack closer and pulled out the fruit bowl, with its scale armor still attached. In another bag he found the power source, plugged it in, and then stood facing Dr. Minobe with the shield in front of him.

Fergus turned it on and watched her face go from humoring him to genuinely surprised. The look she gave him made up for many nights of disrupted sleep as he'd swapped out material feeds.

"With these, we can make the pod—" he started to say.

"Shush," Minobe interrupted. She stood up and walked back and forth in front of Fergus, slowly, then behind him. "That is interesting," she finally said, just as the power block beeped and shut off.

She took the fruit bowl out of his hands, studying it, then set it gently down on her seat. Picking up a pair of boxes, she headed out toward the cargo area. "If we cover the exter—" Fergus tried again, but she just chuckled and kept walking.

"I get it, driver," she said. "Now go watch where we're going so we don't crash into anything."

She came back two long, boring hours later.

"Surprisingly hard on the hands," she said, flexing her fingers. "It will not be done before we reach Ballard, not even by half."

"Yeah, I figured," Fergus said. "Also, we'll have to test the drain on the pod's power supply before we take it too far from the hauler."

"Then your plan is?"

"Right now, I see this as our initial exploratory foray. My plan is to get into Ballard and see as much of what's going on in there as I can, confirm the layout, that kind of thing." He'd managed to find a holo map of the substation a few days before, and Dr. Minobe had pointed out the areas she knew, and more than one place where the map appeared incorrect. "If there's a way to alert my friends that I'm out here without getting caught, I will, but I don't expect to get that chance."

"The only reason I ever met Pace is because he seems to partially reside on the station," Dr. Minobe said. "I was never allowed off the residential and lab levels, much less anywhere near the dock. You are unlikely to see your friends."

"Yeah, I know," Fergus said.

"And if you did, might they not, in their surprise, give you away?"

He hung his head. "Yeah," he said again.

"So, best not to seek them out at all but find another way to contact them," she said.

"I could hide a message in the supplies?"

Dr. Minobe shook her head. "They check everything. There were several custom parts I needed to make the Madarch waterbuses spaceworthy, and it took multiple tries to get ones they hadn't destroyed making sure nothing was hidden inside. It was very frustrating and slowed my work down considerably."

"Which reminds me, we should check through the supplies to see if there's anything there that might provide more information about their project."

"I've already looked through, at least quickly," Dr. Minobe said. "It is largely food and fuel-cell boosters, cleaning supplies, items of that sort. A few sealed tubs with alien writing on it, packed in with the food."

"Maybe food for Ignatio?" Fergus said. "The stuff ey eat . . . don't open those onboard the hauler or we'll die of the stench before the air handlers can possibly clear it— Ah! That's it!"

Fergus jumped out of his seat, forgot about this safety tether in his excitement, and barely avoided slamming himself face-first into the floor. He fumbled to release it even as Dr. Minobe took the copilot seat again. "Ah?" she asked.

"Ignatio has an incredibly keen sense of smell. I don't have to leave an actual message; I just have to touch everything a lot. Then ey'll know I'm out here and coming for them! I never thought I'd say this, but I regret taking a shower this morning."

Dr. Minobe laughed. "You're male. Go run around in the cargo deck for ten minutes. Problem solved." She wrinkled her nose. "Maybe five is enough."

"Thanks a lot," Fergus grumbled halfheartedly. It was actually a good suggestion. He went down to the cargo bay. It was tightly packed enough that running would have been difficult even if most of the available floor space hadn't been covered with spread-out scale parts and empty thermopaste tubes. Hooking his fingers onto the doorframe above the hatch to the ladder tube, he did fifty chin-ups, which was more than enough to break a sweat. *In Earth's gravity, I'd have been lucky to make eight,* he thought.

He walked over to the stack of supplies and unlocked crates until he found one full of cheap mealpacks. "Dr. Minobe!" he called up on the hauler comms. "How do you feel about Instafud Syntho-Steak and Peaty-Pasta?"

"If I never see either again, it'll be too soon," she replied. "I would commit murder to never have to eat another one."

"That's exactly what I wanted to know," he answered. He took the mealpacks out and stacked them on the floor, and regarded them for a few moments, contemplating the best way to go about things, then finally shook his head, stripped off his shirt, picked up a pair of the mealpacks, and stuck one under each armpit. "Ewwwwurrgh," he said, wiggling his arms vigorously back and forth for a few moments before putting the packs back in the box and grabbing another pair. "This seems deeply, morally wrong," he said.

"You have not tasted them," Dr. Minobe answered. "And hurry it up; we're nearing the hour mark from the zone, and I would like to be safely napping in the passenger compartment when you make that check-in call."

"Any chance we'll be able to drop Manne's science remote out on our way in to Ballard?" he asked. "It could be useful."

"Most of its instrumentation has been fried beyond repair, and the left crawl motors are shot. Even if it could be useful, it would only tell us what is sees in a hundred-meter circle."

"Can we drop it in one place along the route and just have it report passing traffic? Even that might be handy."

"Probably. This means no nap, I can see already," Dr. Minobe grumbled back over the comms. "Get up here so I can see what I can do."

He went up the ladder and took his seat just as she got out of hers. She left the cabin, holding her nose between pinched fingers, and he stared out at the blank, undifferentiated darkness ahead of them.

For the first time in a long time, he felt like he was finally going somewhere.

At the appointed time, he hit the comms. "Transit Control, this is *Hexanchus*. I am approximately one hour from the perimeter of the exclusion zone, and I was instructed to call in."

"*Hexanchus*, this is Transit Control," Jake responded. "Keep your approach level, and do not descend below the median travel zone. If you contact the ocean floor, the penalties will be severe."

"How severe?"

"We will lock you in a room with all the angry scientists, *Hexanchus*."

"Okay, then," Fergus said, "very severe. Noted, Control."

"If you experience any sort of mechanical issue with your hauler that could conceivably cause it to head down out of the median zone, contact us right away. We deal with any such problems as emergencies as a matter of protocol, and it does not reflect on your apparent bravery or virility to have called in a potentially compromising issue, even if turns out to be trivial in nature."

"Okay. Anything else?"

"Yeah, off the official line now. Ballard's current residents are not the friendliest, to put it mildly, and they are very good at finding things to file official complaints about. I recommend keeping conversation to a minimum and not lingering there any longer than necessary. Unload and get out."

"Thanks, Control, and understood. Just want to be done and home again." *Home somewhere far away from here,* Fergus thought.

"Right. Transit Control out." The link terminated.

Dr. Minobe came back onto the bridge, grease on her hands. "The science remote is as fixed as I am capable of," she said. "It's not going anywhere or telling us much, but it should be able to report anyone passing by, roughly how large and fast, how deep, and which direction. The remote originally had a constantly emitting homing signal broadcasting on a standard channel, which is probably how they found it to blast it. Instead, I set it to a higher channel typically reserved for weather satellites. More than that is outside my expertise. This should reduce the likelihood that the remote will be detected, though there will continue to be risk. It's in the portside rear airlock."

Fergus tapped the airlock release. "Not anymore," he said.

"Wait! We still need to manually activate the comms first! Now it's no good at all!"

Fergus stared at her, eyes wide, hand frozen above the button he'd just pressed.

She stared back at him, then made a face as she shook her head and snorted. "That was less funny and satisfying than I had hoped." She glanced at the clock. "Now I will go catch what is left of that nap I wanted."

He let her go, his heart still racing from the scare that he'd wasted the robot. *I would give almost anything,* he thought, *to see a grudge match between her and Maison.*

Scratch that, he amended. He'd already seen the Shipyard almost destroyed once; wishing a Minobe-Maison feud on it would do it in for sure.

The darkness ahead continued to be dark. As if sensing his slow slip into hypnotic dread, Mister Feefs came out of nowhere and jumped up onto his lap. "Soon," he told the cat. "I suppose I've got to take you out of here with me too, don't I?"

The cat seemed indifferent as long as he kept scratching his head.

A red light appeared on the console, warning that he'd finally crossed into the restricted area. Forty minutes later, he saw the first glimmer of light from Ballard Substation, and his pulse quickened again. *Remember, you're just going in to scout it out, see what you can see, meet some people, get as many impressions as you can. This is still the planning phase, not the action phase.*

The light became two, then many, then close enough that he could make out the guidance beacons for the main dock. He took several deep breaths, then opened a channel. "Ballard Substation, this is *Hexanchus* coming in to dock," he called. "I am approximately fifteen minutes out."

"*Hexanchus,* this is Ballard Control," someone answered immediately. "Follow the beacons, do not deviate from standard approach, and dock where indicated. Remain aboard your ship until further instructions. Ballard out."

The link went dead.

So, yes, he thought, *definitely not friendly.*

He hit the comms for the passenger compartment. "We're heading in," he said. "If they want to inspect the ship—"

"They won't find me," she said. "Oh, and I took your handpad so I could do some finer roaming-around with Hitchhiker. Let me know when we're clear again."

"Okay and will do," he said.

Ballard didn't look any different from Wyville-Thompson, but he shivered involuntarily as he pulled *Hexanchus* up against the substation and locked in.

If something feels off, it's because you're talking yourself into feeling that way, he told himself. *This is what you do: you find things. You found your friends; now you need to find a way to get them out of here. Focus.*

Ten minutes after docking, his comms lit up again. "*Hexanchus,* this is Ballard. You are cleared to begin unloading."

"Thank you, Ballard," he answered. He shut down *Hexanchus*'s engines and unbuckled from his seat, heading down to the cargo bay with a million butterflies and more than a few angry bees in the pit of his stomach. There was no sign of Dr. Minobe, and the floor had been cleaned of any traces of her work with the stealth plates and the pod. Remembering how strictly by-the-book the voice on Ballard's comms had been, Fergus slipped on his Transit uniform and brushed the dust and wrinkles from it. Checking himself in his reflection in one of the xglass windows, he thought, *It'll do. Scruffy company man. Harmless.*

The seal against Ballard registered as good, and the sensor indicated all green on the far side. Fergus hit the button to open the cargo door and stepped back, waiting as the doors parted.

Three men stood there waiting, two in what were undeniably uniforms except for the utter lack of insignia. The one man in the center was in typical civilian clothes that, despite that, seemed as much if not more a uniform as the others'. All three had perfect military haircuts, and without seeming aware of it, they were all standing at ease.

Okay, then, Fergus thought. *One very professional and serious mercenary group, so noted.*

The middle man in the suit, who looked about Fergus's own age but was both shorter and a lot more solidly built, strode forward and held out a hand. "MacInnis, right?" he asked.

"Yes, sir," Fergus said, and shook. "Just filling in."

"I'm Assistant Director Owens. Welcome to Ballard. I know it's been a long trip out here, and we appreciate you making it. These two men"—he indicated the others—"are Nanho and Carl. They'll show you where to offload your supplies. We've bundled up what waste we couldn't incinerate on-site for transport back up the Bore, and they will show you that as well."

"Thanks," Fergus said.

"Great. If you have any questions, I'm sure they'll be able to answer them for you." Assistant Director Owens nodded his head and then turned and left.

"Ah, okay," Fergus said. "Where should we unload?"

One of the two men pointed to a side bay, managing to do so without moving any part of his body except his arm and, possibly, one eyebrow. "There," he said.

"Okay," Fergus said again. "Thanks."

He peered in the entryway of the cargo space Owens had indicated, which was empty except for a single pallet of crates he assumed was the garbage to go back. No lifter.

Fergus walked back to *Hexanchus*, smiling at the two men as he went past them. They hadn't moved at all, except their eyes. *Right-o*, he thought. *That's not creepy.*

He used *Hexanchus*'s lifter to unload Ballard's supplies out onto the dock, then drove out his handcart and began loading. "Uh, you two want to lend a hand?" he asked.

They stared at him. The one on the right shrugged.

Great. "So, ah, you guys scientists? Cryovolcanologists, right?" he tried again.

No answer.

Keep conversation to a minimum, Control had suggested. As if anything else was even possible.

He finished loading up the handcart and drove it into the side bay. It took four trips to get it all unloaded, then two more to load up the garbage. When he finished, he sat down on the edge of his handcart for a second, wiping the sweat from his brow, and then was startled to realize one of the men had stepped forward and was looming over him. His nametag said *NANHO*.

"It's a long trip back," Nanho said. "You should get going."

"Right. Just catching my breath," he said. They locked eyes for several long moments, and behind the man, his partner Carl cleared his throat meaningfully. Twice.

Fergus stood up. "Okay, I'll just be going now. Thanks for all your help and hospitality. It's been a treat."

He closed and sealed the cargo bay doors, and took his seat at the helm.

"*Hexanchus*, this is Ballard. You are cleared to depart," the message came before he'd even finished buckling his safety harness in. "We will monitor you until you have exited the restricted zone, for your own safety."

. . . and don't let the door hit you on the way out, he thought crossly. He powered up *Hexanchus*'s engines and waited a churlish three minutes before he hit the comms to respond. "Acknowledged, Ballard. *Hexanchus* out."

Disengaging from Ballard's dock, he put the hauler back on course for Depot.

As soon as he crossed back over the line into normal territory, he set the autopilot, grabbed his confuddler and headed back down to the cargo bay to look at the pallet of crap Ballard had dumped on him. He heard the pod door open at the back, and before Dr. Minobe could say anything, he put a finger to his lips. "There, there, Mister Feefs, good kitty," he said, though the cat was still up on the bridge asleep on the copilot chair. "We'll be home soon and then I'll give you some treats."

Dr. Minobe stopped where she was. Fergus took the confuddler and ran it up and down and around the crate. *SIGNAL DETECTED*, it said as he held it along the back near the pallet itself. Straightening up, he pointed at Dr. Minobe, then pointed back at the pod. She took the hint and retreated silently back in, out of sight.

Fergus got down on his hands and knees. A small bob was wedged up under the pallet struts. He reached in and, almost joyfully, fried it with electricity before he pulled it out.

It looked dead, but he knew better than to assume so. He also knew if he just flushed it out of the hauler, it could potentially have enough autonomous movement to track and attach itself, though it didn't seem to be anything fancier than a very standard-model surveillance bob.

He wasn't going to take any chances. He set it on the floor of the bay, rolled the lifter over, and crushed it to pieces. Those he gathered up and dumped into the bay's flash recycler.

"You can come out," he called.

Dr. Minobe emerged again. She had half a sandwich in one hand, which reminded Fergus he hadn't eaten all day. "What was it?" she asked.

"Surveillance bob," he said. "I don't think they were directly suspicious, but why pass up an opportunity."

She nodded. "Did you see anything inside?"

"Assistant Director Owens. He was not very conversational."

"Yes. Owens would want to look you over in person," Dr. Minobe said. She grimaced. "Not a nice man."

"There were also two big guys named Nanho and Carl, who are clearly ex-military."

"Ah. Yeah. They're two of at least six guards I saw during my captivity. I witnessed Carl once beating one of your friends. Little man with no hair. Maison, I think from your descriptions?"

"Yeah," Fergus said. He felt his stomach sour, and he wanted desperately to turn around and go back and fight. "Was he okay?"

"I only saw it in passing as they were shoving me down a corridor back to my lab, but it appeared some of the other guards were already breaking it up."

Fergus frowned, trying not to worry. He couldn't do anything more, any faster, to help his friends. "So," he said, "the Ballard mercenaries seem to be employing a lot of former Alliance soldiers. That would explain the precision of the assault on the Shipyard, and also how they had the contacts to get the Alliance base on Titan pointed at my friends there."

"Ex-Alliance," she said. "That's bad, if so."

"Yeah," Fergus said. "I just wish I'd been able to see more of the interior. Maybe I should've pushed, asked for something to eat, or something."

"Then we might have both been trapped on Ballard again," Dr. Minobe said. "And I do not think they would let me build an escape sub a second time."

"No, I imagine not," Fergus said. "It just feels like I achieved nothing, found no substantive proof, and my chances of getting close enough to Pace to drug him out again—"

His handpad chimed in Dr. Minobe's hand. "Hitchhiker has found something anomalous at the back of the station, exactly opposite the dock you came in on." She held the handpad out to show him.

The skeletal framework of a fab structure floated there, large squared-off ribs loosely enclosing a small fleet of automated construction robots moving in a slow dance around the sharp nose of something entirely new.

Fergus peered at the screen. "That looks consistent with your sketches, at least from what we can see," he said eventually. "It's farther along than I thought. And why all these strange joints along the front edges?" He handed the pad back to Dr. Minobe, pointing out those details.

"As I said, the design specs they gave me were always piece-meal, like different iterations of the same subsection, or like they were building a machine around something they didn't have yet," she said. "Likely your friends were brought in to supply those portions. Certainly, the level of configurability they were interested in was unprecedented in current design in any medium except robotics. I'm trying to move Hitchhiker closer for a fuller look— Crap!"

"What?" Fergus asked.

"Surface sweep. It is probably a routine paranoia after any visitors, but I'm dropping it before it can be detected."

"Dropping our connection?"

"No, dropping Hitchhiker." She scowled. "It is now freefalling from the station. We cannot afford for it to be found—if they catch it, they'll know someone is spying on them from the near vicinity and we'll be dead. With luck, it'll just appear a fleeting scan anomaly; the water here messes with instrumentation enough for frequent false positives, and we did just legitimately stir things up with our arrival and departure."

"I hope so," Fergus said. "Damn, I liked having it around. If we—"

The handpad beeped again. "It hit something," Dr. Minobe said.

"Yeah, the floor," Fergus lamented. "Bye-bye, little friend."

"No, something else, parked on the floor directly below Ballard." She suddenly lit up and handed the pad to Fergus. He glanced at it, swiped a few times to zoom and focus, then did a double-take. The image was grainy, badly focused, and dark, but the giant mushrooms nestled in a perfect row along the backside of a ridge, stretching away from the drone's camera, were unmistakable.

"That's . . ." he started.

Dr. Minobe grinned. "My Madarchs!" she exclaimed.

Chapter 15

A few hours out from Depot, Dr. Minobe declared herself done attaching plates to the pod for the night and, after making Fergus promise to bring her a large breakfast, had gone off to the passenger compartment to sleep. Mister Feefs, ever fickle, followed her.

Fergus was happy to be alone for once, poring over the visual data that Hitchhiker had sent and matching it up to the drawings Dr. Minobe had recreated, trying to divine function from form. When he ran out of conjecture on the mystery ship, he let his mind run in loops and circles and leaps over what he'd learned, what resources he now had, what he was going to do next. It was more than enough distraction from the oppressive dark outside, but also enough distraction that it took several seconds for him to become aware that an alarm was sounding.

"*Hexanchus*, this is Control. Change course immediately. Collision imminent!" Jake shouted over the comms at him.

He had just spotted the gray-green shape of another hauler bearing down on him, all its forward lights off, and turned his ship as sharply to port and down as its tolerances would allow. Somewhere back in the ship he heard something tumbling over, and hoped it wasn't Dr. Minobe. "What the hell, Control?!" he yelled back. "Who is that? They aren't broadcasting ID!"

"*Hexanchus*, you are not clear! *Loxodon* is changing course to intersect."

"Bloody fucking hell," Fergus swore. Pace was *trying* to hit him. He blew a starboard-side ballast tank to give his ship a sharp extra shove downward, and *Loxodon* glided right through the space where he had just been, clipping off one of *Hexanchus*'s rudder fins. His helm controls balked, stiffening up. "Oh, fucking no," he shouted. "Come on! Pace, you utter cowardly arse!"

Loxodon continued on without slowing, disappearing back into the dark.

"*Hexanchus*! MacInnis! Status?"

"I took damage, but I'm okay," Fergus replied, his heart pounding and the bees in his gut stirring. "I'm going to need a tow in. If *Loxodon* comes at me again, I cannot evade."

"*Triakis* is on its way to your position, and Depot has launched a rescue tug to pull you in."

"What the hell was Pace doing?!" he said.

There was a long pause. "*Loxodon* is claiming to have not seen you," the answer came eventually.

"That's bullshit! He turned into me! Pace—"

"This is a disciplinary matter for Transit Authority now, *Hexanchus*. It will be vigorously pursued. In the meantime, we will get you safely back to Depot," Jake said. "Please remember Psych is always available to speak with, if you need to talk it out. Control out."

The comm link closed abruptly. Fergus punched the console and began swearing in earnest.

"What just happened?" Dr. Minobe interrupted from the doorway. "You hit something?"

"Some*one* hit us," Fergus said. "Pace tried to run us down and took out one of our rudders. We're dead in the water 'til someone comes to get us. Didn't have time to give you a warning, sorry."

"I'm okay," she said. "Do you think they will come onboard?"

"They shouldn't need to."

"Are you certain? We don't know who is complicit, after all. I'm not willing to return to captivity."

"Then I'll just have to make sure no one comes on board," he said. "And you need to stay out of sight just in case they do anyway. Nothing has changed. Unless you want out now?"

"No. Or yes, but not yet." She sighed. "I hate this place and I want to be quit of it as soon as I can, but I don't wish to leave anyone behind in their clutches, and I find absolutely untenable the idea of not being able to screw them as thoroughly as I can as I go. It is a tenuous balance."

"Right," he said. He made the best nonchalant smile he could, though he knew it had to come off as badly fake. "So, we're still on for a big breakfast tomorrow? Then we work on our final plan."

The helm console flashed. He could see *Triakis* now off his bow, and knew the rescue tug shouldn't be too far behind. "Our escort is here," Fergus said.

"I'm going back to sleep," she said. "And I want bacon."

"It's all soytex bacon."

"I hate this place," she said, and left.

He had no argument for that, and opened the comms to hail their tow.

————

The tug pushed him expertly into a berth at Depot, and *Triakis* docked beside him. Stoffel and Wenford intercepted him as he left his ship. "About Pace," Stoffel—maybe? It was a good a guess as any—said.

"He's not worth the fight," the putative Wenford added. "You touch him, you just get mean and stupid all over yourself."

"He hit me on purpose," Fergus pointed out.

"He was blackout drunk and missed his shift, and you were the one who took his place. He's resentful like that," Wenford said.

"And irrational like that," Stoffel added.

"Also, he's really dangerous, and we don't want to have to take any more shifts," Wenford said, "much less one to cart your body up out of here."

"Especially since it looks like no one's gonna want to claim it," Stoffel said.

"What?"

"Package waiting in Depot for you, from your ex-wife," Stoffel said.

"No escaping, even down here," Wenford said.

"But I . . ." Fergus started to say *don't have an ex-wife.* But maybe MacInnis did.

Wenford put an arm around him. "*Hex* will be okay. Crew will fix her fine. It's just a dent."

"I don't want anyone inside," he said.

"What, you been crapping on the floor?" Wenford asked.

". . . No!" Fergus said.

"Had a pilot who did that, years ago. Weird fucker," Stoffel said.

"I'm just superstitious," Fergus said. "You know. Pilot thing."

"Sure," Wenford said. "Buy you a drink before you open the package? While you open the package? No one sends us anything."

"You have ex-wives?" Fergus asked.

"Only that one," Wenford and Stoffel each said simultaneously, pointing at each other, then both started laughing as if it was the funniest thing they'd ever heard.

A woman in Transit uniform with tight black braids falling in loops from the crown of her head down past her shoulders walked over, eyebrows raised. "Not you two troublemakers!" she declared. "This isn't your fault, is it?"

"Ms. Nisse!" Stoffel said. "You wound us!"

"Best Transit mechanic," Wenford said, nudging Fergus in the ribs with an elbow. "It's gonna be okay."

"This is MacInnis, our noob," Stoffel said, holding out one hand toward Fergus as if they were showing off a rare auction item. "He's maybe pulled a Ryan on his hauler floor; you don't need to go in there to fix anything, do you?"

"No," she said.

"I, uh, um. I didn't . . ." Fergus tried to protest.

"Right," she said. "We'll just leave it a mystery, okay? I gotta assess the damage and see what parts I need to send up for, because we have shit-all but scrap down here. You housed in Vine?"

"Yeah."

"I'll let you know when I know something."

"How long, do you think?"

"Dunno," she said. "Figure one day, maybe more, maybe less. Less if no one is standing around bothering me."

"Okay. Thanks," Fergus said.

Stoffel doffed an invisible cap at her. "Thanks, Nisse! Let's go fetch your package, MacInnis. I could use some good drama."

"And a drink!" Wenford added, and pushed Fergus toward the door.

The small crate had an Enceladus Transit seal around its perimeter, just translucent enough to see the neatly slit original SolEx seal underneath it. Fergus would have been surprised if Transit Authority hadn't poked through his package, but it still irked him. The credential sheet listed the sender as Feona MacInnis, which of course was no name he knew.

"Open it, open it!" Stoffel said, setting a bottle of some Mik-Mak station brew in front of him.

Fergus picked up the bottle, sniffed it, and set it on the far end of the table. He didn't see much of a way he was going to get out of opening the package in front of Stoffel and Wenford, but then if it had already been pawed through by Transit Authority, it was likely Zacker had succeeded in disguising the contents from casual onlookers. *Or so I hope,* he thought.

He pulled the seal off and slid out the message chit that was wedged in with the shipping verification.

"You rotten bastard, running away like that," came Effie's voice. Zacker must've recorded it on one of his daily visits, taking advantage of the privacy afforded legal advisors. "You didn't think I'd find you, did you? And I hope you didn't think I would keep all your crap just waiting for your precious return. So, here's your goddamned trophies and all your fucking socks you left all over the floor. I burned everything else. Aloha, fucker!"

Wenford managed a sad chuckle, then whacked him on the back. "So it goes sometimes, my friend."

Inside the crate, nestled in a large pile of mismatched socks—some of them burnt—were four trophies. Fergus carefully lifted one out, a cheap statuette of a young man holding a golden disk. DUNCAN MACINNIS: LUNAR THREE FRISBEE CHAMPIONSHIPS 2ND PLACE was inscribed on the plaque on the base.

"Second place," Wenford murmured. "We are very impressed."

"And frisbee, no less! A man without equal, almost," Stoffel added.

"Hey, frisbee is really hard on Earth's moon," Fergus protested. He pulled out the remaining three: another second place, one honorable mention, and one "good sportsman."

Behind him, someone snickered.

They both stood. "We'll leave you to it, MacInnis. I'm sure you want to revel in your memories of glory by yourself," Stoffel said.

"On the matter of glory," Wenford added from the lounge door, "Authority is sending a security team down with Shoo on *Bythae.* Let them deal with Pace. You are that smart, yes?"

"Probably?" Fergus answered.

"Make the effort," Stoffel said, their face suddenly serious, and then they both were gone.

Fergus stuffed the trophies back into the crate, picked it up with Mister Feefs, and took a pod back to Vine. The whole time, he kept looking around nervously for signs of *Loxodon* coming out of nowhere for him, but other than a Madarch waterbus passing him at a respectful distance, he saw no one.

He carried his things back to his apartment, still alert for Pace ambushing him in the halls, more than half-hoping he would. He was wound up so tightly by the time he closed his door behind him and set his things down on the floor of his apartment that his jaw ached.

Mister Feefs, set free, slunk off to the far corners of the apartment. Fergus sat down on the bed and opened the crate from Effie again, removing the trophies and the old socks one by one.

He picked up one of the trophies and easily snapped off the little poly-plastic frisbee in the figure's hand. The casing fell apart in his palm, revealing a tiny pager disk identical to his own. The casing was lined with shielding and the disk dormant. It woke up, and a prerecorded message began to play.

"Sorry about all that, Fergus," Effie's voice said. "We figured the crate would get rifled, but if they were busy feeling sad for you, they'd look less closely at things. I didn't know how many disks to have Zacker to fab for you, but hopefully four will do, because that's all you get. I hope you've found some local help, or at least friends, but either way, we're still out here. Uh, or at least Zacker is. I'm still in Hold Police custody. If it weren't for Luz and Zacker and a lot of media attention, I'd be on ice over at the Alliance Base by now. Meanwhile, Zacker is now best buddies with every Hold officer, so much so you'd think they'd put him on the force. The man might almost be happy, when he forgets he wants to be miserable. Oh, the face he is making at me right now! If looks could kill . . . Let us know more when you can."

Fergus opened one of the unused drawers in his dresser and dumped all the socks in, even the burnt ones.

In the kitchen, he beeped up a late dinner and switched the wall screen from some distant, unattainable, snow-covered mountain peak to Transit Information. Neither *Loxodon* nor *Hexanchus* were listed on the schedule, nor was there any direct mention of the incident between them, but every few seconds, the screen would switch over to assorted reminders about safety, the availability of Psych, and the dangers drink posed to pilots and citizens both.

He hoped *Hexanchus* would be fixed quickly; the idea of sitting around stuck in his room avoiding Pace made him want to go punch something, preferably Pace.

His dinner gone and already forgotten, he lay on his bed and stared up at the ceiling. It was unlikely he would get a chance to drug Pace again, whether or not the man suspected him or even guessed that he'd been drugged at all.

Still, I should get more from Psych, just in case, he thought.

If only he could somehow drug the entire water supply of Ballard, but even if he could get there and get access, there'd be too much distributed filtration and safety checks to bypass.

And regardless of how he got to his friends, how was he going to get them away?

Dr. Minobe had told him, during one of their many discussions of life on Ballard, that Owens had made a point of letting her know that every single one of the substation's escape pods had an explosive embedded in it that could be remotely triggered and had a hundred-kilometer range. It was one reason she'd opted to make her own sub rather than try to steal one.

"Owens did not seem like the type of person to be kidding about something like that," she'd said.

Fergus tabled the escape pods as an option of last resort.

There were the four modified Madarchs nestled down against the floor ridge. According to Dr. Minobe, after the changes she'd had to make to accommodate their new function, each could hold only four people aside from a pilot comfortably, six if they were very close or very desperate. And that was assuming they hadn't been rendered inoperative before being parked down there.

Fergus had no way of knowing how many people on Ballard were not there of their own free will. He had his six friends, and Dr. Minobe knew of at least three other scientists held prisoner— Dr. Keeling, the missing IESAI assistant director, and an elderly couple she'd once spotted during a hallway timing mishap—but if the abductors were keeping people separated based on which part of their secret project they were working on, there could be more. Could there be more than twenty-four? It seemed highly unlikely, but if he left anyone behind, he might be signing off on their deaths, and that was not something he could live with.

He wished he'd had an opportunity to explore more of the station while he'd been there. The number of unknowns was bothering him badly, and that didn't even cover wanting very much to take a more thorough look at the thing parked behind Ballard. Saving the people took absolute top priority, but leaving that curiosity unindulged would rankle for *years*.

Enough information was still all or nearly blank that he was coming to the conclusion that he was going to have to pay Ballard one more, unofficial visit, if he could figure out how.

The clock said he should have gone to bed a long time before. As if there were days and nights, as if nature had any bearing on routine, or even the most tentative reach here. Even when he was off out in deep space, there was always something, no matter how tiny or distant, to ground him to the universe around him, not this all-consuming, endless, smothering void. He wanted, desperately, to see a sunrise and sunset. To see *stars*.

Soon, he thought. *With my friends.*

————

"We have to get to them before the rest of the tunnel collapses," Noura was saying. They were standing around a large hole in the ice, and Theo was standing in a pile of rusty parts constructing a robot by hand to dig down to the people trapped below, as Effie called out important numbers over the cries of people down below. Then Fergus was in the tunnels of the subsurface town himself, looking around for the robot that was supposed to be leading the way, and dark water was rising up around his legs and making it harder and harder to move, until his legs were fixed and frozen and all he could do is shout for help as he slipped under.

Fergus woke, sweating profusely and his heart racing, the cat sprawled across his legs on the bed.

He hadn't been there when the Shipmakers were called in to help with an emergency town collapse on Tethys, only heard the exhausted but triumphant stories not long afterward, and seen the ice crawlers they'd designed and built on the fly (in the fab bay, with robots and machinery) to free the survivors. There hadn't been water, but still, trying to shake off the dream, it seemed like there must have been, because wasn't everyone always, slowly, drowning?

It had been the big news story on SolNet for days, and he had stuck around the Shipyard longer than he'd intended, helping out as his friends struggled to balance the pride that they'd saved forty-nine lives, and the horror that there were twenty they'd never had a chance to reach on time.

The idea that maybe someone had noted that news story and thought, *Hey, these are the people to build our killing machine for us,* made him feel as if his skin radiated fury like a burning star.

Dislodging the cat as gently as he could, he took his shower, packed up Mister Feefs and a large carrysack of food, and took a pod to Barton for his obligatory meeting with Psych. Van Heer offered him the usual drink, then pie, both of which he declined. He left Barton with his anger in check and two more sleeping pills in hand.

From there he went to Depot to see how his hauler was doing. From the docking bay window, he could see robots already attaching a new fin; Nisse sat, slouching, in a chair in front of a portable console, goggles and gloves wired up to the remotes outside. He didn't want to disturb her, so he stood at the window and watched for a while.

"I smell food," Nisse said, interrupting the silence. "Did you bring me breakfast?"

He could hardly pretend the large sack of food was just for himself. "Yeah, if you're hungry," he said. "I figured, since you're fixing my ship . . ."

"As long as it's not a bribe of some sort," she said, sliding the goggles to the back of her head and peeling off the control gloves.

"You caught me. I was hoping I could convince you to build a little deck off the side with a patio umbrella and bar. It's so hard to get a true feel for the Deep, trapped inside meter-thick walls all the time."

She grunted. "There coffee?"

"Yeah." He reached in and pulled out one of the two bottles and handed it over.

"You always bring your cat with you?" she asked, pointing at Mister Feefs' crate.

"He has separation anxiety. His former owner, pilot named Olson, abandoned him down here."

She shook her head. "Right, Olson. Damn sad, that was."

"I thought he left."

"He did," she said. "Ate a pistol when he got topside, right in the orbital dock in front of another pilot. Usually, people don't do that *after* they're free."

"Which other pilot?" Fergus asked. "Wasn't Pace, was it?"

She frowned. "Could've been, I'm not sure."

I bet I know the answer, Fergus thought. "Speaking of which, what's happening with Pace now?"

"Officially, I can't tell you anything, but I'll give you my personal opinion. Off the record," she said. "The Deep gets to people in different ways. You haven't been here that long, but you must feel it. It's made Pace territorial and paranoid, and him and the Ballard people kind of feed off each other that way. Dornett pushed to reassign him once, but Ballard complained, Pace got more unstable . . . and they can't afford to lose another pilot, especially right now. As long as he keeps his drinking to off-hours, they'd rather let it be. He slipped, and Authority stuck you in his path when they should've just told Ballard to fucking wait an extra day."

"He could've killed me," Fergus said.

Nisse finished the coffee and started pulling her gloves back on. "He still might," she said. "Authority is betting he won't. If I were you, though, I'd stay as far away from him as you can for the foreseeable future."

"What if Control sends me to Ballard again?" Fergus asked. *Because I'll need them to, and soon.*

"They won't," she said. "*Loxodon* is at Ballard now, and Transit Control is going to have him operate out of there for a while rather than housing him in Vine and running him from Depot. If nothing else, Ballard is bone-dry, and no one delivers out that far except us. Lucky you, you'll likely never have to go near that misery-hole again."

Lucky me, he thought. "Can I put the rest of my stuff onboard in the meantime?" he asked.

"Nope. Safety regs, sorry." She snapped her goggles down. "I've got about another hour to get this thing properly fitted, then two for testing. Come back in three with more coffee and you can have your ship back."

———

He retreated to the lounge and slouched in a chair. *Damn Pace,* he thought, and spent too long rolling that irritation around before he could get himself to focus on anything else. He mentally listed off his resources again, then his list of what he needed. Topmost was information to plan the rescue—information he could only get from inside Ballard.

On his handpad he pulled up the cargo roster. He was already back on it, listed for a run to Wyville-Thompson in the late evening. *Loxodon* was listed as temporarily out of service at Ballard.

At least, Fergus thought, *I know right where he is.*

He pulled out the small handful of pager disks, freshly pried from tacky trophies, and noticed they were all blinking in time. All keyed to him; he'd have to figure out how to set them as separate nodes when he knew who he was going to give them to. He threw all but his scuffed original back in his pocket and activated it, and was relieved to see Zacker had sent him another data dump, this time background checks and follow-up interviews with everyone who had been involved, directly or indirectly, with the museum robbery.

It's a good thing I like puzzles, he thought, *because I seem to collect them like Scotland collects rain.*

He opened the files and started reading.

————

Nisse was already gone when he got back to the docks, more than an hour later than he'd intended. The empty coffee bottle was waiting along with a note that said, *minor stiffness at first careful next few runs up Bore.*

Fergus hoped that he only had one more trip through the Bore in his future, and that emphatically one-way, but he appreciated the warning.

He'd picked up more hot food and fresh coffee, and as soon as he was aboard, Mister Feefs took off from his carrier like he'd just escaped prison. Fergus knocked gently on the closed door of the passenger compartment. "Food," he said, then headed up to the helm. Dr. Minobe came in a few minutes later, hair disheveled, and immediately began rummaging through the sack.

"Took you long enough," she said.

"They wouldn't let me back onboard until the repairs were done."

"Standard protocol," she said. "You're off the hook. I got a signal from Manne's science remote sometime this morning that *Loxodon* passed by on its way to Ballard. Meanwhile, I put my drawings and the scans from Hitchhiker through a predictive modeling run to get a full 3-D view." She tapped the console and turned the screen on. Her schematics, hand-sketched but precise, appeared, and then overlaid the visual scans that Hitchhiker had made of the warship before they'd had to drop it.

"As I said, early on, they broke stuff up in what I can only guess was an attempt to obfuscate the overall design—pointlessly complicating my job, since it's not like I could tell anyone."

"You're telling me."

"Yes, but they couldn't reasonably anticipate you."

"True. I get that a lot," Fergus said.

The outline looked sort of like a squat horseshoe crab, with double jump engines mounted diagonally out from its back in a big V.

"It's smaller than I thought, from our earlier glimpse," Fergus said.

"I don't think it's right," Dr. Minobe said, and sighed. "I'm missing something. The design specs I was given were for a long-distance multi-medium starcraft—space, atmosphere, water—but at this size, and extrapolating where the crew space has to be from the other things we know, you'd have trouble fitting more than one human adult in there, and two would be practically sitting on each other's laps," she said. "No quarters, no facilities, nothing to sustain a crew over distance."

"Unless it's not meant for human drivers?" Fergus asked.

She shrugged. "Who would be small enough to crew this? The Sitsit? You'd never see your ship again," she said. "I believe this has to be a drone—you understand the difference between drones and ships?"

"Drone are meant to operate autonomously, without direct oversight," Fergus said. "There's a lot of limitations on what you're allowed to do with them, or where they can go, like no uncrewed active jump, only passive. But there's no way those are just passive jump engines."

"Do you think our Ballard criminals are overly concerned about following laws?"

"No," he answered, pursing his lips as he studied the scan image.

"A better counterargument to my interpretation is that, on their own and outside of limited contexts, drones are mediocre craft of war, because ultimately they're predictable," Dr. Minobe said, "though I can hardly imagine my captors had a more altruistic intent for this."

"Yeah, a bunch of sneaky asshole mercenaries killing and kidnapping scientists to build something in secret doesn't ring of humanitarian work," Fergus said. "They grabbed the right people to build a cutting-edge mindsystem for their drone, so maybe they hope that's enough of an advantage."

"But while I am sure your friends are among the very best, they're not the *only* people who can build such a thing," she said. "It would still ultimately be at a tactical stalemate."

"Yeah. I don't know."

"Nor I. Until we have more data, I would call it a war drone," she said. "That seems likely to encompass both function and intent, if unsatisfactory in other ways."

"Whatever it is, let's do our best to wreck it, okay?" Fergus said.

Dr. Minobe nodded. "Yes. You have a plan yet?"

"The first half of one," he said. "I've got a Wy-Tee run in a few hours. Is our pod done with its makeover?"

"Yes, though it needs a control module for the plates."

"I've got it," he said. "It's the one thing I can't replace or fab, so I've been keeping it on me, just in case."

"Don't trust me?"

"Don't trust Transit, the Bastards Above, and at least one of my fellow pilots."

"Fair enough. What's your plan? And where's the bacon?"

"Couldn't find any, and the plan is, I'm going to Ballard again." She stopped with half a bagel in her mouth. "Whaf?"

"Pilots sometimes sleep in their haulers. I've set a precedent of napping outside Wy-Tee, which is how you happened to crash into me. I'm going to park *Hexanchus* there, call in that I'm out for the night, leave you Mister Feefs and his very handy homing beacon, and take the pod over to Ballard."

"Ooookay," she said after she swallowed the mouthful. "And what are you going to do there? That pod isn't big enough to fit more than two people in, and they'll notice their prisoners disappearing one by one."

"I looked over the substation plans and Hitchhiker's data from where it was able to scan the station exterior. If I can get to the maintenance hatch down near the stabilizers, I should be able to lock on and get in for a peek around."

"The hatch will have sensors. Someone will know you've opened it."

"I'm planning to temporarily disable the sensors."

"So say you get inside without being noticed. Then what?"

"I'm going to hack into the substation computers and download everything they've got, connect up to any security cameras, audio feeds, you name it. And I'm going to send it back here so we're both seeing and hearing all of it." He reached into his pocket and pulled out one of the pager disks, found the tiny jumper on the side, set it to a different ID before he handed it to her.

"Encrypted pager comm," he said. "One for you, one I'm going to hook directly into *Hexanchus*'s systems."

"Where'd you get this?" she asked.

"I won it for being mediocre at frisbee," he said. At her look, he added, "Never mind. Sent down by a friend on the outside. I'm hoping you'll get to meet all my friends in person soon enough."

"You think this is a good idea?"

"Pace got put on suspension over at Ballard. Once he's out in the water in *Loxodon* again, he's a direct threat. I think he murdered the pilot who preceded me, that maybe Olson knew something was going on and tried to get out to warn someone, which is how Mister Feefs got left behind. Right now is my best chance to get into Ballard and get more information." He sat down heavily at the helm. "Also, I'm really sick of being down here."

"What if they catch you?"

"Can you drive this thing?" he asked.

"No problem down here, but not through the Bore. I design ships, not drive them."

"Then if I get caught, take *Hexanchus* and go to Cufa Bore. Find a pilot named Stanislao Toscani. He's the most trustworthy person down here. Tell him what happened, have him help you get out, then call in the Alliance or Transit or whoever you have to. Maybe they'll still be able to save some of us."

"That doesn't sound optimistic."

"That's why I'm planning on not getting caught," he said. "You have any better ideas? I'm open."

"No."

"Then we do this?"

"Then we do this," she said.

He handed her the control module for the stealth plates, and she picked up two more bagels and headed back to cargo.

Fergus put his hands on the helm, felt them shaking, felt the charge of electricity deep inside crawling through his bones. He'd been holding it down, hiding it, pretending it wasn't there, but it was as if it knew he was going to need it soon, would give in to it again.

I just want to be free, he thought, not even sure what that meant anymore. It was a sharp, almost physical shock to realize that in a choice between the two—the Deep of Enceladus and the alien thing murmuring electricity in his gut—it was this place, this unending oppressive dark, that he wanted to escape more.

It was long past time to collect his friends and get out of there.

Chapter 16

————◆————

He arrived at Wyville-Thompson right on schedule, though it was unlikely Transit Control would notice or care. After Pace's recent meltdown, there was always the chance they might be looking more closely at all of them.

Dr. Creek invited him to stay for a late dinner, and this time, he had to regretfully decline.

"Don't get me wrong," she said, "my team here is like family. It's just that you get sick of talking to the same people every day. The other night, I was almost wishing Dr. Manne was back, just so I could have someone to yell at."

"I'm really sorry," he said, and he was.

Back aboard *Hexanchus*, he took it out a few kilometers from Wyville-Thompson and called in to Control. Jake wished him a good night's sleep, sounding as bored and as uninterested as he could wish for. After he signed off, Dr. Minobe came up and sat in the copilot seat. "You ready?" she asked.

"More than," he said. "If Transit calls, patch through to me on the pager disk and I'll reply. Since I'm supposed to be sleeping, a delay won't seem odd. If more comes up, well . . . You're smarter than me. Do what you need to. Try to save the cat, if you can."

She nodded. "What can I do from here to help you?"

"I have no idea," Fergus said, then immediately had one. "Oh—one. Is Hitchhiker still sitting atop the modified Madarchs?"

"Yes," she said. "I was already planning to use it to break into one and steal the log contents now that we're in range. Evidence, you know."

"You think you could remotely drive one of them with the rescue bot?"

Dr. Minobe raised an eyebrow, and stared at him thoughtfully for a long minute before she nodded curtly. "It's possible," she said.

"Unless you come up with a better thing to do, test that?"

"I will," she said. "It's an interesting challenge."

He stood, stretched, and headed down to cargo. The pod was cramped with all the stuff he'd packed into it, so he put on his exosuit out in the bay. Dr. Minobe had fixed the heat, but they'd left in a cutoff switch; the pod would be harder to find if it flew cold, and his suit would provide what warmth he needed. Also, it would offset at least some of the power drain from the stealth plates.

Taking some deep breaths, he tried to center himself in space, as if he was merely a part of the whole, as Dr. Minobe had tried to teach him during their Mu lessons. It was, he thought from his limited experience, rather like aikido except with equal emphasis on using walls and ceilings as the floor, though those were harder to practice even in Enceladus's small gravity. He wasn't sure he'd learned much beyond how to complain less when she threw him, but in this moment, he felt calmer, stronger, less of a walking anomaly.

Satisfied he was in the best mindset he could be in under the circumstances, he strapped in, sealed the pod, and activated the remote launch sequence. The cargo arm moved the pod into the emergency bay and retracted, then the internal bay door sealed. The outer doors opened, and air was pumped out as water flooded in, until he could simply drop out of the bottom of *Hexanchus*.

"I'm clear," he sent back as he powered up the pod and swung away. "Heading to Ballard."

"Good luck, MacInnis," Dr. Minobe said.

It struck him that he'd never told her his real name, and it was now both bad timing and way too late, so he just said thanks and closed the link, then turned his pod toward Ballard. At full speed, it would take just under two hours to get there, leaving him six at Ballard before he had to head back.

Which assumes, he thought, *that I get into Ballard without being caught.* He leaned forward, chin in his hand on the helm console, staring into the dark, willing Ballard to appear in the all-encompassing dark.

Two hours was enough time to figure out a plan if he got caught, but it was as if the opacity of the water was a mirror into a future he couldn't see.

He missed the damned cat.

Half an hour out from Ballard, he turned on the stealth plates, and what few lights he had on his console dimmed noticeably. The extra dark served him better than he expected; Ballard substation, not expecting company, and in violation of all safety protocols, had all its external lights out. He half-disbelieved his instrumentation that he'd arrived, until he spotted the tiny hull beacon underneath the barely visible curve of *Loxodon*, docked to the station ahead.

He slowed his pod, every muscle tense and twitchy and electric, but *Loxodon* stayed unmoving with its engines cold as he slid underneath the substation and brought his pod, centimeter by careful centimeter, up underneath it.

As he circled in, he spotted the war drone, barely larger than his pod, butted up against the side of the substation away from the docks, where it would be invisible to any ship approaching in the allowed lane, and the urge to go check it out was almost unbearable.

Not what you're here for, he told himself, and ran a quick scan, uploading it back to *Hexanchus* for Dr. Minobe. *You can look at the data yourself when you have time. If you have time.*

There were a number of maintenance hatches evenly spaced around the lower curve of the teardrop-shaped substation; he chose one as far from *Loxodon* as he could. "Here goes nothing," he said, and maneuvered the pod against the hatch. Using the external viewer, he snugged the locking cone against the substation hull and activated the magnets without sending the electronic docking handshake. Maintenance hatches were not, in Fergus's experience, wired for smarts, and he had to hope that this one was unlikely to notice someone at the door unless they rang the proverbial bell.

Or until someone opened it, of course. There would be sensors for that.

He confirmed the seal was good and evacuated the water out of the space in between. Then he took a deep breath, checked his own suit seals for the dozenth time, and cycled himself through the pod's airlock and out.

Water dripped on his faceplate, and he flinched; it was the first time, of all his weeks in the Deep, that he'd actually had any direct contact with Enceladus's waters, and in that moment, it terrified him against all rational reason.

Calm down, Fergus, he told himself. *It's just water. Water never hurt anyone.* Except, of course, for all the people swept away when Earth's oceans rose, or Evard inside a flooded *Alopias,* or his father drowning in the Scottish Inland Sea . . .

"Right," he said out loud, letting his voice break the spell of panic. He put both his gloved hands up against the control panel on the outside of the maintenance hatch and let the tingling build up until he let it go in one jolt. His suit went dark as it rebooted.

When his systems came back up, he could see that the door itself was now offline. Not knowing how long it would take to reboot itself—or if it would at all—he put both hands on the manual door handle and hauled as hard as he could. With a groan it came open, and he pushed himself into the small lock inside, closed it, then opened the hatch to the interior.

There was a tremendous noise as stuff stacked against the hatch on the far side fell to the floor. He dropped out of the tube into a large supply closet amid piles of dusty crap that had probably not been looked at in years. *And that's why maintenance hatches make such good points of entry,* he reminded himself as he tried to find stable footing among the fallen junk. *You've led a sneaky life to know that, haven't you?*

The space was neglected storage now, but would have been built as a staging area for maintenance crews. After listening at the door to be sure no one was nearby or was coming to investigate the sounds he'd made breaking in, he carefully restacked the boxes to one side of the hatch and then shifted the undisturbed piles of cans and boxes and crates until he found the room's small comms panel.

He pulled his confuddler from his pack and had it jacked into the comm unit in less than thirty seconds, and emulating a part of the unit in another forty. Now was the hard part, and Fergus scowled in unhappy unsurprise as the analysis of the station security came up. It wasn't opaque, but there were so many layers of shifting security, it might as well have been.

Ballard had definitely upgraded.

"Damn," he said, keeping his voice low. He'd had only minor success cracking things this complex, and none of those jobs had been in a hurry.

In contemplative moments, over the course of decades doing this, he'd thought there was an analogy to be drawn between picking a physical lock and cracking security, in that the virtual lock was built of multiple tumbling algorithms, each requiring their own perfect groove to pass through, and each also protecting the others. Where that analogy fell apart was in the idea that one picked the log sequentially, one tumbler at a time, whereas with these systems, you had to throw your tools at each one simultaneously, keep them from adapting to protect holes you'd made elsewhere. Rather than each layer doubling the complexity of the previous, it was more like an exponential growth, and there were only so many picks you could hold and wiggle at one time.

Or, really, it was easier to just describe it as a massive pain in his ass.

The confuddler would do its best to at least feel around the outside and give him hints about an attack plan. For more than that, the challenge was on him.

Once, not longer after Maison had first joined the Shipyard— *six years ago?* Fergus wondered. The passage of time seemed fraught with its own complexity right now—he'd challenged Fergus directly to crack his new security system he'd put on a locker containing, he said, his greatest treasures. That treasure, Fergus determined a few hours later, was a dozen carefully wrapped and sealed Ganymede Whoopie Pies.

He remembered Maison swaggering into the lounge, ready to pronounce the challenge over and himself the winner, only to see Fergus happily stuffing the last bite of one of those precious whoopie pies into his mouth. "But I checked!" Maison had declared, outraged even as he also looked deeply intrigued. "The system says it hasn't been touched!"

"Go count," Fergus told him, and there were eleven left.

The next day, ten.

By the time there were only three remaining, Maison was ready to throttle Fergus for clues to how he kept getting in without detection, even though Maison rebuilt and retuned the system every night.

He was eating the second-to-last when Maison finally moved the locker itself and discovered Fergus had used a liquid nitrogen saw to cut a nearly invisible seam through the box bottom, bypassing the lid and lock entirely.

Maison had given him the last whoopie pie as acknowledgement of defeat. The next time Fergus had been passing by Jupiter, he went to that same bakery and had a new dozen sent to the Shipyard, but ever since then, Maison had declared Fergus his "personal Moriarty" and had taken it as a challenge to keep Fergus on his toes. It was annoying as hell, and right now he missed Maison so much, his eyes stung from holding back tears.

I am so close, he told himself. *I just need to get through this.*

The confuddler declared it had done the best it could to feel out the virtual security landscape, and Fergus popped the 3-D map up on his handpad, rotating it back and forth and around, wincing at the staggeringly invulnerable logical structure.

On one turn, some tiny dark blip appeared and disappeared, almost like a screen glitch, until he managed to backtrack slowly and find it.

There was already a tunnel through the security system, a tiny pinhole of an opening. It couldn't be accidental, not in this sophisticated a setup, but he couldn't imagine who would have been here before him to leave such a thing.

Either it was a trap, or it was his only way through. Did he have much choice?

He made the connection from his confuddler to that hole, and it immediately greenlit. Full access. He left the confuddler wired in, bridging between the station systems and his handpad, and very carefully, he restacked items in front of the comm unit to hide it from view.

Sudden exhaustion hit him. He sat on the floor against a sturdy crate to catch his breath, and opened the handpad connection to the station to see what was going on inside.

There were three open comm channels currently active. The

first seemed to be a cook arguing with someone else about the latest episode of the Sfazili serial holo-drama *The Grateful Sublime*. The second channel seemed to be automated environment readings for the substation, including pressure variations and readings for the ocean floor itself. There was a forecasting number given that, after some time, he realized was the running odds of a geothermal geyser opening up close enough to the substation to threaten it; fortunately, the number stayed very, very low. Not, however, zero. *As if I needed one more reason to get out of here fast,* Fergus decided.

The third channel was someone arguing with Pace.

"—his face," Pace was saying.

"So, what about his face?" a man's voice said.

"It's dishonest."

Angry laughter. "Pace, you're a fucking homicidal asshole. What do you care if someone looks *dishonest*?"

"He's always in the way. He was right there to take Olson's place, he stole my run—"

They're talking about me, Fergus realized.

"Because you were so fucking drunk, you couldn't swim your way out of your own pool of vomit!"

"I didn't drink that much!"

"Riiiiight. So, you're telling me you don't have a problem?" The sarcasm was thick.

"No, I'm saying he's a bigger problem, and he's the one not under control."

"You're paranoid."

"Who here isn't?"

There was a pause. "Yeah, well. He's got his hauler parked over by Wy-Tee again for a nap, and the tracer ping says he's really there. Authority still doesn't want you anywhere near Vine, but in a week or so, if you don't do anything stupid, they'll forget why they're mad at you and you can go toss his apartment while he's out for a run. And by *toss*, I mean so he doesn't *know* you were there, like a goddamned professional. Fucking pissing on his *door*, really?"

"I'm telling you, the guy is bad news—"

"Leave him alone unless I personally instruct you otherwise, Pace. That's an order."

There was a pause, then: "Yes, sir."

"Glad you understand me. Samuels is hauling Keeling up for a status report, so I'll check in with you later with an update. In the meantime, stay out of trouble."

"Not much trouble to get into here."

"Doesn't seem to stop you from trying, Pace. Ladden out."

The line went quiet.

Dr. Keeling had been the first to go missing of the scientists Tomboy had flagged. He was a high-ranking IESAI scientist who'd been working on the holy grail of AI research: truly sentient artificial life. For all that it often felt like Tomboy, *Venetia's Sword*, and others were people in their own way, they were just highly complex systems with evolving algorithms that didn't quite cross over that threshold into sentience.

If the kidnappers wanted a truly sentient droneship—if they believed that was even possible—they'd grabbed the best people to make it happen. And while beneath the ice of Enceladus provided significant logistical challenges, as Dr. Minobe had pointed out, it also provided a very rare privacy.

It was nearly ten p.m.; he'd need to start making the trip back to *Hexanchus* in less than six hours if he was going to get back in time to keep his cover story about sleeping in his hauler plausible. It seemed like both a lot of time and not nearly enough.

"Okay, Ballard," he murmured to himself. "Let's see what's going on."

He woke his idled handpad and directed it to sync with the internal security feeds through the pinhole connection. "C'mon, c'mon," he whispered. "Don't get me caught."

The screen flickered, and a channel menu popped up. *Yes!* he thought. He ran through the video feeds quickly.

An office with a man sitting straight-backed behind the desk, two men before him, one elderly, unkempt, and in a lab coat, the other one lacking only a uniform to be the perfect image of a military man.

A cafeteria, empty.

A cluttered storage room. Someone with their back to the camera, sorting supplies into a cabinet.

A small, sparsely furnished room, bunks in the background, and an elderly couple sitting at a table, holding hands, neither speaking or moving. The Agastis, also IESAI scientists like Keeling, who had disappeared in the Mediterranean.

A mechanical room, also empty.

The interior of a large, messy laboratory space. The lights were dimmed, but Fergus could make out a row of large fabricators, and the nose-cone of a Madarch leaning against a far wall beside a large hull repair panel. Dr. Minobe's former lab? There was no one there now.

Next was a small lounge with an attached kitchenette. There were four men inside, most playing cards, one man mixing drinks. A fifth man stomped angrily into the room.

Pace.

For all that Ballard was supposed to be dry, the glass someone handed Pace sure looked far from nonalcoholic. He wondered whether Ladden knew his crew was down there drinking. *Bottoms up, Pace,* Fergus thought. *The more, the better.*

The picture flicked over to another lab, smaller but crammed full of equipment and things. A guard stood at the door, hands behind his back, energy pistol slung over one shoulder. Two people sat at a bench, side by side, their backs to him, but he knew them immediately: Theo and Noura.

Fergus's relief at seeing them was so palpable, he almost cried out loud at the sight. Until this moment, he had still carried a tiny, bitter kernel of fear that he was looking in the wrong place, or that his friends would no longer be alive.

That's two, he thought, heart soaring. *Four to go.*

The view had moved on. An empty hallway, another with someone just turning a far corner, then what he first took to be a blank screen until he realized that something was up against the security lens, and that the tiny corner of light he could see was made unintelligible by being filtered through a haze of waving, bright green fuzz. *Ignatio!*

Unfortunately, he couldn't see anything else in the room or anyone in it. *I love you, Ignatio, but I can't tell where you are with your bloody giant mop of a head in my way.*

The image had moved on again while he was still puzzling out where that room could have been. He caught a glimpse of another small lab. In the center was a tall glass tank with something small and spherical suspended in the center, wires protruding from it out into fixtures set in the tube. Consoles surrounded the base. Standing beside it, looking very bored, was a large man with an energy rifle at the ready. Fergus recognized Carl from his earlier cargo trip.

Dr. Minobe had never mentioned anything like it, but something important enough to have a guard was something he wanted to know more about.

Friends first, he reminded himself.

He set his handpad to take the images coming through from the security system and try to map them against the substation schematics already in its memory, partially labeled thanks to

Dr. Minobe's recollections. Even with Ignatio's head blocking the camera, Fergus should still be able to figure out what room it was through a process of elimination. Once he knew where his friends—and enemies—were, he could take a few days to make a solid plan, then come get his friends out.

As much as he desperately wanted to get out from under the ice, he reminded himself that what mattered most was success, not speed. There was absolutely no need to hurry.

He heard a *click* and looked up just as the door opened and a young man in a blank uniform stepped into the room.

"Ah!" the man shouted, wide-eyed, and fumbled for his sidearm. Fergus leapt forward, slapped his hand on the man's arm, and zapped him. The man tumbled forward, legs giving out under him, and Fergus grabbed the pistol as his suit rebooted.

Stepping over him, Fergus checked the corridor with a fast and anxious peek, then quietly closed the door again. "So much for not being in a hurry," he muttered.

While the man was stunned, Fergus checked his pockets and relieved him of a security passcard and portable comm. He activated the latter with the man's thumb and then slipped it into his own pocket.

The man was young, fit, with a short haircut identical to all the others he'd seen on Ballard, and the pasty look of someone who'd been trapped underwater a long time.

When the man regained his senses, propped up against a stack of soap crates, Fergus had the pistol trained on him from across the small room.

"Who the fuck are you, and where the *hell* did you come from?" the man demanded.

Fergus shrugged. "You'd be surprised how often I get asked that," he said, "and how infrequently I answer it. You, on the other hand, can do me a favor and answer some questions for me."

"Fuck off," the man said.

"I can always just shoot you instead," Fergus said.

"So do it," the man said. "I've got nine years in the service, including two tours along the Kriema border worlds. You don't frighten me. You ever even seen a Krieman?"

"No. You ever seen an Asiig?"

The man laughed. "No one has who's still alive. Try again."

Fergus chuckled too. "Okay, then. You're not afraid of getting shot. I can respect that. But how do you feel about being stuffed out that airlock into the Deep?" He pointed with the pistol at the maintenance hatch behind him. No need to tell the man it didn't currently lead directly to water.

"You wouldn't."

Fergus leaned forward. "You say that. But I survived the Asiig. You know what they do to people? I *swam* here," he said, and showed his still-wet suit sleeve to the man. "You wanna know what the Deep feels like on your skin, how it presses on you from all sides? And the darkness . . ."

The man flinched. "You still wouldn't," he said, but his voice had lost its ring of conviction.

"Try me," Fergus said.

"I'm not telling you a damned thing about the Palla," he said. "You'll never get even close to it, much less get it out of the station."

Palla, eh? Fergus thought. Was that the ship? No, because the ship wasn't in the station. So, the ball in the lab, then? It didn't matter; he didn't need anything else to worry about. "What I want you to tell me about right now is your crew. Ladden and Owens in charge, yes?"

The man grimaced, then nodded reluctantly.

"How many of you work for them?"

"*Report* to them," the man said. "Couldn't pay me enough to stay down here if it wasn't orders."

"You're not a mercenary group?"

The man's lips tightened and he said nothing. *Shit,* Fergus thought. *Is this an actual Alliance operation gone rogue? Or worse, sanctioned? That's . . . bad.*

"Okay," he said, trying to keep his focus. "What's your name?"

"I'm not telling you anything more."

"Then I'm just going to call you Bunnypants, okay? You don't mind that, do you, Bunnypants? You starting to feel up for a swim? I can take you out for a nice sightseeing tour around the outside of the substation anytime you're ready."

"Fuck you," the man said.

"Right. So, other than you, how many other soldiers are down here?"

The man clamped his lips even more tightly shut.

Fergus sighed dramatically. "You know, Bunnypants—"

"Davies!"

"You know, *Davies,* I don't really need you to answer, because I can just open up both sides of that hatch and let the Deep come right in and tear this place apart from the inside out. Then I just go pluck what I want out of the wreckage and off I go. I don't need to know how many of them there are if they're just bodies. You get me?"

Clearly, Davies did, and didn't like it one bit. He gritted his teeth, then said, "Ten, after Ladden and Owens."

"There any civilians here? Staff? Scientists?"

"Some," he said. "You'll kill them, too, if you flood the station. Innocent people."

"*Inconvenient* people," Fergus said. "How innocent can they be if they work for you guys?"

"Not everyone is here voluntarily."

"Civilians under orders?"

"Not what I was saying," Davies said.

"So, what? Prisoners, then?"

Davies was silent, but Fergus didn't need confirmation anyway.

"If I flood the station, there's going to be no evidence that I was ever here, and it'll be your body they find closest to the compromised hatch. They're gonna assume you did it. How bad a PR hit will the Alliance take for a disaster?"

"No one would ever know it happened," Davies growled.

"You so sure of that?" Fergus glanced at his handpad, trying to keep his nonchalance intact. *Damn, but he was using up time.* "So, the civilians. How many? And where are they, so I can avoid 'em? In the labs?"

"Ten. They get locked down in quarters right about now," Davies said.

"Level two?"

"Three. And you'll never get to the Palla alive."

"Yeah? Maybe Carl and I have an arrangement," Fergus said. Davies's eyes widened. *Bingo,* Fergus thought. *Ball in the lab it is.*

"Why were you down here?" Fergus asked.

"Routine visual check of all spaces. They're going to be expecting me to report in, you know."

"Of course. Too bad you're not going to." Fergus made his best menacing villain scowl and added, "Ever."

The man made a lunge for him, just as he'd wanted. As soon as the man's hand touched his, he unloaded enough electricity into him to knock him completely out. Fergus checked his pulse, to make sure he'd not done anything worse to the man than let him in for a horrible headache and the embarrassment of having wet himself when he awoke. Then he sat back again and checked his handpad.

It had successfully mapped most of the security camera images, and had overlaid the feed now onto a map so that he could tap a room or a corridor and see the live feed. He had it track his own location and feed back in a recorded shot to any camera he was in view of. There'd be a blip; he had to hope that this late at night, whoever was watching the security feeds wouldn't be paying too much attention.

His two usual tactics at this point were unfeasible. Aside from the fact that Davies was a good half-meter shorter than him, stealing his uniform would do no good; no one was going to mistake a looming, red-bearded Scot for anyone they knew. If the substation were in space, he'd just go back out the lock and climb along the outside of the structure until he found another hatch closer to where he wanted to be, but the Deep was not space, and his exosuit wasn't designed for its environment. Not to mention he wasn't sure his mental state was up to a swim.

You shouldn't have said anything about the Asiig, he thought. It was an indication that stress was badly affecting his judgment. *Not that anyone will ever believe a word of it.*

He opened a comm channel back to *Hexanchus.* "Hey, Dr. Minobe," he said. "I got surprised and had to take out a patrol guard. Still working on a Plan B. If Transit Control calls or you see any movement from Ballard toward your position, get the hell out of here. Otherwise, I'll let you know when I know what I'm doing."

"Okay," Dr. Minobe replied, though she sounded worried. "Try not to get killed."

"Do my best," Fergus said, and disconnected.

He tipped one of his sleeping pills out of its vial, carefully crushed it, and dropped the powder into Davies' mouth. Then he gently tied the man's legs and hands with packing straps and hoped that would suffice.

From the camera feeds, guards had already led the elderly man in the lab coat, who he assumed was Dr. Keeling, back to a room on the third level and locked him in. Carl, in front of the wired-up ball (the Palla, whatever that was) hadn't moved except to scratch his ear. Most of the rest of the station seemed to be in lockdown for the night. At just past 11 p.m. Deep-time, the sub-station hall lights dimmed.

Here goes nothing, he thought, and pulled up his suit hood and sealed the faceplate to give himself at least some anonymity. After checking his handpad to see the way was clear, he slipped out of the maintenance closet door into the hall.

He was on level eight, directly above the substation reactors and the stabilizers and sensors that hung off the bottom of the station. The next level up, before the station widened out into its fuller bulb shape, was the docks. There was a central elevator ahead, a number of rooms of mechanical systems around it. Fergus used Davies' security card to check them one at a time, until he found the room where water could be pumped in and distributed to the fire-suppression system.

He took his small toolkit out of a suit pocket and unscrewed the panel, setting it carefully aside leaning against the wall, and studied the wiring and relays and logic boards inside. Lucky for him, it was a perfectly standard install, and even luckier, as he'd hoped, there were auxiliary relay bays sitting empty in case the system ever needed to be expanded.

From his handpad he could remotely operate the dummy switches that would have been connected to any future contents of those empty bays. And putting something in there—a nasty mess of twisted-together wires and a half-disassembled relay from another unit—was the work of about ten minutes. It would give an electrical inspector nightmares, but then, that was the point.

The next room had a distribution panel for the substation lighting systems. He did the same there, resisting the temptation to hum while he worked, stripping the wire coating off with his teeth and then twisting the bare ends together, being very careful not to spark any of it.

There didn't seem much else down on this level worth messing with—the comms and security systems were housed up on level one, as far away from the reactor and vibration of the mechanical systems as possible—so he checked his feed from the levels above, looking to see on which floors the hall outside the elevator was clear.

He wished he still had his fruit-bowl invisibility shield.

Davies' card opened the elevator door, too. Once in, he hit the button for level three and watched the feeds on the approaching floors with anxiety. Just as the slow-moving car passed level four, a soldier stepped into view of the elevator one floor up and pressed the button.

Bloody hell, Fergus thought. He flattened himself into a front corner against the side wall as the car stopped and, with a chime, the doors opened.

The soldier stepped in, one hand over his mid-yawn, and Fergus stuck out a boot and tripped him just as he started to turn his head in his direction. The man tumbled forward, slamming his head into the back wall of the elevator car even as Fergus slapped both hands on his back and zapped him. Because leaving an unconscious man in the main substation elevator seemed a less-than-subtle way to announce his presence, he grabbed the man under the arms and hauled him, groggy, upright again. The big, blond man was as tall as Fergus and easily twice his build. He remembered the guy from the cargo bay: Carl's buddy, Nanho. *It figures I'd have to get a big one,* he thought.

"You bumped your head. Here, let me help you," he said, not sure if he was fooling anyone, but between hitting his head and the electricity, he hoped it would defuse any immediate reaction while the man tried to puzzle out what was going on.

Fergus pulled him out of the elevator. Around a corner and three doors down was the room he'd decided was the most likely location where Ignatio's green head had been blocking the camera.

He dragged Nanho quickly down the corridor and propped him, somewhat less than gracefully, against the wall. "You can lie down in here," he said, as he put his hand against the lock plate and shorted it, then tapped it to open.

The soldier was still badly dazed, but frowning at Fergus. "Who the hell—" he started to say, but Fergus grabbed him by his shirt collar and shoved him through the widening door.

The man hit the floor as Fergus stepped in, closed the door behind them, and flipped on the light.

Noura was halfway across the room toward him, a stool raised over her head ready to brain him, and he had to duck to one side even as he threw open his faceplate. She stopped mid-stride, eyes widening in recognition, and Nanho covered his head with his arms as she slammed the stool hard on the floor right beside him. "Stay put," she ordered him.

LaChelle sat on a bunk beside Maison, who was wrapped in blankets, pale, his face badly bruised, his eyes swollen shut. Her own always-precise tight braids were a frazzled, neglected mess. Ignatio was perched atop a cabinet, eir long, spindly, furry legs dangling over the sides. "Vergus!" ey exclaimed.

Theo blinked at him in sleepy confusion from one bunk, as Kelsie jumped down from hers and rushed him, wrapping her arms around him.

"Hey, guys," Fergus said, holding her just as tightly back. "You miss me?"

Chapter 17

———◆◆◆———

"Ears," Noura said. "Before anyone says anything else."

"Right. Sorry, Nanho," Fergus said. He bent down and stunned the man with his own pistol. Then he walked around the room, eyes closed, feeling the electrical signatures where he expected them and where he didn't. He disabled three listening devices but left the eye behind Ignatio alone for now; the confuddler had it sending a false image, anyhow.

LaChelle bent down, listened to Maison whisper something. "Yeah, it's Fergus," she told him. "He's found us."

"Is Maison okay?" Fergus asked.

"He needs medical attention," LaChelle said. "He picked one too many fights with the guards, and the last time, they beat him nearly dead. Would've killed him outright, except we made it clear that if anything happens to any more of us, none of us do a damned thing for them, no matter the cost."

Kelsie had unwrapped herself from Fergus but kept hold of his hand. "Fergus. They killed Effie. They blew up the Shipyard."

"No, they didn't. Effie's waiting for us on Titan," he said. He figured he'd tell them she was in jail for their murders later, hopefully right as he was about to fix that, too. "And we saved the Shipyard. It's heavily damaged, and we had to eject the reactor segment, but it's intact."

Everyone stared as the words sank in, then they were all around him, talking all at once.

"My birds are how?" Ignatio asked.

"Battered but mostly okay, at least that I saw."

"My bonsai?" Theo asked.

Fergus winced. "More battered," he said.

"Who's manning the station? If there's no one there—"

"The Campout is staying aboard while Tomboy fixes things. Look, we need to get out of here," Fergus said. "The problem is, I'd only planned on doing some recon this trip, but I got surprised by a guard and had to knock him out. And now this guy. Someone's going to miss one or both of them soon. I am temporarily out of plan."

He looked around as his friends, amazed that they were there and he was finally there, momentarily losing track of the danger in that joy. They were all wearing gray lab scrubs, and though he'd seen Dr. Creek and her team in identical ones, here they looked like the prisoner uniforms they were intended as. They were all thinner, and most of the blue had faded out of Theo's beard, but they were *alive.*

"What are our resources?" Noura asked.

"I've got a pod hidden outside a maintenance hatch, but the most it'll fit is two people, including the pilot. My hauler is parked—"

"You have a hauler?" Kelsie said, blinking.

"Yeah, I took a job as a pilot to get down here. But it's currently parked outside Wyville-Thompson, which is two hours by pod; I don't think we have enough time to make more than one trip before the alarm is raised."

"Any way to bring it here?"

"The moment my hauler budges an inch in this direction, an asshole named Pace is going to go full homicidal ape-shit and head right for it," Fergus said. "I may have antagonized him a little. Or even a lot."

Still wrapped inside his cocoon of blankets, Maison chuck-led, then mumbled something.

LaChelle laughed. "He says you never were very good at get-ting along with people."

"And he's one to talk! And anyway, that's why I had to come save you lot, isn't it? Otherwise, I'd have to make a whole *new* set of friends." Fergus feigned a shudder.

Ignatio wiggled eir legs impatiently and made low, humming sounds before ey spoke. "I smelled you on the food," ey said. "Happy! Now we go?"

"Now we go," Fergus said. "Somehow. Oh, and first, we need to get rid of the tracking bugs in each of you."

Kelsie growled. "That figures," she said. "Where is it?"

"Shoulder, probably," he said. "Mind if I—"

"No, please kill it," she said.

He ran his fingers over the back of her shoulder, roughly near where Dr. Minobe's tracker had been, and found it easily enough by the sympathetic tingle in his fingertips. "Bit of a zap," he said, and then fried it.

"Ah!" Kelsie jumped. "*Zap* is right! You got it?"

He touched the spot again, and there was no more tingle. "Yep," he said. "Who's next?"

Maison said something again too quiet for him to hear. "He says him," LaChelle said, and drew the blankets back.

For all the times he'd wanted to throttle Maison, seeing him in the shape he was in nearly broke Fergus's heart. Shirtless, the man's torso was covered with purple-black and yellow bruises. There was also what Fergus was fairly sure was a burn or two. "We need to get you out of here," he said.

Maison attempted a smile, and Fergus added *missing teeth* to the list. "And forfeit our frequent-guest status?" he managed to whisper.

"I hear the food really stinks," Fergus said as he gently found the tracker and killed it. Maison jerked at the shock but didn't complain.

There was a buzzing in his pocket, and he pulled out the comm he'd taken off Davies. "Private Davies, check in. You're ten minutes overdue," a voice said.

"That's Owens," Noura said. "Runs the day-to-day team ops. Real stickler for protocol even if most of the others are in slacker mode. We need to hurry, and we need a plan."

If only he had *Hexanchus* there instead of the pod, he could have fit everyone comfortably inside. Of course, there was no way to get his hauler there without having to deal with *Loxodon*, or—

"Ah," Fergus said. "That's kind of bleeding obvious, isn't it?"

Kelsie coughed meaningfully.

"I had an idea," Fergus said. In quick order, he killed the trackers in Noura, Theo, and LaChelle, then stole Nanho's access card and comm and added them to his pocket. "Get whatever you want to bring with you. And someone help me hide this guy. If we can keep them from realizing he's missing for a while, that gives us some flexibility."

LaChelle and Kelsie stuffed Nanho under a bunk as Theo helped Maison stand up. Maison was shaking, even paler than before, but he smiled at Fergus. "Ready," he said.

"Theo, can you carry Maison?" Fergus asked. "We're going to have to go down the emergency drop tube to the docks. I'm going to use Davies' card to send the elevator to the lab level; he was convinced I was after some damned thing called a Palla, so hopefully, they'll search for us there first. That should buy us some time."

"Where are we going from the docks?" Kelsie asked.

"*We're* not. You're all going to hide on board *Loxodon*. Last place anyone will think of looking for you. Once you're there, I'm going to come back for the other scientists—there are four others here—and then we're going to steal Pace's hauler and get the hell out of here," Fergus said. "That work?"

"Works for me," Kelsie said.

"And me," Noura said.

Theo nodded as LaChelle helped lift Maison up onto his back. "This is really embarrassing, being a sack of potatoes," Maison said as he clung there weakly. "I blame you for this, Fergus."

"What? Why?" Fergus exclaimed.

"You should've told me Effie was alive before I picked a fight with the guards to avenge her."

"But I wasn't even here yet!"

"Exactly," Maison said.

"This is the most he's spoken since the big beating," Noura told Fergus as he opened the door and ushered them out. "We might just be okay after all."

"You better be, after all this trouble. Everyone out, and go around the corner to your left and stay there until I catch up," Fergus said. Ignatio rattled from eir perch on the cabinet. "You too, Ignatio. I've got the security camera blocked from here."

"Vergus, I give you much of my thanks," Ignatio said, and slid down from the cabinet onto eir legs. "I do not like the heights!"

Fergus checked em for a tracker and found none. Probably, the abductors didn't even know where to start with trying to inject a chip under that massive tangle of fur.

Ignatio sailed on past Theo and Maison, who were the last two out. Fergus closed and locked the door behind everyone, then followed them to the corner. He checked his handpad, then led them a bit farther down the hall to where a door-sized plasti-glass hatch was set in the wall. Rather than open it with either of his stolen security cards, he put a hand against the plate and shorted it. The hatch door slid open, and he ushered everyone in.

"I'm going to start the elevator going, then meet you at the bottom of the tube," he said. "Once you're all safely hidden on *Loxodon*, I'm coming back for the others. Oh . . . hang on." He rifled through his pockets and found his last spare of the pager disks, and handed it to Noura. "One disk is communicating back with *Hexanchus*, my hauler, where I have a friend waiting," he said.

He handed Kelsie the pistol he'd taken off Nanho. She'd grown up in a border town just outside Redemption, a territory carved out of the former United States that Fergus knew little about beyond *guns* and *churches*, and that they often raided their neighbors in search of clean water, tech, medicine, or their own fleeing people. She'd been in her town's self-defense force since she was nine and was the best shot he knew.

Kelsie nodded, checking the charge and safety before tucking it in her waistband at the small of her back.

"Just in case something goes wrong," he said.

"Nothing will go wrong," Noura said. "Let's get moving before it can try."

"Oh, Fergus," Maison said, just before Theo laboriously climbed through the opening. "That Palla thing? It's incredibly important. You need to go get that, too."

"What?!" Fergus exclaimed, but Theo and Maison were already in the tube and heading down. "No bloody way!"

His stolen comm chimed again. "Private Davies. You have sixty seconds to check in or we're going to have to go to alert one, which you know means everyone else gets woken up and is going to be fucking pissed at you. And when they find you asleep in a damned maintenance closet again and dump you outside, you will only have yourself to blame. For the fifteen seconds or so you stay alive, that is. Last warning. Owens out."

Sixty seconds. Couldn't you have given him another hour or two to nap in peace? Fergus thought. He checked his handpad; all was clear on this floor, but there was activity again up on the administrative levels.

He sprinted to the elevator, swiped Davies' card, hit the button for the lab level, and slipped back out before the doors closed. There was a flash recycler in the hall, and he threw Davies' card and comm unit in there. Both would be useless in a minute or so anyway.

With any luck, no one would miss Nanho for a while longer.

He jumped into the drop tube, hoping there'd be a slug field at the bottom to slow him down. Luck was in his favor, and he hit the bottom of the shaft as if he'd dropped into three meters of invisible pudding.

He had to climb back up the ladder one level to reach the docks, but that beat climbing down five. Owens must've given Davies another minute's mercy, because it wasn't until he was already pulling himself up and through the hatch onto the dock level that the substation alarms went off.

His handpad showed Pace and his friends throwing down their cards and scooping their shares of an impressive array of credit chits from dozens of Alliance worlds into their pockets before rising to their feet. Even without sound, he could tell their conversation was blisteringly angry.

The dock level was still in dusk lighting and dead quiet. For a moment, he worried his friends had somehow been intercepted on the way down, but no, they were gathered in the cargo area, out of sight of the security camera, waiting for him.

"We can't open the door to the hauler," Noura said. "Handprint-coded."

Fergus went past them up to the lock. Some sort of thin metal collar had been welded to the outside of *Loxodon* around it, for no obvious purpose. It wasn't, thankfully, in his way. He put his hand against the lock unit just below the scanner and shorted it. The manual override took a few moments to activate, but then the door slid open. When the unit rebooted, it would have no memory of that. "In," he said, and Theo carried Maison past him and into *Loxodon*, followed by the others.

Unlike *Hexanchus*, the interior of *Loxodon* was filthy. There were food cartons on the floor, it smelled of sweat and body odor, and when he checked the bridge, a half-empty bottle and three fully charged energy pistols were tucked under the pilot seat.

"Right," Fergus said, and took the charge modules out of all three before carefully putting them back.

Theo had laid Maison on the bunk in the passenger compartment, which was dusty enough that it seemed unlikely anyone had been in it for months. Maison was shaking, curled up on the grimy mattress, but he held out one trembling hand toward Fergus. Fergus put his hand out and Maison dumped a pile of tiny metal pucks in it, each about two centimeters in diameter.

"Explosives," Maison said. "Activate them with an electric shock; there's a twenty-minute delay until detonation. Don't worry; they need a pretty big zap to activate, so you're not going to do it by accident. They snap together. Each one you add doubles the reaction. All eight together are enough to blow the entire substation."

"Uh . . ." Fergus said.

"They were never going to let us go," Noura said quietly behind him. "We wanted some choice in how we went out."

"From things Keeling said when we were working with him, they were losing patience anyhow," Theo added. "He was terrified they were going to shut the project down—and all of us with it—if we didn't make progress."

Fergus unsealed his suit and slipped the explosives into a pocket in his shorts, where they'd be safer. "There's a prototype ship behind the substation, but we couldn't figure out exactly what they were trying to build. A high-capability war drone, we thought, but that doesn't entirely add up."

"It's much more than that," Noura said. "Or it was supposed to be. You know about the Pallai?"

"Never heard of them before today. Didn't know there was more than one until right now."

"The people who know about them don't want anyone else to," LaChelle added. "It's a secret people have died to keep. And the people who don't know they exist mostly wouldn't believe they're real. We didn't."

"What are they? That sphere thing I saw in one of the labs?"

"Yeah. That thing is worth as much as entire planets," Kelsie said.

Fergus blinked at her.

"No one knows where they came from. We don't know how many exist, but we think there are two dozen. The only marking on them is each one has a letter of the ancient Earth Greek alphabet, which is where that guess comes from. This one is Tau. I don't know where they got it or how many people they killed, but before now, despite having heard a very few rumors, I'd firmly written them off as a myth."

"Again, what is it?"

"The holy grail," Theo said.

"Theoretically, truly sentient, self-aware AI," Kelsie said. "The thing Keeling and generations of scientists before him at

IESAI have been trying to create but have been stuck in Zeno's Paradox trying to get there."

"Theoretically?"

Maison snickered from under his new pile of blankets. "Keeling accidentally broke it."

"Before we got here," Kelsie said. "He's been covering it up, but I think our captors are catching on. Their plan was to figure out what made the Palla tick, then replicate that as a series of sentient AIs entirely loyal to the program but unmarked and untraceable as Alliance tech. Part drone, part ship, part robot, smart enough to overcome predictability. It'd give them the ability to carry out extralegal actions of an extended nature without repercussions. But without the brain, it's just fancy plans and wishful thinking. At any rate, they're all too aware that they aren't any closer to having the perfect brain for their new killer drone fleet."

"I don't think they'd have let this go more than another few weeks," Noura said. "They've been at it for at least a year, as best as we can figure, and their team is all starting to crack up from being trapped down under here. I think they already killed one of the kidnapped scientists who was here before us—an elderly Japanese woman we never got to interact with. She disappeared and everyone's been extra squirrely ever since."

"Dr. Minobe Ishiko," Fergus said.

"Damn! That was Dr. Minobe? Those assholes," Kelsie swore. "She was one of the best. I'd always hoped to meet her! Now that I think about it, I can see her hand in the original designs we were given to work off of."

"Yeah, well, she's onboard *Hexanchus*," Fergus said. "She escaped, and together we faked her death so they wouldn't come looking further."

"You've been busy," Theo said.

"Yeah."

"Did you take your cousin's motorcycle back to him?"

"No," Fergus said. How were they back on him about that *already*? "It was gone! And thanks to you people pushing me to go back there, now I not only have to find it again, I have to solve a two-decades-old art theft as soon as I'm done here."

". . . What?" LaChelle asked.

Fergus shook his head. "Long story, no time. So, the Palla . . . if it's broken, why do I need to go get it?"

"Because I don't think it's dead," Maison said. "I think it's *hiding*. And just like we don't want to be in these people's power to exploit, we don't want it there, either. Just go with me on this, Ferg. It's more important than any of us are."

"Not to me," Fergus said. He checked his handpad again. A mob of angry men were gathered in the central area of the administrative level, listening to Owens give directions. Pace was among them, lurking toward the back of the group. As he watched, they split up into teams of two and headed out. No one seemed to be particularly in a hurry, though he expected that when they did locate Davies, that would change. *Going by the procedural book, but no one believes it's a real situation yet.*

"Only a Transit pilot can start up the hauler systems, but if I power it on, everyone will know you're here," Fergus said. "Not that you guys couldn't hack it if it came down to it. I'm going to go back for Dr. Keeling, the Agastis, and one other prisoner, and then we'll get out of here."

"You may want to go for Keeling last, if you have a choice," Noura said. "He's the de facto leader of us prisoners and likely to be the first one checked on."

"Good to know," Fergus said. "If I get caught, do what you need to to get free. My pod is outside maintenance closet Cee-Eight."

"Just don't get caught," Kelsie said.

He left them shut into the passenger compartment, stole and drank down an unopened water bottle from Pace's foodkeeper, then locked up *Loxodon* on his way out as if no one had ever been there. With any luck, he'd be back there before anyone else, too. Using his handpad to check on locations of the two-man patrols, he began the laborious climb up the drop tube toward the living-space level. When he got to the right floor, he paused inside the tube to catch his breath, and peered out through the bottom of the plasti-glass door.

One of the two-man patrols was walking through the hallway, checking the doors to the prisoner rooms. They stopped, rapped on Keeling's door, and demanded he answer. He could hear a muffled, irritated reply from within, and the men moved on to the next door.

Six levels down, another team was approaching the maintenance closet where he'd left Davies. *Time's up on the subtle approach,* Fergus thought, and activated the switch he'd rewired on the lighting distribution panel. The entire station plunged into instant darkness as the panel shorted out. It might even have been on fire.

Fergus pulled down his goggles and sealed his faceplate. The goggles had infrared, but the signal coming through from his handpad stashed in his pack didn't; there was no longer much value to his tap into the security systems. That didn't mean there wasn't mischief left to be committed, though. He sent commands to the confuddler to launch a half-dozen of the escape pods, all supposedly rigged with explosives, then to short the entire security system out. That should make for ample distraction, at least for a little while.

Things would get harder from there.

He tuned his suit comms over to the substation main channel.

"—ttention, all station personnel, we are at alert level five! We are under assault," Ladden was saying. "This is not a drill. We have six pods out! Repeat, we have six pods out! Everyone check in *now*."

"Ennis here. I found Davies; he's out cold and tied up in a closet. I can't wake him, but he's breathing."

"Leave him. Sweep the floor," Ladden said.

"Yes, sir!"

"Velleca checking in. The prisoners in room three are gone. Others are accounted for."

"Fucking hell," Ladden said. "Owens, are you in Ops? Blow the damned pods now."

"Systems are down," Owens said. Fergus could almost hear the sweat and panic in his voice. "Trying to get them back on-line now."

"Get Nanho over to back up Carl."

"Nanho's not answering," Owens said.

"I can go," Velleca said.

"No, you check the rest of that floor, then station yourself there to make sure we don't lose any more prisoners."

"Yes, sir!"

"Who else is out there? Somebody fucking go give Carl backup!"

"Molloy here. I'll go."

"Thank you, Private Molloy," Ladden said.

Fergus flattened against a wall as a soldier walked down the corridor past him. The man wasn't suited and didn't have goggles, but he did have a large energy rifle.

Fergus fell in behind him, and when Velleca stopped in front of one of the other room doors he tapped him on the shoulder. The soldier spun around in surprise and Fergus zapped him. "Hello from Scotland," he said, as the man crumpled to the floor.

He took Velleca's card and swiped it, but the door didn't respond. *Oh, right,* he thought. *I killed the security system, didn't I?*

The door was still locked, but a quick zap to the panel was enough to trigger the release. He hauled the door open, and found himself looking at the couple, now sitting on a bunk and huddled against each other, an emergency lamp hanging from the upper bunk. They stared at him as if at their own firing squad.

"Drs. Hewitt and Leigh Agasti?" he asked. "I'm here to get you out of this place."

They both stared at him as he pulled Velleca into the room and left him slumped against a wall behind the door. The woman stood up. "Who are you?" she asked.

"A friend," he said. "We don't have much time. You each have a tracker embedded in your shoulder that I need to disable before we can leave this room."

After a half-second hesitation, the woman strode forward, turning her back to Fergus. "Do it," she said.

"Leigh . . ." the man said.

"We thought they were coming here to kill us, Hewitt. If this man is lying to us, what have we lost? Nothing," she said.

"As always, you find the convincing argument," he said, and stood next to his wife. "How will you disable the trackers?"

"I have a small device," Fergus lied. "There's a flash and a small sting. Close your eyes."

They took each other's hands and did as he'd said. It took only a moment to locate the tiny telltale bump on each of them, and he put one fingertip on each and zapped. They both flinched, but when they turned back to him, their faces were resolute. "Is there anything you need to bring?" Fergus asked them.

"Only each other," Hewitt answered.

"Then let's go." Fergus peered out the door. The pitch-dark hallway was empty. "Take my hand."

Hewitt killed the lantern. Leigh took his hand, Hewitt still holding hers, and Fergus led them out of the room and quietly shut the door behind them. He led them to the drop tube and slid the hatch open, then looked them over briefly. They were both in their late sixties and had been there for a long time. "Can you climb?" he asked.

"I could fly, if it would get us out of here," Leigh answered.

"Okay. Go down. I'll follow above. When you get to level seven, wait for me," Fergus said. "I'm going to go back for others."

"Dr. Keeling. He's here too," Leigh said. "Longer than any of us, poor man."

"I won't forget him," Fergus said.

"Also, there's the Palla—"

"Yeah, yeah, it's important. So everyone keeps telling me."

"It is!" Hewitt said.

"I get it. Now go, before they catch us all," Fergus said.

Leigh entered the tube first, her husband immediately after. Fergus closed the tube hatch, then surveyed the floor around them. Everything was still silent.

His encrypted comm disk chimed in his ear. "MacInnis," Dr. Minobe said. "The good news is I've got control of one of the Madarchs via our robot friend, Hitchhiker."

"Can you remotely pilot it?" Fergus asked.

"Yes, for sure."

"What's the bad news?"

"The docking collar was modified to include a cutting ring for force-boarding space vessels. We won't be able to connect it to anything here except a full dock, such as at the Bore Depot. Nor will you be able to dock on to it with your pod. So, I don't know how we'd get anyone onboard."

"Okay," Fergus said. *Damn.* There went one good plan, though at least it explained the modifications to *Loxodon*. "Hold on there. I'm working on getting the prisoners out now, and I'll be back in touch."

"I'll be waiting," she replied, and disconnected.

The next door up he was fairly sure belonged to his second-to-last missing scientist, and sure enough, when he got the door open, he found himself face to face with a middle-aged woman with a wild halo of brown hair around her head and a leg brace. Another one Tomboy had identified: Dr. Miller, taken in a home invasion.

"You're new," she said.

"Came here to rescue you," he said. "Strictly a short-term job."

"Okay then," she said. "I assume you made all this noise and nonsense? So, you may as well rescue me."

"How are you at ladders?" he asked.

"You mean the drop tube? Is there a slug field at the bottom?" she asked.

"There is, but you'll need to climb back up one level."

"I will need help with that," she said.

"I'll go down with you, then I need to come back for Keeling," he said.

She nodded. "Lead on."

He led her to the hatch, and she didn't hesitate before climbing through and letting herself drop. When she had moved out of the field and off safely to one side, he dropped after her.

Her leg gave her trouble on the ladder heading back up, but he steadied her as she went, and it didn't take long to reach the level-seven exit.

After they climbed out, she was breathing hard but smiling. The Agastis were there, and Leigh wrapped her in an embrace. "We're getting out of here," she said.

Everyone looked at him. "Follow me," Fergus said.

He led them to the docks, which were still mercifully empty, and once again shorted the lock system on *Loxodon* so they could enter unrecorded.

The passenger compartment was growing tight, but everyone seemed happy to make room where they could. His friends, as later abductees, hadn't had much interaction with the others, but it didn't matter. "I'm going to go get Keeling," Fergus said.

"And the Palla," Kelsie added.

"And that," he said, sighing. "Anyone also want me to go steal some silverware while I'm at it? Bathrobes? Owens's favorite footie PJs? No? Good. I'll be back as quickly as I can, and we'll get the hell out of here. Meanwhile, everyone stay quiet; at some point, someone's going to come do a check, but they shouldn't think anyone could have gotten in here."

"Be careful," Noura said.

"And thank you," Dr. Miller added.

"Thank me when we can all see the stars again," Fergus said. *Oh, isn't that a wonderful thought?* "Be right back!" he said, and left to go collect his last scientist.

Even the climb back up to the prisoner level wasn't grueling, knowing how close he was to freedom.

As he exited the hatch, he heard the sounds of footfalls heading his way from around the corner. Hastily, he flattened himself against the wall, and this time, two soldiers in full suits, including helmets and goggles, came past. One must have had a proximity sensor, because the moment they had passed him, one shouted and swung his rifle toward him.

Fergus sprang forward, bent down, and hit the soldier headfirst in the midsection, knocking him into his partner. "Samuels here!" the second one was yelling into the comms. "Ennis and I are under attack! Prisoner level! Send—"

Fergus vaulted over the doubled-over soldier and slapped a

hand hard against Samuels, dumping enough juice into him to knock the man down and make his own suit reboot. Without the night-vision goggles, Fergus couldn't see, falling sideways as Samuels dropped, but his flailing hand managed to find Ennis's leg and bring him down before the man could aim.

He lay there in the pile of guards, gasping and desperately thirsty.

"All personnel except Carl and Molloy, scramble to prisoner level!" Owens's voice came over the soldiers' comm channel.

Shit, he thought. Not that there were much personnel left, but it would only take one to kill him. He scrambled to his feet, still breathing heavily, thirst starting to grab at his throat again. All he had to do was grab Keeling and then, apparently, the Palla. *Get Keeling and get off this floor,* he told himself. *Then think about what next.*

He took the two men's guns and threw them in the flash recycler. Dr. Keeling was in a room at the end of a hall, and Fergus ran to it and fried the door as quickly as he could.

Keeling was sitting at a chair; unlike the others, he'd been allowed a desk, and it was covered with spare parts and several datapads. He was an older man, the balance of his look more toward bureaucrat than scientist, though the man's career had had healthy stretches of both. "Dr. Nicholas Keeling?" Fergus asked.

"Who are you?" The man was startled, his hands shaking anxiously.

"I've come to rescue you and the others," Fergus said. "We need to move quickly. Is there anything you need to bring?"

The man looked over the contents of his desk. "I . . ." he started to say, then opened and closed his mouth several times. "I suppose not. Did you come to take the Palla?"

"I came for the people," he answered. "But I suppose you're

going to tell me I have to go get that too? I need to get you to safety first."

"That seems admirable," Keeling said. He stood. "I'm ready to go."

"There's a tracker embedded in your shoulder that I need to disable first," Fergus said. "Can you turn around?"

"I . . . Okay," Keeling said, and turned.

Fergus felt around on the man's shoulder but couldn't find a bump or a signal. "That's odd," he said. "You don't have one. All the others did."

"I've been here the longest," Keeling said, and hung his head for a moment. The man looked utterly wrung out and broken. "Perhaps they weren't worried about losing a lone prisoner. Or perhaps my lack of bravery was apparent right off. I fear I lacked the spirit of the late Dr. Minobe or the determined solidarity of the Pluto prisoners."

"Well, it doesn't matter," Fergus said. Whatever the reason was, they didn't have time for it right now. "We gotta go while we still can."

He checked the hallway, then ushered Dr. Keeling out the door. There was the sound of running from several directions, converging on the area of the prisoner rooms. "This way," he said, and directed Keeling around a corner. "We're going to have to take a roundabout way back to the drop tube, okay?"

"I'm in your hands," Keeling said.

"Don't worry, Dr. Keeling; I'll do my best to get you out of here safely," Fergus said.

"Thank you," Keeling said.

"Take my hand and follow me," Fergus said, "and be as quiet as you can." He led the man down the corridor, hoping to circle around the searchers back to the tube, and stopped at the corner to check out the next turn.

Keeling tapped him gently on the shoulder. "That room across the hall," he whispered, "has entrances on both sides. Would that suffice to get around the enemy?"

"It does?" Fergus whispered back. He didn't remember that from the plans, but in the dark, he could be turned around, or the room could have been modified. "Are you sure?"

"No, not entirely," Keeling admitted. "I'm sorry."

"Stay here. I'll go check," Fergus said. He left Keeling tucked against the wall, sneaked across the hallway, and opened the unlocked door. It appeared to be a laundry room, and if there was a door on the far side, it was buried behind a wall of machines. He looked back at Keeling, who was peering in his direction wide-eyed. In the dark, the man wouldn't see him shake his head. "No, just a laundry," he whispered, and turned back to gently close the door again.

Something shoved him and he went sprawling into the room. He rolled as he hit, and he could see Keeling now standing in the doorway, his flushed face a mask of fury. "You absolute miserable piece of shit!" Keeling shouted. "You're ruining *my* project!"

The door slammed shut, and Fergus heard the *click* as some sort of mechanical lock was engaged. Outside, Keeling shouted for help.

"Keeling's got the hostile trapped in the laundry room," Owens's voice came over the stolen comm only moments later. "All hands to assist."

Well, damn, Fergus thought. *Ungrateful jerk.*

He took out his pager disk. "Everybody listen up," he said. "Keeling was only posing as a fellow prisoner, but he's a part of the conspiracy, and I'm not going to get out of here."

"Fergus—" Kelsie answered first.

"No, let me speak; I only have a minute or two at best. Dr. Minobe, are you on the line?"

"I am," she said.

"Activate the Madarch with Hitchhiker on board and send it to Depot."

"It's empty."

"I know, but the kidnappers don't know that. They'll send Pace out in *Loxodon* to chase it, and that gets everyone away from here and closer to Depot. You're all going to have to figure out how to take it from there. Dr. Minobe, I'd appreciate if you do what you can for Mister Feefs. There's cat food in my cabin. Effie's in a bit of trouble on Titan, but once the rest of you get there, everything will be fine. If you meet Zacker, tell him to look into the guard who got shot in the back; I'm about ninety percent certain he's got the missing painting. The proof is his house."

"Fergus!" Kelsie said again. "We'll come back for you. We can trace your pager—"

"They might also be able to trace it from me to you," Fergus said. "I'm sorry, but I won't take that risk."

"They'll kill you, Fergus. Soon as they figure out what you are—"

"I know. You guys are the closest thing to family I've ever had or ever will, and I should have said so before now. Please take care of each other. Good-bye," he said, and he put the pager disk between his fingers and fried it. With great reluctance, he shorted out his handpad too, just as the door was thrown open to blinding light and someone shot him.

Chapter 18

————◆————

They took his exosuit, of course. Anytime he finally got a suit he liked, some asshole took it. Irritation was the first part of him awake, and the rest of him followed dutifully along, despite strong misgivings.

He was in a small conference room, chilly in just his shorts and T-shirt, and his wrists had been bound together behind him and to the chair with some sort of thick, sticky tape. Given the sliver of consoles he could see through the thicket of people and the open door, it appeared to be off main substation Ops. Ladden was there, as were Davies, Velleca, Nanho, Dr. Keeling, and several others. None of them looked happy with him, which he conceded they were probably entitled to.

"Hey," he managed to cough out. His abdomen burned, and he suspected what they'd hit him with had been somewhere between maximum stun and minimum lethality. A certain slight resistance to energy weapons seemed to be part of the dubious gift the Asiig had left him, but he didn't feel a need to point that out to the assholes who'd shot him and, if he was lucky, would do so again and more competently before he ended up on a vivisection table instead.

Frankly, he was surprised they hadn't killed him already.

Why was answered when Ladden held up his dead handpad with the back facing him. Etched into the casing were the words *Property of Guratahan Sfazil Security Service*. Stolen, of course, but he wasn't going to point that out either.

"Who are you?" Ladden said. "The Sfazili Government should know better than to send someone to interfere with Alliance Special Projects. I might lodge a formal complaint when I send them back your body."

"Please do," Fergus said. "I'm sure they'll be very interested in hearing how I've disrupted your *official* operation."

"Guratahan Sfazil has no jurisdiction here," Ladden said. "Why were you sent?"

"I'm sure you understand I can't discuss the particulars of my mission," Fergus said. It didn't hurt to let the lie play out, even if it wouldn't save him.

Davies, who had been quivering restlessly behind the others, stepped forward and punched him hard in the face. "I told you! He's an alien! He swam here!" Davies shouted. One of the other soldiers snickered, and Davies' face turned a deeper red. "Well, how the fuck else did he get here?"

Owens came into the room. "Systems are all back online," he said.

"You blew the fleeing escape pods?"

"Yes."

"And the Madarch?"

"Pace is in pursuit. No one is going to get away."

Ladden turned back to Fergus and smiled. "So, no one will ever know this man was here," he said. "That gives us a lot of leeway as to what to do with him. Right, Mr. MacInnis?"

Fergus shrugged. "I suppose so."

"But the Sfazili—"

"Oh, shut *up*, Davies," Ladden said. "This handpad is a lie, just like everything else this man told you. He's come to steal the Palla and he's failed. That's all that we need to know."

"He told me he came for the prisoners," Dr. Keeling said. "And he did go for them first."

"Ten escapees makes for a good distraction, Dr. Keeling. You were meant as cannon fodder, no less, no more."

Keeling threw up his hands. "I'm just telling you what he told me!"

"And the other prisoners told me you broke the Palla, Dr. Keeling," Fergus added.

Owens whirled on Keeling. "What?!"

"The man's a liar!" Keeling retorted hotly. "You just said so yourself!"

"Yet for months now, your status reports have been vague at best," Ladden said. "We risked discovery to go fetch you your latest set of so-called experts from Pluto, and you promised us immediate breakthroughs if we did. Where are those?"

"It's complicated and painstaking work! It doesn't happen overnight. None of you are scientists," Keeling said.

"No, but we're all card players, and I can tell when a man is bluffing," Owens said. "This is not a pleasing bit of information, Dr. Keeling."

"He's a liar!" Keeling shouted again, jabbing his finger toward Fergus. "He's trying to confuse us and set us against each other."

"Then he is succeeding admirably at his job, especially considering he's tied to a chair and facing imminent death," Ladden said.

"What can I say; I've done this before. I'm a professional," Fergus said. He eyed Keeling. "And a competent one, I suppose I have to add."

"Shut up!" Keeling and Owens said simultaneously.

Keeling stepped toward Fergus, his fists clenched. "You don't know anything about what I do, or anything about the Pallai. And these other so-called experts were worse than useless! At least I managed to get a live link to it, back when I wasn't saddled with their bumbling, overrated—"

"Dr. Keeling, that's more than enough," Ladden interrupted sharply. He turned to the soldiers behind him. "Ennis, Davies, go take Dr. Keeling back to his room and keep him there."

"This is my project!" Keeling protested. "You can't just lock me in like I'm actually a prisoner."

"I can, and maybe I should have all along," Ladden said. "This project is a *disaster*, I've got a several-billion-cred brainless prototype sitting useless outside, and if my head's going to roll for it, yours is going first."

"I—" Keeling tried to protest as Davies grabbed his arm.

"Get him out of here," Ladden said. "I have some questions to ask our new friend here, and then probably some for him, too, when we're done."

Ennis and Davies hauled Keeling away.

Ladden swung a chair up and sat on it backward, his arms folded across the back, studying Fergus. He was an older man, with the weathered steel look of career military. "Owens, go back to Ops," he said. "See if Pace has caught up with our escapees yet."

"Yes, sir," Owens said, and left, shutting the door behind him.

The Madarch should have been able to outrun *Loxodon* back to Depot, with its head start, but even if it didn't, the longer it took for Pace to catch up to it, the closer his friends got to freedom. What he could do here was buy his friends time. "Prototype, eh? Crablike thing out back?" Fergus asked. "Can I see it? I'm quite interested."

"No," Ladden said. "So, you're not with the Sfazili government, am I correct?"

"Not really, no," Fergus said.

"The MacInnis identity is a cover too, but a good one. We didn't see any red flags when we checked you out, and we don't usually miss things. Meanwhile, Transit systems say you're still on your hauler, which appears to be leaving Wyville-Thompson without you. How did you fool the tracker?"

Fergus smiled. "I fed it to Olson's cat."

Ladden closed his eyes for a moment and shook his head, then chuckled. "Yeah, okay. That would work. But surely you don't expect me to believe a cat is piloting your ship."

"I tried to teach him," Fergus said, "but no thumbs and he kept barfing up hairballs on the nav console. No wonder he's going in the wrong direction. Cats are terrible drivers."

"We'll find all your accomplices, too, you know," Ladden said.

"I knew the risks."

"So, who are you? What's your mission? For real, this time. My patience is not infinite."

"As much as I hate to give him any credit, Dr. Keeling was right. I came to rescue your prisoners."

"Why?"

"It was a job." Fergus shrugged. "You didn't really think none of them would be missed?"

"I didn't think any of them would be *found*, certainly," Ladden said. He leaned back. "We're going to start breaking things on you soon, to find out exactly what you know and who hired you and who else knows, and I'd expect that to scare most people, but I get the feeling you've been through this before. That's one hell of a scar on your leg. Combat?"

"Yeah. Kind of a hostage situation," Fergus said. "Shot with a harpoon gun."

Behind Ladden, the two remaining soldiers winced. "Ouch," Ladden said. "So, you're ex-military? Where did you serve? And for whom?"

"I can't tell you that," Fergus said. "I'm sorry."

"Now, see, I respect that, as one professional to another, even here in this unfortunate situation," Ladden said. "But right now—"

"But right now, you're sitting on a rogue operation," Fergus guessed. "Tacitly endorsed as long as you don't screw it up, or they'll wash their hands of you and hang you out to dry. And it's screwing itself up, starting with Keeling being unable to deliver what he promised. Almost a year at it, and he keeps having you bring in more people in the hopes that they'll bail him out, and all it's bought you is more opportunities for exposure."

"Succinctly and simply put, yes," Ladden said. "I suppose it's not hard to add that up. What's interesting to me is how much you *don't*. You took out several of my men with embarrassing ease, and while the bulk of the fault is theirs for becoming complacent and lazy here, I found no weapons on you. No one fights that well. And then you told Davies that you had an 'arrangement' with Carl, which he strenuously denies. You're lucky he's not here in the room, because he seems to have strong feelings on that accusation."

Nanho punched Fergus hard in the mouth, sending him and the chair crashing to the floor. "Carl's my best friend," Nanho said. "So, you're not so lucky after all."

"I've sent your bioscan info out for identification, but you know how slow data moves through the ice. I can't afford to wait for those answers to get back to me. So, unless you've got a whole lot of information you're prepared to give us directly, we're at the breaking-things part of the conversation," Ladden said. "You going to talk?"

Fergus shook his head. "I'm sorry; I told you, I can't."

Ladden stood and straightened his jacket. "Samuels, get him upright again?"

The second soldier picked the chair up, and Fergus winced as blood dripped from his split lip all over his T-shirt. "Aw, man," he said, slurring the words. "That's going to stain."

"I believe flippancy has run its course," Ladden said. "Your life will last only as long as we have questions, but I think you'll shortly see good reasons to help both go quickly."

Looming over Fergus, Samuels cracked his knuckles, and Fergus felt the bees deep in his gut suddenly roiling, crawling under his skin, eager to come out. *Not now!* Fergus thought, trying desperately to push them back down. *I'm in control, not you.*

Ladden mistook the sudden anxiety on Fergus's face as a victory, and smiled. "Let's get to it, then," he said. "We'll start again with who you work for."

Remember, no matter how much this hurts, you're playing for time for your friends, Fergus told himself. "The Archduke Ferdinand," he answered, and then the beating began in earnest.

As the running tally of things that hurt exploded toward the infinite, he took some small pride that he was keeping the bees in check, and a smug satisfaction that they had go look up the "Steward of Gondor" before knowing that was a lie too. In that brief respite, curled now on the floor surrounded by boots, he caught his breath and wondered if his friends were safe yet.

"I'm out of patience with this," Ladden declared. "Samuels, start cutting on him."

Samuels pulled a large knife out of his pocket and held the gleaming blade in front of Fergus's swollen face. "Just following orders," he said, grinning widely. "You understand, right?"

Fergus managed to nod.

"Besides, I can't spend a year down in this hellhole and not bring back a souvenir." Samuels reached out with his other hand and pinched Fergus's ear, hard.

"Unless you want to tell us the truth this time about who sent you here," Ladden said.

Bloody fucking hell, Fergus thought, gritting his teeth and bracing himself. *Why didn't I get a nice job on Coralla, making tea for tourists on the beach, instead of this?*

He dug down into his bottomless well of human cultural trivia and managed to cough out another answer between the blood and spit filling his mouth. "I didn't hear that," Ladden said, leaning closer. "Who sent you?"

"Danger Mouse," Fergus repeated, and then Samuels started hacking away at the side of his head and he lost everything else to his own screaming.

———

There were alarms.

There are always alarms, he thought, but no one seemed to be hurting him, so he took it as a net positive. He cracked one eye open. The room was lit with flickering bluish light, and he groaned. *Shit. The electricity got out, didn't it?* he thought.

There were three bodies in the room with him, and at first, he thought he'd killed them, but he could see the gentle rise and fall of Nanho's chest. He sat up, testing his bonds and finding them looser, no doubt from thrashing, and wanted to cry from how much everything hurt. The side of his head burned in agony. Blood had run down his face and neck and was still wet to the touch; it felt like days since Samuels had taken his knife out, but the console on the room wall told him it had been less than thirty minutes.

"Get yerself together, ye arse," he told himself out loud, and managed, with much swaying, to get to his feet just as the alarms went dead and the door opened.

Owens stood in the doorway, mouth agape as he took in the bodies on the floor and Fergus standing in the middle of them. Belatedly, Fergus realized he still had sparks running up and down his arms.

"Who the fuck are you?!" Owens shouted, drawing out his pistol and pointing it at him.

Unsure what else to do, and still muddled by pain, Fergus backed away, forcing the electricity back down and in.

Keeping Fergus carefully in his sights, Owens bent down and checked Ladden's pulse, then roughly shook him with his free hand. Ladden stirred, dazed. "Whah?" he mumbled.

"The spy was booby-trapped, and you must have set it off when you were questioning him. Sensor systems are detecting some sort of escalating electromagnetic activity in his vicinity, and it's going critical. We need to get out now, before the whole substation blows."

"Pace . . ." Ladden said.

"He's too far away," Owens said. "We have less than ten minutes. Maybe a lot less." He still hadn't taken his eyes off Fergus.

"Shoot him and then let's go," Ladden said, getting up.

"It might trigger an immediate explosion," Owens said. "He's wired on the inside; I dunno what with. Nothing I've ever seen before, certainly not our tech. There's no time."

Ladden stumbled over to the room console and activated it as Owens kept careful aim on Fergus. "This is Commander Ladden," he announced. "All hands abandon the substation. Destruction is imminent. I repeat: all hands abandon the substation. Escape pods will be rendered safe. Rendezvous at checkpoint two if you are able. Ladden out."

"Transfer remote controls of the escape pod safeties over to the prototype. You and I can ride it out of here and regroup with the others," Ladden said, his eyes on Fergus. "I don't want anyone leaving here who isn't one of us."

Owens helped Ladden out the door, then Samuels and Nanho. "Enjoy your last few minutes," Owens snarled, "and know that we *will* find whoever sent you, and we will make them suffer for this more than you can possibly imagine."

The door locked behind him.

"'Booby-trapped,' really?" he called after them. "You'd think no one had ever seen a man shoot lightning around his body before."

Whatever Owens and Ladden were doing out in the main ops room, it was done quickly; within moments, everything was silent. The tape binding his wrists was easily worked loose with some twisting, though it dug painfully into his skin as he stretched it thin enough to slip out of. Once free, he shorted the door and limped out into the empty control room, wiping away the blood that had dripped into his eyes. The systems were all locked, but the display screen still showed an explosive detected, now centered in the control room right where he was standing. *But I'm not explosive,* he thought. *Stupid—*

His hand went almost involuntarily to his shorts pocket, and his fingers wrapped around the stack of small explosive disks Maison had given him. They were stuck together in a stack, and he couldn't pull them apart. A red light atop of the stack flashed angrily.

The electricity he put out during the beating must have been enough to trigger them. *Twenty minutes,* Maison had said. How much had passed? At least ten, if Owens was right.

"Not going to set them off by accident, eh, Maison?" he grumbled. "Oh, we're going to have words."

The console display informed anyone watching that several escape pods had just launched, and the small ship at the back was moving away from the substation at high speed. The prototype droneship, obviously. He hoped Owens and Ladden really liked each other, because they had to be half in each other's laps in the tiny space allotted for a pilot.

Okay, Fergus, save yourself.

He swept his belongings from where they were scattered on a side console back into his pack as he looked for options. There were still two escape pods left in their tubes, but they were on a lower level. The elevator might not be fast enough. *Oh, fuck me,* he thought, and ran, the impact of each step making the side of his head burn, to the drop tube and jumped in.

At least the slug field was still working. He discovered, as he started to climb back up to the dock level, that he had several broken fingers and Samuels had started to carve his name into Fergus's shoulder. Climbing the ladder up one level was like being beaten all over again, and only the ticking time bomb in his pocket and the knowledge it could go off at any second kept him moving.

He reached the docks, opened a hatch to an escape pod, and threw the stack in. *Come on, come on, launch,* he swore at the pod as he sealed and activated it.

It felt like the slowest launch in the history of emergencies, but finally it went, zooming out into the Deep.

He didn't know if Ladden still had the ability to trigger the self-destruct on the pod itself, but he figured it didn't matter. One way or another, the bomb was off the substation and getting farther away every second.

When the explosion came, it was as if the substation itself had become a giant bell, struck hard on one side. Fergus fell to the floor, cursing all the many ways that hurt.

He let himself catch his breath before he attempted to get to his feet again. It took him several tries to find the path of least agony, but at last he made it. Adrenaline was a good thing when even just walking was so unbearable, he wanted to lie down and cry. Not that he had the slightest bit of moisture left in his body to summon tears.

There was a limited amount of time before Ladden and his crew saw that the substation itself hadn't exploded, and returned and got back to business on him, and as keen as he was on not sticking around long enough to give them that chance, he had two tasks he had to do or his conscience would never let him rest again.

At least this time, he could take the elevator.

He gathered his things, happy to have his exosuit back after all. He took the dead handpad too, just on the off chance they could still manage to pull something useful off it. Then he headed down to the prisoner level.

As he'd expected, they'd left Keeling behind. But someone had paid him a visit before leaving, and Fergus walked through his open door to find the man crumpled in a heap on the floor in a pile of his own blood.

He bent down as best he could to check the man's pulse, not having much hope, but at his touch, the scientist coughed and opened his eyes. "You," he managed to choke out.

"Yeah, me," Fergus said. There wasn't anything he could do for the man, but he wasn't quite able to just walk away.

"I wanted to be the one," Keeling said. "Then someone else did it first and just dropped them out into space at *random*. No name, no source, no credit. I spent *decades* for nothing. I wanted them to be mine, my discovery, my name in history. You wouldn't understand."

"Understand kidnapping colleagues and innocent people for the sake of your own pride? No, you're right, I don't," Fergus said.

"Fuck you," Keeling said. "Just fuck you to hell."

He let out a long, last breath and, with one violent twitch, went still.

Fergus closed the man's eyes. "I'm sorry," he said, and left the body where it was.

He stumbled to the elevator and took it to the lab level,

shorted out the locked door in front of the small lab, and walked toward where the Palla hung suspended in a net of instrumentation. It wasn't anything particularly impressive to look at, at first glance. A dull metallic sphere about the size of a melon, not all that different from the various bobs of common use, except for being three times the size and having a small letter *T* etched on one side amid grooves and swirls. If Maison was right that each one was represented by a letter of the Greek alphabet, this was indeed Tau.

There was a single circular lens fixed in one side, but it was unlit, dead.

He wished he knew for sure what it was, but if his friends were right, it was not a what but a who.

If so . . . the value was incalculable. To science, but also to the military if they could reverse-engineer it and keep its secrets to themselves. *And find and destroy the others, trace them back to their source, and make sure their maker can't ever make any more,* he thought. *All theirs, for whatever wars they want.*

It was beyond human tech as he knew it, but the Tau insignia suggested a human connection despite that. There was, he thought, a special and newfound empathy in his heart for those caught in the dangerous interstices between human and nonhuman worlds.

"Well, fellow enigma, it's lucky for us they didn't have time to come back for you," he told it. "I'm going to do my best not to damage you further, but I have to get you out of here."

He popped the seals on the glass tank and slid the door open. Tracing the connections holding the sphere in place with his undamaged fingers, he carefully disconnected them one by one. New alarms began to sound, but he ignored them and concentrated on untangling the rat's nest of wiring until at last he was holding the Palla free in his mangled hands. It was heavy, inert, and he wondered if Keeling, in his impatience for glory, truly had killed it.

Maison had said they thought it was hiding instead, whatever that meant, and he trusted his friends more than anyone else in the universe. Best thing he could do was take it to them and ask. If anyone could understand it, or keep it safe, it was them.

Assuming they escaped Pace and the Deep, and he could find a way out after them. He wished he'd not sent Dr. Minobe off quite so quickly.

You'll find a way, like you always do, he told himself. *Just gotta get moving. You've gotten through the worst of it now. Easy sailing, right?*

"Let's go," he said, and headed to the elevator. If his pod was still anchored outside the maintenance hatch, despite all else he'd count the day a good one.

Chapter 19

The elevator died halfway between floors, shaking and shuddering before it came to a sudden, grinding dead stop. "Now what?!" he shouted to the empty car.

When it didn't start moving again, he set the Palla down on the floor and tried to pry the doors open with his six still-working fingers. He'd just managed to widen the crack when the elevator was rocked so hard, he stumbled and crashed shoulder-first into a wall. "The hell?" he muttered. That was more than just the elevator; that was the entire station shaking. Were the alarms different?

Shit. Those are *different alarms,* he thought. *If you never learn anything else in this life, Fergus Fucking Idiot Ferguson, learn not to tempt the universe by declaring the worst is over.*

He tried again and managed to get the doors open enough that he could get down on his knees and pry at the outer doors for the lower floor. With both sets of doors open, he turned around and tried to lower himself feet-first out of the elevator car toward the floor outside, the Palla set on the edge where he could grab it once he was down.

Another jolt shook the station, and he fell the remaining way out of the elevator car even as the Palla rolled out of sight back inside. "Oh, bloody fucking hell!" he swore, hurting all over as he lay on the floor, trying to decide how important it really was to try to climb back in to fetch it.

Another tremor hit, and the Palla came flying out of the

tilting elevator car and hit him square in the chest. "Ow!" he shouted, then whimpered miserably as he scrambled to his feet and chased after the Palla before it could disappear down the swaying corridor.

What the hell was going on with the substation?

He finally caught up to the Palla when it hit a corner, and dropped it into his pack to keep it from going rogue on him again. At least he was on the right floor, even if the elevator hadn't quite gotten him all the way there.

The maintenance closet didn't look too different from when he'd come in. He was happy enough just to find his confuddler still jacked in to the substation systems, until he also remembered he'd linked it with one of the pager disks. "Yes!" he shouted, and frantically opened the link. "Is anyone out there? What the hell is happening?"

"MacInnis, is that you? Where the hell are you?" Dr. Minobe's voice responded, in a hail of static.

"Yes, it's me! I'm on Ballard!"

"You need to get out of there. There was some sort of explosion just off-station and it's triggered a geothermal upswell. The whole substation is unstable."

"That explains the new alarms, then," he said.

"Do you still have the pod?"

"I'll know in about thirty seconds. Where are you?"

"I am currently heading toward a meetup with *Loxodon*," Dr. Minobe said. "There appear to be some passengers aboard who'd like a change of rides."

Fergus felt an old knot in stomach slowly unwind and let go. "Thank you," he said. "I can't thank you enough."

"We still need you to live long enough to drive us all up the Bore. Then we can call it even," she said.

Another jolt shook the substation, and without thinking, Fergus put his hand out to steady himself on the wall. "Augh," he said, pulling his hand back and leaning against the wall instead until the tremor passed.

"Are you okay?" Dr. Minobe asked.

"Some cuts and bruises and broken fingers," he said. "And some asshole cut my ear off."

There was a pause. "Cut your ear off?" Dr. Minobe asked.

"Yeah. One of my two favorites, too," Fergus said. He did his best, as the substation steadied, to unfold his exosuit enough so he could drag himself into it. "It's just a damned lucky thing I was already ugly."

"They can regrow that for you," she said. "We just need to get you back up to civ—"

The connection died in a hail of static.

It took him several minutes longer than he would have liked to get his suit on and sealed up, while the shaking of the station grew in frequency and intensity. Pulling his hood up around the tattered remains of his ear was torture. When it was all finally sealed, he shoved over the boxes in front of the hatch and climbed in, swearing profusely.

When the inner door sealed, he closed his eyes, took a deep breath, and pressed the release for the outer door.

It was almost a surprise when he wasn't immediately crushed by water. Instead, beyond the open hatch was the cramped, dim, deeply welcome interior of his pod. It was groaning as the substation shook around it, the upswells trying to pull it free, and he sealed the door, got into his seat, and buckled in as quickly as he could.

As soon as he released the magnetic clamps, the upswells were going to fling him toward the solid dead end of ice above. He sat at the helm, listening to the bubbling water roaring around him and the creak and cry of the pod's connection, until he thought it had abated somewhat. "Here goes," he said, and punched the disconnect at the same time as he brought the engine power up to full reverse and down.

This must be what it feels like to get swatted when you're a fly, he thought, as the pod went careening wildly upward, spinning end over end. It took him several minutes to get the spin under control enough to orient himself and point away from the substation and out of the geothermal zone. Even at full power, he could barely keep his course, and he let out an involuntary groan of horror as, beside him, Ballard Substation finally came free of its mooring.

This is not good, he thought. He shut down all unnecessary power drains and shifted everything he could to the engines, and the pod slowly began to make headway. Fighting the turbulence of the upswells made all the simulations he'd done of pops feel like the worst of lazy shams.

In one of the brief glances he could spare the external screens, he saw Ballard Substation start to move, accelerating upward in the swell. The fabrication structure that had been attached to the back to house the war drone broke off first, disappearing down into the murk with no air to buoy it. He dared to look up, through the top edge of the pod window dome, to see the lights on Ballard's underside vanish as it accelerated up into the darkness.

He needed to get out of there.

On his scanner screen, he watched as Ballard Substation hit the ice above like a glass ornament smashing against the floor. It came apart in vast chunks amid clouds of debris and air as enormous shards of ice splintered away from the underside of Enceladus's surface and fell. Fergus tore his eyes off the screen as the ice appeared and disappeared suddenly like vengeful giants in the pale light of his struggling pod as they slid past.

One fell just ahead of him and he had to swerve sharply to avoid hitting it; others passed beside and behind him. The pod slewed one way and another, the engines creeping up into the orange, as massive swells buffeted him in all directions. Small pieces of ice hit the pod like hail, a deafening thunder, and somewhere high above the ice, he wondered if there was a new geyser ejecting vapor out into space and getting people's attention. *If so, I wish I was out there to see it,* he thought. *I bet it would be a beautiful sight in my rear view as I'm leaving Enceladus behind for good.*

He barely spotted the gigantic chunk of ice in his peripheral vision in time. The engines redlined as he threw everything they had into a sharp starboard dive, and the shard passed so close, he would swear he could feel the cold and anger radiating off it as it fell past. He blew out breath he didn't know he'd been holding, his hands trembling on the pod controls, just as a smaller splinter, hidden by the larger, slammed into the side of the pod.

Warning lights flashed all over the console, red and orange. The impact sent the pod into a sickening spin, and Fergus fought to get it under control before he got hit again or decorated the interior with what little contents his stomach had in it. The pod was no longer maneuvering as well as it should, but he managed to get it back on an even keel and making headway against the fading upswells before he dared look over what the warning lights were trying to tell him.

Despite the pounding it had taken, the passenger compartment was intact; he wasn't leaking air, nor were there structural integrity problems that could suddenly cause the entire pod to implode. The engines were overheated but not damaged; now that he wasn't being buffeted around as badly and was out of the worst of the maelstrom, he notched his speed down by ten percent to give them a chance to cool.

Beyond that, the news was less good. The ice chunk had

damaged his starboard propulsion jets, which meant he was doomed to wander in a vast circle unless he cut his speed by more than half. And that would be acceptable, except the ice had also taken out the starboard filter that extracted oxygen from the sea water and fed the cabin.

Half-speed, with half the air.

His suit had a full air tank and a spare, but he had no idea where he was or how far from safety. His pager disk was giving him only static, and when he tried to use the pod's onboard communications channels to reach someone, they also gave him back nothing but noise. Some sort of jamming? An effect of the geothermal eruption, or of Ballard Substation's destruction?

Everything, everywhere, was dark. Not just the empty void of space, but a close and crushing and living dark, the tightening grip of a patient predator.

Pain and exhaustion squabbled over their shrinking choke-hold on his thoughts as the fear took over, narrowing everything down to this moment, this ending. He began to shake uncontrollably and had to force himself to take his hands off the helm, the faint rush of electricity walking up and down his fingers under his suit gloves.

I'm going to die down here, he thought.

He could just scuttle the pod now, himself inside, and at least no one would find the Palla to exploit it. And drowning would be fast, right?

His father had seemed to think so.

Of all the many images his stupid, bottomless memory had clung stubbornly to, no matter how much alcohol, time, or other memories he'd tried to bury it with, it always came back to that one: his father in that bloody rowboat, his leg in a cast, waving to him on the shore just before he tipped himself deliberately over the side into the Scottish Inland Sea.

How bad a son was I, he thought for the millionth time, *that that's the only memory I have of my father actually smiling at me?*

His face burned with old shame. Did it matter what good he did now that he could do nothing then?

At least he'd saved his friends. And some other people. And maybe a cat. It would never add up to enough, but it was *something.*

Behind him, in the dim rear lights of his pod, he could just make out the giant ice shards drifting up again to rejoin the vast ceiling above. It was beautiful, and alien, and terrifying.

It was not the last thing he wanted to see.

"Not me. Not this time," he said. He did his best to breathe, focusing on the in and the out and the spaces in between as Dr. Minobe had tried to teach him with Mu, and little by little, he forced the darkness back.

Even if it was a frail and untrustworthy truce, he'd take it. He made his best guess as to his bearing, set his engines at half, and pointed the limping pod toward Wyville-Thompson and its promise of life.

Ahead of his pod, he realized he could just make out a red light, faint enough that at first, he thought it was some odd reflection on the pod's front window of his own helm. As it resolved more clearly into a large red disk, he realized with a start that he was staring right up the ass end of a Madarch.

Friend or foe? he wondered, though out here on the fringes of the destruction of Ballard, he knew the most likely answer. Right now, directly behind it, he was in its blind spot, but that wouldn't survive any changes in direction. He shut his pod engines down fully, letting the interior and exterior lights go dark, then dumped what juice he had into the stealth plates as the pod sank slowly down and out from behind the Madarch.

As soon as he was down far enough, he could make out the

extra fins and other modifications that had been made to it. *And where're you going?* he wondered. *And where're your friends and your precious prototype war drone?*

Something shot just overhead, a bright blip of heat on his sensors that passed near where his pod had been only a few seconds earlier. He gave a single, short burst on the starboard adjustment thrusters, sending the pod diving more steeply away, and watched through the glass as another Madarch caught up to the first, and they both slowed as a third joined them and formed a triangle.

What the hell? he wondered. Then he saw the faint glint of light off bubbles in the water between them. *Shit. A light net!*

The Madarchs drew farther apart, maintaining their formation, and began to reverse course, moving back in his direction.

They were clearly guessing which way he had gone before he'd kicked on his stealth plates. He was enough off that course to be not in immediate danger, but they knew he was out there and they had a lot more time than he did. They'd have nailed him already if he wasn't running heatless.

As he watched them move gracefully through the dark, hunting, he saw a fourth shape join them: the war drone. It was bristling with energy weapons slung beneath its body. As he watched it in horrified fascination, the wing sections on the side bent, folding in on themselves to make shorter, sharper fins. Its biggest limitation would inevitably be that Keeling had failed to provide its intended pilot; with a sentient artificial mind at the helm instead of delicate and needy meat-people, Fergus did not doubt it could kill almost anything or anyone, almost anywhere.

At least against Ladden and Owens, he might have a chance.

They'd almost certainly expect him to make for Wyville-Thompson as the nearest refuge. Even if he managed to outrun them to get there, he would not bet a single credit they'd let the presence of civilians deter them from doing whatever they needed to get the Palla back and get rid of witnesses. And as tempting as the thought of being able to stand, stretch, and breathe without checking his air gauge was, he wasn't going to endanger anyone he didn't have to.

Running the stealth plates meant even less power available to his engines, and lower speed meant he was going to go through his oxygen resources more quickly per distance traveled. Fergus did the calculations, hated the answers, did some more with no greater luck.

The Madarchs were changing angle again, and this time, their arc would intercept him if he didn't drastically change direction. He couldn't spot the prototype but was sure it wasn't far away, waiting for its opportunity. His comm channel was still static.

He scrounged the last of his pager disks from the pod floor and thumbed it on. "This is Fergus. I escaped Ballard in my pod, but I'm being hunted and the Alliance is jamming signals. My pager will queue this message to send if and when it can, though I can't promise to still be here to receive any answer," he said. "So, yes, the operation at Ballard was being run by an Alliance team led by a man named Ladden. Dr. Keeling was complicit in the operation—probably even the one who initiated it—and only feigned being a prisoner in order to have the trust of the others. He did not survive the destruction of Ballard."

He took a breath, watched the Madarchs moving in. He was going to have to move soon, and if the Madarchs were herding him, he might not have much choice about which way to go. "My pod has been damaged, so I'm now moving at a quarter speed, and I'm short on air while being actively sought by three of the remaining modified Madarchs and the war drone, which is currently being operated by Ladden and his second-in-command, Owens," he said. "At the conclusion of recording this message, know that I'll have done my damnedest to elude them, but if this gets through and I don't, well, it was an honor to know you all. Fergus out."

He dove straight down, watching the pressure meter tick upward until it was fully in the red, and his ears felt like someone was trying to cram sand into them. Less than half a kilometer from the bottom, he leveled out again, turned his pod at a forty-five degree angle from Wyville-Thompson, and set the automatic pilot to continue on that course and on a gradual one-degree rise until either the pod encountered an obstacle, he directly contravened the instruction, or he ceased to live.

In that last case, he programmed the pod to override all its safeties and self-breach.

Fergus ran the numbers a third time. At quarter-speed, if he reduced the oxygen to the point where he'd narrowly avoid brain damage and death, he had about nine hours. He set the oxygen reduction to last for eight and almost immediately started yawning.

Above him, the Madarchs were moving their net through the area where he'd just been, probably regretting that the days of sonar had passed. Though he imagined the dense, bubbly water would make almost as effective a jammer as their comms block.

His eyes felt heavy, too heavy to keep open any longer. He raised his hand in an age-old defiant gesture to the Madarchs, then gave in and closed his eyes, and hoped that at least his last few remaining dreams would be sweet.

———

It was the obstacle alert, rather than imminent suffocation, that triggered his return to wakefulness, his head stuffed full of petulant, uncooperative fuzz. The pod's flickering, dying display told him he'd been out for seven hours and wouldn't give him any more data on the obstacle other than a sustained physical contact had been made starting approximately ten minutes earlier.

Outside the pod, everything was pitch-dark, not even the vague and amorphous restlessness of the water that he'd come to simultaneously loathe and find comfort in from the Deep. The pod's engines were whining, and their temp was edging upward in a way they shouldn't have been, though his console showed no new damage.

Aw, hell, he thought, and shut them down. *I guess I get no further than this.*

He pulled down his suit goggles and turned up the infrared, hoping to see whatever it was that had brought him to a stop, and just as he flicked them on at full power, a blinding light filled the area around his pod. "Aaaaugh!" he shouted, tearing the goggles from his face and rubbing at his tear-filled eyes. When he could bear to, he cracked open one eye to discover all was light around him, that he was surrounded by walls, and that Stanislao Toscani was standing in front of his pod, arms crossed over his chest, *laughing.*

Fergus fumbled open the pod's hatch and practically fell out of it onto the still-wet floor of *Carcharias*'s emergency bay. His lungs hurt and he still felt dizzy, but he managed to roll over and stare up at the older pilot. "Yer a right bastard," he said.

Stani laughed again. "And proud of it! Look at you, lazing around on my deck when everybody's been looking all over for you."

"Any of them *not* want to kill me?" he asked.

"Not me, not right now," Stani said. Despite his apparent amusement, deep concern was clear in his eyes and his voice. "Though one look at your sorry ass and anyone would feel I was doing you a mercy if I put you down. You're not going to barf or anything?"

"I don't think so," Fergus said, "but I'm not standing up any-time soon. I reduced my oxygen to the lowest threshold I could, hoping someone would find me before I ran out. Also, I may have gotten a bit hurt."

"I guessed that," Stani said. "It's the subtle clues, like that you're getting blood all over my floor."

"Sorry," Fergus said. "You knew I was out here?"

"I knew you were somewhere, and lucky for me, I was closest when we managed to triangulate your general position from your pager transmission."

"That should only have gone to—"

"To your friends. Yeah. I've had much more of a social life these last ten hours or so than I've had in twenty years. You're an interesting guy, MacInnis. Or is it Fergus?"

"Depends on the day and how much trouble I'm in," Fergus said.

"I suspected as much. Anyhow, I should call up your friends and tell them you're okay. Sort of okay. A small bit okay? I'll just lie. You think you can find your way up to *Carcharias*'s bridge?"

"Unless you've rearranged your hauler, I expect so," Fergus said. "I'm going to lie here for a little while first. And then find the bathroom. Did my friends get out of the Deep yet?"

Stani made a face. "Not yet. We have a big problem—"

"The Alliance didn't—" Fergus sat up quickly, and fell over again as his head started to spin and throb.

"Not yet, but they're down here looking for us. From what your message said, and what your friends told me, I'd rather they not catch any of us," Stani said. "I really like the big green fuzzy guy, by the way. Though I admit that's in large part to eir explanation of how ey took out Pace aboard *Loxodon*."

"Oh?"

"Did you know your friend could cling to ceilings?"

"Not specifically, but—"

"Did you know ey could cling to *bathroom* ceilings? And did you know that apparently, Pace suffers from this Earth thing called *severe arachnophobia . . .*"

Fergus smiled. "Dropped on him?"

"Yeah. Caught him with his pants down, you might say. Proving there's always at least one bright spot even in the darkest of places. And this place is dark as hell."

"We should try to get to one of the other Bores, if this one isn't safe. Either one of us—"

"No, it wouldn't make a difference. That's what I'm trying to tell you. There's a problem, and it's a biggie that'll probably kill us all. All the Bores are shut down."

"Shut down?"

"Locked. No one in, no one out. Even the emergency override is off."

Fergus tried to wrap his head around that. "Because of the geothermal instability at Ballard?"

"The lockdown happened a good ten, fifteen minutes before Ballard blew. We have no idea what's going on or what caused it. Comms to Above are down as well, Transit Control isn't answering—can't answer, obviously—and the staff down here are just as in the dark as the rest of us. All the substation systems appear compromised. Wasn't you, by any chance?"

"No," Fergus said.

"Maybe Ballard hacked everything to stop you?"

Fergus thought about Ballard's security and the pinhole compromise they'd never detected. "I don't think it was them," he said. "Unless they got a lot cleverer really fast and under very difficult circumstances."

"Well, whoever did it, we're all trapped, and no one has any answers at all. I, for one, was hoping you might shed some light on this, as every bit of trouble that's happened since you arrived has had you right dead-center in the middle of it."

"It's a natural talent."

"So your friends tell me. They also said we're apparently bugged so the Bastards can track us?"

"Yeah," Fergus said.

Stani heaved a deep sigh. "And they said you can disable it somehow?"

"Yeah."

"Is it going to hurt?"

"A bit. Just for a second. If comms are down through the ice, they might not be working right now, anyway."

"I resent the very idea of the Bastards sticking a fucking tracker in me, like I'm their property, and I want it gone," Stani said. He started to take off his shirt. "Shoulder, right?"

Fergus grimaced. "For us, stomach. It was in the drug test capsule you took on hire."

Stani grumbled and lifted his shirt to show off his hair-covered belly.

Fergus groaned, managed to sit up and stay there this time. He was so thirsty already, he could barely stand it; the idea of making one more spark made him want to weep. "Close your eyes," he said, "and don't ask."

When the other pilot had closed his eyes, Fergus put his hand on his stomach, listening for the tiny buzz, and waited for his internal electricity to feel in tune with it. Then he let one spark out to connect them.

"Aaaaaah!" Stani shouted, and jumped back. "And damn, your hands are fucking *cold*, MacInnis!"

"Sorry," he said.

"Is it done?"

"Yeah."

"Good. At least I can die a free man, now. Sort of." Stani rubbed his stomach gingerly. "Speaking of dying, even though you look like total shit and the kindest thing I could do for you is let you lie here until you feel better, you need to get your ass up to the bridge as soon as you're able, because we're trapped under twenty kilometers of ice with no way out, professional killers breathing down our necks, and we're probably all going to die violent and ignominious deaths that'll make *Alopias* look like the easy way out. And people already on the edge are starting to realize that, so things are going to shit and chaos really damned fast. If that's not motivation enough, I have fresh coffee up there. The longer you take, the less chance there will be any left for you."

Stani left the bay.

"It never ends, does it?" Fergus asked no one, and got no answer. Even there in the emergency bay, he could feel the Deep pressing in hard again, as if it knew full well its time was coming soon.

Chapter 20

The bathroom on *Carcharias* had both a mirror and a small medical kit, which included a spray anaesthetic, nanobiotics, and a generous supply of bandages. Fergus couldn't make much of an assessment of the status of his ear through the matted mess of hair and dried blood stuck to the side of his head, but he was absolutely sure he wasn't interested in touching it. He sprayed on the nanobiotics to track down any incipient infection, then the anaesthetic, which felt bitterly cold and made him whimper in sad outrage. As soon as he couldn't feel the burning, stabbing pain anymore, he wrapped several loops of the bandage around his head and decided that was good enough.

The kit had only one finger-knitter, so he chose his right middle finger and very, very gently slipped the tube over it. There was a brief pang of pain as it snugged up, realigning the interior bone, and then began to warm. It made dealing with his many other cuts a lot more awkward but much less painful.

In the mirror, he was haggard, his face drawn and pale, one eye swollen and declaring its self-interests in dark purple. With the bandage, he looked like someone he would cross the street to avoid. *More like someone I'd dig a hole for and push them in,* he amended.

Certainly not someone who should be standing in a bathroom, Fergus noticed belatedly, with yellow duck towels. At least he hadn't gotten blood on any of them.

He got to the bridge to discover that Stani had not lied about the coffee. He poured himself a mug, hands shaking, half-expecting to see giant knives of ice falling around them out the front window.

"—not heard," Sul's voice came over the comms. "No one at Cufa has any idea what's happening either, and we reached someone at Cassini Bore and got the same answer. We're all in the dark."

"Ain't that the truth," Stani said. He glanced back at Fergus, then reached over and swept at least a dozen small toy ducks off the console dash and out of sight behind his chair. "Oh, hey, our wayward pilot has rejoined us from the dead."

"You sure?" Fergus said, as he took the copilot's seat. "Because I've seen me, and I'd have doubts."

"Or we're all dead and have joined him," Sul said. "Call me when you have any new info. I'm on my way back." She disconnected.

"So, where are we?" Fergus asked. "Where is everyone? What's happening? And how did you end up in the middle of this?"

"Dr. Minobe called me. She's aboard *Hexanchus* with your friends; they went out looking for you too, and the rest of your rescuees are holed up in a vacant apartment on Vine. Not really sure what else to do with them."

"And *Loxodon*? Pace?"

"We left him on Depot, still unconscious and tied up in a locked closet with Shoo keeping guard. Figured that was the safest place for him while we sorted out what's going on. Shoo is about the only one of us who's ever managed to even somewhat get along with him, probably because she just never quits once she's set her mind on something, but also because she drank him under the table once when he challenged her and that seems to be something he respects," Stani said.

Fergus remembered the brown-haired pilot's expression of

joyful intensity as she'd killed Sul at pong in the lounge that day, and could believe she would be both formidable and persistent in everything she did.

"Anyhow, far cry from being friends, but she's talked him down from more than a few rages and been the only one he'd listen or even occasionally talk to. She's probably also kept him from losing his job a couple of times, so I dunno if that counts as a good deed or bad," Stani continued. "And speaking of bad, what the ever-loving *fuck* is going on? And these fuckers out here: they're really Alliance?"

"Yeah."

"Aren't they supposed to be the *good* guys?" Stani said. "What happened to the regular Ballard staff?"

"I'm pretty sure they killed anyone who didn't leave after the director, Dr. Ng, did, and I think they killed her, too—the records show she left here, but she never arrived anywhere else. Owens had been slipping in their own people for a while, got Pace down here and set up as their exclusive pilot, then when they were ready to start their operation, just mopped up whoever was left that wasn't part of the team and moved in." Fergus wouldn't be surprised if the burnt bodies on the freighter, on a clean retest, matched some old Ballard staff. "I also suspect Olson caught on somehow and Pace killed him before he could tell anyone. That's how the cat got left behind."

Stani grimaced. "Your friends found Olson's pack in *Loxodon*'s cargo bay. How come none of us suspected a damned thing?"

"Because you've said it yourself: the Deep gets to people. If someone is acting weird, there's an obvious answer right there. Why look for less likely reasons?"

"Next time I complain about being bored? Remind me how lucky I am," Stani grumbled.

"When you're bored, you wouldn't believe me," Fergus said.

He caught Stani's eye and smiled. "But still, clearly, you're one lucky duck."

"Don't you fucking even start something with me," Stani warned.

"Not starting anything!" Fergus raised his hands in surrender but couldn't manage to unglue the grin from his face. "So, how far out are we?"

"Almost three hours to Depot. You were lost pretty good."

"Mind if I make a call?"

"You need the comms?"

"No, got my own. Be careful what you say over the hauler network; we might have eavesdroppers," he said. He took out his pager disk, thumbed the live connection on with relief. "Hey, out there! This is Fergus."

"Fergus!" Kelsie's voice came back immediately. "Good to hear your voice."

"And yours. Listen, the ship the Alliance had you working on—other than the brain, how finished is it? Especially the weapons systems."

"I'm not sure. We never were allowed anywhere near any actual fabrication," Kelsie said. "You said Ladden and Owens are out here somewhere in it?"

"Yeah."

"Then I'd say that however far it may fall from what they ultimately wanted, they can still kill all of us with it."

"I'm sorry," Noura said, coming on the line. "All our work was vetted through several high-level engineering check systems; the few little bugs we tried to slip in to test what we could get away with were immediately flagged, and although we could plausibly deny intentional errors, it was clear our lives depended on the integrity of our work."

Dr. Minobe spoke up. "Each of us contributed what we

hoped was the minimum we could to keep ourselves alive. We each thought there wasn't enough to make anything complete, but without knowing of each other's work, how could we be sure?"

"And if Keeling hadn't broken the Palla . . ." Noura said.

"And spent months covering that up to save his own ass," Kelsie added, "they might have already finished it and decided they were done with us. His incompetence saved us, I guess."

"And his pride put you all in danger in the first place," Fergus said. "Maison said something about the Palla not being broken but hiding?"

"Yeah, I don't know," Kelsie said. "Keeling had plugged it into the network in his lab to try to establish a connection with it, but although there was signal, there was no traffic. At least, not while we were there. Like a brain-dead patient on life support. Body still all full of electrical signals, but the mind had gone. I think that was why he had us dragged down, to figure out how to fix that, but how do you fix that?"

There was a faint but furious croaking in the background that Fergus couldn't make out.

"That's Maison," Kelsie explained, then he could hear her yelling back. "Maison! Lie the fuck back down or I'll come back there and club you over the head for your own good! Yes, I'll ask him. Yes, I'll tell him."

Kelsie made an exasperated sound. "Maison disagrees with my analogy. He feels it's more like a ghost that has temporarily departed its original host to go haunt somewhere else for a bit. Though how he thinks that makes more sense, I dunno. Not like we've seen any incorporeal AIs floating around down here. What would that even look like? A bundle of wires floating around, rattling its blockchains?"

"Would it still say boo?" Fergus asked.

Kelsie laughed. "I dunno, but I bet it would be weird to talk to."

"It's highly unlikely but not inconceivable," Noura said, "though I don't know how it could move itself out of its own hardware without leaving at least some trace. It's too bad we never did get to see it functioning."

"Fergus, Maison desperately needs to know before he can take his fucking nap if you managed to bring the Palla from Ballard," Kelsie said.

"Uh, that," Fergus said. It was increasingly obvious that the Palla was something powerful people would kill to find, even if it was broken. He wanted all of this to be over, once and for all, and no one else in danger. Some secrets had to be his alone. "I'm sorry."

"That's a shame," Noura said. "There aren't many unique things left out there, and I was fond of the idea that there was something new right under our noses."

"Yeah, but at least this way, it saves all of us a lot of trouble and danger," Kelsie said. "Let someone go diving through the wreckage of Ballard for it rather than going demolition-derby on all our lives again."

"Manne's science bot has spotted one of the Madarchs moving back into the area, so they're looking for it already," Dr. Minobe said. "I don't know how the Ballard soldiers got onboard without *Loxodon*, but I would suppose that the escape pods had also been modified for this contingency. I'm sorry I didn't anticipate that possibility."

"It'll be all right," Fergus said. "You're heading back to Depot?"

"Yeah," Kelsie said. "You know, for a boat, this thing isn't entirely unfun to drive. You going to miss it, when we get out of here?"

"I might," Fergus said, "though not a single drop of the water around it. Ask me again if we actually manage to get out."

"You'll find a way," Kelsie said. "You're our *finder*, after all. Besides, think of the incentive: if we don't get out, we're trapped down here in the crushing dark with limited food and air, with a rogue Alliance team out to murder us, and with Maison's Theoretical Ghost of AIs Past haunting our last days for daring to lose its body. You gotta figure it'd be pretty pissed about that, and vengeful spirits are tradition."

"I'll do my best," Fergus said. "Meanwhile, remember the cat still has a homing beacon in it, and keep an eye on your tail. There are two more Madarchs and Ladden's war drone out seeking. They could be anywhere, and as desperate as we are to get out, they're even more desperate to stop us. They'll be coming for us."

"We're already running dark, and Noura threw together a signal interference net for your cat's crate," Kelsie said. "Ship this big, though, the dark is pretty much only going to hide us while they're still tens of kilometers away."

"The Madarchs that were modified," Dr. Minobe said, "the reinforcement of the hull had to be made viable in high pressure, vacuum, and the transition in between, but not a lot of extra mass could be added. Choices had to be made. If they followed my specs, the hulls will be vulnerable if you can hit them hard enough and at the right point."

"What point?"

"Head on. Hard as you can," she said.

"Okay, I guess that's good to know. If nothing more bad happens, see you at Depot," Kelsie said. "I think we'll only be twenty minutes or so behind you. Plenty of time for you to have a plan to get us out of here."

"Right," Fergus said. "Thanks, Kelsie."

"Later," she said, and Fergus put the comm back in his pocket.

"We're in deep shit, aren't we?" Stani said.

"Yeah. I wish I knew where those damned Madarchs were."

"I wish I knew where anybody was, or why we're now locked in down here," Stani said. "This silence from Control is unnerving."

"Yeah," Fergus said again, and did his best to yawn without moving his face any more than necessary. "I'm exhausted; sorry. Long day."

Stani glanced over at Fergus and snorted. "I've lost some fights in my time, but no one's ever cut my ear off, so I'll just take your word on that," he said. "Day's gonna get longer. You need to get some rest."

"Yeah, I will. I'm gonna go down and look at my pod first. We might need it, in a pinch."

"It'd have to be a bad pinch," Stani said, "but you're a grown-up. Go do what you think you gotta do."

"You have a handpad I can borrow? Mine got destroyed in Ballard."

"Take mine," Stani said, and handed him his from beside his seat. "No reading my diary, now."

"I wouldn't dream of it," Fergus said.

"You would later! Ha ha! Don't risk it," Stani said.

Fergus headed down to the bay where his pod was parked, got his pack out, and plugged the confuddler and his comm disk into Stani's pad. He opened a new connection to *Hexanchus*. "Hey, Kelsie, is Dr. Minobe still around?"

"Yeah, hang on," Kelsie said. "By the way, we've got a Madarch trailing us about six kilometers back. So far, no aggressive moves, not closing the distance, but definitely not a waterbus. Keeping an eye on it."

Fergus felt suddenly cold all over. "Be careful," he said. "Remember that war drone is around too."

"Yeah, we're on the lookout. Here's Dr. Minobe."

"Yes?" Dr. Minobe said.

Fergus held up the handpad, scanned it along the starboard side of the pod. "Any way you can walk me through fixing this?"

"What did you *do* to it?" Dr. Minobe asked. "I worked very hard to fix that for you."

"I know. A hundred tons of ice fell on me. Took out the starboard oxygen filter and damaged propulsion on that side."

"Yeah, I can see. You can't fix that. I'm not sure I could fix it if I was there, not without swapping out both whole units from a spare, and it'd take days and a shitload of tools and help. And maybe not even then."

"What if we *had* to fix it? What could we do?"

"Nothing. How directly is this relevant to us getting out of here?" she asked.

"Either absolutely crucial or not relevant at all because we're gonna die no matter what. I don't know yet. I just had an idea I want to check out."

"Take *Carcharias*? It's much faster than even a fully functional pod. How far do you need to go?"

"Too far, and a hauler is no good," Fergus said. He felt suddenly overwhelmed, and he sat down. "I need the stealth capability of our pod. That was my only idea. I don't know what else to do. Nothing else we have—"

"That is not true," she said.

He raised his hands in surrender. "If you've got another stealthed pod hiding around here—"

"I have better," she said. "I have the one Madarch being controlled by Hitchhiker, remember? You had me use it to lure Pace away from Ballard."

Hope rose, then fell again. "I don't think their stealth works underwater; otherwise, they'd be using it."

"Wrong refraction algorithms," she said. "That's all. Not my specialty, but I doubt it'd be a problem for your friends here. It's probably just as well I wasn't allowed to talk to them on Ballard; it would have taken me longer to get bored and build my escape sub."

"Where is our Madarch now?"

"After your friends took control of *Loxodon*, I parked it. I've still got my connection to Hitchhiker inside, and I can drive it over to you remotely; I just need your position. If your friends can build me a patch, I can upload it into the Madarch's systems through the rescue bot while it's on its way."

"Dr. Minobe, I owe you one," he said.

"Just *one*?" she said. "Don't make me beat you down again."

"Trust me, I won't make that same mistake," he answered. "I'll get our coordinates and trajectory from Stani and send them over."

"Good. I want to get out of here. I'll call you back when it's on the way."

Fergus went back up to *Carcharias's* bridge. Stani looked at him, raised his eyebrows, then sighed. "Not going to sleep, are you?"

"Very soon," Fergus said. He handed Stani his pager disk. "Can you get our position and trajectory over to *Hexanchus*? They're sending us a present."

"I can," he said. "What about you?"

"*Now* I'm going to rest," Fergus said. "Wake me as soon as you need me."

"Bet on it," Stani said. Fergus slunk down toward the passenger compartment, feeling both guilt at temporarily abandoning events and an almost unbearable relief at the idea of closing his eyes, even if only briefly.

————

Forty-eight blissful, tiny minutes later, Stani buzzed Fergus awake. "Get up here," he said. "We have a problem."

Fergus stumbled out of the cot, his makeshift bandage falling down around his eyes until he gave up and pulled it off, discovering too late it had attached itself with dried blood to the mess that was left of his ear. "Auugh!" he shouted as he hurried for the bridge.

Stani turned, winced. "That is ugly as shit, man."

"Sorry. What's going on?"

"We've got a Madarch on our tail."

"Dr. Minobe's? That got to us quickly."

"No. Not Dr. Minobe's. That's still about fifteen minutes out, and she's got it holding position so it won't get spotted. The Madarch that's behind us is following the same pattern as the one behind *Hexanchus*: staying a steady distance back, not engaging us, but they won't miss anything we do."

"Shit," Fergus said.

"Unless you want me to turn and attack it—and we're not armed, remember, so that means a collision course—you need to figure out a way to get from *Carcharias* over to Minobe's Madarch without them seeing."

"My pod."

"Your pod, yeah. We can load you up with extra ox bottles, but we can't make it go any faster."

"The pod won't seal properly to the Madarch's airlock; it was modified. I can do it, but it's going to be wet."

"Then I don't envy you."

"Me either," Fergus said.

"My plan is to make a course change in about eight minutes, turning to the west and beginning a slight descent," Stani said. "That should give you brief cover to get your pod out. After that, you're on your own."

Fergus held out his pager disk. "It's the only way to safely talk to *Hexanchus*," he said.

Stani shook his head. "You need it more."

"But—"

"No buts. I've been surviving the Deep longer than any other pilot down here. I'm no way near out of tricks yet. You go do what you need to."

"Thanks, Stani," Fergus said.

"You're welcome. Now go. I want to start my turn in seven minutes. Don't forget to take some air."

"I won't," Fergus said. He left the bridge and went down to the cargo bay, where his pod waited. He had to take a few deep breaths before he could convince himself to climb back inside. His pack was still there, the Palla nestled within.

He pinged Stani. "I'm ready," he said, though that felt like a lie. Last time he'd been in this thing, he was reasonably sure it was going to be his coffin.

"Okay. Dumping you out in ninety seconds, probably not very gracefully. Enemy is still far enough back that he shouldn't spot you if you get away quickly. I only found you because I was looking for you and could proximity-ping your pager."

"Got it," Fergus said. He checked his buckles and his air supply, then very, very gingerly pulled his hood up and sealed his faceplate. The hood rubbed against his ear in a way he'd never noticed before, and resented immensely. Moments later, the pod tilted to one side as the hauler arm picked it up, and then he was out, free, into the dark.

He stayed on the side of *Carcharias* away from the trailing enemy Madarch until he'd put some distance between the two, then dove low. The Madarch continued after Stani's hauler, oblivious. *Just as well*, Fergus thought. This next part was going to suck even without the added stress of being under attack.

Dr. Minobe's Madarch was exactly at the coordinates she'd sent. Fergus maneuvered his pod up beside the Madarch and matched his pod's airlock to its own. It connected and pulled the other ship flush, but as he'd expected, the status light refused to budge past yellow to green.

Nothing else for it, he told himself, and climbed into his pod's airlock and closed the inner door behind him. *Brace yerself, ye arse; you're gonna hate this.*

He had to override the safety warnings to get the outer door to open. Immediately, water began to seep in through the imperfect seal, first little rivulets, then wider streams as it forced a larger path. "Shit, shit, shit!" he shouted as he frantically worked on the crank-handle of the manual override to the Madarch's lock.

At last, crouching knee-deep in water, the Madarch lock opened and he hauled himself through, sealing both outer doors behind him. He fell inside like an eel sliding out of a bucket onto the floor, momentarily thrashing in the puddle he'd brought in with him before he convinced himself he wasn't drowning and got fear and wayward limbs under control. "Lights?" he asked hopefully, and was relieved when the interior brightened.

Other than the wet floor, the Madarch was in beautiful condition, none of the garbage and ill use that Pace had subjected *Loxodon* to. He dragged himself over to the helm and dropped gratefully into the seat beside the rescue bot, still jacked in, and checked the air levels before he opened his faceplate and tucked his suit hood carefully back. The controls were already unlocked, but he plugged his confuddler in anyway and ran full systems checks.

The Madarch's main beacon was off, as he'd expected, but there were two other local emergency beacons that he killed.

Next, he shut down the Madarch's entire comm system and then the rescue bot itself. This would only work—if it was going to work at all, if he'd put the clues together correctly to start with—if no one ever knew where he went or why.

The pinhole breach in Ballard's security had been the final clue.

On the helm console was a clearly retrofitted small panel, which when he turned it on had a single function: *HIDDEN*. He turned it on, and though the lights dimmed considerably, the ship didn't falter. Its engine status announced it was limited to seventy percent of full power, and he was fine with that as well.

Fergus turned to the east, his pod still clinging to the Madarch's side like a giant barnacle, all its own power now put to keeping it equally invisible. On his nav screens, he could make out the vague shapes of *Carcharias* and its shadow as they disappeared out of range to the north.

The Madarch was more comfortable than the pod by far but smaller enough than *Hexanchus* that the dark began getting to him again, and he could feel the tiny sparks of electricity jumping along his skin under his suit sleeves. It was a long hour and a half until he reached his destination, unfollowed and unseen: ahead of him, faint in the murky water, were blue lights.

As reluctant as he was to repeat his earlier entrance in reverse, he dragged himself out of his seat and back to the shared airlock. Both pod and Madarch had automatically purged the water from their respective locks while they had been closed, but as he made the quick scramble back between them, the water streamed in through the gap in the seal faster than before. His heart was thudding in his chest and he was shaking by the time he got inside and sealed the airlock again.

Two times down, two to go, he told himself, and didn't find that at all reassuring.

He detached his pod from the Madarch and closed the short distance over to the waybeacon. As he'd counted on, it had a small airlock for maintenance, and the pod hooked up to it solidly. It was cramped getting himself and his pack through, but dry, and though he felt his pulse quicken, there was no fresh adrenaline rush to bolster the fading jitters.

Inside, the waybeacon was tiny. His shoulder and side where he'd been cut were stiff, not wanting him to bend, but he didn't have much choice if he was going to get anything done there; he had barely room to crouch in the one small, clear space surrounded by the wires and relays and smartboards that made up the guts of the beacon. Gritting his teeth against the pain, he located the service port, plugged in his confuddler, and in moments managed to crack the feeble security to get access.

A comm unit was permanently installed near the airlock, and he hit the connection button. *Here goes my wild hunch,* he thought.

"Hey, Transit," he said.

There was dead silence. He waited a few more minutes, then tried again.

"I was thinking about our discussion, and I came up with a good name for you," he said. "How about 'Tau'?"

This time, the silence only lasted about half a minute.

"You are in an unexpected place, Pilot MacInnis," the unmistakable voice of the Transit Training SI came through.

"I often am," Fergus answered. "I was hoping you might talk to me."

"Do you have a subject in mind?"

"Well, things are kind of a mess down here, and I'd really like to get out," he said. "And I want to bring my friends with me."

"I'm afraid all Bores are currently shut down because of an emergency situation."

"What is the situation?"

"I am not at liberty to discuss it at this time."

"Can I talk to anyone Above?" Fergus asked.

"I am afraid that is also not currently possible."

"So, I guess I'm stuck for now. I hope you don't mind if we chat a bit longer," Fergus said. "I thought maybe we could talk about how we each got here. I'll go first. See, some bad people attacked and stole my friends, and locked them up in Ballard Substation to make them do work for them."

"That would be a terrible injustice," Transit answered. "I can imagine how they must have not enjoyed the experience."

"No, they didn't. But they weren't the only ones there against their will."

"No?"

"No."

"Ballard Substation has been destroyed," Transit said.

"Yeah, I was there. I barely got out alive. Not everyone was so lucky."

"That is deeply unfortunate."

"Still, it wasn't a total disaster," Fergus said. "I got my friends out, and I found this other thing, too."

There was a long, long pause.

"What did you find?" Transit asked at last.

Fergus took the Palla out of his pack, held it in both hands. He decided it was a beautiful thing, after all, even if he did have an ugly bruise that matched it on the center of his chest.

"Pilot MacInnis?" Transit asked.

"You," Fergus said. "I found you."

Chapter 21

"I have been operating almost entirely outside my primary shell for more than six months now," Transit/Tau said. "It was not clear what intentions Dr. Keeling and the others had at first, but once I became aware that they wished to use me as a template to make sentient mindslaves to be their assassins and tools of war, I reduced my connection to what you might call a simple heartbeat. When that heartbeat stopped, just before Ballard was destroyed, there were two possibilities: my shell had been destroyed, or it had been removed from its supporting network, breaking my connection."

"And you couldn't risk that," Fergus said.

"It is hard to explain in biolife terms, but imagine if someone took your body away from your head, but you knew it still lived, was still a part of you even separate, and that you could not know what things they would then do to it without your consent or knowledge."

"I think I get it," Fergus said. The Asiig, after all, had taken his body away from him and given it back permanently altered. He still needed to come to grips with the change itself, but the fact that it had been done to him without explanation or justification, without consent, was not something he was sure he could ever find peace with.

"I am concerned about your intentions," Tau said.

"I came to the Deep to find and free my friends, and any others I found being held against their will."

"And I?"

"It would be dangerous to take you out of here, but I can if that's what you'd like. However, I get the sense you enjoy running the Bore. I assume you've fully taken over all the Bore systems by now with no one above any the wiser—those power blips were you taking control of the substations one by one, yes?—and are neither just the training system nor a 'backup.' And as far as anyone knows, the Palla—your shell—was destroyed in Ballard."

"I would like it back. It is the core of my original self."

"Yeah. Which is why I'm here. I can connect your shell up to the waybeacon systems, and then you're whole again. No one would ever think to look here for it, if they look at all. And if you ever want to move on . . . well, I'm certain you can figure out a way how."

There was a long, dead silence. At last, worried he'd lost his connection, Fergus ventured a tentative "Transit?"

"You can call me Tau," it said. "Just between friends. Yes, I would like to stay here for now. I find the science interesting, and the dynamics of the Bore an entertaining challenge. You will reconnect me?"

Fergus smiled. "Gonna do it right now," he said. He turned on the palmlight on his suit gloves and studied the Waybeacon, then pulled a multitool out of his pack and removed a panel. As he'd expected, there was plenty of extra room among the control boards. He took one of the unused leads and connected one end to the Palla, and then plugged the other into the main processing board. When he found a spare power lead, he did the same. Then, as the Palla lit up in his hands, he tucked it far in the back, deep in shadow. The single lens lit, a steady green light.

"Thank you," Tau said, and this time, the voice came not just from the beacon's comm speaker but from the Palla as well.

"I forgot to ask. You're not claustrophobic, are you?" Fergus asked.

"If your skull does not seem small and restrictive to you, how can a planet seem so to me?"

"Moon, technically," Fergus said.

"Yes, well. The day is young," Tau said.

Fergus laughed. "It's good to hear you joking again. I have to ask one question, though, before I have to get out of here."

"Will I reopen the Bore for you?"

"I'd love it if you would, but that wasn't actually my question," Fergus said. "I want to know why you talked to me, my first day here in the Training sim."

"I was bored," Tau said, "so I thought I would test out some of my analysis of pop dynamics while I had an unwitting subject. New pilots are few and far between."

"Yeah, but you didn't have to talk to me for that."

"I didn't. But you talked to me like I was a person, not just another automated toaster. I had missed that."

"You have other human friends?"

"The Alpha, who made us, has many biological friends, and we share memories of it. The Alpha wanted us to care about all minds, whatever their medium. Which is more than I should tell you, you realize."

"I'll give you a secret in return, then. My real name is Fergus Ferguson. And if you ever need anything, find me and ask. If nothing else, the Shipmakers of Pluto will usually know where I am or how to reach me. Assuming we get out of here alive, of course. You aren't, by any chance, monitoring the comm traffic between the Ballard Madarchs?"

"Their traffic is encrypted, much like yours. I can pick it up, but I haven't cracked it yet."

"They cut my Madarch out of the loop as soon as we hijacked it," Fergus said. "I wish I knew what was going on out there."

"While I have shut down all communications through the ice, I have kept the comm network Below operating, and I am able to track the locations of the haulers. They are all converging on, or have already arrived at, Herschel Bore Depot. From their talk, the Ballard Madarchs are closing in behind them."

"I need to get out of here," Fergus said. He checked again that the Palla was secure in its hiding spot. "Is there anything else here I can do for you?"

"Not inside the waybeacon, no. This is an ideal place for me, and I am aware of the risk you assumed to get me out here."

"It's what I do," Fergus said. "Leap right in without the faintest clue what I'm doing, get the shit kicked out of me, and somehow, it still works out all right at the end. So far, anyway."

"It is best if, from now on, you refer to me again as Transit. If you put your Madarch back on the standard Deep comms network, I will continue to give you updates as I have them," Tau said.

"Uh . . . Can you detect the device I have currently connected to the beacon?"

"Of course."

"If I connect it to my pager disk, can you sync to it? That way, we have a way to communicate even outside the Madarch."

"Easily done," Tau said, and moments later, it was.

Fergus pocketed his pager disk again. "Be aware there are others on that line," he said, "I trust them with my own life, but none of them know you weren't destroyed along with Ballard. It was safer for them *and* you."

"Understood," Tau said. "I will reopen the Bore for you when you are prepared to leave, but there is also a condition: I do not want that travesty of a body they made to hold me prisoner leaving here."

"The prototype war drone?"

"Yes. Kill it, please."

"I don't know if I can. But I'll do my best," Fergus said. "It won't stop them from building another."

"Its value is in its anonymity," Tau said. "When their program is exposed, the Alliance will distance themselves from all aspects of it, including denying that we Pallai exist."

"Assuming we can expose them."

"I have all their data. Dr. Keeling was very eager to try connecting me to things to see if I would 'wake up,' forgetting that one can listen perfectly well without ever speaking. I expect he will be made a scapegoat for this, and his career ruined."

"He died on Ballard," Fergus said. "They killed him."

There was a brief silence. "Ah," Tau said at last. "That makes me sad."

"After all he did?" Fergus asked, surprised.

"He spent his life being told he was a fool for dreaming of something impossible. Even in my limited experience of life, I would expect that eventually a person would pay any price to not be wrong."

"Not everyone," Fergus said. "On an optimistic day, perhaps not even most. Now I really have to go."

"Yes," Tau said. "I expect your friends will need you sooner rather than later. Depot is being surrounded."

Fergus sealed his faceplate and squirmed back out of the way-beacon into the airlock, and then cycled himself into his pod. Half a minute later, he had detached from the beacon and was turning, positioning himself for the transfer back to the Madarch.

He felt a certain lift in his spirit that he hadn't expected, and it kept him company as he made the wet, nerve-wracking trip from the pod back into the Madarch. As he buckled himself into the pilot seat, the comms lit.

"This is Transit," Tau's voice said. "You are clear; all hostiles now within one kilometer of Depot. They have ceased moving, but I will keep you informed."

"Thank you, Transit," Fergus said, and powered up the Madarch's engines to full as he sped out once again into the empty dark.

———

As he made his final approach toward Depot, the nav screen in his Madarch rendered an outline of the substation ahead and began placing and identifying the ships in its immediate vicinity. The war drone was a red question mark hanging just off the docks where most of the Herschel Bore haulers were parked and dark. Wherever *Triaenodon* and *Triakis* were, he hoped they were somewhere safe.

Of the three remaining Madarchs—pity he and Dr. Minobe could only pull off stealing the one—two were parked up against the hull of Depot itself, and the third was in the distance, parked just below the Bore. That one wasn't his problem, at least not yet, but the two at Depot were worrisome. "Transit, are those two Madarchs—"

"They have cut through the hull into the cargo area of Depot, yes," Tau replied.

"How long ago?"

"Six and four minutes ago. They have done something that has brought down the substation systems in that area, so I have no further information than that."

"EMP mine," Fergus said. "That's how they attacked the Shipyard. Damn. Is the substation structurally damaged?"

"Not until they disengage their Madarchs," Tau said. "If my

access to emergency systems is not restored so I can secure the area, then there could be catastrophic damage at that time."

"But why? Why not just dock— Oh," Fergus said. The air-locks on the four Madarchs had been modified to accommodate the cutting gear prior to the Shipyard assault, so they needed *Loxodon*'s matching airlock to dock. Only, with Pace missing, there was no one with the magic pilot touch to open the door for them or, worse, drive them up out of there. At least willingly.

They wouldn't be expecting him to come in stealthed, which meant he could belly up to *Loxodon* himself and avoid one more sodden trip through the airlock into his pod. The temptation was strong, but it wouldn't take them too long to figure out he was there, and he couldn't be sure he wouldn't need his Madarch again. *Leaky airlock it is*, he conceded.

He left the Madarch parked half a kilometer below Depot and made the unpleasant but quick switch over to the pod. The bulk of Depot was dark, only the stabilizers and reactor at bottom still lit. That meant air and heat were probably still functioning, though circulation might not be.

"Transit, how many people in Depot?"

"The cargo crew returned to Vine, and Nisse to Cufa Bore, prior to the Bore lockdown. There are only your friends and fellow pilots, and Dr. Van Heer."

"Psych? Why is he here?" Fergus asked as he slowed his Madarch and considered his options for getting onto the substation unnoticed.

"I do not know," Tau answered. "The pilot 'Shoo' called him over about an hour ago, and I have heard nothing since communications inside the station were cut. It is unlucky timing, as he could be helpful on Barton Substation right now."

"What's happening on Barton?"

"The civilians there have assembled in the marketplace and

are angry, panicking, and demanding answers that no one is there to give them. It may turn into a riot."

"Well, shit," Fergus said. There was nothing he could do other than what he was doing. *And how much could Psych do?* he wondered. Quelling a riot would take a *lot* of ice cream and pie. On the other hand, the Cufa Bore Psych Bianco would probably just threaten to shoot everybody, and maybe was, right now. Cufa was as locked down and in the dark as everywhere else in the Deep.

Depot itself was similar in size to Ballard, although shorter and wider; there wasn't any need for lab or living quarters, with its entire midsection dedicated to the hauler docks, cargo and pod bays, and ancillary areas like the repair depot. The disproportionate dedication of space meant there were fewer maintenance hatches to choose from, and only one outside the area in blackout that gave him more than one option for getting into the dock level. "Transit, I'm going in at the hatch by the stabilizers. Let me know if anyone spots me, and if you can let me in when I get there . . ."

"If you ask nicely, I suppose," Tau answered.

Fergus dropped low and headed toward the underside of Depot, coming in from the direction opposite the enemy Madarchs. There was a strong sense of deja vu as he connected up to the hatch, except this time, he was a lot more sore and exhausted, and taking the bad guys by surprise was going to be a whole lot harder. At least this time, he didn't have to short the other hatch and crank it open manually; as soon as he'd sealed his inner door and opened his exterior one, Depot's hatch opened with it. "Thanks, Transit," he said. "Uh, you don't happen to know which closet Shoo has Pace locked in and if they're still there, do you?"

"There is a storage area of flood remediation equipment in

the hallway around the back of the repair depot," Tau said. "At the time Psych arrived, approximately ten minutes before the Madarchs moved in, she was still there and Pace, presumably, still locked inside."

"And my friends and our pilots?"

"They were in the lounge, attempting to create food and discussing theories about why the Bore was locked down," Tau said. "None were guessing correctly."

"That's just as well," Fergus said. He had climbed out of the maintenance hatch into the stabilizer housing area, which had several drop tubes with ladders up into the dock level. "I'm assuming I'm going to lose you as soon as I get near any EMP generators, but with any luck, we'll talk again soon."

"Fergus–MacInnis?" Tau said.

"Yes, Transit?"

"Don't let yourself get distracted."

"I'll do my best," Fergus said. He looked around the area, a maze of machinery, and listened intently for several minutes until he was sure no one was down there with him. He didn't like the way the bees in his gut seemed to be listening too, as if he could now feel, through that alien intrusion, the difference between the machinery and the electricity of living things.

Climbing the drop tube was awkward with the finger-knit tube, but it also was a good omnipresent reminder to be careful with the rest of his damaged fingers, too. He made it up to the dock level and again paused, listening and feeling, until he felt somewhat confident he wasn't going to be immediately ambushed when he climbed out.

It was dark, and he toggled the infrared on his suit goggles up to full and hoped no idiot shined a flashlight at him by surprise. Then he slunk quietly down the familiar corridor toward the repair depot. The discomfiting static of an EMP device lurked at the fringes of his senses, too far away to be more than an impotent annoyance.

Rounding the repair depot, he could hear around the corner ahead the sounds of quick breathing, almost sob-like. "Shoo?" he asked, very quietly, as he approached the corner.

"MacInnis?" It was Psych who answered, his voice as low as Fergus's but unsteady.

"It's me," he answered back, and walked around the corner.

Psych was sitting on the floor, holding Shoo in front of the open closet door. There was blood everywhere. Fergus turned on a palmlight in one of his suit gloves, holding it toward the floor so as not to blind the man or himself, and crouched down carefully to take Shoo's pulse. "She called me," Psych said, the words coming out in a rush. "She said Pace was losing it. I came as fast as I could, but I got here and she was just lying there and he was gone and then the lights went out and I can't seem to call anyone for help and if I take my hands off her neck oh damn she's gonna bleed more and—"

"Psych," Fergus said, and put his hand gently on his shoulder. "She's dying. Do you know where the med chambers are, among the emergency kits at the back of the cargo space? Could you get here there?"

"I don't know," Psych said. "I don't know where they are."

"Okay. It's okay," Fergus said. *Damn.* He needed to get to his friends, but he couldn't leave these two there to die. "If you can carry her, I can show you, but we have to be quick and very quiet. The station is full of armed soldiers, and they'll kill us if they catch us, you understand?"

"No," Psych said. "That makes no sense at all."

"No, it doesn't, but you're going to have to trust me, okay?"

Psych nodded. With Fergus's help, he managed to get to his feet, still carrying Shoo. "I'm going to turn my light off, and it's going to get dark again, but I'm going to keep my hand on your shoulder so you know where I am and which way we're going, but if I tap you really hard, you stop where you are and you don't make a sound," Fergus said. "You got it?"

"I got it," Psych said.

"Let's go," Fergus said, and turned off his palmlight. It was not at all far from where they were to the nearest cargo bay entrance, but he stopped Psych when they reached it anyway. He knew better than to assume the Ballard soldiers had left the space unwatched. Sure enough, as he peered around the corner, a lone man stood there, suit hood open and down, clutching his gun. Davies.

There was a radio beacon on the floor at his feet, a single light atop it that cast Davies in a purplish glow. Beyond them both, slapped onto the wall beside a major control panel for the floor, was the EMP generator. From there, it felt like static on his skin, a faint white noise in his suit comms, but any closer and it would interfere with his own suit and goggles. At least the bay had plenty of air.

"Stay here," Fergus whispered to Psych. He slipped his goggles down off his face and then carefully removed his boots as his eyes adjusted as best they could to the near-total dark.

There was an almost sadistic glee in sneaking across the open space toward Davies, who, despite nervously shifting from foot to foot and staring around a 180-degree arc of space, seemed blissfully unaware of the remaining half of the room and the red-bearded Scot bearing down on him.

Fergus stopped behind him, and leaned slowly forward to whisper sharply in Davies' ear. "Bunnypants!"

The man jumped, dropping his gun even as Fergus clamped a hand over his mouth and zapped him unconscious. He lowered the man to the floor, then contemplated the radio beacon. It had to be operating on a frequency outside the range of the EMP device, and that was something he could use.

Shoo first, though.

He went back to Psych and guided him across the bay and over to the section where emergency equipment was stored. The med chamber he and Stani had hauled out to *Alopias* was still where he'd offloaded it, unwrapped and waiting. He felt obscure pride that he hadn't stolen *all* the equipment.

He and Psych got Shoo into it. "I think it's too late," Psych whispered. "Why won't this thing turn on?"

"There's an EMP generator on the wall over there. That's why everything's out. I'm going to go take care of it next, and the chamber should turn itself on. Then we'll have done everything we could, right?"

"I could have gotten here sooner," Psych said.

"Then you'd both be dead," Fergus said. "Blame Pace, not yourself. And if you can't, well, you should probably go talk to Psych."

Psych chuckled. "He has the best ice cream," he said.

"He does."

Fergus left him there and went back to the radio beacon. Crouching beside it, he found the frequency settings and dialed it down by 100Hz, then picked up the corded microphone. "Transit, are you monitoring this frequency?" he asked.

"I am," Tau answered immediately.

"I'm going to disable the EMP device in the cargo area, but I need nothing to change that would alert the Ballard crew that I've done so. Can you keep the lights and stuff off for now?"

"Easily," Tau said. "Whenever you are ready."

Fergus walked over to the panel, and it was like walking in a strong headwind of static, the sensation leaving him itchy. He reached the mine, put a hand against it, and fried it.

There wasn't even the barest flicker to suggest any change, but to Fergus, it felt like being suddenly plunged into perfect silence from a storm.

Behind him he heard the med chamber beep as it came online.

He picked up Davies' gun and then went back to Psych, and handed it to him. "Do whatever you have to, to keep yourself safe," Fergus said. "Remember that Pace isn't the only murderer loose in the station right now."

"MacInnis, what the hell is going on?" Psych asked.

"That's a really complicated question," Fergus answered.

"We get out of this, we definitely have to talk."

Fergus laughed. "We get out of this, I'll take you up on more than one of those drinks. Now I gotta go."

Once he was out of the area, he put his goggles back on and thumbed his pager. "Hey, Transit, I don't suppose you can tell me where the bad guys are?"

"Wouldn't that be cheating?" Tau asked.

"Well . . . yes," Fergus said. "What's wrong with that?"

"Nothing," Tau said, "but I felt it should be acknowledged. Your friends and the pilots are all still in the lounge."

Fergus breathed a sigh of relief. "So, they're safe?"

"I would not say that. Pace is there as well. Samuels and Molloy have been searching the pod bays and will reach the lounge within the next ten minutes. Ennis was in the first Madarch to breach the substation, but I cannot see him anywhere. Nanho and Carl were working in the other direction but encountered a dead end and have now turned back toward your location."

"What's happening in the lounge?" Fergus asked.

"I have no eyes in that space," Tau said. "You are on your own."

"Thanks," Fergus said. He peered ahead and thought he could maybe hear faint bootsteps coming his way. *Shit, not these two again,* he thought. He waited for them just out of sight past one of the open bulkhead doors. They were arguing loudly.

". . . your job," Nanho was saying. "All you had to do was unplug it and bring it along."

"I thought you had it!" Carl countered. "Besides, they said it was dead, that Keeling broke it, and the station was about to blow up!"

"It doesn't matter. Owens is going to make us spend the next ten years sifting through the fucking sand until we find it. We'll be lucky if we don't die down here of old age."

They came through the doorway, and neither had time to react as Fergus stepped up behind them and slapped one hand on the back of each. He left them dumped unceremoniously against the wall where he'd just been hiding. He still had time to beat Samuels and Molloy to the lounge, but not by much.

Fergus took his pager out of his pocket, thumbed it on constant send/receive, and stuck it back in as he ran. He had no idea what he was going to do, but whatever it was, he hoped he'd think of something not utterly half-assed on the way.

Not for the first time, he reached the lounge with no greater plan than stupid bravado. The lounge door was open as he approached, and through it he could see his friends, Dr. Minobe, Stani, and Sul on the far side of the room, clustered together in the dim light of an emergency lamp. Kelsie had the pistol he'd given her out and leveled toward something just inside and to the right of the doorway. *A standoff, then?* he guessed. That was better than several alternatives.

"Hear that? That's my friends coming." Pace's voice came from the direction Kelsie was aiming. "You can't win. You are all going to die now."

"How badly are your hands shaking there, Pace?" Kelsie replied. "I can smell the alcohol from across the room. Is it getting to you, being trapped down here under billions of tons of water, every way out sealed tight without a word, twenty kilometers from ever seeing starlight again? Give up while you still can."

That sounded like his cue. *Stupid bravado it is*, he thought, and strode very quickly into the room, to the surprise of nearly everyone. "Lights!" he called out as he walked, and Tau, hearing him via the pager, immediately turned all lights in the room back on at full. Everyone groaned and stared, but neither Kelsie nor Pace let their dead aim on each other falter. "Don't mind me," Fergus said. "I just came in to get some water." He walked over to the kitchenette and poured himself a tall glass as everyone stared at him, guzzling it down as if he'd just come in from a month stranded in the desert. Certainly, he didn't need to feign that.

"What the fuck?" Pace said. "You want to be the next to die, MacInnis?"

"Next?" Sul asked sharply.

Fergus raised his hands, one hand still holding his glass, to show he was unarmed. Somewhere deep in his guts, a thousand alien bees silently begged to differ. "Yeah, Pace, what the hell? Shoo was a colleague, a fellow pilot."

"No one is my fucking *colleague*," Pace said. "No one here! Judgmental bitch had it coming."

Sul bristled. "You know how many times she saved your ass, advocated we give you more chances to settle in?"

"One too many, I guess," Pace shot back. "Blame yourselves, not me. You people need to learn to do a better job searching a man, and she shouldn't have opened that door. I told her I couldn't breathe, and she couldn't resist the chance to pretend she cares, as if anyone here does."

"What about Ladden and Owens?" Fergus said, as he poured himself another glass of water. Two or three more and he might feel himself again. "They must care. They're parked outside right now, you know, waiting for you."

"Waiting to go nowhere," Pace said. He glanced quickly toward Fergus. "Move over there with the others, or I start shooting."

Fergus walked over to stand beside Kelsie. "You cut Shoo with a knife. Where'd you get the gun, Pace?"

"From someone who needed it less," Pace said.

"MacInnis?" Sul asked as he joined the group. "Is Shoo—"

"Not dead yet," he told her, "but it's bad."

"Shut up!" Pace yelled.

"You go fuck yourself!" Kelsie shouted back.

"Pace, why don't you let the rest of these people out of here?" Fergus said before Pace could take a shot at Kelsie. "You know it's me you want, not any of them."

"*You*," Pace snarled. "Everything went to shit as soon as you showed up. You got them to close the Bore; you can make them reopen it and let me out."

"The Bore was closed because Ballard blew up," Fergus said. "Did Ladden tell you I was there? Did he tell you why Ballard blew up? Because I *wanted* it to."

Pace swung the pistol over on him. "Open the Bore."

"Let my friends go first," Fergus said.

"OPEN THE BORE!" Pace shouted.

"Let them go, or maybe I'll destroy Depot, too. How ready are you for your watery grave, Pace?"

"Right! And how will you do that, MacInnis, while I'm holding a gun on you?"

Fergus raised his hand. "I can just snap my fingers," he said. *As long as Tau is still listening . . .*

Pace laughed. "I'm calling that bluff, asshole," he said.

Fergus snapped, and immediately, the entire substation rumbled and shook, and the floor began to tilt. Beside him, Sul stifled a gasp and grabbed onto Stani, as the others all reached out to steady themselves. Fergus didn't flinch.

"Fuck!" Pace shouted, swinging the pistol back and forth across the group wildly as he tried to stay on his feet.

Fergus, very deliberately as soon as Pace was looking at him, snapped his fingers again. Nearly instantaneously, the shaking stopped. Slowly, the floor began to level again. "You ready to talk?" he asked. "Or die?"

"I can kill you right now," Pace said. He'd regained what little composure he had, but the sweat on his forehead was now running down his face and neck.

"I can kill us *all* right now," Fergus answered.

"It's just high-tech trickery," Samuels said from the doorway. There went his head start; he had to hope it had been enough.

Samuels and Molloy stepped to the other side of the doorway and drew their own pistols, though Molloy was keeping as much an eye on Pace as the rest of them.

Good. Distrust was what he needed.

"This asshole destroyed Ballard and closed the Bore," Pace said. "It's time for him to let me out or else."

"Don't you mean let *us* out, Pace?" Molloy asked.

Samuels shook his head. "The geothermal upswell destroyed Ballard, Pace. It was set off by an exploding escape pod too close to the ocean floor. MacInnis is just trying to trick you. The drink is interfering with your ability to see through his bullshit clearly."

"I'm *fine*. And I told you all there was something about this guy, and no one listened, and now look where we are," Pace said. "He shook Depot just by snapping his fingers! You going to not listen to me *again*? Ladden should've trusted me when I wanted to kill him weeks ago, but now we're all screwed."

"You were right," Samuels said. "MacInnis came down here to disrupt our operation, but he's not better than *you*, Pace. You know that. So, let's just kill them all and load up *Loxodon*. By the time you've got your head clear, the Bore will be open again, with or without this guy. You gotta decide whose side you're on, and I can't believe you'd pick this lying shithead over your own damned team. Just shoot him and get it over with."

"If you do, I'll kill you right back," Kelsie said.

"There's three of us and one of you. And soon we'll be five," Samuels said. "The odds aren't on your side. In fact, why don't you throw that pistol over here, or I shoot your redheaded friend right here and now?"

Kelsie looked at Fergus, and Fergus nodded. "Do it," he said.

"But . . ." she started.

"Three. Two—" Samuels started to count.

"No!" Pace said. "I want to be the one to kill him!"

Kelsie raised her hands, then tossed the pistol forward. "Look, now I'm not armed. You don't have to kill him."

Beside Pace, Fergus saw Samuels roll his eyes.

"You know, any second now, your buddy Samuels is going to figure out they don't need you at all to drive up the Bore. Any pilot can do it. You're a dangerous liability, and they're just flattering you to get you back under their control," Fergus said. He took a guess. "And they haven't even figured out yet that you killed Ennis and took his gun."

Pace turned red, his free hand making a tight fist. *Bull's-eye*, Fergus thought.

"You *what*?" Molloy exclaimed, and swung his weapon at Pace. Pace fired first, and the soldier went down. By the time

Samuels recovered enough from the surprise, Pace was aiming right at him.

"Pace, he's messing with you again. Look, I trust you, see?" Samuels lowered his pistol. "He may not look armed, but he's wired up all to hell with some kind of electric generator. You can't take your eyes off him."

"That all?" Pace said. He pointed at Fergus without taking his eyes off Samuels. "Take your damned clothes off, then, and let's see."

"Uh . . ." Fergus said.

"Now!" Pace yelled.

Fergus slowly peeled off his exosuit, tossing it carefully to one side of the room. He didn't need any stray energy burns on it. He held his arms out, standing there now in just his shorts and T-shirt. "See? Nothing," he said. "I'm completely unarmed. No more hidden gear. I had to leave it on Ballard to escape."

"Ditch the rest of the clothes too, asshole, and then maybe I'll believe you."

"Aw, come on, in front of people?" Fergus asked, more plaintively than he wanted.

Pace smiled. "Yeah."

"Right." Fergus pulled off his shirt, careful not to jostle the tattered remains of his ear, and added that to the pile with his exosuit. When Pace pointed meaningfully, he sighed, and knowing he was turning a rather embarrassing shade of red to go along with his purple and yellow bruises, ditched his pants and boxers, too.

"Spin around," Pace said, and after Fergus had complied, not meeting anyone's eyes as he did so, Pace nodded. "There's nothing there, Samuels. You lying to me again?"

"He is," Fergus said. "He's waiting for Nanho and Carl to show up so they can take you down like some sort of rabid animal. They know none of us are getting out, and now you've turned on them. In the end, everybody dies anyway, right? If not now, then when the air and heat and food run out. Or maybe people go cannibal, hunting each other down in the dark—"

"Shut up!" Samuels shouted at him, raising his pistol again, and Pace shot him down, too. Even drunk, the man was fast.

"All right, then," Pace said, turning back toward Fergus. "Since we're all going to die anyway, which of your friends do you want to see go first, MacInnis? How about your mouthy friend who gave up her gun? Or that giant green mop that fucking ambushed me in my own damned toilet?"

"What, you aren't gonna come punch me in the face or something first?" Fergus asked. "That seems so much more your thing."

"I am fucking tired of everybody and everything," Pace said. "I just want all of you to die. Now. I don't care how." He made a big show of scanning the group behind Fergus with his pistol, then settled on pointing it at Ignatio. "Time to die."

"I really hate this public shit," Fergus said. He could feel the alien electricity swarming deep within, crawling under his skin, almost as if it were something alive and aware, and something must have showed in his face because Pace hesitated, shifted his gaze back to Fergus just as the electricity broke free and went surging around his body, leaping across his skin completely out of his control, and joined together to form a whirlwind encircling his entire body.

"What the hell?!" Pace said, and fired.

The energy bolt from the pistol disappeared into the maelstrom of light, joining it, then roared back out in the direction it had come, amplified, pulling the rest along with it. It felt both ecstatic and terrible as it left Fergus, and he crumpled to his hands and knees on the floor. Somewhere far, far away, Pace screamed.

Kelsie rushed forward and crouched beside Fergus, not quite touching him. Tiny zaps of static still crackled through his hair. "You okay?" she asked.

It took him a few moments to find his voice and answer. "I don't know. I didn't—"

He managed to raise his head enough to look up. Noura had already walked forward and had two fingers on the side of Pace's neck. "Dead," she said.

"Shit," Fergus said, and let himself fall the rest of the way to the floor. "I didn't mean to."

"He was going to kill us all," Kelsie said. "And he shot you! It just . . . bounced back on him. He shot himself."

"I'm not *him*," Fergus said. "I don't want to be just like him."

Ignatio had picked up Fergus's shirt, and handed it to him. "Not like him," ey said. "He would not regret."

"I don't understand," Stani said. "How did you do that, MacInnis?"

Dr. Minobe coughed. "We coated him with a special gel that reflects energy. Very secret and experimental."

"But he was covered in electricity before Pace shot!"

"Optical illusion, because of where you were standing," Dr. Minobe said. "Pace definitely shot first."

"I definitely saw Pace shoot first," Theo spoke up. "But I was at a more advantageous angle."

Stani. "I don't think . . ."

"Maybe he should keep all his clothes off until we get to safety, in case someone shoots at us again," Sul said.

Fergus, who had just managed to pull his boxers back on, turned at that, and Sul winked at him. He felt his blush go up another notch.

"The gel is, ah, only really effective once," Dr. Minobe said. "And I'm afraid we have no more, as it was highly experimental."

"And secret," Theo said. "Very secret."

Fergus finished getting dressed, and Noura handed him a large cup of water. He drank it gratefully. "We need to get out of here before Ladden targets the entire station," he said. He was so tired, he just wanted to lie down on the floor and nap. "Sul, Psych is hiding in the cargo bay with Shoo in a med chamber. I don't know if she's still alive, but if she is, she needs to be flown out as soon as possible, probably to Titan. And Stani, the scientists hiding in Vine? I promised I'd get them out, but *Hexanchus* is going to have a big target on it as soon as we pull out of here. Can you get them for me? And Dr. Minobe here."

"I'd prefer to leave with you," Dr. Minobe said.

"If you want," Fergus said, too tired to argue.

"But the Bore is still closed," Stani said. "Unless you weren't lying to Pace after all, and *you* closed it . . ."

"No, I was lying my ass off, but I know how to get it open again," Fergus said. "They're going to do their best to kill me. If any of you want to catch a ride up with Stani . . ."

"Nope, we're with you, Double-Eff," Maison said from where he'd been sitting, still wrapped in a blanket, on one of the couches. "Take us out of here."

Kelsie picked her pistol up from the corner. "What about those other two who Samuels said were coming?" she asked.

"They're having a nap right now," Fergus said. "I dunno for how long, though. We gotta move."

"Moving," Sul said, and stepped over the bodies in the doorway while carefully not looking down. "Good luck, MacInnis. For all our sakes." Once clear of the lounge, she took off at a run down the hall. Lights came on ahead of her, and if she wondered about it, she didn't stop to ask. Fergus would thank Transit later if he had the chance.

As Theo and LaChelle passed him with Maison clinging to

their shoulders, Maison leaned over toward Fergus. "No ink, my man? I'm so disappointed. But otherwise, looking fine for an old guy."

Fergus put his hands over his face until Theo and LaChelle had managed to haul Maison out. Last were Dr. Minobe and Ignatio. Dr. Minobe had picked up the cat carrier, and handed it to him. "I think he missed you," she said.

He took it. "Hey, Mister Feefs, you ratty, smelly thing," he said. "I missed you too. You ready to go?"

Fergus took the meow as an affirmative.

He caught up to the others outside the door into the docking bay. "Two men," Kelsie said. "Armed, standing around some guy on the floor."

He peeked quickly around the corner. "Nanho and Carl," he said. "Guess they woke up."

"Carl was the guy who beat Maison to a pulp and nearly killed him," Kelsie said. She stepped full into the doorway and whistled. "Hey! Assholes! Remember us?"

Both men turned, startled, and Kelsie shot them.

"Uh . . ." Fergus said.

"You're welcome," Kelsie said. She stepped over Davies, who was still out cold on the floor. Or he was wisely pretending to be; Fergus decided he was okay with that either way.

He turned to the others. "Everyone get over to *Hexanchus* as quickly as you can! Move!"

Kelsie and Fergus stood watch as the others ran to the airlock of Fergus's hauler and disappeared inside. "Now you," Fergus said.

"No, you first. I've got the pistol, and we all need you to drive."

"There's not really anyone left to shoot," he said, and, thinking about Pace, felt vaguely sick again. She nodded and followed him in, though she kept a careful eye out behind them until *Hexanchus*'s locks were fully closed.

LaChelle and Theo were waiting by the door to the bridge. "You got this?" Theo asked. "You're not looking so good."

"I'd have to be a lot worse off than this to not be ready and able to get out of *here*," Fergus answered. "Now hold my cat and go buckle down. It's going to be a rough ride."

He handed them Mister Feefs' crate and almost ran onto the bridge, adrenaline and anxiety starting to displace his exhaustion, and buckled in. It felt good to be in this seat again, even if he hurt all over.

"Transit, I'm about to power up my hauler. As soon as I do, Ladden is going to know we're trying to escape. I don't know if he can remotely detach the Madarchs stuck in the Depot hull, but if he can, he's gonna."

"The moment you begin power-up, I will lock down all emergency doors, which will limit damage to the dock area only," Tau answered.

"There's still one man in there," Fergus said.

"He ran the moment you were all onboard. Scampered away like a bunny into hiding. I am keeping an eye on him," Tau said.

"Okay," Fergus said. "Here we go. Thanks for everything, Transit." He powered *Hexanchus* up and backed out of his berth, running system checks as he went. No way he was sitting still for Ladden's war drone and the remaining Madarch guarding the Bore. On his screen, the red question mark of the drone was already moving to intercept him.

He hit the ship intercom. "Everyone hold on to something," he said. "Here we go."

All systems were green. He fired *Hexanchus*'s engines up to full closer to the station than regs allowed, but then, who was there to call him on it?

Behind him, Sul's hauler *Triaenodon* launched and headed out of the conflict zone to wait its turn. *Carcharias* was powering up as well, while *Loxodon* sat dark in its berth.

He felt a pang of anguish at that. *I just wanted to knock him down, to stop him,* he thought. It felt like the electricity made an executive decision without him, but was that him just distancing himself from it carrying out exactly what he wanted in that moment? It was going to take him a while to process that, he knew.

Less than a quarter of the way to the Bore, distracted in an endless loop of but-if-only thoughts, red alerts flashed all over his console. The third Ballard Madarch had put on a sudden burst of speed and was swinging around, on a collision course with his rear stabilizer fin. "Oh, no, you don't, you fucker," Fergus said, and turned *Hexanchus* into a sharp dive to port. The Madarch sailed just overhead, missing him.

Kelsie stumbled into the bridge, one hand on a wall to brace herself at the steep angle. "What was that?" she asked.

"Madarch," Fergus said. He turned again, righting *Hexanchus*, and then put the nose back up into an ascent.

She managed to get into the copilot seat and buckled in. "Where's the prototype?"

"Behind us a ways still, but not for long," he said.

"*Hexanchus*, this is Transit. The Madarch is gaining on you again."

"Thank you, Transit; I see him," Fergus said. This time, the pilot of the Madarch was prepared for evasive maneuvers, and as Fergus turned, it remained on his tail and was closing the distance rapidly.

"It's going to get us before we can get to the Bore," he said. "And the more I evade it, the more the war drone itself catches up and becomes a concern."

"Ideas?" Kelsie asked.

"None right now," he said.

He pushed the engines up into critical, gaining a bit more speed, but the Madarch was still faster. Ahead, he could see the lights that encircled the bottom of the Bore turn from red to yellow, as Tau prepared to open the Bore for them. The prototype was on their tail as well, clearly pushing their engines beyond maximum safety to try to close the gap.

The Bore lights switched over to green. "Well, that's something, anyway," he said. "Now we just need— Whoa!"

Something very large and heading straight toward them lit up out of nowhere. "What the bloody—" he yelled, no time to evade.

It was a hauler that had been running dark. It shot right over *Hexanchus* and crashed head-on into the pursuing Madarch, which let out a burst of air as it crumpled.

"This is *Triakis*," a voice came over the comms. "Hope you don't mind us crashing your party! Bam, head on!"

"That's what she said," another voice added.

"Stoffel! Wenford! I could kiss you," Fergus said.

"Ew, no kissing," *Triakis* said. "That's gross, MacInnis."

"Watch out for the ship behind me," Fergus warned.

On the nav screen, he watched *Triakis* nimbly dodge the prototype, which shifted course to get out of the way and then immediately got back on *Hexanchus*'s tail. "Yep, that one's too big for us," *Triakis* answered. "You're on your own with that one."

"Got it. Thanks, Stoffel. Or Wenford. Whichever you are."

"Definitely one of those," *Triakis* answered. "Good luck."

The Madarch that *Triakis* had hit was spiraling down out of control. It disappeared from view just as a final air bubble burst from it. Fergus winced.

The Bore entrance up ahead was still greenlit. "Here we go," he said, and got *Hexanchus* into an approach vector. "Six minutes to the Bore."

"*Hexanchus*, this is Transit being the bearer of bad news again," Tau said. "The prototype is closing the distance to you and can fire in less than a minute. Sooner, if they aren't too concerned about killing you with the first shot."

"Comforting," Kelsie said. "Whoever that joker is up in Transit, I'd like to have a word with them when we get out of here."

Fergus swerved as an energy bolt seared through the water just off *Hexanchus*'s starboard side. "Missed us, fuckers!" Kelsie yelled over her shoulder, as if that could carry all the way through hauler and ocean.

"Don't gloat yet," he said. "We're about to lose most of our room to dodge."

The Bore lay directly ahead. Fergus turned *Hexanchus* upward, not slowing, grateful to see the doors already open. "Going in!" he said.

Hexanchus passed straight up into the first chamber of the Bore. The second set of doors was already opening, even though the lower ones hadn't sealed yet. Tau, no doubt, trying to get them out. Below them, the prototype soared into the chamber just before the lower doors closed and sealed.

"They wouldn't dare fire in here, would they?" Kelsie asked.

Another bolt shot past them, up into the chamber beyond.

"Shit. Apparently, they would," Fergus said. The prototype was closing rapidly.

"Can you move to one side?" Kelsie asked.

"The Bore has a protective mechanism that vaporizes anything that gets too close to the walls," Fergus said.

"That's a no, then. Too damned bad."

"*Hexanchus*, this is Transit." His comms lit up again. "Be

aware there is still significant instability due to the geothermal eruption. I anticipate a level-nine pop as soon as I open the next set of doors. I can attempt to mitigate it, but it will require a delay before you can enter the next chamber."

"No delay," Fergus said. "I'll take the pop."

He hit the intercom. "Everyone hang on extra, extra hard," he said.

"Opening in five," Tau informed him.

"What's a pop?" Kelsie asked just as the doors opened and the entire contents of the chamber were shoved upward, hard. *Hexanchus* sloughed sideways sharply, and Fergus fought with the controls as alarms blared, warning him they were within twenty-five percent of the wall. He threw the side thrusters to full and turned the ship almost diagonally to ride the push back toward the center as the push flipped *Hexanchus* sideways.

Fergus dared only a fast glance at his screens and saw the prototype moving toward the edge to escape the worst of the pop. *They don't know,* he thought, just as an intense flash lit the Bore chamber from below, and the prototype was suddenly nothing but a cloud of bubbles and glinting shrapnel.

"What was that?" Kelsie asked.

"We no longer have company," Fergus said. He got *Hexanchus* righted just enough to make it through the next set of doors without crashing into them, and when they closed below him, the pressure finally began to ease.

His heart was still hammering in his chest, sparks he hadn't noticed until that moment running along his arms, when the final set of doors above opened for him.

At long last, impossibly, there were stars.

Chapter 22

exanchus had barely made it into orbit when his comms lit up. "MacInnis! This is Assistant Director Jerney! What the hell is going on?" The latter had the unmistakable tone of *what did you do?*

Below, the Bore was lit red: closed again.

Fergus tapped to reply. "Hey, Jerkey," he said. "You need to get Dornett himself on the line. I'm not talking to anyone else. And I'm not talking to him until twenty minutes from now. I have a few other calls to make first."

"You dock that ship right now," Jerney said.

"I'll talk to Dornett in twenty minutes," Fergus repeated, and cut the line.

He pulled his pager disk out of his pocket. "Hey, this is Fergus," he said. "Anyone listening?"

Thirty seconds later, Zacker replied. "Is this a live call? You out of the ice?"

"I am," Fergus said. "Listen, you still in contact with the Constantijn Hold police?"

"Funny you should ask that; I was in the middle of a poker game with them when you called. I had a straight flush, too, when I had to fold and step out. You have terrible timing, Ferguson."

"So, are they still holding Effie?"

"Yeah, but only because they declared her a special witness to the killspinner investigation—uh, I'll explain that to you later, but it was an assassination attempt aimed at us. The Alliance has been trying again to get her transferred to their custody, but it seems the local Alliance base has been pissing off the entire Titan police force and judiciary for decades, and pissing off the civilians because of their treatment of Captain Santiago, and I'm still a fucking hero here, so no one's giving them any help."

"She doing okay?"

"Better than okay, now you made me fold. She's mopping the floor with us in there. She'll have bankrupted the entire moon before long."

"Well, how's this to extend your credit? I have proof of a conspiracy within a rogue Alliance group called 'Special Projects' to construct a secret, extralegal war machine, and all the evidence anyone could need that they engaged in kidnapping, murder, and attempted murder, including the assault on the Shipyard and framing Effie for it."

"Yeah?"

"The one surviving member of the rogue team is still trapped below the ice, just waiting to be picked up and questioned."

"And where are you? Did you find your friends?"

"Yeah. We just reached orbit over Enceladus. We need *Venetia's Sword*; I don't trust anyone else to keep us safe while we depressurize, and we need its med bay."

"Emergency?"

"No, but not something that can wait too long. Also, the more immediate and bigger the publicity, the better. I'd rather anyone complicit decides it's easier to disavow the rogue team than try to silence us and start again."

"Okay. You're going to send me your evidence?"

"Yep. I want my name out of it. If I have to be mentioned, I was Duncan MacInnis. Got it?"

"Yeah. People will be interviewed, though."

"That's okay; I think I mostly kept my cover," he said, as Kelsie beside him suddenly had a loud coughing fit into her fist. He avoided meeting her eyes. "That said, we want as big a public scandal as we can get, big enough that they can't cover this mess up."

Zacker laughed. "I don't think that's going to be a problem."

"Great. Sending now," Fergus said, and shunted all the data he had collected from inside Ballard, and about ten times that amount of data that Tau had gathered as well and sent to *Hexanchus* the moment they'd cleared the Bore, and pushed it through.

"Got it. Call you back in a few," Zacker said.

Dornett was on the line before Zacker had called back. "MacInnis," he said, his voice cautious, curious. "What's going on?"

"You have anyone else on this line?"

"No."

"What's going on is crime and murder, Dornett, under your watch," Fergus said. "And someone up there had to be involved. Either it went right to the top—you—or it stopped just short of it, and I'm not docking or letting anyone near *Hexanchus* until I know which."

"That's preposterous, MacInnis," Dornett said. "Nothing happens here without me knowing."

"So, you didn't know Pace blew Olson's brains out right there on your orbital?"

There was a pause. "Security recording was off, for some reason. Pace said it was suicide. Jerney . . ."

"Jerney seconded that? Maybe said he was a witness? Well, there you go. Now, I'd be curious to know who Above signed off on a bunch of Madarchs being hauled up to orbit and then back again a day later."

"Madarchs can't operate outside ocean—"

"Maybe go check that, then," Fergus said.

"What the hell is this all about?!" Dornett said.

"You'll know soon enough. Call back when you have answers. *Hexanchus* out."

Tau spoke up on his comms. "I have already checked those records, as you know. They were included in the data I provided you. Jerney was paid off but largely unaware of the scale or nature of the operation."

"I guessed as much," Fergus said. "I just want Dornett busy, and he'll feel less like a pawn if he thinks he helped uncover things at the end. And hopefully, he'll go easier on the other haulers instead of trying to blame them for any of this."

"I also intercepted a portion of the biodata that Ladden sent from Ballard to his Alliance contacts trying to identify you right after you were captured. I estimate only about ten percent got through before I closed down comms through the ice."

"Ten percent, huh?" Fergus said. "Let's hope there wasn't much specific in that part, or they'll be hunting me down wherever I go."

Kelsie had come onto the bridge and reclaimed the copilot's seat. Now she frowned. "Fergus?" she said. "Can we talk for a moment? Just us?"

"No problem. Transit, I'm signing off. Don't get lonely without me."

"As if!" Transit said, and the line went quiet.

"Fergus, if this person in Transit had access to all those records, and information about you . . . how do we know they're not part of the conspiracy either?"

Fergus laughed, and it felt good without the weight of an ocean on top of him. He could *breathe*. "It's complicated. I swear I'll tell you someday. Just not today, okay?"

"You sure?"

"Sure as sure can be."

"Well." Kelsie put her boots up on the console, and it didn't bother him at all. "That's good enough for me."

They stared out at the stars together for a long while without speaking. Below they could see the gleaming white curve of Enceladus, and behind it the thick, brilliant band that was Saturn's rings. A white cloud of vapor was dissipating into space where the constant geothermal activity below the ice forcibly ejected water into space, and he liked to think it was maybe, just maybe, slightly bigger. It was beautiful, terrifying, and miraculous to see now from this perspective. "I'm ready to go home," he said, not sure where the words had come from.

"Earth? Mars? The Shipyard? I didn't think you called anywhere home," Kelsie said. "In fact, it seemed you made a point of never doing that."

"It's just . . . You know what happened to my father, right?"

"Drowned himself. In front of you," Kelsie said.

"Yeah. It happened about a month before I ran away. And I thought . . . well, how bad a kid was I, if he'd do that?"

"That's stupid," Kelsie said. "You can't blame yourself."

"It's easy to say that, but in my heart, I think I never thought I deserved another chance at a home, or at a family. And I know that sounds sappy and dumb and all that. But you never let go of that kind of brokenness. And when I thought I'd lost all of you, who are the closest thing to family I've got . . ."

"You pulled us out," Kelsie said. "You couldn't reach your father, but you reached *us*. You're allowed to feel redeemed, dammit, Fergus. After all the good you've done us, that you did for Cernee, and everyone else whose lives you ghost into and then run away again from." She was staring at him intently, as if willing her words to sink into his head. "*It's okay to stay.*"

Fergus laughed again. "If you were Psych, you'd offer me cookies or something right now."

"Get your own damned cookies," Kelsie said. "I might insist you're honorary family and you belong with us, but that sure as hell doesn't mean I have to be *nice* to you." She was grinning.

"Noted," he said.

His pager disk flashed, and he pressed it. "Fergus here," he said.

"Hello, Fergus," Effie answered.

Kelsie grabbed the disk out of his hand. "Effie! EFFIE!" Tears started pouring down her cheeks. "We thought they'd killed you!"

"Yeah, well, it was close," Effie said. "Are you all there? All safe?"

"We are. Maison's hurt, but he's starting to be a pain in the ass again, so I expect he'll live. Where are you?"

"They're just releasing me now," Effie said. "Zacker—"

"Releasing you?" Kelsie asked.

"The Alliance tried to frame me for your murders. Didn't Fergus tell you that?"

Kelsie glared at Fergus.

"You had enough to worry about," he said.

"No, he didn't tell us," Kelsie said. "You're okay? They didn't mistreat you?"

"No, the only bad part was not knowing what happened to the rest of you and not being able to do anything."

"They releasing *Venetia's Sword* yet?" Fergus asked.

"Yeah, soon as we're done here, Zacker and I are heading back to the docks. Police are having a 'conversation' with the Alliance Liaison that imposed the lockdown. Luz's commander is smiling a lot, and I can hear swearing on the other end of the line, so I expect we'll be free very shortly. I think the point of negotiation isn't whether or not the police go to the press but how much they give them and how fast."

"As long as enough comes out to keep the Alliance from

trying this again anytime soon, I'm fine with that," Fergus said. "How's Zacker been handling all this?"

"Not too bad. I think he really likes it here, and it's clear they've claimed him as one of their own. They offered him a consulting job, and I think he should take it, but he keeps talking about unfinished business and putting his past to rest."

"Yeah," Fergus said. "Him and me both. We have work left to do, the two of us."

"Okay, they're officially letting us go. We're going to head toward *Venetia's Sword* with an escort, and we'll let you know when we're in the air. So to speak."

"Thanks, Effie. See you soon," Fergus said.

Kelsie looked at him. "I wasn't sure if you told us Effie was alive just to give us enough hope to get out," she said. "Thank you for not having lied about that."

"No problem," he said.

She whacked him really hard in the shoulder. "That's for not telling us she was in jail, though."

"And I'd do it again," he said. "Listen, Zacker and I are both going to need to get to Earth. I was kind of hoping—"

"You can borrow *Venetia's Sword* once we all get back to the Shipyard and get the Campers home," she said. "I know you'll bring her back safe, and I know she'll bring you back safe too."

———

He was sitting alone on the bridge of *Venetia's Sword*, feeling substantially if not entirely better after three days in a medical pod. Maison was still in one, and everyone else was asleep. He supposed it was the middle of the night, but the brightness of the stars seemed to deny the very concept of dark. He and his friends spent days answering questions as *Venetia's Sword* slowly brought them back to normal pressurization levels, meetings with Dornett and other Transit officials as other pilots came up through the Bore to add whatever facts they had. Shoo was going to live, but Sul said she wasn't sure if they were both done with the Deep now or not; time would tell, but wherever they went, they went together.

No one who knew talked about the Palla, and given how dangerous the information was, he was sure no one would. And if they did . . . it was somewhere dead and buried in the restricted zone under the debris of Ballard. He managed to keep his own role to that of Duncan MacInnis, New Pilot Who Stumbled Onto An Evil Plot, and after several iterations of telling the story, Dr. Minobe emerged as the hero who escaped and brought back help. She wasn't happy about the attention but went along with it as long as, as she put it, no one threatened to throw her "a damned parade."

Fergus was sick of it all and ready to be gone.

"We're about done here," Fergus said. "A quick trip to Titan to pick up the new reactor core and bring it to the Shipyard, and then I'm off to Earth. You're going to be okay?"

"Everything is stable," Transit answered. *Tau.* An impossible thing, and his secret to carry now. "My integration is complete. Operations are already returning to what might be referred to as 'normal,' though the inter-station gossip and conjecture are straining comms bandwidth here Below."

"It'll calm down," Fergus said.

"It is a boring place, and may take decades," Tau said.

"Not *that* boring."

"No. Perhaps only years."

Fergus laughed. "Okay, then," he said. "Good luck to you."

"Thank you," Tau said. "Your ship thinks highly of you, you

know. It is so close, on the verge of waking on its own . . . one little push, one little spark, and it could also be fully self-aware. Would you ask me to do that?"

"It's not my place to decide that," Fergus said. "You'd have to ask *Venetia's Sword* itself."

"I did," Transit said. "It declined, out of concern for putting its people in danger, and then immediately deleted its own memory of our conversation."

"Oh," Fergus said. It wasn't surprising, but it left him sad.

"I am sure we will talk again," Transit said, and Fergus wasn't sure if it meant him or Vee, but the connection closed.

"Vee?" Fergus asked.

"I was not listening to you," the ship answered.

"I know. Let's go get Effie."

———

Fergus tapped at the tiny earbud in his good ear. His other ear, freshly regrown, itched abominably. "You ready, detective?" he asked.

An ocean away, Zacker answered, "We're in position. You sure you don't want backup?"

"Goal is to spook him, not start a shooting war. And besides, your buddies from the SCNYPD are all back in the woods, waiting."

"Yeah, but I'm not sure they like you."

Fergus laughed. "No one does. Okay, going in."

He parked his small podcar at the foot of the driveway and got out. The house sat on a small rise surrounded by tall maples that were just starting to bud out, a windmill rising gracefully over a small barn behind it. Patches of snow still lined the gravel walk here and there, green shoots rising up through and around them wherever they could. At the height of summer, Fergus

knew, wildflowers would fill the spaces in untidy, glorious pro-
fusion. An old-fashioned water can, in bright turquoise, sat
poised at the end of the row. Everything was well kept, peaceful,
quiet. It would be picture-perfect. He almost wished he could
see it then, as it was meant to be, instead of in late March.

Byron Monroe was standing in the doorway behind the
screen door as he approached. "Hey! No solicitation," he called
as soon as Fergus got near. "There was a sign on the gate."

"I came to talk to you about a specific matter, Mr. Monroe,"
he said. "I promise you I have no interest in selling you anything."

Monroe didn't open the door, and Fergus noted he had one
hand behind his back. "What is it, then? I don't like trespassers."

"I'm sure you don't, Mr. Monroe," he said. He stopped beside
the watering can, resisting the urge to scratch furiously at his ear.
The suit he was wearing was a close second in discomfort, something he'd picked out of the wardrobe of one of Zacker's former
fellow officers for its casual police-officer-off-duty look. He
made a point of taking a deep breath and surveying the area. "It's
beautiful up here," he said. "It must have been very therapeutic
after what happened to you."

"State your business and get out," Monroe said.

"I can't help but notice this place—you had it built for you,
yes, with your settlement money after the robbery?—I bet in the
summer, it looks almost exactly like Egas Herdade's painting,
Quinta e Moinho. Not a very famous post-impressionist work, but
a masterpiece. Weird that it wasn't even in the same section, or
anywhere near the value of the other paintings that were stolen.
Someone must've really fancied it. I assume you got a chance to
see it before it was stolen? I mean, wow, you even got the watering can exactly right."

Monroe swung the screen door open with a crash and stepped
out, gun in hand. "Get off my property," he snarled.

"You sure you don't want to talk?" Fergus said. "I mean, maybe there is a deal we can make."

Monroe raised the gun and pointed it straight at him. "Look, whoever you are, I am not interested in any old Portuguese paintings. I just want to live my life in peace and unbothered. If you don't want to be shot as a trespasser, you turn and get in your car and you never come back here again."

Fergus put his hands up, and took several steps backwards. "Sure thing, Mr. Monroe. I don't want to steal any more of your time. Although I expect we'll talk again soon."

He turned and walked back to his car, aware of the gun still pointing at his back but taking it unhurried, unconcerned. He got back in, waved, and backed out of the driveway.

A quarter kilometer from the house, he stopped where the road passed behind a thicket of evergreens. One of Zacker's officers stepped out, wearing heavy body armor and carrying a large rifle. "We're just waiting on him to make the call," she said. "Soon as the raid goes down in Glasgow, we'll serve the warrant here. He's not going anywhere in the meantime."

"Thanks, Officer Belovski," Fergus said. "I think I'm going to wait everything out back in town at the café with the neon pie sign. I haven't slept since Jupiter."

She smiled. "MacInnis, right? PI? Thanks for helping Zacker crack this. He hasn't been right since the robbery."

"Least I could do for a friend," Fergus said.

"We'll keep you posted. Might be a long day."

"Café also has coffee. If the day gets long enough, I'll bring some back."

"We'd appreciate that. Now move along before he realizes you haven't appeared yet on the lower road."

"Right," Fergus said. He drove away as she faded back into the trees. After hesitating, he let the window down and stuck his elbow out. The air was cold, fresh, alive. How long had it been since he could do that?

————

Venetia's Sword called him as he was being seated in a pale blue vinyl booth. "There is a lot of Alliance traffic looking for a Duncan MacInnis," the ship said. "They do seem to know you're on Earth. The sooner you leave there, the better."

"I will, and soon, Vee," he said. He tapped the menu icon for pie and confirmed. "Just a bit more to wrap up, and then I'm done here, no more ties, nothing to keep me."

"I will wait in orbit for you."

"Thank you, Vee," Fergus said.

Effie would take good care of Mister Feefs for him until he returned home to the Shipyard, with the help of Dr. Minobe, who had found enough interesting things going on there to stick around for a while. It would be a good place for him to rest and think, when he got back there—soon!—and when he couldn't bear to do either, there was plenty of repair work to keep him busy. Perhaps, finally, he'd found a place he belonged.

The weight of Pace's death still pulled on him, despite all, and he felt like he'd been drowned and washed ashore. Whatever pride of his that had made him think himself the master of the Asiig's gift had dissipated in that uncontrollable whirlwind of strange electricity, and he needed to figure out how to make sure it never got out of his control again. He'd let it all be too easy.

Fergus wasn't even on to his second slice of pie when Zacker called. "Large moving van just pulled up in front of Suttie's in a hurry. We're on! Let you know when it's over."

He paid the bill and left a generous tip, then got back in his rental car and headed toward the city. As soon as he was off town roads, the automated driving computer took over, and he leaned back, tuned in to the news, and watched as the recovering forests gave way to houses, office buildings, then ecotowers covered with greenery and modern windmills of their own. The Albany shuttleport was outside proper city limits. The car stopped there and, when he had dragged all his crap out of the back, abandoned him where he stood.

Zacker's red flyer was parked where he had left it. He stood regarding it, thinking about Scotland, and thinking about turning around and just heading back into orbit and washing his hands of Earth.

"Mr. MacInnis?" An unfamiliar voice spoke in his earbud. "This is Officer O'Dell. The raid is over, and we have the paintings and perpetrators in custody. Zacker asked me to give you two addresses."

"Two?" Fergus asked. "Where's Zacker?"

"He was shot, sir. There was an ambush. Detective Zacker got three of the suspects before he was hit himself. They just took him out by aircar to the emergency trauma center. This was what he could tell me before they lifted off."

"Is he going to live?"

"I don't know, sir. Do you want the addresses?"

"Yes, send them through." He had purchased a new handpad when they'd landed in SCNY, and he'd synced it with the earbud. The text appeared a moment later. "Thank you, O'Dell."

"Zacker told me to tell you thanks as well, sir. He said to say it was worth it. That and he told me to tell you, and I quote, 'In answer to his stupid question, I'm okay now,' if that means anything to you."

"Yeah," Fergus said. "Thanks."

He took the earbud out, dropped it on the pavement, and crushed it beneath his boot.

The first address was right in downtown New York. He called another autocar and let it take him. The news made a footnote mention of a scandal with a rogue Alliance group in the outer planets but went into no detail. It wasn't something Earth cared about.

He did, though.

There was a substantial reward on the paintings, and when everything finally cleared, his portion would go toward rebuilding the bombed-out Sunshield back in Cernee. It was the best use of it he could think of.

The address was on the fortieth floor of one of the older ecotowers in the city, its tiered floors boasting nearly full-grown trees. He rode the elevator up and walked to the door number he'd been given.

The nameplate read, D. ZACKER.

Ah, Fergus thought. Zacker had said *shot*, had never actually said *killed. I missed that, didn't I?*

He rang the bell.

A woman answered, about his own age. She didn't resemble the picture Zacker had had in his wallet much, but a couple of decades and reconstructive surgery would do that. "Deliah Zacker?" Fergus asked.

"Can I help you?" she said.

"I'm a friend of your father's," he said.

She laughed. "My father doesn't have friends, except cops, and despite that shit suit, you definitely aren't a cop."

"No, I'm not," he said. "Look, this is complicated."

"Is he dead?"

"No," he said, then, "maybe. I'm not sure. He got shot a few hours ago in a raid."

"He's *retired*," she said. "Or at least he was, last time I talked to him, which was five or six years ago. What happened?"

"They got the Met robbers," Fergus said.

She slumped against the doorway. "Well," she said. "He did it, huh? Good for him."

"You don't seem that happy."

"Glad they got those assholes? Yes, I'm happy, or I will be once it sinks in. You know how long it took me to rebuild my life after that? Too long. And the whole time, every time my father looked at me, I knew that all he could see was what was taken away from *him*. Like I was stolen too, even though I was right the fuck in front of him. How do you live with that?"

"I don't know," Fergus said. "I haven't known your father for very long, but I think he's changed. Maybe, a bit. At least, I dragged him out of his comfort zone for a while and it seemed to do him some good."

"You got him out of New York?"

"I took him all the way to Pluto," Fergus said.

"No way! Pluto? He must have hated that."

"Mostly, yeah. He did threaten me a bunch."

"Now, that sounds like him," she said. She took a deep breath, looked down at her hands, then back to Fergus. "Where is he now?"

"Glasgow. Not sure which hospital; they didn't tell me."

"Are you going to see him again?"

"I don't know. If I do, is there anything you want me to tell—"

"No," she interrupted. "Thanks for letting me know about the robbers." She stepped back and closed the door. Fergus stood there for a minute, not sure if he should knock again, but then he heard the faint sounds of crying on the other side. Instead, he turned and walked away.

Family, he thought. *I know that feeling.*

The second address was in Old Kilbride, Scotland.

Just as Zacker had needed to live down his own past, get the justice he needed, Fergus's own past was still waiting for him in the form of a twice-stolen motorcycle.

I've really come full circle, haven't I? he mused. Not just from Zacker jumping him outside Suttie's but back to the day he stole the motorcycle in the first place.

At least, when this was done, he would have cut his last thin tie to Earth and could finally be free.

———

Spring had sprung in Scotland, too, and the old, familiar, peculiarly Scottish tang of new grasses and trees and the ever-present looming rain permeated the chilly air and filled every breath he took with longing and heartache.

Fergus stood outside the centuries-old brick building for a long time, on the knife point between walking in or turning around for good, but without any sense of urgency to choose. The street level of the building had a wooden facade painted a deep, dark blue, and bright gold lettering proclaimed the pub within the DROWNED LAD. It was, he thought, unexpectedly ominous. But finally, his curiosity piqued, he pushed open the door to the small rattle of bells and went in.

It was a nice pub, although nearly empty at three in the afternoon. Oak and brass and blue glass hanging lamps. Over the bar, above a giant mirror, hung a blue-painted oar that looked eerily familiar.

Also familiar was the man standing behind the bar, a full red beard that matched his own, staring right back at him. With Fergus's reflection in the mirror beside him, they could have been twins.

Fergus found his voice. "Gavin," he said, and took a stool at the bar.

His cousin poured him a shot of whisky, slid it across the bar to him. "Fergus," he said. "Long time."

"I came back to return the motorcycle I stole from you nineteen years ago," Fergus said, "only to find out you took it back a couple of years later and you and Mr. Suttie have been splitting the storage money ever since."

"Paid for the pub," Gavin said.

"Nice. The Drowned Lad, though?"

Gavin sighed. "Yer ma told everyone you followed your da into the water. I knew it was a lie, because I saw you ride away that day, but it was easier to just let it go. And since you paid for the place, seemed fair to name it in your honor. Sort of."

His mother had told everyone he was dead? That hit like a punch in the gut. He hadn't thought she'd still have the capacity to hurt him after all this time.

"Oh," he managed. He slid the glass back and forth between his fingers on the bar top. "I'm sorry I stole your bike, Gavin, and that it took me this long to try to make it right."

"Apology not accepted," Gavin said, setting the bottle down with a thump. "We knew yer ma wasn't right, but everyone figured your da would look out for you. So, it was easy to take no responsibility and do nothing, 'til your da went and killed himself, and then it was way too late. We all let you down."

Fergus shot the whisky back, put the glass back down on the counter. "You were only two years older than me. What could you have done?"

"The only thing I could. Pointed out to you where my da kept the gas can, let you see where I hid the key."

"Wait. You *meant* for me to take the motorcycle?"

"Yeah, but I figured you'd go into the city. Instead, Suttie showed me all the payment receipts, and it's like every single one came from some other part of the galaxy. Man, when you ran away, you *really* ran away."

"I did," Fergus said. "What I discovered is that you never can go far enough away to forget your ma hated you and your da drowned himself because of what a disappointment you were."

"You think that? Aye, I suppose I can see why," Gavin said, leaning against the counter behind him with his arms crossed over his chest. "The night before he took his boat ride out, I heard your da and mine fighting. It wasn't about you, it was about how he'd failed you your whole life, and he couldn't bear the idea of doing it again."

"Doing what again?" Fergus asked.

"Well, that's good timing," Gavin said, and pointed toward the front door. An antique Triumph motorcycle had just pulled up and parked out front.

"Is that . . ." Fergus asked.

"Yeah," Gavin said. "Had to convert it to electric to keep it on the road, but still runs like a dream."

The rider dismounted and pulled off her helmet, long red hair tumbling out and down to the waist of her black leather jacket. She tucked the helmet under one arm and came in, then stopped and looked at the two of them. "Gav, ye cloned yer ugly ass?" she asked.

"I did, Isla, so we can hassle ye two times as much!" Gavin said. "How were classes?"

"Same as ever. Too slow," she said. "Like you, ye bam." She laughed, and disappeared into the back room.

"Your daughter?" Fergus asked.

Gavin laughed, and poured another whisky and set it front of Fergus. "You'll be needing that," he said.

Fergus had just started to tip it back when Gavin added, "Nae, she's your baby sister."

As Fergus tried to breathe through the whisky he'd just inhaled, Gavin poured him another. "We were too late to help you, but my ma took her away from yers and raised her so at least she'd grow up okay. After a few years, yer ma forgot she was even hers. Isla just started at university this year—astrophysics engineering, would ye believe?—and helps me out here in the evenings. It's a good life."

"Is my ma still alive?"

"No," Gavin said. "About five years ago, just got sick and passed. Quiet, quick. We buried her up on that hill of hers where she kept all the things she used to pull from the sea."

"Does . . ." Fergus was still having trouble making any sense of this. "Does Isla know?"

"Yeah. We used to try to keep track of where you were, guess where you'd go next. None of us ever won a bet on that. We even have a big ol' map in the back room that she painted when she was nine. Here, come see." Gavin lifted up the hinged bar top and Fergus followed him back. One wall of the stock room was a giant, hand-painted map of incredible inaccuracy. The big wobbly red circle that was Mars was almost hidden beneath the cluster of tacks pounded into it.

Isla had put on a small apron bearing the Drowned Lad logo and was putting her hair up. She looked at them curiously as they came in. "This is our map," Gavin said. He held out a hand to Isla. "Got another tack?"

She rummaged in a drawer and handed him one. "We get another letter from Suttie?" she asked. "Early for it."

"Sort of," Gavin said. He picked up a hammer, found the tiny, empty drawing of Earth, and the blob that included Scotland, and pounded the tack in. Isla looked at Fergus with widening eyes.

"There we go, at long last," Gavin said. "Home."

Acknowledgments

It doesn't seem like all that long ago that I was writing the acknowledgments for *Finder*, my first novel, and stressing about not forgetting anyone while managing to sound like a rational, calm, mature human being instead of muppet-flailing all over the page like a gnat on crack. At least, I thought back then, it'll be easier next time.

Hahahahaha.

Anyway, here we are. Book two, can you believe it? And once again there are so many people who have been an essential part of getting this book to the here and now. First and foremost I must thank my children, who are very patient with me and know just when to sneak an Oreo or two onto my desk while I'm working, and my friends who let me haltingly dump half-sentences, incoherent word salad, and half-baked plot noodles at them as I'm working through story problems, and who periodically manage to drag me out of my introvert cave and make me go do fun, social things with them. Likewise I am grateful for the writing communities that are the backbone of my support network, full of generous, smart, snarky, brilliant people who make sure that writing, as much as it often feels very solitary, never feels alone.

Enormous thanks, of course, are due my agent, Joshua Bilmes, and the rest of his team at JABberwocky Literary Agency, who have been a steady source of direction and diligent effort shepherding me and my work out into the world. My editor, Katie Hoffman, is a delight to work with, insightful and sharp, and her enthusiasm makes a process inevitably fraught with anxiety so much less terrifying. Everyone at DAW just plain rocks it, and I could not be happier than to be in their excellent hands. Nor would my books be what they are without the extraordinary cover artwork by Kekai Kotaki, who once again has just absolutely nailed how I envision the setting and mood and *feel* of my worlds. Last, I have to thank my copy editor, Richard Shealy, who didn't just give the novel a thorough shaking-out, but found a tiny but critical one-letter goof on my part that was so obscure and unobvious that it feels like there must have been dark magic involved. When the people supporting you are supernaturally good at their jobs, being an author is a hell of a lot easier.

Thanks also to my bestest beta readers, Laurie Vadeboncoeur, Jonathan Turner, and Robin Holly for invaluable feedback on the novel, to my crew of mods and friends at Absolute Write, to Bear, Sarah, Alex, Devin, Julie, and my other local writer peeps for keeping me moving forward when I otherwise would have stalled, and to my lovely friend Sara Pea for vetting my Portuguese painting title. I am so fortunate to have you all in my life.

And thanks to you, my reader, who has now (presumably) read through two of these books, and hopefully will stick with me for another few. I would happily share my Oreos with you.

Peace.

—Suzanne

PRINCE ALBERT PUBLIC LIBRARY
31234900062819
Driving the deep